SLINGSHOT 1918

Danny Creasy

Acknowledgments

I am especially grateful to the following members of my *Slingshot 8* team:

Edit – Elizabeth Brown

Cover art – Mike O'Brien, freelance illustrator, wheelhouse-art.com

Map art – Delano (Deno) Ellis and Ellen Creasy Ellis

Veterinary medicine – Dan M. Whitlow D.V.M.

Horses and tactical equipment – Mounted Police Officer Lee Smith and Police Sergeant Hal Howard

Radio communication – Jack Belew, U. S. Army, U. S. Navy, Alabama National Guard, and municipal law enforcement

Proofreading and general consultation – Jim Watson, retired chemical engineer and avid science fiction reader; Mike Zacharski, U. S. Army and municipal law enforcement; Glenda F. Oldham, retired English teacher and very good neighbor; Bob Barclift, Bradshaw High School classmate (1975 – Go Bruins!) and lawyer; Monty Shelton D.M.D., best friend and eternal scholar; and my Saturday lunch buddies, Dwight Pilkilton, Andrew Butler, and John Butler

Back cover text – Jim Watson (compressed over three hundred words of query letter into a seventy-three word grabber)

Intellectual properties – Meredith Cheney, attorney

Self-publishing – Angela Hoy, BookLocker

Love and support (enablers) – my wife, Karen Creasy (also a proofreader); my daughters, Ellen Ellis (proofreader) and Katie Mahany; and my sons-in-law, Deno Ellis and Matt Mahany

Inspiration – William Shakespeare and a dream. Folks, this is *Henry V* (1599) including my stylized renditions of the Duke of Exeter's ultimatum to King Charles and The Dauphin, the *St. Crispin's Day Speech*, the Duke of Burgundy's plea for peace, King Henry's marriage proposal, and King Charles's marriage blessing.

Table of Contents

SPARED TERRI

TENNESSEE

NORTHERN

LAUD

Central

Natchez
Trace Bridge

Oakland

Cherokee

MISSISSIPI

COL

SOUTHERN

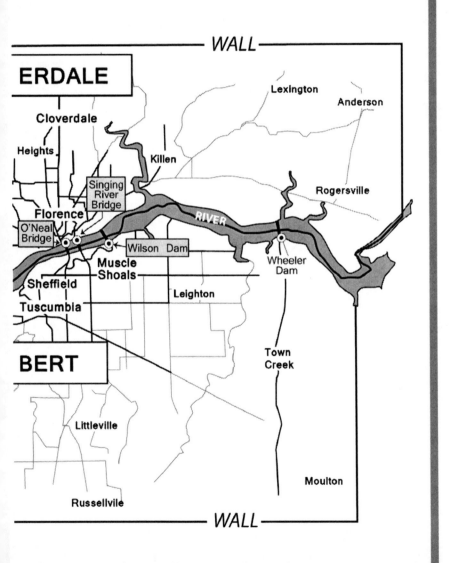

TORY- YEAR 70

WALL

ERDALE

Cloverdale

Heights

Killen

Lexington

Anderson

Singing
River
Bridge

Florence

RIVER

Rogersville

O'Neal
Bridge

Wilson Dam

Muscle
Shoals

Wheeler
Dam

Sheffield

Leighton

Tuscumbia

BERT

Town
Creek

Littleville

Moulton

Russellvile

WALL

THE LAUDERDALES

"Henry" Wade Smith III – Former President, long-deceased

Henry "Wade" Smith IV – President

Henry "Harry" Wade Smith V – Son of the President – Overall
Slingshot Commander

Philippa Smith Carter – Daughter of the President – Director of
Ladies Auxiliary

Ben Smith – Brother of the President – Florence District Leader –
Overall Commander, Lauderdale Militia
David Smith – Brother – Central/Waterloo/Oakland/Cloverdale
District Leader
Clifford Hayes – Brother-in-Law – Green Hill/Lexington/Anderson
District Leader
Peter Hayes – Brother-in-Law – Killen/Center Star/Elgin/Rogersville
District Leader
Curtis Campbell – Nephew – Council Representative
Biscuit Gray – Nephew – Council Representative
Bill Snope – Nephew – Council Representative

Church Leaders

The Reverend Arthur Canterbury – Lauderdale High Church Leader
Brother Eli Stram – Lauderdale Low Church Leader

The Slingshot Defense Force Commanders

Slingshot 1 – Colonel Phil Goins – Cloverdale – North Wall Defense Command
Slingshot 2 – Major Donna Flurry (Phil's daughter) – North Florence
Slingshot 3 – Major Wayne Morris – Anderson
Slingshot 4 – Major William Fuqua – West Florence
Slingshot 5 – Captain Clara Smith (Ben's daughter) – East Florence
Slingshot 6 – Captain Bedford Smith (David's son) – Waterloo
Slingshot 7 – Chester Hayes (Clifford's son)– Killen
Slingshot 8 – Overall Slingshot Commander's Humvee

Slingshot 8 Crew Members

Sergeant Mortimer "1911" Johns
Corporal Chance Bardolph
Corporal Thomas Nim
Falstaff's orphan – Robby

Commanders of Combat Arms and Support Units

Major Donnie Smith – Logistics
Captain Thomas "Scooter" Shelton – Lauderdale Artillery
Captain Jesus Juarez – Lauderdale Cavalry – mount's name is *Chain Lightning*
Lieutenant Neva Lazo de la Vega – Communications
"Crazy" Ned Flanagan – Air

Enlisted Personnel, Lauderdale Cavalry

Sergeant Mark Gillespie – Platoon Sergeant – mount's name is *Noble Deed*
Corporal Michael Williams – Squad Leader, 1st Squad – *Dungee Boy*
Private John Bates – Assistant Squad Leader, 1st Squad – *Black Jack*
Private Alexander Court – Trooper, 1st Squad – *Cider* and later, *El Truenos*

Private Betty Sands – Trooper, 1st Squad – *Double Knot*
Private Cameron Brown – Trooper, 2nd Squad/Buffalo Soldiers –
Sugar Rhea
Private Clive Bennett – M249 Gunner, Weapons Squad – *Hector*
Private Jake Connelly – M240 Gunner, Weapons Squad – *Margie
Sue*

Enlisted Personnel, Slingshot Teams

Sergeant Annie Slocomb – Tactical Team Leader, Slingshot 2
Corporal Ruff Creasy – Asst. Tactical Team Leader, Slingshot 5
Private Deb Romine – Shooter, Tactical Team, Slingshot 2
Private Judy Kelley – Shooter, Tactical Team, Slingshot 2

Militiamen, Zip City Squad, East Low Church Militia

Sergeant James "Pastor Jim" Dayton – Squad Leader
Corporal Mary Dayton (Pastor Jim's daughter) – Assistant Squad
Leader
Private Tim Gray – Rifleman
Private Jaybird Rhodes – Rifleman

Lauderdale Telephone System

Sarah Haney, Senior Operator

Miss Nell's Place – Inn, Restaurant, and Brothel

Nell Quickly – Proprietor and Madam
Ginger Davis – Prostitute
Cold Zee – Prostitute

THE COLBERTS

"Big" Charles Edward Ragland V – Former President, long-deceased

"Little" Charles Edward Ragland VI – President

Isabel "Izzy" Ragland – Wife of the President

Charles Edward Ragland VII – Son of the President – Director of Operations for Wilson and Wheeler Dams

Catherine Isabel Ragland – Daughter of the President – Liaison to the Colbert People

Daniel "Danny" Ragland – Nephew of President – Constable of Colbert – Commander of Black Force Knights and Colbert Militia

Lawrence Foster – Adjutant Constable of Colbert

Coffee Club Members

Pickard Thompson – Leading Colbert Industrialist
Midge Burkett – Credit System Director
The Reverend Thomas Utter – Colbert High Church Leader
Brother Donnie Butler – Colbert Low Church Leader

Ragland Staff Members

Johnny Montjoy – Envoy to Lauderdale
Alice Boyd – Catherine Ragland's Personal Assistant and Body Guard
Knight Holt – Head of Security, Ragland Palace

Gail Atkinson – Black Force Communications Assistant

Colbert Militia Roving Sniper Team

Corporal Jimmy Putnam – Shooter
Corporal Ted Creasy – Spotter

DAY ONE

Henry "Harry" Wade Smith V shifted his arms and legs ever so slightly to ease his stiffening muscles and joints. He had been flat on his belly for almost an hour. Harry let his heavy binoculars rest on the ground for a moment; his arms were cramping. If the tip was accurate, the swimmer should have already shown. Harry's traitorous cousins, Curtis Campbell, Biscuit Gray, and Bill Snope, made their appearance as the morning sun broke over the horizon; but their Colbert messenger was late. Curtis and Biscuit perched on the tailgate of Bill's big 4X4 pickup truck while Bill stood in the bed anxiously watching the ancient river. Curtis, this sector's River Watch commander, must have given the early shift a morning off with a promise to cover for them.

Chance Bardolph, Mortimer "1911" Johns, and Harry arrived well before sunrise. They had also brought along the orphan named Robby. After parking Slingshot 8 well off the Gunwaleford Road and covering it with some brush, the three Lauderdale men left Robby with a 12 gauge pump shotgun. They told him to stay close to the vehicle and be quiet. Harry then led his old soldiers down to a remote earthen boat ramp on the river where they carefully selected an advantageous spot from which to observe the rendezvous. The colors were turning, but few leaves had fallen; the men had no trouble concealing in the dense foliage.

According to Harry's spy, the Colbert scuba diver was supposed to emerge from the Tennessee River around sunup and meet with Harry's cousins. Harry did not know what information or items were to pass, but he knew it had to be dangerous. The plotters hated Harry's father, President Smith, and they had been jealous of Harry since the four were boys.

Could it have been too cold for the diver? thought Harry. Typical for November in Northwest Alabama, it bottomed out around 40 degrees as they departed Florence. The water temperature would be close to the same. *Properly suited up, the messenger should be fine*, Harry optimistically reasoned.

As soon as Harry finished his internal argument, a head bobbed up from the shiny green water. The conspirators shuffled down the old earthen boat ramp to help the diver remove his flippers and tank. They walked him back up to the truck and Biscuit poured the cold Colbert man a cup of coffee from his battered stainless steel thermos.

"Damn," Harry whispered to Bardolph at his side, "That son of a bitch used to drag out that same old thermos when we hunted whitetails at Waterloo."

"Shh," Bardolph responded from Harry's side. He patted Harry's shoulder with a calming touch that was no stranger to the young heir apparent.

The meeting lasted only a few minutes. The diver removed a plastic bag from inside his thermal suit and handed it to Cousin Curtis. The distance was only about 80 yards. Harry easily made out folded papers in the clear plastic bag. Curtis didn't even open it. The messenger and the traitors talked intensely and quietly for a few minutes before and after the exchange.

As the covert meeting was concluding, Bill went to the cab of the truck and retrieved a manila envelope. He handed it to Curtis; and Curtis proceeded to open the plastic bag. The Colbert contents and Lauderdale contents were swapped, and the freezer bag was sealed and returned to the diver.

After the diver secured the bag and zipped his suit, Harry's cousins appeared to offer physical assistance to the messenger as he lifted his diving tank. However, he waved them off and urged the Lauderdale men to depart. Harry's nervous kin gave little argument, climbed into the 70-year-old truck, and noisily departed. As the bio-diesel fueled truck passed from view, the diver shuffled over to a tree stump near the riverbank, sat down, and stiffly began putting on his flippers.

Harry looked back over his shoulder at old 1911 and softly commanded, "Mort, hand me my rimfire."

The 62-year-old subordinate anticipated Harry's need and had the sleek .22 caliber rifle ready. Staying low, he slid the rifle to

Chance. Chance eased it over to Harry. Harry rolled on his back and exchanged the binoculars for the bolt action rifle. As Bardolph focused the field glasses on the distant diver, Harry ran his left arm through the loop in the decades-old supple leather rifle sling. He cinched it tight above his bicep and rolled back over to assume a prone firing position. Earlier, Harry told 1911 to set the variable scope on 8-power, set the adjustable objective halfway between the 50 and 100-yard marks, insert a five round magazine of sub-sonic hollow points, cycle a round in the chamber, and place the rifle's safety on. With a trust forged since his childhood, Harry had no reason to check these settings.

The diver stood and turned towards the river. He was fiddling with his mask, and the pause provided a perfect silhouette. Harry eased the safety off and centered the scope's reticle on the back of the frogman's head. The shooter took a deep breath, let most of it out, raised the point of aim a couple of inches over his victim's noggin, and began to press the trigger. At the shot, the six-inch silencer, threaded to the rifle's 16.5-inch barrel, suppressed the report. Not a bird on the river fluttered. The Colbert man's knees buckled and he fell forward jerking and prostrate at the river's edge with his head in the water.

Harry cleared his weapon and passed it back to 1911 in exchange for the team's LLSR-10. A 7.62X51mm battle rifle based on a scaled up M16 receiver, Lauderdale Loads had manufactured a dozen of these powerful and accurate weapons for the Slingshot Teams in ST year 65. The development of the Lauderdale Loads Slingshot Rifle Model 10 was one of Harry's earliest administrative assignments. Facilitating projects requiring the fulfillment of governmental needs by privately owned enterprises had become one of Harry's fortes.

The typical river fog was rising in the channel, so the visibility from the Colbert side was obscured. Given the shroud, they all advanced slowly to the motionless body. No Barrett wielding marksman from the south side of the river could threaten Harry and his men.

Bardolph rolled the man over, unzipped his suit, and retrieved the plastic bag. He handed it to 1911, and then removed the diver's oxygen tank, mask, diving weights, and flippers. Harry scanned all directions for observers or interlopers. 1911 had brought along a large nylon bag and rope. After he and Bardolph filled the bag with a couple of hundred pounds of rocks, they wrapped the rope around the dead man's mid-section and tied the loose end to the bag. Bardolph grimaced in the cold water as he waded the body out into the river. When Bardolph was waist-high, he slid the diver into the current and watched him float away. The insulated diving suit provided some buoyancy, but the bag of rocks soon pulled the body beneath the surface.

As expected, the little soft-lead bullet did not exit, thus the dead man's face was intact. Harry thought he recognized the middle-aged courier, from a ball game or some such event — back during The Peace. "Was that a Chandler?" asked Harry. "He looked like one of them Chandlers from Colbert Mountain."

Bardolph shrugged and answered, "Coulda' been. Some Colbert gal will be missin' her man tonight."

"Damn, Harry, your mole was right on with the info about this drop!" commented 1911.

"That's true enough," added Bardolph, "Harry, that poor Colbert bastard had a nice little knife and a stainless .38 Special on him. Can I keep 'em?"

Harry thought a moment and said, "No. Well, you keep the knife, but give the revolver to Robby. He ain't got a handgun."

"Will do, Harry," Bardolph acknowledged without hesitation.

The tired men divided the burden of the scuba gear and hurried back to Slingshot 8. Harry had securely donned the heavy tank, not only to help out his aging companions, but this would keep his arms and hands free to operate the LLSR-10. Fortunately, Harry's skills as a killer got a rest. They made their way back to young Robby without incident. The mist from the river swept them ahead of it.

The observant young man shivered as he watched his seniors approach. He wondered if his chill was caused more by the cold or the eerie white cloud following the returning Slingshot team. Robby raised his gloved hand high above his head and saw 1911 respond with the same recognition. Robby was relieved that all three men returned. They'd soon be headed back to the warmth and sustenance of Miss Nell's place. He could only imagine how good the hotcakes, bacon, and chicory would taste. He knew nothing of this mission's objective, but he had found it best not to concern himself with such matters.

"Hello, preacher!" greeted Arthur Canterbury.

The Low Church leader, Eli Stram, responded, "Hello, Arthur! At least you didn't have to bring your kneepads for my church. I guess that's a relief."

Reverend Canterbury played along with the jibe and said, "Yes, that will give these old arthritic knees a rest."

The two men chuckled then shook hands. Brother Stram gestured for his old friend to have a seat on the front row. Eli glanced around the sanctuary to make sure they were alone and joined Arthur on the pew.

Both men sighed with the pleasant relief of getting off their feet. They each had a busy morning.

"How're Grace and the family, Arthur?"

"Fine. Just fine, Eli, and how about your Mary and that new grandbaby?"

Eli knew better than to deceive his old High Church friend, and decided to quickly dispense with the painful news in his life. However, always the optimist, he opened on a high note, "The little girl is healthy and happy, and beautiful to boot!" Then he dropped his smile, looked into Arthur's eyes with his own watering ones and said, "Doctor Flynn says that Mary's cancer is growing and all we can do is try to keep her comfortable."

Reverend Canterbury's joyful smile dropped, "Oh no, Eli. That is sad to hear. Yes, very sad news. God bless you and your family, my old friend."

"Thank you, Arthur."

"I take it, you have her at home?"

"Yes, we hired Betty Flynn to come take care of her."

"Ah, there is none better than Nurse Betty."

They both looked around to escape the anguish, and in unplanned unison, wiped away tears with their wrinkled hands.

" Let me know what I can do to help, Eli."

"I will, my friend. I will."

After a moment or two, Eli asked with a businesslike tone, "What is the latest on Brother Wade?"

Arthur answered, "I fear that President Henry Wade Smith will not survive the day. I only left the hospital because of the urgency of our meeting."

"Was Harry there when you left, Arthur?"

"No, our would-be leader slipped out around midnight after receiving a visit from Mortimer Johns."

"Dear Lord! 1911 Johns? Arthur, that old reprobate should have been hanged a dozen times."

"I agree, Eli. Nonetheless, he and his two cronies have always had Wade's back. All three are bound even tighter to young Harry."

Eli asked, "Do you think it had something to do with those trouble making sons of the Smith sisters?"

"I'm almost sure of it, Eli. Those three are like a pack of wolves at the kill. They will never be satisfied with the Smith Ascendancy, even as successful as it has been. Their busybody mothers have pushed for free Lauderdale elections for years, and the whole lot of 'em see this as an opportunity."

Eli considered for a moment and then said, "Some of my Low Church elders have told me that Biscuit, Curtis, and Bill have been talkin' up their ole Colbert friendships and griping about everybody's lost trade."

"Eli, I would not put it past 'em to conspire with the Colberts and sellout Lauderdale in a power grab — all under the cover of elections."

"There must be good reason for Ben Smith's placing the militias on High Alert Status."

"These are grave matters, Reverend Canterbury."

"Yes indeed, Brother Stram."

"The two of us need to meet with Harry real bad, Arthur. Surely, he will call a meeting of the Lauderdale leaders after his daddy's passing."

"Yes, he will, Eli. Wade's brother Ben told me that Harry asked his four uncles to plan for a council meeting within a half-day of Wade's death — no matter the hour."

"My Low Church congregations are sick of the Colberts' escapades over the past two months. They are ready to fight. How 'bout your uppity ups?" asked Eli while giving a teasing poke of his finger to Arthur's forearm.

Arthur feigned insult and answered, "Some of my people will need urging, but there is as much High Church blood soaking these fields as Low. My parishioners remember, my friend, they remember."

"I know they do, Arthur. Please remember to keep me informed."

"I will, Eli. Now, I must get back to the hospital. Give my regards to Mary and your kids. You are all in my thoughts and prayers."

"I will, Arthur. Be safe, and Jesus be with you."

The Reverend Arthur Canterbury departed the Petersville Church and checked his watch. It was half-past ten, and there was still much to do. *War! Well, if it has to be.* He put on his cuff-clips, climbed on his bicycle, and pedaled off to the hospital.

Harry slowly awoke from a deep sleep at noon. As he had requested, pretty Ginger Davis had come in to wake him up. Ginger was never brusque about this task. She was perched cross-legged on the corner of the bed. Unaware that Harry was awake, the nineteen-year old was looking at herself in the mirror while softly singing along to a song on her tiny Old World media player, which was a gift from Harry. It had hundreds of pre-Mad Flu songs stored on it and was her most treasured worldly possession. He grinned as he watched her long red tangles dance back and forth. She had an earplug cord in each hand and gently swayed them back and forth with the beat of the song. She had a nice voice, and Harry had no trouble determining the song. Given all his troubles, he couldn't imagine a better way to wake up. Harry had every intention of letting the song play out, but Ginger glanced at his face and saw his open eyes.

She exclaimed in embarrassment, "Oh, you and that shit eaten' grin!" She pulled the earplugs, tossed them aside, and dove on top of Harry, flailing away in a half-hearted beat down.

Harry took the hits with no resistance, and his smile turned to laughter. This just frustrated Ginger more and the mock punishment continued until she tired and collapsed at Harry's side. He rolled over and kissed her. Their lips parted. She shyly smiled.

"Hey, what ya' got to trade for a tumble, your highness?"

He chuckled at the working girl and replied, "I got a box of .22 long rifle cartridges over in my coat pocket."

"Is it a full box?"

"Well, there's one round missing."

Ginger considered for a moment and countered, "Two boxes?"

"Hell, nah. I ain't got two boxes with me. It's one or nuthin', darlin'!"

"Hmm. Okay, one it is," said Ginger. She stood facing her vanity's mirror. After pulling loose the bow of her pink chiffon robe, she let it slip from her shoulders to the floor. Her gaze never left Harry's reflection.

Harry had always thought she had the best figure in Lauderdale, and with her standing there naked, at five feet two and a hundred pounds, he had no reason to change his mind.

She knew she was as hot as a firecracker and loved mesmerizing the soon to be most powerful man in Lauderdale.

Harry asked, "Where'd ya' get that tan this late in the season, girl?"

Ginger pivoted to Harry and giggled, "See what ya' miss when you're gone for more than a couple of days? Nell just acquired the last workin' tannin' bed in the Spared Territory. She keeps it down in the basement and guards it with her life. We been takin' turns using it.

"Why don't you just tan without a stitch and not have them bikini lines?"

"No way. That little white ass gets you boys going and out of here in half the time. Why?" She turned and looked back over her shoulder at the mirror, "You don't like it?"

"Aw nah — I like it just fine. Now, get it over here."

Harry reached out and grabbed Ginger's arm. He gently tugged her back onto the bed and pulled the thick covers over them.

She cooed, "Not that I want you to take 'half the time', Harry."

He smiled, "I wouldn't dream of it, darlin'."

Later, Harry sat up on the side of the bed and pulled on his BDUs. He stood and walked over to his coat. Harry fumbled around in the coat's side pockets for a few seconds. Ginger watched his shuffling about with curiosity and anticipation.

Harry neatly stacked three boxes of *Lauderdale Loads* rimfire ammunition on the dresser and said, "That's three, Ginger. I have to head back to the hospital. I shouldn't have been gone this long. After I leave, go down and bring Robby up here and show him what's what. I'm sure it will be his first time. So, be extra sweet and patient with him. Deal?"

"Deal!" said the elated redhead.

Harry finished dressing, put on his pistol belt and coat, and walked back over to the bed to kiss the beauty good-bye. Without another word, he winked at Ginger and then closed the door behind him on the way out.

Ginger looked at the stack of ammo on her dresser, and thought, *Damn, me and Nell have enough to trade for a new wind generator now.*

She laid on her back for a moment. After a couple of minutes of daydreaming, she said quietly, "Ginger girl, you got paid in advance. Now, you best go earn it." She chuckled and thought, *Oh well. That Robby is kinda' cute.*

President Charles Edward Ragland VI glared at his son, Charles Edward Ragland VII. Charles leaned back in his sumptuous leather desk chair while Eddie sat across from his father. The Colbert President's office was on the third floor of the Ragland Building high atop Sheffield's river bluff. The wall behind Charles was dominated by a large picture window providing a magnificent view of the Tennessee River, the O'Neal and Singing River Bridges, and downtown Florence. The entrance of Constable Daniel Ragland broke their stares. Danny Ragland had entered without knocking. He had no fear of reprimand from his Uncle Charles. As Constable, he was second in power to Charles, with direct control over all of Colbert's defense and law enforcement personnel. Charles trusted no one more than his nephew.

Danny caught the air of tension hanging in the room. He exchanged glances with the two men and asked, "What's up with you two?"

Charles smirked at his son and responded, "Oh, we're fine. Aren't we fine, Eddie?"

Edward slurred, "Just fine, Cousin Danny, everthang's peachy."

Noting the sarcasm, Danny decided to invest little in the fuss and move on, "Okaaay then," After sitting in the chair next to Edward, he announced, "Chandler has not returned."

Charles shot back, "What the hell? That was hours ago. Wasn't he supposed to meet Biscuit and his cousins around sunup? Shit, even this pussy over here"— pointing at his son —"could've scuba dived the Tennessee River three times by now."

Danny showed no weakness or sense of responsibility. He felt no need to respond to the obvious.

However, Edward did, "Didn't you have spotters watchin' him from our side?"

The president snarled at Eddie, "Of course he did, and they couldn't see a damn thing through the fog on the river. Right, Danny?"

Danny Ragland simply nodded affirmatively and added, "My observers didn't hear a shot, but that doesn't mean much. I have had them spot-checkin' ever since the fog burned off, but no luck. No sight of a body — nothin'. They did hear a vehicle, but that was probably just Biscuit and them other two traitorous sons-uh-bitches."

The three men pondered in silence for a moment.

Edward knew that he would get his head bitten off once more, but he chose to press on, "Now we don't know when, where, or how they are going to kill Harry."

His father and cousin frowned at Edward.

Knowing he would probably have to answer to the president's son someday, Danny invested in his future by shrewdly inserting himself between the disgruntled father and son. He turned his head to Edward and said, "That's true enough, Edward. I thought about all this on the way over here, and I have an idea." Quickly, he turned back to President Ragland and continued, "We know that Wade is on his deathbed, and we can guess that Harry will call a full council meeting as soon as his daddy has passed. I say we gamble and send an ambassador across the river under a flag of truce."

"What good will that do?" asked Edward.

Charles said nothing, as he contemplated about the direction his nephew may be going.

12

Danny continued, "If we send the right person over there, openly, he can at least assess the situation and see if Biscuit, Curtis, and Bill are still in the mix. If they are missing from the meeting, then we can assume that they have been found out. We know that they weren't going to move on Harry for at least a day or two after Wade's death."

Charles said, "It would need to be quick."

"Absolutely," responded Danny.

"Who do you have in mind, Danny?" asked Edward.

As the constable pondered, Charles said, "Johnny Montjoy."

"What the hell? That old fag?" blurted Edward.

Danny interjected, "Yeah, Montjoy. He's perfect - smart, unthreatenin', an' charmin'."

Charles chuckled and said, "Those Smith bitches loved that guy back in The Peace. He was invited to every party, wedding, and funeral. And, he knows 'em well."

"But, Daddy! —"

"Nah, that's enough son. Johnny may be gay or just a big sissy. Whatever. But, he is loyal, kin, and downright fearless. You two don't know this, but I used him as a spy when Johnny was a teacher in Florence. He worked at their college and rented a room from that rich ol' widow lady, Mary Parker. He went around on sightseeing trips. Under the guise of documenting the flora and fauna of Lauderdale, he plotted the Slingshot patrol routes. That's what enabled us to knock most of 'em out on the first day of the Three Day War."

"No shit?" uttered Edward.

Danny indicated no surprise. The Colbert Constable was, in fact, aware of Montjoy's contributions to the field of espionage. He asked, "Uncle Charles, how's his health? What is he? Like seventy somethin'?"

"No, no, not that old. Miss Isabel, on her good days, keeps me up on him just like everybody else in our territory. He's pretty spry. If memory serves, he celebrated his 65th birthday this year."

"You know we need to respond to the Lauderdales' formal complaint about the electrical supply anyway, Daddy. Could that give us an angle?"

Shocked, the two territorial leaders smiled at the young man.

"Damn, son. That's a good thought. Maybe there is hope for you yet."

Proud, but embarrassed, Edward sat up with his chest pumped.

After a moment of mutual contemplation, Charles jumped in, "Okay, I better go see Johnny, myself. I know he'll do it. Crap, it's almost three o'clock. Danny, prepare an escort for Mr. Johnny and break the ice with the guards at the Dam — both sides, ours and theirs. I will have Johnny here at seven tonight for a briefing. Both of you be here a few minutes before that. Clear?"

Edward and Danny simply nodded, stood, and departed. Both men always knew when Charles Ragland was done.

Charles waved them out and walked to his big office window. He stared out over the Tennessee River, across to Florence, and beyond. He would normally imagine Wade Smith staring back at him, but at this moment he smirked, and figured his old Lauderdale foe was probably staring at nothing but the ceiling, if that.

Harry Smith stared out of his father's office window. His trip to the hospital was delayed by a meeting with his uncles. The meeting at the Lauderdale Building started at two o'clock. An hour later, it was over. Ben Smith, David Smith, Peter Hayes, and Clifford Hayes had departed. Ben and David were his father's brothers. Peter and Clifford were his late mother's brothers. He loved and trusted all four of the men. Each one ruled a different section of Lauderdale. Ben controlled the center of the territory and lived in Florence. David lived in Waterloo and saw to the west end. Peter did the same for the east end out of the Lexington community. Clifford held down the heavily populated Killen area just east of Florence.

He had disclosed the contents of the diver's envelope. It angered and hurt all five of them. Harry's traitorous cousins were making a power play. They had cut a deal with the Raglands to kill Harry, sabotage the Slingshots, and generally panic the Lauderdale populace. These activities would pave the way for an invasion force already assembled at the Colbert's Nitrate City Training Center. When a new order was restored, the Raglands would rule both sides of the river. The three traitors and their families would hold positions of power. Unfortunately, the envelope did not contain a disclosure of the invasion's river crossing or a battle plan. The Raglands were too wary for that.

Biscuit wrote that he would transmit a coded spark-gap message as soon as Wade died. He further promised that Harry would be assassinated within 24 hours of Wade's death followed by his accomplices' simultaneous attacks on the Slingshot Teams. He could not guarantee the destruction of all eight Slingshots, but he assured the Raglands that the force would be crippled.

The hot-tempered Hayes brothers wanted to go shoot all three of the conspirators and jail their wives and parents immediately, but Harry calmed them down and presented a plan. The five men worked out the details and promised to say nothing of this matter to anyone — not even their Slingshot team commanders.

Harry urged himself to go to his daddy's side, but he dreaded the pain of seeing the most important and beloved person in his world pass. He glanced at the Ragland Building on the Sheffield bluff and growled, "I'm going to send you to hell, Little Charles, and I'll make sure your goddamn son and nephew are there to keep you company!"

Harry's Uncle Ben was waiting to drive him over in his old pick-up. Two of Ben's men sat in the back. No weapons showed, but Harry knew the boys had heavy firepower concealed in the truck bed. As they drove away, Harry wondered if his next visit to this building would not be to his Daddy's office, but rather his own.

Robby came down the long staircase at Miss Nell's on wobbly legs. A moment earlier, Ginger had gently escorted the young man to her door, tousled his shaggy brown hair, and sent him on his way. Robby floated over to a big leather chair in Nell's front room and plopped down to stare out the room's picture window.

Shortly, Robby's orphan friend Brud Tate came in cockily strutting across the room. "What the hell is up with you, Dude?" asked Brud.

Robby shook off his dreamy state and glanced at Brud. Embarrassed, he mumbled, "Aw nuthin', Brud. What are you up to?"

Mean chuckles emitted from the shadowed corner of the room turning the orphans' heads in their direction. After a blink of their eyes to adjust to the dim view, they recognized the profiles of Slingshot 8 crewmen Chance Bardolph and Thomas Nim sitting at the corner's small table and two chairs.

"Nuthin' — my ass" growled Bardolph. "Our little Robby just lost his cherry. If that ain't enough; Ginger got it!"

A bunch of feelings came over Brud, but he thought it best to not respond. There was not only jealousy in Bardolph's words but anger, too. Bardolph and his old buddies had repeatedly begged Ginger to be with them ever since she started working for Nell the year before. However, the beauty would have nothing to do with them at any price. She sold her favors dearly to only those men she liked and to whom she was physically attracted. Her clients were usually young men from the gentry. Occasionally, a handsome construction worker or farmhand would get spruced-up, travel to *Miss Nell's*, and proffer a week or two's pay in exchange for Ginger's favors.

After Brud assessed that the two soldiers were probably too drunk to do anything but cuss and stare, he looked back to Robby and asked, "No shit, man?"

Robby said nothing, but his expression answered his friend.

Suddenly, 1911 and Nell burst in from the back. They were giggling, hugging, and kissing like a couple of lovesick school kids. The couple straightened up a bit after they became aware of their audience. They had obviously just departed Nell's quarters in the back of the cavernous inn.

Brud broke the silence, "Hi, Miss Nell! Hey, Sergeant Johns!"

Nell and 1911 slowly shifted their gazes from the cloistered Nim to the boys. Their smiles returned as they said, almost in unison, "Hello, fellas!" Neither addressed the dark corner.

1911 continued, "Well, my young friends, it is no longer Miss Nell, but Mrs. Nell or better yet, Mrs. Mortimer Johns."

Robby blurted, "Y'all got married this afternoon?"

Nell nodded with excitement.

The boys went over and gave congratulatory hugs to Nell and handshakes to 1911.

1911 teasingly added, "And, we have had our honeymoon as well!"

The embarrassed young men looked down while Nell smirked at 1911 and jabbed him in the ribs with her elbow. She was a curvaceous blonde in her mid-fifties, but she looked ten years younger at this moment. The six-foot two 1911 seemed a strapping six-foot seven.

Nim stood and fired his chair backward into the next table. The noise caused the boys and the newlyweds to turn and step back defensively.

Everyone knew what was up. Nell Quickly, the madam of Lauderdale, had not turned tricks in years. She let her string of ladies handle that traffic. She saw over them, her restaurant and bar, and the attached hotel. Nell steadied with a series of different men since her "workin' days." Nim was one of them. She had long since gotten over him, but he could not claim the same. 1911 honored his friend's broken heart for a long time. He and Nell, friends for years, recently realized they loved each other and began keeping time a few weeks ago. Nim had cooled towards them, then smoldered. He missed their dawn mission because he had "hung-one-on" to try and bury his depression over the situation between 1911 and Nell.

17

This marriage news was just too much. Nim staggered towards 1911, flipping open his combat folder, and extending it threateningly. Quick as a cat, Bardolph, leapt from his chair, sending it crashing to the floor, and grasped the wrist of Nim's knife wielding right arm and twisted it up towards the ceiling and leaned into his friend to bring him down. Robby and Brud raced to Bardolph's assistance. Nim finally let Bardolph wrench the knife from his grasp and began to sob uncontrollably.

1911 started to advance from his defensive stance. Nell stepped in front of him, put a firm palm on his chest, and commanded, "No, no, you go to the back! Go on, get out of here!"

1911 sullenly departed — slowly backing away from the scene.

After 1911 was gone. Nell went forward and knelt at the distraught Nim's head. With her knees gently touching his crown, she bent her head over his, clasped her hands on his cheeks, and wiped away the tears. She motioned for the others to let Nim loose and move away. They complied cautiously. Robby subtly picked up Nim's blade as he rose, closed it, and handed it to Bardolph. They watched the madam and Nim carefully, but could not discern the cooling whispers Nell bestowed upon her past lover.

After a few minutes, Nell rose. Nim rolled over and then stood up. Embarrassed and beaten, he tried to stand up straight and take a proud stance — chest out. He seemed to want to step forward but was stiffly holding back. He finally said, "How about a shoulder, boys?"

Brud and Robby came to his sides. One under each arm, they walked the old warrior to the door. Bardolph looked at Nell, shrugged, turned, and followed them out.

Nell watched the door close behind them. She turned to take in and assess the damage. It was just overturned chairs and a broken glass. She caught the time on the big clock back above the bar. She called to her staff cowering in the bar and kitchen, "Mae, Mary, get out here and help me straighten up this mess! It's after four and the first guests should be here any minute. We got an establishment to run."

Harry had been sitting by his father's bed in the old Smith Hospital for a couple of hours. Slowly, the other friends and kin left the room. Wade Smith's congestive heart failure was sapping the life from him. His eyes were clinched shut as he gasped for breaths. He was not going away easily.

Shockingly, Wade rose up on his elbow, looked around the room then fixed on Harry. Harry leaned forward and gently pressed his father back down. However, Wade's eyes never left Harry's.

Wade began to speak — broken occasionally by gasps for air. "Harry, my strong, handsome son, you've had your good times. I can't fault you for that, but I hope you have burned up that wild hair up your ass. You're a good soldier, a good leader, a smart tactician, tougher than I ever was, but with a gentle heart. Son, I overheard the nurse telling y'all that Ol' Jack had just died, right down the hall. Well that leaves you on your own, man. Time to step up. The shit's about to hit the fan again with the Colberts, and you know what that means. Be hard when you have to — even ruthless — but save sumthin' for the gentler times. God, I hope for gentler times."

Harry watched Wade's eyes glaze over and he said, "So long, Daddy. God bless you."

Robby was jarred from his sleep by Bardolph's angry voice. "Goddammit, Robby, answer that phone!"

In deep sleep, the boy hadn't even heard the jangle of the old wall phone. He sat up, rose, and stumbled to the phone. He paused a second at the wall, shook off the sleep one more time, and picked up the receiver.

"Slingshot 8." Robby stated in a surprisingly coherent voice.

"Is that you, Robby?" asked Ben Smith.

"Yes, sir."

"Robby, inform the 8 Team that President Smith passed away earlier this evening."

"Uh…Oh…Yes, sir. I'll tell them."

"And, Robby."

"Yes, Mr. Ben?"

"You know your ol' guardian, John Falstaff? He passed away tonight as well."

"Cap'n Jack is dead, too?"

"That's right son. I'm sorry. I know he was like a Daddy to you."

The boy could only manage a muted, "Ohhh."

"Somebody should have come and got ya'. You know…to be at his side. I guess with all the hoopla over Wade's condition and the fact that Jack went down so fast and unexpectedly…well, it just didn't get done. I hate that, son. If it's any consolation, Captain Falstaff was unconscious the whole time. The ladies from the home said that his head just tilted forward in the dining hall at supper, and it was like he went to sleep. They couldn't rouse him, so they sent for an ambulance and had him brought to the hospital. He died a couple of hours before Wade. I guess those two old hard-knots just had to go out together."

The boy had regained his voice and asked, "Is there anything else I need to tell the crew, sir?"

"Uh, yes there is, Robby. Someone will call in the morning with the details about both funerals. In the meantime, tell 1911 and the rest of 'em to have Slingshot 8 all serviced, armed, and ready down at the council hall just before noon tomorrow. That is straight from Harry. Okay?"

"Yes, sir. The whole bunch, in the 8, outside the council hall, before noon."

"That's right, Robby. Good man. Now, you try and get back to sleep, son. Tomorrow is going to be a long day."

"I will, Mr. Ben."

"Okay, goodnight."

"Goodnight, sir."

Robby returned to his bed, but sleep would be a long time returning. The recollections of a young man's life shared with an elderly soldier flooded his mind. Captain Falstaff had been hard on Robby but never cruel or unreasonable. There were many more good memories than bad. Robby was glad the old man went peacefully.

I'll miss you, Cap'n. God rest your soul.

DAY TWO

Despite the passing of President Wade Smith around midnight, the Lauderdale council members were notified immediately of his death. They were summoned to a ten o'clock meeting with the newly ascended President Henry Wade Smith V. Of course, the location was the council chamber in downtown Florence. As of five past ten, fourteen of the sixteen council members were in attendance. Harry was late. Not surprising — his father had always been late. The low rumble of conversation in the council chamber stopped abruptly after the chamber doors were thrust open by two guards. The council members stood.

Harry entered. He was almost unrecognizable to some — clean-shaven, in a coat and tie. Harry was twenty-six years old, six feet tall, had short light-brown hair, and weighed about 190 pounds — it was mostly muscle. He had killed his first deer at age seven and his first man at age fourteen. As the leader of the elite Slingshot Defense Force, he stayed in immaculate physical condition. He was skilled in the martial arts, close quarters battle (CQB), demolition, munitions, military tactics, and first aid. There was no better marksman in the Spared Territory no matter the weapon: long range rifle, assault rifle, sub-machine gun, shotgun, revolver, pistol, bow, crossbow, or muzzleloader. From his earliest memories, his parents had engaged tutors of writing, literature, history, math, chemistry, biology, physics, and agriculture to ensure he was a scholar as well. He could easily converse with and bond to any Lauderdale citizen — from a trapper at Panther Creek, through the mill workers of East Florence, up to the landed gentry of the big farms. He had one sibling, his little sister, Philippa. Both parents were dead and he was unmarried — a bachelor by choice. The finest ladies of Lauderdale had sought him out and failed. He had one past love that he kept secret. And now, by the Spared Territories' Laws of Ascendancy, he was the absolute ruler of the 700 square miles and twelve thousand occupants of the Lauderdale Territory.

He walked between the two rows — seven substantial chairs on each side and two simple padded stools, one on each side of the president's chair; Harry's new "throne." He made eye contact with all but gave no other acknowledgement — a neutral smile and set jaw were all he offered the assembly.

To focus his racing mind, Harry reviewed each council seat as he passed between them. His blood pressure rose at the sight of the first two. To his left was Biscuit Gray, his Aunt Sadie Smith Gray's only child and a Smith Family Representative of the Council. To his right was Bill Snope, his Aunt Jane Smith Snope's oldest son also a Smith rep.

The next pair was a contrast in character. On Harry's left was Captain Chester Hayes, his Uncle Clifford Hayes's oldest son and commander of Slingshot 7 stationed at Killen. If Chester was Simon Peter then to Harry's right stood Judas Iscariot. Curtis Campbell was his Aunt Samantha Smith Campbell's only son and the oldest of the three Smith Family Representatives on the council.

Next were his closest cousins, most stalwart soldiers and constant training companions. To the left was Captain Clara Smith, his Uncle Ben's only child and the Slingshot 5 commander operating out of East Florence. Captain Bedford "Bed" Smith, Harry's Uncle David's middle son, stood across from Clara. He commanded Slingshot 6 out of Waterloo.

The first three Slingshot commanders were in their early thirties. The next pair served as Majors after surviving arduous Slingshot missions well into their fourth decades. To the left was Major Wayne Morris of the Anderson community. He commanded the Slingshot 3 Team. Morris was short and thin, but he was wiry and tough. In contrast, Major William Fuqua's six-foot-four 280-pound frame towered to Harry's right. He commanded the Slingshot 4 Team out of West Florence.

Next on Harry's left was the head of the North Wall Defense Command, Colonel Phil Goins. His personal military vehicle was the Humvee of the Slingshot 1 Team, and he tended to have a bevy of support vehicles in tow, Light Medium Tactical Vehicles (2.5 ton LMTV) and Medium Tactical Vehicles (5 ton MTV). His HQ was in Cloverdale. Across from the Colonel was his daughter, Major Donna Flurry. A 35-year-old widow, she commanded the vaunted Slingshot 2 Team. Her all female team was stationed in North Florence.

Harry's four uncles, the District Leaders of Lauderdale, occupied the seats closest to his. Clifford Hayes, Leader of the Green Hill/Lexington/Anderson District was on the left across from David Smith, the leader of the Central/Waterloo/Oakland/Cloverdale District. Ben Smith, the Florence District Leader, stood across from Peter Hayes, the Killen/Rogersville District Leader.

As Harry cleared his uncles, he noted the two empty stools. Without pause, Harry turned and sat down. The council members sat as well. Henry asked, "Where are the preachers?"

Before a response could be uttered, the doors opened again. Eli Stram and Arthur Canterbury scurried in nodding at those in attendance and offering short nervous glances to their new president. They took but a few seconds to assume their perches on the awaiting stools.

Harry knew they would not have been late without good reason and continued, "Brother Stram, please open our meeting."

Eli was prepared. It was the Low Church's time to say the opening prayer. The Smiths cherished and honored both churches. Henry Wade Smith III and Charles Edward Ragland V got tired of dealing with the plethora of congregations and denominations. Over time, they and their sons amalgamated the populace into two churches. Originally, they were officially named State and Evangelical. However, the two congregations seemed to prefer the teasing-nicknames of High and Low when referring to one another. Eventually, the slang became badges of honor and the official titles were changed accordingly. The actual order of worship and dogma varied among the congregations of each official body, but administratively, a church member was in one or the other. The two ruling families had worked diligently for two generations to maintain the respectful and cooperative coexistence of these two community churches. The High Church, the Smiths denomination, was heavy in membership in and around the Florence District with small but devout congregations scattered about the rural areas. All of the High Church congregations reported to Arthur Canterbury, as did a handful of Jewish families that maintained a temple in Florence. Arthur's rolls also included seven Muslim members, four Buddhists, three Hindus, and a single follower of Confucianism. Without the Vatican, the Spared Territiory's Roman Catholics dwindled. However, they maintained two devout High Church congregations, one in Colbert and one in Lauderdale. Geographically, the Low Church was weighted to the opposite; Brother Stram oversaw several small and large community churches across Lauderdale and a single downtown church located across from Smith Park. He maintained an administrative office at his own church, The Low Church of Petersville. It was the Low Church's largest congregation — numbering close to a thousand members.

"Let us pray," directed Eli with his deep resounding voice. "Our Heavenly Father, thank you for the privilege to assemble and conduct the business of this blessed community. We will miss our dear friend and leader, Wade Smith. However, we take solace knowing that his earthly suffering is passed and further comfort knowing that he now resides with You in heaven. The image of Wade, reunited with his long departed, but dear wife, Mary, brings further joy to our hearts."

Harry visualized his mother. Although she passed in his thirteenth year, he could still see her face and feel her touch.

His voice elevated a bit for effect, Eli finished, "Lord Jesus, look over and guide us to make the right decisions — the brave decisions — for the citizens of Lauderdale. It is in your name we pray. Amen."

Harry said, "Thank you, Brother Stram. Now, on to the business of the day, Reverend Canterbury, are the arrangements for my father final?"

"Yes, Mr. President, they are. The service is tomorrow. It will be at the Florence High Church at one o'clock. A graveside service, with full military honors, will be held at three o'clock at the Smith Family Cemetery. That information will go out in today's copy of *The Lauderdale Messenger*. By the way, the late Captain John Falstaff will be buried at three o'clock this afternoon in the Soldiers

Cemetery. Captain Jack had no surviving kin. I will conduct a service at the graveside. I urge all of you to come and pay your last respects to this hero of the Three Day War. He surely had his frailties, but as Wade Smith often reminded us, the brave actions of Captain John Falstaff on the Singing River Bridge turned the tide in our favor during that brief but cataclysmic confrontation."

After a thoughtful silence, Harry moved on, "Thank you, gentlemen. Now, Reverend Canterbury, what is the stir among the congregations?"

Arthur paused to collect his thoughts and replied, "Well, Mr. President, after extensive conversations with our flocks, the Low Church Leader and I recommend you and the Council take a bold, even aggressive, stance in dealing with those south of the Tennessee. The Colberts are holding us for ransom with their control of the dam and they continue to use their old relationships to foment trouble among the congregations. Yes, Harry, we feel hesitation in addressing these issues is a mistake."

Harry now turned to look into the eyes of Eli Stram. The old fundamentalist simply nodded affirmatively.

Suddenly, the Council Secretary, Bonnie McGee, approached. She maintained a small desk in the corner behind the president's chair. Bonnie's goal was to be invisible during council meetings. Her quiet distraction was thunderous in its rarity. She handed a handwritten note to Ben Smith.

Ben took a few seconds to read the communication. One could tell that he had to decide just how to relay this news. Addressing his nephew for the first time as his new Commander in Chief he calmly said, "Mr. President, it seems that 'those south of the Tennessee' have sent an envoy. He crossed Wilson Dam this morning, alone, under a flag of truce. A Slingshot 5 security detail has him waiting in the foyer."

"Who did they send?" asked Harry

"Johnny Montjoy," answered Ben.

Harry chuckled and looked around. His ears filled with the hum of the surprised chamber. "Alright, calm down, folks. Calm down."

Harry extended his arms toward both preachers and waved them forward. Without hesitation, the two old men leaned in to confer.

Harry's eyes darted back and forth between Arthur and Eli. The men noted his expression. It was as if Wade looked at them instead of young Harry. It was the Smith war face. The old men had not seen it in years.

"Listen, you two. I must know. Are your people willing to go to war? I hate that things are moving this fast, but they are. Tread gently. Your response is vital."

Arthur spoke, "Harry, I know most of their hearts and they will support you. You must reestablish our bargaining position with the Colberts, and I fear it has come to violence. The Ragland's message Montjoy brings will tell us a lot. If they are reasonable, I will be the most surprised of all."

Eli nodded and said, "I have the same report, Harry. The Low Church members have had it. Many of my members remember all too well the blood and losses of the last war. The last thing they want is violence, but after hearing that the Colberts locked our monitors out of Wilson Dam, they feel we have no alternative."

"Very well," said Harry. He grasped the ministers' right hands and stood, pulling them up. He patted their shoulders as they returned to his sides. "Bonnie, have Johnny brought in."

A few moments later the chamber doors opened and in strode Johnny Montjoy accompanied by Tim Bratton, of Slingshot 5. Sergeant Bratton carried a beautiful pine box. Montjoy stopped a few feet in front of Harry.

Harry spoke, "Hello, Mr. Montjoy. What news do you bring us from the Ragland family?"

Arthur moved forward with his stool and placed it next to Johnny. As Arthur returned to stand by Harry, the President gestured for Johnny to sit.

Johnny responded, "Thanks, Arthur. President Ragland sends his best to you, President Smith. He mourns the passing of your father and urges you to call on him if he can be of any assistance during this trying time."

"Be sure to thank him for his condolences and the offer of counsel. How are you doing, Mr. Montjoy? Let's see. I have not seen you since I was a boy — back during The Peace — at my Granny's church."

"That's right Mr. President. You were a strapping lad with your father's hair and complexion but your mother's eyes. Now, I see them again. I remember President Wade Smith at your age. You could pass for him."

In spite of his attempt at a severe demeanor, Harry was moved by this charming courier's words. His eyes watered and he had to swallow hard. Harry realized why Charles had sent Montjoy.

Johnny Montjoy observed this emotion and provided a merciful distraction for the young Lauderdale leader by addressing Harry's perfunctory question as to Montjoy's well being. "As for me? Well, I was enjoying the solace of a peaceful retirement at my cottage until Cousin Charles called upon me to visit our northern neighbors on his behalf. Actually, I had not heard from him in over a year. I think he was surprised to find me alive and kickin' when he called!"

Mild laughter came from the council members. Harry even heard the demure Bonnie giggle off to his right.

"Well, it's good to see you again, Mr. Montjoy. What have you there, Sergeant Bratton?"

Surprised, Bratton responded, "A gift, sir. This gentleman carried it with him across the Dam. Don't worry, Harr ... I mean, Mr. President. We have examined it for chemical and explosive threats."

Johnny gasped and exclaimed, "Well, aren't I the scary character?" He glanced about the chamber and rolled his eyes.

Raucous laughter ensued.

Harry chuckled along then asked, "Is this the sole purpose of your errand, Mr. Montjoy?"

Johnny replied, "No, President Smith, Charles and Edward Ragland have discussed the Lauderdale's formal complaint. They conferred with their hydro-electrical engineers and community leaders. The electrical power needs of the eighteen thousand Colbert residents and their thriving economy are taking a toll on the generating capacity of Wilson Dam. Their only option has been to increase the number of periodic power shut downs for our Lauderdale brethren. No reversal of this current policy will be considered at this time. They apologize for the lack of notice about these shut downs and hope to give ample notice of any future changes. Oh, and President Ragland asks that you forgive the locking out of your monitors. He said it was just a mix-up between his son, Edward, and some of his people. The monitors will be allowed…uhm…rather, welcomed, back upon my return with a positive Lauderdale response."

Harry solemnly stared at the emissary. "By changes, do you mean the number of power shut downs could increase?"

"The Raglands fear that may be the case. And uh, not just the number but the duration."

The chamber had a hushed silence.

"In duration!" parroted Harry.

A meek "Yes" was all that Montjoy emitted.

Harry caught his Uncle Ben's eyes, "My dear uncle, let us see what treasure Montjoy brings."

Montjoy nervously began to chatter, "Actually, this gift is from Edward. He remembers the competitive sports relationship he shared with young Henry Wade Smith V in the summers of The Peace."

All eyes watched Ben Smith release the clasps of the pine box held by Sergeant Bratton. Ben lifted the hinged lid and peered in the box. "It's tennis balls, Mr. President." He retrieved one of the metal tubes of sealed tennis balls and held them up. "Six tubes I make it. A treasure, indeed, these days."

Harry mockingly repeated, "A treasure, indeed."

Harry calmly but grimly continued as his eyes burned into Montjoy's, "Tennis balls? Tell Edward thank you. Johnny, convey this message as well, we will soon have fun smackin' 'em around at the Colbert Sports Park. I will personally bounce one or two off Charles Ragland's head. However, it won't be attached to his body. Also, this match will only take place after the cries of a thousand Colbert widows have been heard and the gutters of Sheffield, Tuscumbia, and Muscle Shoals run red with the blood of many a brave Colbert soldier. Edward Ragland's joke is not a joke. He pokes fun at me, but I will poke a bullet in his little heart. Now, be on your way, Johnny Montjoy, and take Edward's balls with you. Perhaps they should have been made of brass. Curtis, Bill, and Biscuit, as Smith family representatives, please go with our good sergeant, and see to Mr. Montjoy's safe return."

And with that, the unexposed traitors, envoy, and balls exited.

After the chamber doors closed, Harry, announced, "Ladies and gentlemen, we have plans to make."

It was time to reveal his cousins' treachery and the Ragland's conspiracy.

Harry walked out of the council chamber around noon and found Slingshot 8 and its crew waiting for him. 1911 was at the wheel, Bardolph and Nim were in the back seats, and Robby stood in the open top hatch next to the secured M240 machine gun. Harry hopped into the passenger seat.

1911 simply asked, "The Arsenal, Harry?"

Harry smirked and nodded.

A Humvee's engine is not conducive to conversation but years of practice had the occupants trained to communicate in clear and loud voices. The crew all knew better than to ask about the goings on of a council meeting, but they each expressed their condolences to Harry. He thanked them, reached back and up, grasped Robby's shoulder, and pulled the boy down to address him face to face. "I'm sorry about Jack, Robby. We will all miss him."

"Thank you, Harry...uh...I mean, sir."

Harry smiled, squeezed the boy's shoulder, gave it a slight shake, and released him to return to the cold embrace of the brisk Alabama air.

Cheered by the show of affection, Robby smiled for the first time that day. He looked about at the traffic in town. It was slow for a Tuesday. He spotted some of his friends and acquaintances — most on bikes, horses, or in wagons. Only the most important or vital Lauderdales traveled in fuel burners. He thought to himself, *Here I am without a pot to piss in, no folks, no nuthin', and riding around in a motor vehicle with the president. Damn!*

As he pulled off his tie and suit coat, Harry said, "Fellas, we are going to check on my special project, have some barbeque at Benny's, and then come back in to see Captain Falstaff laid to rest at the Soldiers Cemetery."

"Sounds good Harry," said 1911, almost yelling.

The others laughed and 1911 shared an embarrassed grin.

Robby exclaimed from above, "Even I heard that!"

Nim, feeling better today, gave the boy's leg a hard pinch.

Robby emitted a short howl and screamed, "Mule bite!"

They all chuckled.

It was five o'clock p.m. and Johnny Montjoy sat by himself in Charles Ragland's study. The study was off the Ragland Palace's grand foyer directly across from the residence's entrance. He sat on one end of a brown leather couch — it could have held five men as thin as he. He was supposed to meet with Charles, Edward, and Danny at five. A Black Force Knight named Holt had personally escorted Johnny from the holding office at the Wilson Dam and brought him straight to the president's office. Holt handed Johnny off to the president's secretary, and she showed Johnny into the study. Johnny politely declined an offer for libations. He wished he had accepted a drink now that the big grandfather clock in the hall chimed the passing of the hour.

At about ten past, the three Raglands strode into the study. Charles warmly smiled and shook Johnny's hand.

Charles sat down in the chair behind his study's walnut desk, and spoke first, "Well Johnny, I'm glad you made it back from the north side of the river safely. How'd it go?"

"Quite well, Charles. Young Henry Wade seems to have taken to his role with surprising maturity given the rumors of his debauchery."

"Maturity? My ass!" expressed Edward.

"Shut up, Eddie," warned Charles.

"Did you find our Smith traitors intact?" asked Danny.

"Yes, Constable. They even escorted me back to the dam after I was dismissed from the meeting. Before we reached the dam, I tried to nonchalantly discuss our diver."

Danny pressed, "Did they actually see the diver swim off?"

"Well, I didn't specifically ask that question, but I don't think they did."

"Oh," responded Danny with a concerned glance at Charles.

Charles asked, "You didn't tell them that Chandler was missing did you?"

"Heavens no," said Montjoy, and he continued, "I lied. I just mentioned we were worried that Chandler might have been spotted. That led to their expression of total confidence in the secrecy of the exchange and a remark indicating that Chandler was last seen at the river's edge as they departed the rendezvous. They would be in a panic indeed, if they knew the diver was missing."

Charles looked at Danny and said, "Danny, do you still have people looking for a body?"

"Yes, Uncle Charles. Of course, all we can cover is the Colbert side of Pickwick Lake. If he drowned or was shot in the water, he could have washed up on the Lauderdale side, or he could be half way to Savannah by now."

A prolonged silence in the room was broken by Montjoy, "We don't know what happened to our courier, but Biscuit and his two cousins are going to assassinate Harry Smith tonight and light the fuse of a coup d'etat. There seems to be no reasonable way to stop it now. And Charles, I don't think you will want to stop it when you hear Harry's response to our position on the hydro-electric power supply."

"And what was that, Johnny?" asked Charles eagerly.

33

"Well, after I delivered the negative news about the electrical power and then presented Edward's gift—"

Danny interrupted, "What gift? Did you approve a gift, Charles?"

"Hell no!"

A nervous Edward squirmed a bit in his chair and then softly said, "Tennis balls."

Danny and Charles glared at Edward, then at Johnny.

Johnny simply nodded and said, "He asked that I return them. They are in the foyer."

"God dammit, Eddie, what were you thinking, son? I bet that went over well, huh, Johnny?"

"Harry told me to thank Edward. He would enjoy knocking them around at the Colbert Sports Park and would make it a point to direct a few at your severed head, Charles."

Edward put his face in his hands. Danny moaned as he leaned back and stared at the ceiling, but Charles laughed.

"I bet he would! I just bet he would!" exclaimed Charles.

Edward blurted out, "That whoring asshole! He just wishes he had half the forces to back up that kind of threat."

Charles ignored Edward and addressed the Colbert Constable, "Danny, we best be ready to attack at dawn on the day after tomorrow."

"We will, Uncle Charles. Actually, given that they are killing President Harry tonight, should we move the attack up to tomorrow?"

"No, Danny, those three Lauderdales have accumulated quite a little band of followers. Let's just see what mischief they can cause tomorrow. We will hit 'em after the wounds have had a day to fester."

"Very well, Uncle Charles. See you bright and early."

Charles turned to his son and said, "Edward, you better take Harry Smith seriously. He may seem irresponsible and immature to you with all the gossip that has filtered over in the past few years; but he comes from tough stock, and he has good council. Respect your enemy, son. While you have been spending your twenties with your sweet little wife, dabbling in questionable business ventures, and kissing the asses of the Colbert gentry, Harry has been turning himself into some kind of super warrior, SOB, badass. Hell, he crewed one of those damn Slingshot Humvees when he was just a boy during the Three Day War. The time I spent with him during The Peace was short, but I always thought he was a sharp kid. I know you hated his guts and the two of you just slammed away at each other in all of your silly games — tennis, golf, archery, and boxing. His father and I were going to try to get you two to bury the hatchet, but when we found out that your sister, Catherine, had fallen for Harry, we had to break off all the family social interactions. No daughter of mine was going to marry a Lauderdale Smith. Could've played hell with the ascendancy on both sides."

Edward sheepishly mumbled, "Okay, Daddy."

Charles turned to Johnny, somewhat embarrassed by forgetting he was witness to this last exchange, and quickly ordered, "Now, Johnny. You know what is said in here, stays in here. Right?"

"Absolutely, Charles."

"Good."

Charles stood and spread his arms as if to sweep the other three up, "Gentlemen, I'm starving. Y'all get on to your homes, and meet back here at eight in the morning. Johnny, Holt will drive you home."

"Thank you, Charles. Do you mean you want me back in the morning as well?" asked Johnny with a bit of surprise in his voice.

"Oh, yeah. You are back in the state department full time now, my man."

As Johnny nodded and turned to depart the President's study, the front door opened and two laughing women burst into the foyer.

Catherine Ragland and her personal assistant/security guard, Alice Boyd, were sharing a joke as they returned from the markets. Their smiles quickly vanished after they glanced at the four men and perceived their serious demeanors.

Recovering, Catherine smiled at Johnny Montjoy and said, "Why Cousin Johnny, it's been ages. How are you?"

Johnny grinned and hugged the beautiful blonde, "I am just wonderful, Catherine, and what a stunner you are. Still not snatched up by some favorite Colbert son?"

She laughed and responded, "No, thank goodness. Not yet."

Johnny smoothly shifted his charms to Alice, a contrasting but just as attractive brunette. "And Miss Boyd, it is good to see you as well. I thought you were the prettiest Knight Sergeant I'd ever met when you took my business correspondence seminar at the Black Force Training Center, and here you are even lovelier."

Alice blushed a bit and replied while flirting in kind, "Thank you, Mr. Montjoy. You should visit more often!"

Charles asked, "Busy out there, ladies?"

"Yep, yep, very busy, Daddy. Where's Momma?"

"She had a headache and went up for a nap a couple of hours ago."

"Well, Alice and I will take these groceries into the kitchen, so Miss Mable can start supper."

" Sounds good, sweetie. I'll go up and check on your Momma in a few minutes."

Catherine addressed Johnny, Charles, and Danny, "We bought the food market out. Would you gentlemen like to stay for dinner?"

Charles and Danny smiled and shook their heads to decline the invitation, while Johnny responded, "Thank you, Catherine, but I've been out and about all day and simply must get home."

Catherine said, "Well then, some other time."

"Of course, and tell Isabel I'm sorry I missed her," said Johnny.

The women smiled, then turned, and headed for the kitchen as Charles held the door open for the departing men. As he watched them walk away into the twilight, he noticed the pleasant temperature and breeze. *It's mild for November. I hope it stays like this for the next few days.*

Charles returned to the Grand Foyer and found his daughter standing with arms crossed staring at him.

"Daddy, what's goin' on?"

"There's no foolin' you, huh, girl?"

"No."

"Get Alice and come to my study. I need to bring you two up to speed."

"Is it war, Daddy?"

Charles maintained his poker face and said, "Go on, girl and get Alice like I said."

Catherine Ragland relented and left the room as Charles strolled to his study.

At the end of the morning's council meeting, Harry had directed Donna Flurry to put tails on Biscuit, Curtis, and Bill. After a busy afternoon and somber evening meal at his sister's house, a courier from Major Flurry reported that the three cousins were together at Biscuit's house in North Florence. Harry ordered the courier to have Major Flurry and the Slingshot 2 Team meet him and his Slingshot 8 crew at eight o'clock. The rendezvous point was to be the parking lot of the long-abandoned Seven Points Shopping Center — just a half-mile from Biscuit's place.

The Slingshot 8 crew patiently waited in the sizable garage of Philippa Smith Carter's house. Philippa had plates sent out to them with a selection of Lauderdale Soda soft drinks. The men set up lawn chairs around an old ping pong-table and were enjoying the home cooked meal. Nell Quickly and her staff were fine cooks, but it was a treat to take a break from the inn's fare.

Robby pushed his empty plate back, and after a long draw of his "coldrank", took a thoughtful look at their Slingshot 8 Humvee. He turned to 1911 and asked, "Hey, Mr. Johns, are there any Humvees left in storage?"

1911 paused a moment in consideration of "need to know." He concluded, *Hell, this kid is 'inside' now.* He looked the boy in the eyes and spoke, "Robby, son, this is inside stuff I'm about to tell you. You know what that means, right?"

"Yes, sir. I only share this info with Slingshot team members."

"Good, that's right, son."

Knowing this was an important conversation, Nim and Bardolph turned to listen. He would be a team member, official or not, after this.

Robby looked around at the old soldiers and settled on 1911's gaze.

1911 asked Robby, "How much Spared Territory history do you know, Robby?"

"Well, I know that 70 years ago some sort of sickness was killing people all over the world. The Lord spared Colbert and Lauderdale counties, or what was better known as the Muscle Shoals Area. It was then part of the State of Alabama of the United States of America. God sent doctors with special medicine to keep us from getting the sickness. Two best friends, Henry Smith of Lauderdale and Charles Ragland of Colbert, bravely took charge of their counties and worked together to keep the sickness, The Mad Flu, out of their land. People started callin' the two counties the 'Spared Territory' cause everybody else in the whole world died. Mr. Ragland and Mr. Smith had their people put up walls and fences around the territory to keep infected people out. The Mad Flu made people crazy just before they died and the Spared Territory's citizens had to use guns, flamethrowers, bombs, and even poison to keep the crazy infected old world people out.

"For a while, things went well in the ST. We even tried to venture out into the Old World to look for supplies, but none of the search parties ever came back. It's like somethin' in the OW just snatched 'em up. Since then, the only activity that has occurred outside the walls is some logging — not far out and heavily guarded. Later on, the two friends had a fallin' out. In year 21, the two families tried to kill each other off. A feud started between the two sides of the river. It lasted to year 26. Thousands of militiamen were killed from both sides, but all of the fightin' took place over here. We now call that the Long War. The Lauderdales blew up the center of the Natchez Trace Bridge to prevent western invasions from Colbert, and the Colberts did the same to the traffic bridge over the Wheeler Dam in the east. In 25, Big Charles and Henry Smith died a few months apart. They passed the power on to their sons, Little Charles in Colbert and Wade Smith of Lauderdale — who we bury tomorrow. They called a truce and signed a treaty. That was when The Peace started — with the Treaty of 26.

"There was no fightin' for a long, long time. Then in 61 the Colbert and Lauderdale churches got into it and a Colbert High Church official shot a Lauderdale Low Church preacher at a public meeting. A Lauderdale Low Church militia group ended up taking over the Wilson Dam and shut off the Colbert's power feed. Wade Smith was tryin' to get his militiamen out of the Dam and return control to the dam back to the Colberts, as per the Treaty of 26. Little Charles wouldn't wait; he ordered a sneak attack on the Lauderdale defense forces. The eight Slingshot teams were all nearly destroyed the first day — 'cept for Slingshot 8 commanded by Captain Falstaff and Slingshot 4 commanded by Major Fuqua — 'cept he was a captain then. Ragland's Black Force Knights lead Colbert Militia attacks across the Singing River and O'Neal Bridges at the same time. It went real bad for us at first.

"On the second day, those last two Slingshot teams provided cover for our combat engineers. Using fertilizer filled semi-trailer trucks, they blew the O'Neal and Singing River bridges to keep any more Colberts from comin' over and enabled our militias to get the upper hand on those Colberts who were trapped north of the river. With no supplies or reinforcements they didn't last long. On day three, Wade offered to spare the captured Colberts if Little Charles would negotiate a new peace. A day later, the treaty was signed. President Smith let his prisoners return to Colbert and he even tendered the operational control of the dam back to President Ragland. We got to keep armed monitors in the dam crew and they would make sure that Lauderdale received half the power from the generators. Also, the Colberts had to transfer 10,000 gallons of bio-diesel fuel to Lauderdale, and take down their four big 200-foot observation towers at Wheeler, Wilson, Sheffield, and Riverton. Also, both sides chose to cut off trade and travel between the two counties and limit communication. That was the Three Day War."

After a reflective pause, the boy added, "Oh, and Harry was on Captain Falstaff's Slingshot 8 crew when they blew the Singing River Bridge. He was only 16 or 17 years old, right?"

The three older men stared at the boy for a long few seconds until Nim asked, "You listened to them teachers and preachers real good didn't ya', Boy?"

"I tried, sir.'

1911 began, "Yep, they filled his head with all the usual Lauderdale crap — the half-truths and lies. Well, Robby, where did those doctors with the miraculous medicine come from and how did they get here?"

"I don't know. God, uh, ..."

"God!" 1911 cut him off and continued, "What have they taught you of the Old World? The world before The Mad Flu?"

Robby shrugged and answered, "It was a crazy time. There were billions of people, spread all over the world, in hundreds of countries. They had big wars, little wars, lots of different churches, lots of electricity and gas, H-bombs. They traveled all over the earth in airplanes, ships, cars, and trucks. People would sit around for hours and watch movies, videos, play electric games, talk on wireless phones, and eat any kind of food they wanted. Food was everywhere and it was cheap, but the weird thing was that lots of people in the Old World were starving and poor."

"That's good, Robby. You've done some readin' on your own haven't ya'?"

"Yes, sir. I did, Mr. Johns. Captain Jack had a library and he would let me read anything I wanted. He had an old computer too — until it finally conked out. He showed me how to use it to search for information stored on his discs and thumb drives. He also had a big collection of CDs, DVDs, and VHS tapes. The VHS movies usually broke in his old VCR — they were brittle but not the discs. The Captain had squirreled away a bunch of different kinds of disc players, speakers, telephones, radios, and the like. He loved all that stuff."

"Well, Robby, let me tell ya' some other things — some truths that don't get aired. Them preachers would like ya' to believe that divine intervention saved these two pissant counties here on the Tennessee River. That's a load of crap.

"This Mad Flu got started in the Old World and it spread really fast. Wade told us once that it was what they called a weapons grade virus. This bunch of crazy-ass terrorists from overseas used some worldwide gathering to infect people from all over the world. They didn't show symptoms for several days, so nobody knew they were carrying it until they got back to their home countries. One of the most advanced places for fighting disease in the Old World was in Atlanta, Georgia — the Centers for Disease Control. You know where Atlanta, Georgia is don't ya', boy?"

"Yes, sir. It's southeast of here."

"That's right, son. The CDC actually found a vaccine, but things were going to Hell so fast in Atlanta, they had to load the vaccine, equipment, supplies, and personnel on a plane and head for Cheyenne Mountain."

"The big fort the United States built in a cave, right?"

"That's right, Robby!"

The three men shared grins at the knowledge the unschooled orphan had accumulated on his own.

"The plane, a C-130, took some small arms fire on its takeoff from Atlanta. They developed an engine fire and started searchin' for a place to land. They ended up puttin' 'er down hard over at the airport in Muscle Shoals. Henry Smith and Big Charles Ragland had already become dictators of their counties and word of the landing got to them quickly. The military head guy on the C-130 got killed when the plane crash-landed. The main CDC doctor on the plane was named Dr. David Patel, and he was impressed by the amount of control Smith and Ragland were managing to maintain considerin' the way the rest of the world was falling apart, so he told them all about their flight.

"Dr. Patel lost his key scientists in the crash and some equipment. They could not produce anymore of the vaccine. However, they did salvage a bunch of the vaccine that had already been produced. Smith and Ragland would not let Patel contact anybody at Cheyenne Mountain or any other Old World government officials. Their only priority was to save as many local people as possible. Dr. Patel didn't put up much of an argument. The U. S. government had pretty much fallen apart anyway. Robby, it must have been unreal how fast that flu spread and what it did to those folks that caught it."

"What did it do, Mr. Johns? I mean I have heard old folks talk about it, but you know …"

"Hmm, from what Wade Smith told me, you start running a high fever, runny nose, cough, and then a horrible headache starts. Within an hour or so of the headache, you start losin' it. I mean … you go insane, and finally violent. This erratic behavior was the key to the Mad Flu's rapid spread, I reckon, and the worst thing was that the virus was airborne — what the scientists called a spore-borne virus. Doc Harris told me once, 'The virus quickly mutated and its incubation period shortened.' The time between comin' in contact with the virus and starting the fever got down to only a couple of hours. If an infected person didn't kill himself or get put down they would finally collapse after a day or so and die of internal organ failure."

Robby asked, "Was that probably sick people in Atlanta that shot at the CDC plane?"

1911 answered, "I imagine so, but who knows?"

"What'd they do next, Sergeant Johns?"

"Well, the two Shoals leaders worked with Dr. Patel on a plan. They decided to vaccinate everybody in the counties that wasn't already showing signs of the Mad Flu. They were ruthless about it — cold. Hell, they had to be. The vaccine covered a few thousand people in both counties and the rest were put down or isolated to die. They developed a border defense force that turned back or killed anyone from the outside world that would try to enter the area. The Colberts actually extended their territory to the east in what used to be Lawrence County, Alabama. Both sides thought it was best for the Colbert border to extend to a point just across the Tennessee River from the Lauderdale's eastern line of defense at the mouth of the Elk River. The Colberts established theirs at the mouth of Spring Creek on the Lawrence County side of the Tennessee. This would be more defensible. Plus, the southern approach to the Wheeler Dam was in Lawrence County and Spring Creek was a few miles east of it. The Raglands established an Eastern Defense Wall that meandered down to and along Ol' Alabama 33 running down to the town of Moulton. They decided to come straight across back to Mississippi in the west putting up the Southern Defense Wall along what was then Alabama Highway 24. That actually clipped the top of Franklin County off giving them Russellville and the Cedar Creek Reservoir. Ragland's move was a logistics gamble, but it paid off. The fine farmland, timber, and fisheries he picked up made for a richer economic environment than Lauderdale. The remaining population of Courtland, Moulton, Town Creek, and Russellville were more than willing to knuckle under to the Raglands and get the vaccine.

"All the old local governments and laws were dissolved. President Smith called the shots in Lauderdale and President Ragland in Colbert. The two men would not tolerate any bickering between the north and south sides of the river. They appointed family or trusted friends to run things in the two counties.

"At first, a mixed bag of old TVA employees and locals ran the two dams. Over time the Colberts, with their bigger pool of engineers and skilled laborers, took over operational control of the two dams. The hydroelectric power is vital to the survival of the ST. Of course, the spillways have to remain open almost all the time, as some of the upstream dams have failed. As you have seen in even your short life, Robby, the flooding gets out of hand a lot. Wheeler Dam's traffic bridge was destroyed in The Long War. It no longer produces power; they had to rob it of parts over the years to keep Wilson Dam producin'.

"As to your first question about the Humvees, Robby, Ragland and Smith stored all of the Army Reserve and Alabama National Guard equipment at the main National Guard armory in Florence. Also, the governor of Alabama deployed a National Guard mechanized infantry company to the Shoals just as things headed south. Those soldiers quickly surrendered their weapons, vehicles, and services to the locals after they saw the writing on the wall. They got vaccinated and assimilated into the community.

43

"Smith and Ragland created their own defense forces and chose to use some of the Humvees dispersed throughout the ST. The other Humvees, Bradleys, LMTVs, and MTVs were partially taken down for long term storage and carefully housed at the Lauderdale Armory which used to be the old National Guard Signal Battalion's headquarters. We had a total of 60 Humvees, about half that number of trucks, and two Bradleys. A lot of the Humvees had the Signal Battalion's metal boxes on the back. We slowly converted 'em to the assault vehicle versions over the years. They even had two Blackhawk helicopters that landed here looking for a haven. The Blackhawks were stored at the Muscle Shoals airport, and Big Charles gave the flight crews VIP status.

"The Colberts used the Blackhawks against us in the first war but they were shot down at the Battle of First Creek. Ol' Colonel Flurry ordered the use of his four Redeye missiles. Thank goodness his boys figured 'em out on their second tries and got hits on the Blackhawks. We fielded the two Bradleys in that same war, but they were taken out early on by the Blackhawks' TOW missiles.

"The Colberts lost their much smaller supply of Humvees in the first war, and they just used cobbled-up armored pick-ups in the Three Day War and have ever since. After the first war, Wade Smith developed the Slingshot Teams as a kind of flexible defense force that could not only defend us from the Colberts but help out at the OW borders as well. He chose to have eight heavily armed Humvees each accompanied by one to three LMTVs or MTVs active at any one time. Each was assigned its own combat team of elite troops. These were dispersed throughout Lauderdale County. The remaining Humvees and army trucks were held in reserve with their tires and canvas off, up on blocks, all greased down, and covered. Tires are the big thing, Robby. The Guard armory and the Army's mechanized unit had a goodly supply of spares, and the Smiths stored them with great care, but after 70 years even the sealed and temperature controlled inventory has degraded. At least some dry rot has gotten to all of them. They pop way too often."

Robby asked, "Why did he call 'em Slingshots?"

1911 answered, "Cap'n Jack said the Smiths just came up with that one day. He would joke and say the Smiths would, 'Sling 'em here and sling 'em there' as needed."

Robbie chuckled.

1911 continued, "During The Peace the Slingshot force intimidated the hell out of the Colberts and most political, religious, and economic confrontations went our way without a shot being fired. But, as good as they were, they proved to be very vulnerable to espionage and sabotage — two skills that the Raglands were very good at. The Smiths did not realize how big a 'fifth column' the Raglands had until it was too late."

Robby blurted a question, "Fifth column?"

Bardolph interjected, "Spies and saboteurs. You know... they blended in with the Lauderdale citizens."

Robby simply glanced at Bardolph and then nodded.

1911 continued, "Yep, they even blew up some of the stored reserve vehicles — a dozen Humvees and twenty trucks were lost all together."

Bardolph scoffed, "Vehicles? What about the lives?"

Robby mournfully said, "My folks were killed the first day in Florence."

1911 responded, "That's right Robby. Cap'n Jack pulled you out of the basement of a burning house and dropped you off at Nell's. We lost over a thousand people the first day and almost as many on the second. That changed quickly after the bridges were blown. They attacked with a force of close to three thousand. Our Low Church Militias finally got moving. Without reinforcements and supplies, the Colbert invaders were cut to pieces. Only a couple of hundred survived to surrender. Some criticized Wade for suing for peace so quickly, but dammit, the losses were so high and so quick.

"Anyway, Robby, after all the years, loss to combat, loss to attrition, and cannibalization, we have the eight teams' vehicles and only one Humvee and one LMTV in storage. Even carefully preserved, the reserve vehicles have been sitting there aging for seven decades. It's thin, son, real thin."

Robby observed, "Slingshot 8 ain't got any trucks or tac teams, does it?"

1911 answered, "Naw, Son. Just our sorry-asses."

Bardolph and Nim chuckled and bumped knuckles.

Robby absorbed the information in silence as he retrieved his new .38 revolver. He unloaded the gun, took a cleaning kit from his pack, and began to meticulously clean his new acquisition. After he finished, he reloaded the stainless five-shot revolver, wrapped it in a clean facecloth, and slid the bundle in his field jacket's right pocket. Harry had handed him ten rounds of *Lauderdale Loads* .38 Special ammunition earlier in the day and, best of all, they were riding in two speed loaders. Robby dropped those in an old freezer bag from his horde, sealed it shut, and carefully slid the baggie in his left coat pocket. He didn't have the luxury to test fire the weapon given his meager round count, but Cap'n Jack had taught him to shoot with a .22 revolver when he was just seven.

Nim had been watching the boy and spoke, "That's a nice piece, Kid. Just remember — never show up at a rifle fight with just a handgun, but if push comes to shove, stick it in their gut or face and let 'er rip!"

"Yes, sir," Robby uttered.

As on cue, Harry emerged from the house. The Slingshot 8 crew sprang to their feet and huddled for instruction.

"Okay, it's 7:30 PM. Let's head over to Seven Points to meet up with Slingshot 2. You guys ready for this?"

"Absolutely!" announced 1911.

"Hell yeah!" exclaimed Bardolph.

Nim gave a thumbs-up.

Robby nervously said, "I won't let you down, Harry."

Harry smiled at the boy, and said, "I know you won't, Robby. Jack would be proud of you."

1911 asked, "Harry, how 'bout the other Slingshot Teams?"

Harry answered, "2 is working with us, while 1, 3, and 6 are hitting Biscuit's cronies in Cloverdale, Anderson, and Waterloo respectively."

"When, Harry?"

"Between eight and nine, Mort."

"Wow!"

"Exactly! Guys, Let's roll."

Nell Quickly fretted over the lack of business. The dinner crowd was light, the gambling crowd lighter, and the whoring crowd almost non-existent. She heard the grandfather clock in her foyer chime eight. As if it were a signal, she moved from the bar to the parlor to check on her girls. Molly and Peg must have nabbed Johns and headed upstairs. Donna Lee, Cold Zee, and Barbara were tidying up the room for what must have been the third time, and Ginger was playing solitaire on the coffee table.

Nell walked over to Ginger and said, "Ginger-girl, you look tired sweetie."

"Naw, I'm fine, Nell."

"Fine, huh?"

"Yes, ma'am."

"I talked to Benny Stultz today. He took us up on our barter offer for a wind generator."

"Really? Well, ain't that nice," said Ginger with a big grin.

"Yep, he's gonna get a crew over here next week to install one."

Ginger turned back to her cards. Nell reached in and played two cards for her and giggled.

"Smarty pants!" said Ginger.

Nell, in a caring tone, suggested, "Ginger, somethin' big is stirring. The gentry know about it. That's why they are not comin' by tonight. Well, and the funerals, too. 1911 wouldn't have left me to go out on a cold night like this unless Harry really needed him. Whatever the reason, I don't think any of your fellers will be in to see you tonight. Why don't ya' go on to bed, darlin'? I'll watch a movie with these three and wait up for 1911. If Harry shows, I'll send one of these girls up to wake you. Okay?"

Ginger started to protest but noticed the look in her friend's eyes and relented. She said goodnight to her co-workers and headed upstairs. She thought to herself, *That bed is going to feel so good!* She looked back down from the second floor and saw Nell smiling up at her.

"I love you, Miss Nell."

"I love you, My Ginger-girl. Sleep tight."

As usual, the ancient radios weren't working. They had to approach the old shopping center with caution. Bardolph blinked the flashlight code in the direction of the vehicles parked in a dark corner of the lot. The proper response blinked back at them. This mission warranted the investment of some of their precious-few batteries.

Harry knew Donna Flurry and her women would be there ahead of him. They always were. As he stepped out of Slingshot 8, Major Flurry and her tactical-team leader, Sergeant Annie Slocomb, greeted him.

"Hi, Harry. How did Jack's funeral go?" asked Donna.

"Hi, ladies. Oh, it went as well as could be expected. Not many showed, but Jack would have laughed that off."

"Yes, he would. What a bunch of pricks."

"Exactly."

"Well, your cousins are still at Biscuit's. I got two gals over there watchin'. Whatcha think, Boss?"

"Let's take 'em down Donna."

The soldiers expected this, but hearing it so succinctly caused them to stiffen.

Without being asked, Harry turned to Annie and continued, "Annie, you handle the assault how you see fit. I don't want any of your team hurt unnecessarily, so tell your girls not to worry about bystanders or any surrender offers. Just go in hard and shoot for center of mass. If y'all don't have to kill any kids or wives, then don't, but don't jeopardize yourselves either. Remember, all three of those SOBs have been on the teams at one time or the other. They will know quickly that they are being hit and react accordingly. How much time do you need to brief your team and get into position?"

Donna deferred to Annie with a glance.

Without hesitation, Annie checked her watch and replied, "It's 8:05. We'll go in at 8:30."

"That's not much time, Annie," cautioned Harry.

"We don't need much. We already have an assault plan. All we need to do is get over there, move into position, and go. Besides, I'm afraid of them jack rabbitin' on us."

"Good enough, where can we position ourselves so not to be in your way, Donna?"

Donna spoke, "Annie, head on girl. I got this."

"Yes, ma'am!" said Annie and she jogged towards her tactical team.

"Harry, it's not exactly as close as you would prefer, but you will have an unobstructed view from a crest on a street two blocks over. Katie Cook can ride with y'all and show you exactly where I'm talkin' about."

"That's fine, Donna. Good luck! C'mon, Katie. Climb up in the turret with young Robbie and show us the way."

Katie got them to the observation position. Harry wondered just how long he could nurse any remaining service life out of their decades old night vision devices. It was 8:25 by the time they settled in. Harry could make out Annie's team as they positioned around Biscuit's split-level. Robby and Katie lacked the night equipment, so all they could do is stare at the glow from Biscuit's windows surrounded by the murky outline of the house against the darkness.

Bardolph was keeping an eye on his watch for them, and as he whispered "8:30" the lights in the house went out.

"She's cut their power," whispered Katie to Robby.

A series of explosions came from inside the house as the grenade launchers fired. It was quickly followed by the crackle of suppressed machine gun fire. A couple of retaliatory unsuppressed shots indicated that a cousin was fighting back. After a final explosion, there was silence.

A moment later, Donna Flurry shouted, "Harry, c'mon in."

The Slingshot 8 Team sprinted down to the house, leaving Robby and Katie to drive the lumbering Humvee down to join them.

Donna met Harry just outside the house and reported, "We got 'em Harry, and there weren't any women or kids in the house."

"What about your people, Donna?"

"Not a scratch."

"That's great! Well done! Say, they're all dead?"

"Yes, we count three."

Elated, Harry and Donna bear hugged only to be interrupted by Annie's voice from inside the house.

"Dammit to hell!" exclaimed Annie.

She stepped out just as the power was restored and the house lights came back on. She blinked and shook her head as her pupils adjusted.

Donna demanded, "What's wrong, Annie?"

With anger in her eyes, Sergeant Annie Slocomb answered, "Snope and Campbell are in there, but the third guy is not Biscuit Gray."

"What?" exclaimed Harry. "Who is it?"

" I don't recognize him, but one of my gals says it's a guy named Bart Dobbs from West Lauderdale."

Harry's heart sank. He knew Dobbs back from their teenage hunting trips. He was the same height and build as Biscuit. Harry darted into the house and had one of the Slingshot 2 tactical team show him the bodies.

Harry growled, "That's Bart alright."

Donna and Annie caught up with him and Donna loudly asked her team, "Have you searched the entire house and grounds?"

Several answered, "Yes, ma'am!"

Donna reluctantly surmised, "Harry, they must have pulled a switch on us somewhere, and I had my best surveillance people on them."

Harry stared at the bodies for a few seconds, sighed, and then calmly said, "Don't agonize over it Donna. They are, well, were in some cases, a slippery bunch, and Biscuit Gray is the slipperiest. But we gotta find him fast — real fast."

Ginger slowly brushed her flaming mane as she stood in front of the dresser's mirror. Her pink flannel pajamas felt marvelous compared to the slinky lingerie she usually donned at night. After Harry gave her these frumpy PJs last Christmas, he told her she looked "sexy as Hell" in them.

Suddenly, Ginger's heart began to race. Men are often confounded by the opposite sex's sense of smell. Ginger tried her best to not show her suspicion, but she knew she was not alone in her room. There was a man in there with her, and as hard as she tried, she could not tell where he was hiding. Was he under the bed or in her closet? She had gone in the bathroom to brush her teeth, so that was out. Her closet door was closed — almost shut. She had tossed her evening outfit in the bathroom hamper and then taken the pajamas from her chest of drawers. She hadn't been in the closet since before dinner and she could not remember if she pushed the door to or not.

I can't remember.

Could this just be one of her regulars pulling a mean prank on her? No. The scents of her clients cataloged in her olfactory memory cells; this was none of those. Besides, it was not just a hint of aftershave, booze, or tobacco, but something else all together. Suddenly, it came to her.

Back in the Three Day War, at ten-years-old, she had huddled in a ditch as her family's house burned. Her Daddy was shot dead trying to defend them from the black-clad Colbert Knights. Her mother threw dirt and brush over her and told her to lie still and not make a sound. "No matter what, Ginger. Make sure these soldiers are gone before you move."

She watched as one of the Knights raped and killed her mother just a few yards from her hiding place. At one point a gentle breeze carried the scent of her mother's perfume towards Ginger. Unfortunately, it was mixed with the soldier's randy smell as well. Now, the nauseating odor was in her room.

Upon the terrifying recognition, her composure began to fade. She could call out for Nell and break for the bedroom door, but any assailant in the closet could cut her off. The closet and bedroom doors were to her left as well at the end of her dresser. If he was under the bed, she could make it. The worst would be a bullet in her leg or slashed ankle. She instinctively flipped the brush in her hand to a stabbing position.

Biscuit pounced from the closet and drove a powerful right jab into the left side of Ginger's face. He was quick. She did not have time to call out. He caught her tiny frame so as to prevent any noise. He eased her onto the floor alongside her bed. He put his big hand over her mouth and carefully listened for sounds in the house — nothing but the speakers from the TV in the parlor. He double-checked the girl. She was out cold.

Biscuit smirked and whispered to her, "I'm afraid I broke that pretty jaw, you little whore. You never would take my business would ya', Miss Ginger? Just too fancy for Ol' Biscuit, huh? Well, your precious Harry will be along shortly and I'll take care of him too." He held his lock blade hunting knife up to her face, and pressed the knife's point into her forehead until a drop of blood appeared and ran down her temple. He thought to himself, *Fuck yeah, you're out cold, ain't ya', girl? I should cut your throat and be done with it, but I probably have some time to kill until our president shows up. Wonder what this bitch has got around here that I could tie her up and gag her with — then I could have some fun while we wait for Harry.*

Biscuit rose and passed the knife to his left hand, as he pulled up his sagging jeans with his right. The holstered 9mm pistol on his belt had pulled them down a bit, and the gravitational challenge imposed by his big belly didn't help either. He opened the closet door, pulled the light switch chain, and peered in — seeking a scarf and a couple of belts.

Ginger felt a searing pain above her eye. Then she felt as if she were floating out of a cave. This journey seemed to take forever. She managed to open her eyes and immediately saw a hulking figure rambling through her closet. The closet's overhead light was in her eyes and she had trouble focusing on him. As he glanced back, she quickly closed her eyes, feigning unconsciousness. She heard him resume his search and she turned her head left towards her bed. Clarity was returning; she saw her gun. Nell had given her an old single-shot .410 shotgun a few months ago. 1911 had sawed off the barrel just ahead of the forend and the buttstock just behind the grip. Ginger had taped it to the bottom of her bed board.

Biscuit turned back to check on Ginger and noticed her turned head. He said, "Aw hell, never mind," he muttered.

He transferred the knife back to his right hand, slumped over on top of Ginger, and slit her throat. He stood and glanced at his bloody work for a moment and turned to find a piece of clothing to wipe his hands and edged weapon.

Biscuit was not quite the efficient killer he imagined. As her life drained away, Ginger slid her left hand under the bed, found the grip of the little shotgun, jerked it free of its tape, and in one smooth motion pulled it free to meet her right hand. Her right thumb cocked the hammer and just as her killer turned towards her, the little south-pawed girl from East Florence squeezed the trigger.

In spite of the intervening years, Catherine Ragland could still feel Harry Smith's kiss on her lips, the look in his dark-brown eyes, and that smile of his — not a grin, not a smirk, just something in the middle. She had gone to bed early after she and Alice had eaten supper with her father, President Charles Ragland. Her mother had declined the evening meal. That was just before eight and now her bedside clock glowed nine. She knew it would be hours before she fell asleep, if at all. The information shared by her father was very troubling. Not obsessed over her personal wellbeing, she feared the possible loss of her friends and family in this new war. She thought to herself, *Daddy is so confident about how quick and devastating Danny's offensive is going to be against the Lauderdales. He carefully left out anything about killing Harry, but I know that is 'priority one' for him, Eddie, and Danny. Why do they hate the Smiths so much? Why can't we just get along for the good of the entire ST?*

Her father said he would tell her mother after he retired for the evening, but Catherine doubted his willingness or ability to do so. She dreaded the thought of having to tell Isabel herself in the morning. Even if he did man-up and tell her, it would be difficult dealing with her mother. Isabel was frail, both physically and mentally. A war could push her over the edge.

Moving away from thoughts of her troubled mother, Catherine imagined what she would say to Harry if she could magically pick up the phone and call him. That would take magic indeed, the phone lines across the river were all severed years ago. It was actually against the law to reach out to anyone across the river. *What foolishness!* With that, the worrisome sleep-robbing circle began again.

Harry ordered Donna to take every member of her team and search for Biscuit. He gathered his crew to devise a call plan, alerting everyone who needed to know about Biscuit. Robby jotted down call lists for each man as they brainstormed. Harry was going to work his list from Biscuit's phone, but he quickly opted to leave the site of such carnage and asked 1911 to swap with him. Traitors or not, two of the dead were his cousins, and in their youth, they had been his buddies.

The thick-skinned old warrior never blinked an eye. He suggested Harry call from a nearby friend's house and then plopped down at Biscuit's kitchen table and picked up the phone receiver. Somewhat selfishly he had the operator, Sarah Haney, ring Nell, at the inn, first. As the phone rang, he heard Harry, Nim, Bardolph, and Robby outside deciding who was going to call from where and how they would all get there. 1911 chuckled at their disorder in spite of the dire situation, and thought, *This isn't the first dance for this old bunny.*

The phone rang a long time. 1911 checked his watch to find it was five after nine. Finally, Cold Zee answered, and 1911 impatiently barked, "Zee, where's Nell?"

"She's upstairs."

1911 could tell from her voice that she was distraught. "What's wrong, Zee? Y'all got trouble there?"

He heard the phone shuffling and Cold Zee's voice, "Nell, it's 1911."

Next, he heard Nell's voice, "Give me that. Now you go sit down, Zee. Try to calm down! Mort, you need to get over here."

Not questioning the urgency, 1911 replied, "Well, I'm supposed to be looking for Biscuit Gray, but I'll get the 8 and head over."

Nell exclaimed, "Biscuit Gray is here, Honey! He just murdered Ginger!"

There was a pause as she choked back the sobs.

"But not before she blew his head off."

1911 was crushed by emotion, "What the hell? Naw! Aw, naw!"

With a sudden calm firmness, Nell ordered, "Mort, just hang up and get over here!"

1911 heard a click on the other end. He slammed the receiver down and immediately hollered, "Harry, don't leave! I found Biscuit!"

He got no response, and he heard the 8's engine crank. "Shit!"

Harry saw 1911 burst from the house waving both his arms. Thomas Nim, at the wheel, was looking back as he reversed.

Harry loudly commanded, "Whoa, Tom!"

The vehicle halted its backing-up with a jolt, and Harry jumped out of the passenger side. "What's up, Mort?"

"Get back in, Harry! I found Biscuit! I'll tell ya' on the way!"

John Bates and Alexander Court waited patiently for their friend and fellow cavalryman, Michael Williams. It was a cold, clear, and windless night with a three-quarter moon beaming down — sufficient to read by. When they arrived, around ten, at Michael's home on McKelvey Hollow Road, he seemed all packed and ready to go. As if he had forgotten something, Michael handed Dungee Boy's reins to John and walked back into his little house. Michael's wife, Tassy, was standing in the open doorway, and Michael quietly said something to her as he gently put his hand on her waist and directed her into the house. The couple moved away from the doorway, out of sight.

Alex and John exchanged grins and chuckles. Breaking the awkward moment, John addressed Michael's gelding, "Ol' Dungee Boy, I bet you think your master has lost his mind, don't ya'? 'I mean — gettin' me out of my cozy stall to go traipsin' off into the cold night'!"

Dungee Boy shook his head as if to confirm John's supposition. Both men laughed at the response. They needed to laugh. Since time immemorial, it's how warriors often dealt with impending battle.

Michael stepped out of the doorway and moved quickly to join the riders. Tassy once again stood in the doorway. He had a small sack in his hand. After mounting his horse, he brandished the sack at his friends and claimed, "Tassy made cornbread for supper. She had plenty leftover. I thought it would hit the spot for us around midnight."

"No sugar?" teased John.

Alex laughed again.

56

"Fuck you, Bates!" Michael, embarrassed, snapped and then grinned.

Michael slowly turned Dungee Boy to head down the road, but as he did so, he waved to Tassy.

She proudly exclaimed, "I love you, Michael! Alex, John, y'all take care now, ya' hear?"

Alex nodded affirmatively, and John shouted, "Yes, ma'am!"

Michael choked down the lump in his throat and managed just a choppy, "I'll be back soon, Darlin'! Watch over our babies!"

Corporal Williams heeled Dungee Boy. Horse and rider galloped off ahead of Privates Bates and Court. The latter two soon caught up with their squad leader. After the cavalrymen splashed across the first of three shallow creeks that crossed State Line Road, they slowed to a trot. It was going to be a long ride, and they couldn't push their horses too hard.

Michael asked, "Have y'all seen any more wolves?"

John answered, "Hell, yeah — two big greys. They killed one of my old man's dogs two nights ago and carried him off."

Alex spoke little, so when he did, it was a bit shocking, "Gettin' bold, ain't they? I saw a whole pack last week in broad daylight back down on the river over near the Northern Wall."

Michael said, "Yeah, I shot one trying to get in my barn a couple of weeks ago. It scared the crap out of the kids. I hate to leave home with those things lurkin' around. I tacked his hide up on the side of the barn — thought it might scare his buddies away."

Alex again, "Probably just piss 'em off." After a pause he pondered out loud, "I can't tell if they're slipping through a hole in the border wall from Tennessee or swimming the river from Mississippi."

Michael added, "The watch tower crews are reporting huge increases in the number of timber wolf sightings in all the lands around the ST. We even got word last month that the Colbert watch towers were reporting higher wolf counts to the south."

John interjected, "The Colberts? Must be a big deal if they felt moved enough to pass that along."

"Well, the eggheads still communicate even when the politicians don't. Those guys spark-gap back and forth all the time. Yep, the report even mentioned that wolves took a boy just west of Russellville."

"A boy? No shit?"

"That's the message they sent."

With no verbal exchange, the riders had their horses pick up the pace.

They turned onto Pea Ridge Road, and fifteen minutes later, wound down into the town of Waterloo.

Michael announced, "I got a surprise for you boys."

"What's that?" asked John.

"That fine gentleman and esteemed Slingshot 6 commander, Captain Bedford Smith, arranged for our motorized transport. They have a 5-ton and eight-horse trailer waiting in Waterloo. We can load up the ponies and ride into Florence. We'll pick up the Bennett brothers in Wright, Naddy Smith at Gravely Springs, and Tim Tate and Betty Sands in Oakland. Harry ordered trailer transportation for the whole platoon: Central, Cloverdale, and Underwood. Smart move — keep the horses fresh for tomorrow."

His fellow cavalry troopers grinned after finding they would not have to ride all through the cold night on horseback. With no spoken command, all three broke into a canter.

Harry held Ginger's lifeless body in his arms till midnight — in the same spot she died. 1911 and Nell seemed to take turns preventing the others from going to the comfort of their boy, President Harry Wade Smith V. The twelve chimes of Nell's clock finally pulled him from the dark place he had been for the past two hours.

A patch on her forehead was free of dried blood. He kissed the spot, eased his arms fully under, and then rose on stiff legs with

Ginger in his arms. He gently placed her body on the bed, turned to Nell, and asked, "Miss Nell, will you call Mr. Wiggins and have him come see to her? Make her pretty?"

"He's already here, Harry. We'll see to it. I'll watch over our girl, darlin'."

Suddenly, Harry saw himself in Ginger's dresser mirror and was aghast at the reflection. His clothes were soaked in her blood. He fought the urge to start crying again.

Mortimer Johns moved quickly to Harry's side and hurried him from Ginger's room. "C'mon, Harry, let's get you home."

1911 knew he would have to push Harry. He wondered silently, "How hard, though?"

Harry had lost much in the past two days, his father, a childhood hero and mentor, and the only woman he had ever seemed to care about. His three treasonous cousins deserved to die but the lack of loyalty causing their deaths was distressing. If that weren't enough, Harry had pressing domestic and military decisions to make in the morning. In the afternoon, he had two funerals — one state and one, definitely not.

1911 stayed at the inn, as did the stunned, young Robby, while Nim and Bardolph drove Harry to the Smith Complex. Harry had not been home in days. The guards were shocked when Slingshot 8 pulled up at the gate. Nim rolled down the window and scowled at them. The guards almost fell over each other racing to open the gate and flag the Humvee through.

Before they left the inn, 1911 whispered to Bardolph directing him to keep a close eye on Harry. With Nim at the wheel, Bardolph witnessed Harry's melancholy turn to a grim resolve. At his front door, Harry exited the vehicle and told them to be back at seven o'clock sharp. Bardolph moved to the front seat, exchanged a glance with Nim, and uttered, "He'll be fine."

DAY THREE

As Nell's clock chimed the noon hour, 1911 asked, "Are you sure you don't want to go to Wade's funeral, Nell?"

"Yes, Mort. I would love to stand at your side and pay my respects, but I just can't handle the looks from all those hoity-toity bitches."

1911 opted not to press his love on the issue any further. "Well, I won't be able to come back by here, Sweetie. Harry is riding to the funeral with his sister and uncles. Nim, Thomas, and Robby have the 8 all packed, so when the one o'clock funeral is over, we will be heading out."

"So, we are going to war again! Oh, what the hell! We'll probably all be dead in a week!"

"Now, Nell, quit talkin' like that. We got a good plan of attack. We'll kick their ass this time — they'll be beggin' for a treaty before the week is out."

"Uh-huh, well listen here, Ol' Man, just you be careful and make sure you come back in one piece."

"Yes, ma'am. I have every intention of doin' just that!"

They kissed and hugged for a moment and then the sound of Slingshot 8's diesel engine cranking caused them to break the embrace.

Nell softly said, "Mort, thank you again for all the help with Ginger this morning. I still can't believe that Harry, you, and all those others insisted on hand digging her grave. Do you like the spot — out by the pond?"

"I love it. That girl loved to sit out there by that pond. She would read and listen to her music for hours. An' we wouldn't have dreamed of messing up the place with some noisy backhoe. Kinda' amazin' how fast a dozen strong men got it done, huh?"

"Yes, it was, Mort, and Harry never took a break, did he?"

"Nope."

"Lawz yes! He loved that girl."

"Well, Nell Honey, I gotta go."

"I know you do."

"I love you, Miss Nell."

"I love you, Mr. Johns."

A last kiss and 1911 turned towards the big foyer's exit.

As he climbed in the 8, Nell hollered, "1911, make those rascals behave!"

He simply laughed out loud and shrugged helplessly.

They quickly departed and just as they turned on the main road and began to accelerate, Nim hit the horn.

Nell stood for a long minute or two after they were out of sight. She was trying to be optimistic, but found it impossible. This was all just a bad start to a bad time. Mercifully, Cold Zee joined Nell, hooked her arm inside her madam's, and slowly walked her back to the inn.

Colonel Phil Goins and Harry carefully peered through their binoculars at the far end of the Singing River Bridge. They stood atop the gutted ruins of what once was the Shoals Area's state of the art, eight-story, hospital. The structure stood on a hill to the northeast of the Florence end of the bridge.

"Are you sure you don't want me along on this operation, Harry?"

"Yes, Colonel. Absolutely. I can't be worrying about the wall after we cross the river. I need you and your people taking care of it just as you always do."

The old man sighed and relented, "Okay, Harry. We got your six. Of course, we'll keep an eye out for any flanking attacks from the Colberts as well — either across Wheeler or Pickwick Lakes."

"Thank you, sir. I'll be surprised if they don't try something in one or both of those areas even if they are small scale incursions."

The two men stood in silence for a moment and scanned to the south.

"Harry, I just want to say what a beautiful service that was for Wade. I miss him so much. He was a fine man, a great leader, and a loyal friend."

"Thank you, Colonel. He always thought the world of you too."

"I noticed those three aunts of yours were not there."

"Oh, yeah. I've got 'em under house arrest."

"Hmm, good idea. Just gonna deal with them later?"

"Yes, sir."

Colonel Goins took one more look at the southern approach to the bridge, the machine gun bunkers on either side, and then back across the bridge to the ragged-edged gaps in the bridge's roadways. He asked, "Your invasion plan is brilliant, Harry, but its brilliance is only outshone by its riskiness. A hundred things could go wrong, and more than a few of them could cause failure — catastrophic failure."

"I know, Colonel, but my Colbert agent tells me they are preparing to invade us. They have been amassing their forces up near Nitrate City for the last two days. I feel that we must hit them first and hurt 'em real bad."

"Not suing for peace this time, huh, Harry?"

"No, Colonel. We must end it once and for all."

"Harry, won't this probably burn the last of our Humvees and expend virtually all of our .50 cal', 7.62, and 5.56 ammo?"

"Yes, sir, and I anticipate heavy losses of personnel in not just the Slingshot teams but the militias as well. Unfortunately, I see no alternative."

"Did your mole report on how they planned to cross?"

"No, sir."

"Shame. If we'd known that, I assume you would have played defense."

"Correct, Colonel — that woulda' been a hell of an ambush."

"How many militiamen answered the call, Harry?"

"Around fifteen-hundred, give or take."

"Geez, I would have thought at least half-again as many!"

"Yep, Colonel. It's hard to leave those families, farms, shops, and mills."

"Well, I'll give ya' this; the Raglands would never imagine your launching an operation like this one just a couple of hours after burying your daddy, and the traffic from the state funeral even disguised your assault groups — once again, brilliant, Son. Reminds me of Wade. Hell, he'd be proud of ya', Harry."

That one got to Harry and he simply nodded and smiled as he choked back his emotions.

Sparing his young leader any embarrassment, the colonel shifted his eyes to the sky and declared, "And, what a gorgeous day to start a war! I pray the weather holds like this for us Harry." After an anxious glance back to the north he turned back to Harry and said, "Well then. Good luck, Harry, an' give em hell!"

After Colonel Goins turned and headed for the stairs, Harry picked up his field phone's hand set and calmly ordered, "Sarah, get me Captain Shelton."

"Yes, Mr. President. Connecting now."

As he waited, Harry asked, "Sarah, have the civilian lines been turned off?"

"Yes, sir. Only the hospital, and the designated lines are active."

"Good goin', Sarah."

"Artillery!"

"Artillery, I have President Smith for Captain Shelton."

"Oh, yes Ma'am. I'll get him. Just a minute."

"Fine, we'll hold," monotoned Sarah.

As they waited Harry asked, "Sarah, what time is central showing."

"Uh, it's coming up on 3:05, Harry … I mean, Mr. President. Sorry, sir."

"That's okay, Sarah. Give me a mark at the minute."

"Yes, sir. It will be 3:05 p.m. in eight seconds … five, four, three, two, one, mark."

"Got it, Sarah. Thanks. You okay, girl?"

"Oh, yeah, Harry. I'm doing great."

After a few more seconds, Sarah asked in a totally different tone, "Harry, I'm sorry about your daddy, and Gin ... well, everybody. You know."

"I do know. Thanks, darlin'."

They heard a shuffle over their receivers.

"Captain Shelton, here. Harry is that you?"

"Yeah, Scoot. It's me."

"We're all ready, Boss. Everything is set."

"Good, Scooter. You got all four of the 30 pounders battle ready?"

"We do, Harry. I thought one was never gonna make it in time, but those folks at the arsenal pulled it off. Get this, Harry, they managed to deliver 40 rounds last night and promise to have a couple-a-dozen more rounds here in the morning."

"Scoot, how many rounds did you end up with for each of the 57mm guns?"

"Eight each, Harry. Now, as I cautioned earlier, we could only afford to use ten rounds each for testing down at Gravely Springs, but they all went bang and the zero should be close enough for what you have in mind. It's a long shot even for an anti-tank gun — right at one-mile. My guys can do it though!"

"That's great, Scooter. We'll holler back soon."

"Okay, Harry. I can't wait! Damn, this is gonna be cool!"

After hearing the click on the other end, Harry continued, "Sarah?"

"Yes, sir."

"Sarah, connect me to Captain Juarez."

"Right away, Mr. President."

As they waited, "How's your momma, Sarah?"

"She's good, Harry. She was all packed, and as soon as the funeral ended, Uncle Tim was taking her out to Grandma's to stay."

"At Central Heights?"

"Yes, next door to Tim's place."

"Good thinking."

"I pray so, Harry."

"Lauderdale Cavalry."

"Yes, President Smith is calling for Captain Juarez."

"Speaking."

"Jesus, Harry here. Are y'all ready to go?"

"We are, sir. Every damned trooper answered the call — 48 men and women, 60 horses, and four mules for the wagon."

"Armed and ready — rations, bed rolls, and water?"

"Absolutely, Harry. They are all fired up! Some are even wearing sabers."

Harry laughed and cautioned, "Well, Jesus, tell them that Harry said, 'If yer close enough to cut 'em, by Gawd, yer close enough to shoot 'em'!"

Captain Jesus Juarez guffawed and responded, "I will, Harry. I will."

"Very well, Jesus. I'll see ya' south of the river."

"You betcha, Mr. President. We'll be there. Good luck catching up to us."

"Hey, Harry?"

"Yes, Jesus."

"Do you really think that bridge contraption will work?"

"It's got to, my friend. It simply has to."

"That's good enough for me, Harry. Hey, Michael asked me to say hi."

"Waterloo made it, huh? Well, give him my best, okay?"

"I will."

"I'm countin' on y'all, Jesus."

"We won't let you down, Harry."

"Good deal."

"Bye, Harry."

"Bye."

Harry heard the disconnect and started to hang up as well but hesitated, "Sarah, get me the arsenal."

"Uh, they're gone Harry."

"Already?"

"Yes, sir. They checked out about half an hour ago."

"Oh, okay. Good."

He paused.

Sarah gently asked, "Can I connect you to someone else, Harry?"

Harry emerged from deep concentration, "No, Sarah. Not right now."

She couldn't help but add, "Everybody is in the right place, Mr. President."

"Yes they are. Thanks, Sarah."

He placed the hand set back on its base.

Benny McPeters stood and stretched. It was cold in his bunker, and none of the late afternoon's sunshine was hitting his firing port. The light was all coming from his back and left. The sunshine bathed his view in gold. He made his periodic scan of the Singing River Bridge and the opposing shore. He jotted down his log entry, *No activity*. Benny silently read Big John's entry from the previous hour, *Saw people on top of the old hospital building*. Benny brought his binoculars back to his face and took another long look at the monstrous Florence structure.

"Hm, nothing now," he mumbled to himself.

His watch-shift buddy, John Claggett, was in their little break room finishing an early supper. John could never wait once his stomach started growling. "Big John, get yo' black ass back up here. It's your shift."

"Fuck you, Hillbilly. It ain't my black ass's shift until four o'clock and the bunker clock reads, two 'til. Besides, you need to recall that I stood watch until ten after three for your white ass, so you could finish that love letter to your girl."

" Love letter? Aw, hell naw! I was studying for the Black Force Academy entrance exam."

"Give it up, asshole, I just read it, 'Dear Mary, I miss you so much' … hah! 'I wish your momma would get over my past' … ha-ha!"

"God dammit, John! You had no business looking in my pack. You better not have gotten any food on that letter."

"Nuthin' but some chocolate pudding. It kinda smeared when I tried to wipe it off."

"Big John, you better be kiddin'! I mean it."

"Yeah, what's your scrawny 145 pound ass gonna do about it?"

"Don't even go there. I'm quick and deadly. I could be duckin' and jabbin' all around and over that six-foot-four 300 pound frame of yours."

Big John laughed uncontrollably for a few seconds and conceded, "Okay, little man, I give up. Let me just rinse off these dishes and I'll be right there."

Benny was tired of thinking up clever comebacks and chose silence. He peered back across the Tennessee and concentrated once again on the hospital building. Something on the third floor of the old ruins looked a little different. He blinked at a flash from that area.

The 57mm solid metal shot struck the concrete face of their bunker just at the sloped edge of Benny's firing port. A shower of concrete and metal decapitated Mary's suitor.

The concussion sent Big John to his knees. He shook it off for a moment and then crawled towards the front of the bunker while screaming his best friend's name. In spite of the dust and smoke, he spotted Benny sprawled on the floor. He started to make his way to Benny's side, but a second shot smacked the outside of the bunker and changed his mind. It didn't have the deleterious effect of the first hit, but John figured more would be coming. Given the mangled state of their bunker's M2 .50 caliber machine gun and telephone, he decided this was no place to fight. The concrete bunker was designed to fend off rifle and machine gun fire — not artillery projectiles. John darted back through the break room into their magazine. He grabbed their backup weapon, a 7.62mm M60 MG and a single can of ammo, and exited outside. He quickly realized that his options were few and unattractive. A move away from the bunker exposed him to Lauderdale fire. A third shot impacted the bunker, and a glance back through the exit revealed that the front had caved.

As John sat with his back to the rear of the bunker, he glanced across the bridge's southern approach at his matching bunker on the east side of the bridge. Given his traumatic last few seconds, he hadn't even noticed that his compatriots across the road were getting the same treatment. He saw no signs of life at the other bunker — just smoking rubble. It had lost all structural integrity. Big John realized he needed to move or the next hit would probably mean his death. He firmly grasped the carrying handle of the M60 in his right hand and the flat little handle of the steel ammo can in his left. He decided that a climb up the hill behind the bunker either straight away or to his right would be futile. He leapt to his left and sprinted down the treacherous slope towards the road. A fourth projectile struck his bunker as he ran.

Big John made his goal; an ancient drainage ditch that ran along the road. Now in defilade, the Colbert soldier made his way towards the bridge. He crept along the ditch until he reached the steel grate at its end. He knelt on the grate. His hands shook as he flipped open the lid of the olive drab ammo can, pulled its belt of 7.62 FMJ ammunition free, and loaded his weapon. A new series of impacts rattled him further. Having finished off the bunkers, the Lauderdales were reducing a set of Jersey barriers; placed years ago to block the bridge's entrance, they were only a few yards from John.

Captain Thomas Shelton, commander of the Lauderdale Artillery, heard the fire from his 57mm antitank guns. He had entrusted their deployment and engagement to his youngest but very talented battery commander, Lieutenant Smithfield Cox. Shelton's position was atop the old seven story bank building in downtown Florence. From his high vantage point, he could see the muzzle flashes from the little artillery pieces on the Lauderdale side of the Singing River Bridge and the resultant hits on the Colbert side.

His adjutant, Lieutenant Bill Walker, watched through his spotting scope as the two Colbert bunkers crumbled. "Scooter, Smitty is taken 'em down, sir!

"And the barrier?"

"Not yet. Whoa! Wait! He's on 'em now!"

Captain Shelton counted the rounds off. After he counted the 16th, he announced, "That's all of them, Bill."

Bill Walker studied the barrier for a moment and then reported, "The barrier is all busted up, Scoot, but there's a lot of debris in the roadway. It won't be a clean path for a vehicle."

"How about a horse?"

"It'll be fine for that — just fine."

"Okay, Bill. I'm sure Harry sees that from the hospital ruins. His orders are to proceed if at least cavalry will be relatively unfettered. Crank up the 30 pounders!"

"Yes, sir!"

Bill picked up the field phone's receiver. He already had the gun commanders on hold. "Gun commanders, fire!"

Within seconds, the four pre-sighted 4.2-inch repro-Parrott rifles fired. There was one gun each, on floors five, four, three and two. The once majestic ivory colored bank building had been gutted in the Three Day War and rendered dark grey, but its strong frame and steel reinforced floors made for excellent artillery platforms.

Scooter and Bill watched in awe as the Ragland Building on the south river bluff received the first volley of explosive shells.

"Bill, order them to fire at will."

Bill nodded and barked in the receiver, "Gun commanders, you may fire at will!"

A couple of minutes later, the next four shells departed within a few seconds of each other. The bank building vibrated from the recoils and muzzle blasts.

Scooter and Bill timed the reloading operations on their wristwatches. They raised their eyes from the timepieces and grinned at each other. They were proud of their gunners. No words were necessary.

One of the projectiles must have hit a loadbearing wall or support beam, as the right side of the Ragland Building began to slump.

Scooter carefully observed the results on the opposite side and chuckled as he saw people fleeing the structure. He wished out loud, "Damn, I hope that SOB is working today."

Harry watched President Ragland's offices collapse. Some sections actually tumbled down into the river just east of the south end of O'Neal Bridge. It had only taken a dozen of Scooter's precious Parrott rifle rounds to bring it down. There was now a deathly silence over the entire Shoals. Harry knew that Captain Shelton was now busy regulating his 30 pounders to their secondary and tertiary targets. The old black powder guns could shoot "nigh on four miles." Not far enough for downtown Tuscumbia, but they could raise hell in Sheffield and Muscle Shoals. Harry glanced back northwest at downtown Florence and admired the great cloud of gun smoke enveloping the old bank. There was a slight breeze, so the smoke was dissipating slowly. It formed a black pall over the Sheffield bluff, now ablaze, and a glorious grey crown over Florence almost turned golden by the setting sun. He thought it a positive omen.

Still only moments into his attack, Harry loudly spoke into the phone, "Sarah, do you have Slingshot 4 holding?"

She confirmed, "Yes, sir."

"Major Fuqua, are you ready, sir?"

"Yes, sir. Ready to go."

"Is Terrence Brown at the wheel, Major?"

"He is!"

"Good," said Harry, and after confirming the time as 4:15 PM, he continued, "Is the cavalry in place?"

"Yes, sir"

"Major, good luck to you and your team. Let 'em roll!"

"Yes, sir, and good luck to you, Harry."

Harry walked to the west edge of the roof and anxiously gazed north, up Helton Drive.

As Black Force 12 returned to Muscle Shoals from a security check at Wheeler Dam, Knight Second Class Jeff Connor heard the sound of explosions from the northwest and directed his driver, Corporal Trent Akers, to head towards the Singing River Bridge. They kept their vehicle in defilade on the Wilson Dam Road and crouched up to the crest of the southern approach to the bridge. Jeff scanned the destruction of their bunkers with his binoculars. Were that not enough, he was stunned by the sight of what looked like a building approaching the Florence end of the bridge.

Terrence Brown had the M984 Recovery Truck, a 10 ton wrecker, traveling about as fast as it would go. He could feel the swaying of the 80-foot tall steel and aluminum structure standing upright behind the cab. Fifteen miles per hour was all he dared as he crested the northern approach to the Singing River Bridge. Major Fuqua's oldest grandson was only 20-years-old, but he had demonstrated an innate ability to master even the most massive and complicated wheeled and tracked vehicles. He laughed nervously as he recalled a video he watched as a boy at Captain Falstaff's place. It was about the Old World's space program and one segment showed the massive vehicle used to transport a Saturn V rocket from its hangar to its launch pad.

Terrence actually had to brake as he rolled down the slope and crossed Huntsville Road. As he climbed towards the bridge, his confidence began to build, *Hell, I'm gonna pull this off!*

He glanced at the daunting hospital ruins to his left. Even with his diesel's deafening noise, Terrence could hear .50-caliber machine gun fire coming from the river-facing side of the eight-story structure. It was comforting to know the suppressing fire was being provided as promised.

A Lauderdale work crew had pulled a section of the northern Jersey barrier a few days earlier under the auspices of inspecting their end of the beautiful old bridge. Terrence smoothly geared up the big Army wrecker after passing through the opening. Now at 20 miles per hour, his heart pounded in his chest as he spied his target. The gap in the bridge was well over halfway across. Terrence had about a half-mile to go.

Actually, the Singing River Bridge consisted of two parallel concrete box girder bridges. To the west was the old southbound traffic lane and to the east was the northbound. The Lauderdale's Three Day War fertilizer bombs took out a couple of hundred feet of the northbound roadway. A couple of sections of deck and girders were completely gone leaving a lonely, naked, pier and pier cap in the open space. Just 55-feet of the southbound lane was missing. The deck and girders were missing from between just one pair of piers. The first half of the spans crossed over the Wilson Dam lock's channel and Patton Island while the second half crossed over the vast open water of the Tennessee River. The gaps were located well out over the river closer to the Colbert shore. The massive explosive charges only damaged the deck and girders beyond practical use originally, but in a post-war joint operation, Colbert and Lauderdale demolition engineers blew and torched away the remnants making a clean job of it. They gave the older O'Neal truss bridge running between Florence and Sheffield the same treatment.

Terrence stared at the smoking Colbert bunkers that straddled the southern approach to the bridge. He could not believe he was not taking any fire; even from small arms. His grandfather, Major Fuqua, had pulled ahead of him in the Slingshot 4 Humvee. Terrence's best friend, Darnay Ingram, was standing in the ring mount with his M240 belt-fed machinegun trained on the Colbert end of the bridge.

Terrence eased his M984 to a halt only 10 feet from the edge of the abyss. He put the transmission in park, set the brakes, and exited the vehicle. As he sprinted towards the rear, his crewmembers, two of the armory geeks, were already working fastidiously to start the tandem hydraulic winches that would lower his payload.

The armory boys eased "Harry's Bridge" down and its far end only made a gentle thump as it settled on the Colbert side of the gap. An old crane truck had followed Terrence in his mission. Its crew secured their crane to the nigh-end of the gapping bridge. After they disconnected it from the M984, Terrence returned to the cab and backed his vehicle clear. The crane crew lowered the Lauderdale end and quickly freed their equipment.

Just as Terrence and the crane crew raced their vehicles back to Florence, a LMTV disgorged a dozen workmen in hard hats and goggles. Armed with pneumatic equipment and giant steel pins, half of them dashed across *Harry's Bridge* while the rest went to work on the near side. Finished in seconds, they had successfully set securing pins in both ends.

Darnay broke from his MG's sight picture and glanced at the departing LMTV. Movement from the Lauderdale end caught his attention. Upon recognition, he laughed and loudly proclaimed, "Major, here come those hillbilly nightriders from the west end of the county!"

The major looked back and sarcastically reprimanded his gunner, "'Hillbilly nightriders?' Hell, son, that's the Lauderdale Cavalry leading Smith's First Invasion of the South!"

Despite the occasional .50 caliber ricochet, Jeff Connor continued observing the bridging activity on the Singing River Bridge.

Trent Akers suddenly pointed to their end of the bridge and said, "Jeff, one of our soldiers is down there off to the left side of the road."

Through their field glasses, both Black Force soldiers intently studied the figure hunkered down in the gutter.

After a few seconds, Trent continued, "My God, Jeff, if that ain't Big John Claggett down there with an MG!"

"I think you're right, son."

"Oh, crap!" exclaimed Trent and continued, "Lookie there, Jeff! Here they come!"

Knight Connor did not need his field glasses to make out several dozen cavalry troopers rapidly crossing the bridge.

"Let's go, Trent!"

"What about Big John, sir? We just gonna leave him?"

"We have no choice, Corporal! We have to get back to the Black Force station on Avalon and call this in."

They sprinted to their vehicle and were soon headed south towards Avalon Avenue. As Trent depressed the accelerator, he scornfully growled, "Damn, I hate to leave John Claggett back there."

Jeff simply stared at Trent for a couple of seconds and then focused his attention forward shaking his head in exasperation.

Corporal Michael Williams spat his chaw to the right and fought the urge to close his eyes as he spurred Dungee Boy across the relatively tiny aluminum bridge. At least the bridging crew added sturdy six-foot high side rails to the structure before departing. The workmen cheered his cavalrymen on as they passed.

Michael's squad of eight troopers led the cavalry assault. Behind him, trotted Captain Juarez's headquarters element followed by the remaining two mounted rifle squads and the weapons squad.

Bringing up the rear were the handlers with the remuda and the supply wagon.

None of the 1st Squad's disciplined mounts balked as they crossed the precarious bridge. Michael slowed Dungee Boy to a trot as the others crossed and now they were back to a full gallop. He removed his right hand from the reins and drew his three-screw single action .44 Magnum.

His granddaddy had traded for the big revolver at a gun show back in the Old World days. Michael's father carried it in the Long War and passed it along to Michael just before he died in ST Year 60. The story goes that the barrel was originally over seven inches long and the weapon was in bad shape. Michael's granddaddy had a local pistol smith take the barrel down to five inches, re-crown the muzzle, perform an action job, and polish and re-blue the whole thing. It was an early long-grip model. The handgun always possessed an almost magical balance. Even after all those years, the handgun's action was still in-time, very accurate, and cocked "as slick as owl shit." Michael and the revolver became inseparable when, during the Three Day War in 61, he used it to kill two Black Force Knights ransacking his mother's house. This tie between man and gun only strengthened as scores of deer, hogs, coyotes, and most recently, a hundred pound timber wolf fell to the old handgun. Lauderdale Loads developed a decent pistol powder in 65. They didn't produce much of it, but his long ties to the Smith family and his cavalry service earned him the right to purchase five pounds of the smokeless flake powder. Michael used moderate charges of that powder and his own hand-cast 240-grain lead semi-wadcutters to generate about a thousand feet per second from his cherished supply of .44 magnum cases.

Each Lauderdale trooper was responsible for his primary mount and weapons. Sure, the Smiths helped them out with secondary mounts, ammunition, reloading components, tack, and food to some extent, but most prided themselves on their self-reliance and style. This carried over to their uniforms. Other than the standard issue tan briar pants, dark-brown dusters, and the Smiths' chocolate colored rendition of the Andrew's hat it was "to each his or her own." To this ensemble, Michael had added handmade tall brown cavalry boots, brown gauntlets, a green and blue plaid flannel shirt, green kerchief, and brown leather suspenders. His pistol belt and holster were brown leather as was his rifle scabbard. The scabbard contained a Short Magazine Lee Enfield No. 4 Mk II rifle. His belt knife was a handmade eleven and three-quarters inch Bowie.

Michael and Tassy had dropped the kids off at her momma's one morning a couple of years ago. They took the day by themselves to have a picnic on the Natchez Trace and pursue a favorite pastime. They loved to rummage through old abandoned residences and farms for undiscovered treasure. Over the years, Tassy had developed an almost sixth sense for locating the hideaways used by the prior OW occupants to horde their cherished possessions. That particular outing yielded an underground survival vault. It contained some spoiled food stores, mildewed clothing and blankets, deteriorated batteries, and some pots and pans. However, in the back corner was an efficiently sealed plastic drum containing two virtually unissued SMLEs and a couple of thousand rounds of military surplus .303 British ammunition.

The rifles had been partially disassembled and greased. The .303 rounds were still in their sealed factory shipping containers — all loaded in five round stripper clips and in turn, cloth bandoliers. Best of all, they were corrosive primed. Michael had learned from his old gunsmith friend, Hubie Moss, that the corrosive primers had a prodigious shelf life when properly stored. The guns functioned superbly and a sampling of the ammunition all fired safely and accurately. The use of this corrosive ammunition required extra attention to cleaning, but Michael and Tassy developed a meticulous regimen to address that challenge. Michael chose to carry one of the Enfields off to war and left the other for Tassy's use. The woman could "flat-ass shoot" and it was comforting to have her armed with more than a shotgun, crossbow, and longbow.

Michael's peripheral vision revealed John and Alex coming up on his sides. As planned, the two were to pass ahead, and when in range, lob grenades from their M79s into the rubble at the Colbert entrance to the bridge. The 40mm grenades would have little effect on the shattered concrete barrier, but Captain Juarez hoped they might nullify any hidden Colbert defenders. Michael slowed Dungee Boy enough to let his men get out front about ten yards.

The .50 caliber machine guns stopped after they passed the gap. Now, it was just the sounds of the horses' hoofs on the concrete road surface, their panting, the jangling equipment, and the sporadic emboldening shouts of his troopers. Then — pop, pop, boom, boom. Michael had feared, for just an instant, his hard charging friends would reach the blast radius of the grenade launchers' projectiles, but the almost simultaneous explosions occurred 40 or 50 yards from the lead riders, well out of range.

These were the last-two M79 rounds in Lauderdale inventory, so the pair of troopers simply tossed the fired weapons to the left and right, respectively. In unison, the two drew their handguns and began to rein back their mounts to better negotiate the debris. As John and Alex closed on the barrier, they discovered an opening in the middle. The 57mm antitank guns had managed to set a section of the Jersey barrier ajar and the two cavalrymen exchanged grins as they both mentally calculated it was wide enough for a vehicle to pass. The troopers were almost embarrassed by the total absence of Colbert response. The bunker crews must have been it; that was understandable, great, but an emotional letdown for the pumped warriors.

Michael halted the rest of the squad about 20 yards back and hollered to his men at the barrier, "Whatdya' think?"

John yelled in reply, "It'll do, Michael. A Humvee will fit through here from right to left — no problem! We can pull a crane truck and backhoe up in here tonight and clear all this shit out!"

Michael turned in his saddle to Private Naddy Smith who was anxiously waiting with a flare gun in hand, "Shoot the flare, Trooper!"

Captain Juarez was holding near the middle of the bridge after crossing *Harry's Bridge*. He saw the 1st Squad's flare and immediately ordered his 1st Sergeant to have the rest of his platoon advance at a canter.

As the cavalry departed, Major Fuqua ordered one of his Slingshot 4 privates, Billy Urban, to proceed. Billy eased his vehicle, a barely functioning old pickup, onto the aluminum bridge. The armory geeks had cut the cab's top off, and Billy donned a harness with a rope attached. The other end of the rope was tied to Slingshot 4 just in case the bridge gave way. It held. Billy parked his rusty ride to the side of the bridge and stepped free, firing two thumbs-ups back to his team.

As Major Fuqua climbed into the passenger seat of his Humvee, Darnay finished untying Billy's rope. After reclaiming his position in Slingshot 4's ring mount, he gave Billy, now at Slingshot 4's wheel, the command to cross the aluminum span. Harry's geeks warned that his bridge would not support a LMTV, so Fuqua's twelve-man tactical team jogged after his vehicle. Behind them rolled their two lightly armored pickups with ammunition, water, food, and light equipment. Identically manned and equipped, Slingshot Teams 2, 5, and 7 followed. Less than a mile to the west, the four companies of the High Church Militia Battalion departed the middle school. From a like distance in the northeast, the eight companies of the two Low Church Militia Battalions departed the high school.

Harry had been darting around the hospital's rooftop observing his army's progress, while anxiously scanning the Colbert side for signs of activity. Machine gun fire from the Colbert end of the bridge caught his attention. He switched from his binoculars to his spotting scope and adjusted the focus to clarify the image at the opposite shore's Jersey barrier, a mile away.

John Claggett heard two smaller explosions up on the bridge followed by the clopping of horses' hooves on pavement and finally, some shouts. He once again considered chunking the heavy M60 and making a mad dash up the hill towards Muscle Shoals or scampering into the thick brushy woods to the west to make his way to Sheffield. To further his confusion, he had distinctly heard distant explosions from both of those directions as well — more Lauderdale artillery fire he suspected. He cautiously stood and turned towards the bridge's entrance hoping to catch a glimpse of the enemy's activity and better assess his situation. John saw two Lauderdale Cavalry troopers direct their mounts through the shattered remains of the barrier. His blood boiled as he studied them. They were dashing country boys with long coats, dark hats, and brightly colored shirts, sitting atop big jet-black horses while brashly brandishing their pistols. A contrasting image entered his mind — his friend Benny sprawled on their bunker's floor with the torn remnants of his head strewn about. That was it.

Big John had enough machine gun practice to know that shoulder firing his weapon was challenging, but by going prone and employing the M60's bi-pod, he would lose sight of the two Lauderdales. He impulsively took a couple of strides up and out of the big concrete gutter, took a firm stance, raised the 24-pound MG to his shoulder, and began to fire repeated bursts at the horsemen.

After he saw their horses crumple to the ground, he laughed and screamed, "That's right you redneck motherfuckers! Take that! Take that, you Lauderdale trash!"

Big John drug his dwindling belt of linked cartridges behind him as he walked towards the bridge and point fired the M60 from his hip until he suddenly realized that one of the downed troopers was firing at him. He felt a numbing blow to his left thigh that brought him to his knees.

At full gallop, Michael and Dungee Boy cleared a shell-impacted section of the barrier. About 50 yards away, Michael saw the hulking frame of a large Colbert militiaman slumped to the right of the road. He drove Dungee towards the Colbert defender. As he closed the distance, his adversary recovered a bit and was bringing his belt-fed weapon to bear. The seasoned horseback warrior seemed to throw two shots at his target as his outstretched right arm snapped forward, then back, with the recoil from each shot. He knew both connected. The big Colbert soldier paused, still on his knees, but upright with twin spurts of blood pumping out the front of his chest. After a couple of seconds, he fell to his left side with his hands still clutching the smoldering machine gun. Michael shot him again, in the head this time from just a few feet, as he turned his horse to see to his men.

Nearing the bloody melee of writhing horses and screaming men, Michael leapt from Dungee in a sprint and knelt at John Bates' side. He pulled his friend's head and shoulders up to his own chest.

Blood accompanied each word as John spoke, "That sumbitch shot me, Michael. He machine-gunned me and my Black Jack both. What the hell, Michael? What the hell?"

"Okay, John. That's okay. Just relax now, son. Lie back and relax."

Michael shifted his attention to Alex. Alex was trying to use his right leg to pull his left leg free from under his big gelding, Cider. Cider was gasping for his last breaths. He had stopped kicking, neighing, and snorting. Just a series of peaceful groans emitted from the almost still creature. Michael transfixed on the surreal scene for a few seconds. It seemed like an eternity.

The rest of 1st Squad dismounted with Betty and Natty holding the stock, while the Bennetts and Private Tate, now armed with their rifles, scanned the hillside for threats. Black Jack was a few yards away, off to the west of the roadside, thrashing and limping about.

Michael, back in the moment, barked at his riflemen, "God dammit, somebody shoot that poor animal!"

His men nervously looked at each other — stunned.

Michael impatiently growled, "Aw, Hell!"

In scary smoothness he drew and aimed his revolver once again. Just after his arm finished its full extension and the third click of the revolver's cocking crescendo sounded, one of Michael's meticulously hand-cast 240-grain semi-wadcutters mercifully passed through Black Jack's brain.

That seemed to embolden the Bennetts and they scurried to Alex's aid.

Horace demanded, "Alex lie still!"

After handing his rifle to his brother, Horace drew his double-action 9mm pistol and put a killing shot into Cider's head, safely angled to not hit anyone if it happened to exit the animal's massive head and ricochet.

Horace and Eulis managed to free Alex. The blood covered trooper immediately stood and walked over to recover his pistol from beside his horse. The .45 caliber pistol's slide was locked back. Alex smartly ejected the spent magazine, slid it in his pocket, and reloaded the weapon with a magazine from the double-pouch at his hip.

Shocked, Michael inquired of Alex, "You ain't hit?"

"Uh, naw. I don't think so. Hey, I think I hit that Colbert. Did I?"

"Fuckin' A, you shot him in the leg. Thank God! It took him down for a couple of seconds and let me get on him."

Alex holstered his pistol and joined Michael at John's side.

As they stared at their buddy's face, Michael softly said, "He's gone."

Alex's voice quaked as he responded, "Oh? Yep, I guess so. Damn."

Jeff and Trent burst through the door at the Muscle Shoals Black Force Station. Knight Third Class Jason Miller was on duty with his communication tech, Marty Monroe.

"What the hell, Jeff?" exclaimed Knight Miller.

Panting from his sprint, Jeff spoke directly to Marty, "Soldier, get on the phone to Tuscumbia and tell them our machine gun bunkers on the Singing River Bridge have been destroyed. The Lauderdales have bridged the hole in the middle of the western lane and are crossing cavalry. I'm sure that vehicles and infantry will follow — if they haven't already. After that, get on the radio and report the same to Constable Ragland's HQ. I think he is in the field amassing the invasion force up near Nitrate City."

"Yes, sir!" complied Marty.

Jason asked, "Cavalry? How many, Jeff?"

"Looked like forty or fifty."

"A platoon?"

"Yeah, I guess so."

Redirecting, Jason said, "We have had some incoming artillery reported in both Sheffield and Muscle Shoals. The operator at the Ragland building put out an all-station report that they were under attack and evacuating the building."

Jeff and Trent just stood there for a few seconds — speechless.

Marty got through to Tuscumbia and did a fine job passing on Jeff's report. He had moved over to the radio and was trying to reach the Constable's people.

Jeff walked back to the barracks. He was gone for less than a minute. Upon returning to the ready room, he asked, "Jason, did they call all of your Muscle Shoals Knights out for the invasion?"

"Yes, sir. Well, almost. They left me Ben Jones and Put Springer. They left just before this all started — just to make our usual rounds."

"Damn, Jones and Springer? Crap, how old are those two — 60?"

"Older than that, I think?"

Jeff's mind was racing, and after a moment, he announced, "We gotta organize a defense. I'm surprised that the Lauderdale cavalry is not already here."

"I don't have any way to reach 'em, but those old guys should be back here any minute, Jeff."

"Okay, fine. In the meantime, let's open the weapons locker and see what we have. Trent, go outside and keep an eye out for Ben and Put. Marty, stay on that radio!"

In unison, both soldiers complied, "Yes, sir!"

Immediately, all four men halted after hearing two more explosions.

Jason glanced out the west window of the ready room, "Just a little west of here, Jeff! Where the hell did Smith get those guns from?"

Jeff responded, "Well, intelligence reported a year or two ago that the Lauderdales were trying to build a foundry in their industrial park. I wouldn't be surprised if they built some black powder guns. Well, we got some too!"

Jason glanced once more out the western window and said, "Jeff, the sun is down, an' it'll be dark in a half-hour."

The two Knights continued to the rear of the barracks, and as they hurried along, Jeff said, "Yeah, you're right, Jason, it'll be dark soon. I just hope that by attacking this late in the day, their plan is to establish a bridgehead and advance no further tonight. Bad luck on their part, we have almost all of the Black Force Knights and over half the Colbert Militia assembled just a few miles southeast of them. In the morning, we can push 'em right back into the river!"

They both nervously laughed at that prospect, and after a few steps more, Jason slowed and queried his superior, "What if they don't stop, Jeff? I mean, break out tonight?"

Jeff halted in front of the weapons storage locker. He chose to ignore his subordinate officer's last question, and simply commanded, "Unlock this damn thing!"

Captain Jesus Juarez halted his cavalry and dismounted his stallion, Chain Lightning. He passed the reins to Betty Sands. He ran through the barrier to assess the situation. It was a mess. He knew decisive command was called for.

Michael was trying to get his squad back on task.

Jesus wisely concluded the best course was to support his corporal's effort, "Troopers, I hate that we lost John Bates. He was as fine a horse soldier as there ever was or will be. You know what Ol' John would say, though, don't ya'?"

He had their attention now. They were fixated on their cavalry commander.

"He'd say, 'Hell, Troopers. Remember me later — maybe name your kid after me or somethin'. We got a war to win! I'm in God's hands now! Y'all go kill some Knights for me.' Now, let's get off this damn bridge before we all get shot or blown away!"

All within earshot emitted teary-eyed laughs and began to move.

He looked back to his horse platoon and shouted, "Corporal Jackson, get a couple of your 2nd Squad troopers to carry Trooper Bates's body to the side of the road bed. Doc Hayes will be along shortly and will have some militiamen take him back to town."

Michael loudly ordered, "1st Squad, mount up and let's get on recon as planned."

Michael and Jesus walked over to Alex. He was standing by Cider solemnly, eyes fixed on the dead animal.

Captain Juarez put a hand on Alex's shoulder, and after a few seconds pause, said, "Alex, you need to wait here for Doc Hayes. He is in one of Slingshot 4's vehicles. If he checks you out and gives the okay, you can join me at my HQ. You can rejoin your squad after they return from patrol tonight. I'll have the handlers in the remuda pull ya' a solid replacement mount, okay?"

Alex glanced at Michael and then his captain and said, "Yes, sir."

Juarez said, "Good man!"

The two men returned to their horses. Michael led his five remaining troopers east to his assigned patrol area.

With the 1st Squad as an example, all the mounted troopers passed through the barrier within minutes and were deploying to their designated patrol areas. After Juarez established his HQ in a wooded area at the crest of the southern approach, he checked his watch. It was 4:46 p.m.

By 6:00 PM, it was dark. Harry crossed with the Slingshot 8 team and established his headquarters just behind Slingshot 4's defensive position. The other Slingshots were similarly dispersed about a semi-circular perimeter that spanned a half-mile from the southern end of the bridge. After crossing the Slingshot teams and the West Lauderdale Low Church Battalion, Harry had his other two militia battalions hold in Florence. As planned, the bridging units returned to *Harry's Bridge* and they were feverishly increasing the strength of the structure. When they finished, the Lauderdales could start crossing their heavier vehicles and equipment — then the balance of the militia could cross. Harry feared that whatever artillery the Colberts possessed would begin firing on his bridgehead and the bridge itself at any time. He wanted to cross his assault force en masse as soon as possible.

Harry ordered Juarez to have all his cavalry squads back at the bridgehead by 9:00 p.m. He did not want to lose any of them stumbling across some Black Force fire team in the dark. Harry's precious few sets of night vision equipment were on the perimeter in the hands of his Slingshot Teams. He was betting it all on this military venture. He even pulled all of the .50 caliber machine guns from Slingshots 1, 3, and 6 and left each of those three teams with just a handful of grenades, and a few hundred rounds of 7.62 and 5.56 ammunition.

Harry's lower ranks were surprised by the lack of Colbert forces in the bridgehead area. He only informed the Slingshot team leaders and his militia commanders of the enemy's invasion plans and their amassing of forces in another zone. As fortuitous as it was, he knew it was a coiled snake in the corner. If his plans on the morrow were not as successful as those of today, he would be in trouble.

Danny Ragland had rushed to make Charles's 10:00 p.m. meeting. His driver pulled up in front of the Colbert President's house. The six foot three constable strode to the front door with his five and a half foot adjutant, Lawrence Foster, struggling from behind to keep up. They would have sprinted but their sense of decorum deferred them.

Security was now triple strength at Ragland Palace with black uniformed guards in abundance. All were armed with assault rifles issued from the Colberts' dwindling supply of serviceable OW weapons. It was the "first string" just as Danny detailed in his wordy contingency plan from the prior year. Charles always insisted on keeping his river bluff administrative building, but not blind to its vulnerability, he supported the plan. All of the Ragland Building's vital governmental functions were duplicated at the family's estate, Ragland Palace, just south of Tuscumbia.

A pair of guards opened the front doors for Danny and Lawrence. They entered the Grand Foyer. A couple of Charles's aids helped the new arrivals with their coats; it had already dipped into the thirties outside. Without further delay, the men headed down a circular marble staircase and upon reaching the bottom, found the mansion's council room doors open. Inside, one would have thought there was no crisis other than the fact that Charles, Edward, and all four members of the Coffee Club were already present. They stood in two cliques, drinks in hand, with all heads turned to Danny and Lawrence. Upon recognizing the occupants, Lawrence raised an eyebrow to Danny, stepped out of the room, and closed the doors. He hustled back upstairs to find an office and phone to use.

The Coffee Club was a nickname, actually the only name, for a group of cronies close to Charles Ragland. In the OW, prior to the Mad Flu, they would have been called a cabinet. The Colbert President would die before officially admitting the need for such counsel. In spite of Ragland's pride, the Coffee Club members felt honored to hold these positions of influence.

To the left of the long wooden conference table stood Brother Donnie Butler with a soft drink in hand. He was the head of the Colbert Low Church and lived in Muscle Shoals with his wife, surrounded by the numerous members of their extended family. Next to him were President Ragland and Pickard Thompson. Mr. Thompson owned a mill and two factories in Sheffield symmetrically located around his estate. An OW city in decline, Thompson had transformed it into the industrial, commercial, and cultural model for the ST. He micro-managed his two thousand employees with Fordian fastidiousness; ironically, they worshiped him, right down to his company stores.

The threesome on the right of the room consisted of Edward Ragland, The Reverend Thomas Utter, and Midge Burkett. Reverend Utter was the head of the Colbert High Church. A widower, he lived alone in Tuscumbia in a rambling old parsonage just across the street from his leading congregation's church. Midge Burkett was a striking woman, tall and thin with perfectly coiffed silver hair, piercing blue eyes, and an aristocratic almost blade-like nose. A widow, she ran Colbert's monetary system, thought to be the brainchild of her late husband. However, upon his demise in 62, it became apparent that Mrs. Burkett was its creator. Everyone knew that Midge and Thomas kept company, but it was perplexing to try and figure out why they tried to keep it a secret. The Coffee Club member's ages ranged from late 60s to early 70s.

Charles looked at Danny and thought him taller than usual. Charles reasoned his nephew's height was accentuated by the low ceiling of the council room. The Raglands tended to be on the shorter side. He thought of his late sister-in-law's family, *what a tall bunch they are.*

Charles knew what Danny was up against with Harry Smith's surprise offensive and forbade any war talk until his constable arrived. He wanted open minds occupying the assembly.

"Hello, Danny. Well now, let's all have a seat. Drink, Danny?"

"No thank you, sir. I had a bottle of spring water on the drive in."

After they all took their normal chairs at the table, Charles asked Thomas to say a prayer. Charles kept a mental record of this formality — it was the High Church's time. The prayer was succinct, and upon its conclusion, Charles spoke, "Catch us up, Danny, and please, everyone hold your questions and comments."

Danny was just as direct, "These are the facts as best I know. Following artillery fire at four today, the Lauderdales crossed the Singing River Bridge lead by cavalry. Their Slingshot forces and approximately 90% of their militia crossed within a few hours of the first shot.

"All of our bunker personnel at the bridge were killed. Fortunately a Black Force Knight, Jeff Connor, was in the area and observed the initial assault. He reports that the Lauderdale engineers employed some sort of portable bridge to span the gap in the middle. After the Lauderdale Cavalry crossed, Knight Connor withdrew to our Muscle Shoals station to report his observations. I might add that Jeff led a handful of Black Force Knights to prepare a defense for the facility that, as of last report, has not been attacked.

"I was organizing our own invasion force near Nitrate City at the time of the attack and got word of the Lauderdale action via radio. I went to the Black Force Training Center's administrative building and called in to Tuscumbia by phone. My intelligence folks informed me of the artillery shelling of the Ragland Building and other targets throughout Sheffield and Muscle Shoals. At that point, I activated Black Force Contingency Plan C; Black Force squads deployed to Muscle Shoals, Sheffield, and Wilson Dam.

Some of you may not be aware that we only have two functioning sets of night vision equipment. I keep one in my vehicle to be deployed when and where the greatest need arises. I sent the other set with Black Force 3 to Wilson Dam. After dark, that team used it to good effect. They carefully moved to a position west of the dam and observed the Lauderdale activities for a couple of hours. They pulled back closer to the dam after a Lauderdale cavalry squad skirmished with them at approximately eight. However, before retreating they observed the Lauderdales reinforcing their portable bridge followed by their crossing of a dozen or so heavy military trucks and as many SUVs and pickups, all probably 4X4s. The last thing they were able to observe was the crossing of multiple infantry companies.

"The Lauderdales seemed to have stopped with the establishment of a bridgehead. Whether wise or foolish, is to be determined as events transpire. Our verified losses so far are nine military personnel and 26 civilians. President Ragland lost ten of his people at the offices on the bluff and 16 other civilians died in the random shelling. I lost four of my soldiers at the bridge's bunkers, assumed dead. Four more have been killed in skirmishes with the probing enemy cavalry, and I lost one at our Sheffield supply depot to an artillery shell burst.

"That segues well into an assessment of this artillery attack. It seems they used a pair of high velocity guns firing from the ruins of the Florence hospital to take out our bunkers. I think several much heavier muzzle loading cannon were used to shell the Ragland Building and the commercial centers of Sheffield and Muscle Shoals. Those formidable artillery pieces are located in the scorched remains of Florence's old multi-story bank building. Reports of collateral damage are too spotty for me to discuss confidently at this time.

"That's about it Uncle Charles."

"Thank you, Danny. Questions, anyone?"

Edward couldn't have waited a second longer, "Danny, do you think they actually manufactured those high velocity artillery pieces that were used on the bunkers?"

Danny anticipated this, "Here is my best guess; I think they re-manufactured them. Do y'all remember those two old 57mm anti-

90

tank guns that used to sit outside the Florence American Legion Post?"

Nods occurred across the room.

"Well, they were there before the Three Day War when I was a teen, but sometime late in The Peace, maybe 59 or 60, they disappeared. I bet Wade's arsenal geeks managed to break the old welds, take the dozen coats of paint off, make a few key parts, clean up the rifling, and get them working. Making a sighting system for them would not be that difficult, and *Lauderdale Loads* can pull some near miracles in the ammunition department — especially if they had managed to come across some old 57mm shell casings or even dummy rounds in some collector's basement or den."

Pickard Thompson spoke, "Excellent theory, Danny. I have some thoughts on the big guns."

Charles interjected, "I bet you do!"

Chuckles and some laughter ensued around the table.

Pickard grinned and continued, "During The Peace, Ben Smith and some of his buddies, talked us out of some of the foundry equipment that was rusting away in Sheffield. I raised a flag, but no one listened. I'll give ya' two to one that those sons of bitches have turned out a batch of American Civil War type cannon."

Eyes passed from Pickard to Danny.

Danny affirmed, "My thoughts exactly, Mr. Thompson."

Edward, in a concerned voice, asked, "What about ammunition for those?"

Charles growled, "Hell, Son. There're just big muzzleloaders! Both sides got shit loads of black powder now. An' a mid-nineteenth century exploding artillery shell is very doable. We built some mines like that for land and water in the Long War."

"Oh," responded Edward.

Danny moved on, "Whether that be the case or not, did you all notice how the artillery fire stopped dead in the first hour. I estimate that they have expended their entire inventory of ammunition for both types of weapons. Harry used them for what he needed to do and is now done with them."

Thomas Utter commented, "I pray you're right, Constable."

Donnie Butler added, "As do I!"

Midge Burkett said, "I have old family photographs of my grandparents posing by big guns like that down near Mobile, Alabama."

"Ft. Morgan or Ft. Gaines, Midge," added Charles.

"Whatever, Little Charles. My point is that the things are so big and heavy. Harry's people couldn't carry the damn things around! Hell, they'd break his little bridge!"

All the men, including Charles, laughed at Midge's assessment for a couple of reasons. One, she was one of the few people that could get by with calling their president "Little Charles" to his face and two, her last statement conjured images of a big black cannon tumbling down into the Tennessee River surrounded by flailing Lauderdales.

Charles returned order by asking, "Well, Danny. What do you think he will do next?"

Actually, that was the one question to which Danny had no confident response.

"I don't know, Uncle Charles. I do know what I would like to do."

"What's that, Constable?"

Whether he has any clue that we are amassed at Nitrate City or not, I would like to attack his bridgehead at full force in the morning. By all reports, he has even reined in his cavalry. Thus, the likelihood of him continuing his attack tonight is scant. Lawrence has a battle plan that my staff and I have drawn up. I would like to present it to you."

Charles pondered a moment, reached for the phone console in front of him, lifted the handset, and said, "Pam, find Lawrence Foster up there and send him down."

As they awaited Lawrence, Pickard asked, "Danny, do you at least have some snipers firing down into Florence from the Sheffield bluffs — with their .50 BMG chambered rifles or something."

"There is no point, Mr. Thompson. My observers see virtually no movement in downtown Florence. I have scout sniper teams on the bluffs, but they have had no targets of opportunity, and we cannot afford to waste the centerfire cartridges. The Lauderdales were well prepared for this offensive of theirs. My scouts have reported the sound of generators drifting over from Florence and even the rural areas along Gunwaleford Road to the west. They knew we would immediately cut off their hydroelectric power allocation with the first shot from Harry's artillery. They have obviously been stockpiling fuel. By the way, I have not received one single report from my spies or collaborators. They must all be in captivity or dead."

With the last statement, Danny raised his eyebrows and glanced at the two Raglands.

All eyes turned to the chamber's doors as a guard opened them for Lawrence. He carried his briefcase in his left hand and a fistful of maps in the right.

It was after midnight when Danny and Lawrence exited Ragland Palace and hopped into their awaiting vehicle. Lawrence got in the front passenger seat and Danny in the back. The Black Force Knight at the wheel turned to his commander. The Constable of Colbert calmly but firmly said, "Drive."

DAY FOUR
THE MORNING

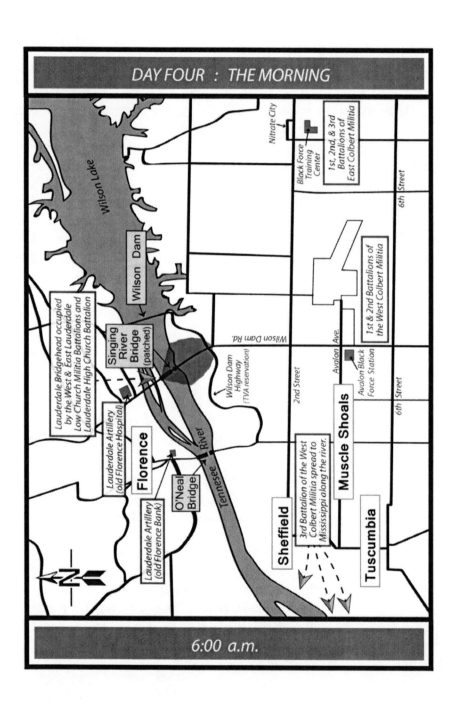

DAY FOUR : THE MORNING

6:00 a.m.

Wilson Lake

Wilson Dam

Singing River Bridge (patched)

Lauderdale Bridgehead occupied by the West & East Lauderdale Low Church Militia Battalions and Lauderdale High Church Battalion

Lauderdale Artillery (old Florence Hospital)

Florence

O'Neal Bridge

Lauderdale Artillery (old Florence Bank)

Tennessee River

Wilson Dam Highway (TVA reservation)

Wilson Dam Rd.

2nd Street

Nitrate City

Black Force Training Center

1st, 2nd, & 3rd Battalions of East Colbert Militia

6th Street

1st & 2nd Battalions of the West Colbert Militia

Avalon Ave.

Avalon Black Force Station

Muscle Shoals

6th Street

Sheffield

3rd Battalion of the West Colbert Militia spread to Mississippi along the river.

Tuscumbia

N

Harry dangled his bare feet in the warm water of Shoal Creek while sitting on their pier. The July rains of the past few days had caused the creek to rise; normally, his feet would have fallen well short of the surface. He turned his head towards the shoreline as he spotted the kaftan clad Catherine Ragland approaching from the back of Smith Lodge. She walked across the estate's manicured lawn and then stepped onto the pier. Harry could not take his eyes off the beautiful 13-year-old blonde, as she seemed to float towards him with an air of poise-driven grace the likes of which he had never seen.

"Why, Henry Wade Smith V, what are you doin' sittin' by your lonesome out here in just your swim trunks? Haven't you already had enough sun today, boy?"

"Oh, I don't know. It was nice to finally have a sunny day again. I guess I don't want it to end."

"May I join you?"

"Sure."

Harry was shocked by what the Colbert girl did next. She removed her cover up and dropped it to the deck unveiling a white bikini — quite the contrast from the more sedate floral-print one-piece she wore earlier that day. The sun was nearing the horizon in the west. Bathed in the orange light, she was too much for the 14-year-old boy's visual senses. Harry looked away towards the horizon in embarrassment.

Catherine sat down by him and cooed as her feet hit the water. Harry glanced at her and found her eyes firing right back at him. She laughed. Even his lightly sunburned face could not hide his blush.

Trying to recover his pride with a tougher tone, he parroted, "Why, Catherine Isabel Ragland, what are you doin' down here sittin' in your white bikini — just you and Wade Smith's son?"

She leaned in and whispered, "Just this."

As he settled into the heavenly press of her lips on his, a distant burst of automatic weapons fire brought him back into the present.

Surprisingly, Harry Smith had quickly fallen asleep around ten the night before. He had just emerged from that mysterious semi-consciousness one often experiences while waking with a troubled mind, a mental state in which actual memories view like dreams. The lamp was on in his tent and he checked his watch. It was exactly one o'clock.

Catherine Ragland had not slept at all. Earlier, she had watched out her window as Danny, Edward, and the Coffee Club departed the house. She tried to lie down and fall asleep, but it was futile. Catherine walked down the hall to check on her mother and found her fast asleep. She heard the occasional scurry of a servant on the first floor.

At half past one, Catherine went downstairs to check on her father. She found him sipping coffee in his study. Not at his usual spot behind the big walnut desk, but in a chair facing the window. She glanced out the window to find only darkness there.

He acknowledged her approach, "Hello, Sweetie. Can't sleep?"

"Hi, Daddy. No, too worried."

"How's your momma?"

"She's fine — sound asleep."

Catherine knelt beside her father's legs and rested the side of her head on his knee. He patted her head with his left hand.

"Love you, Daddy."

"Love you, Cate. Girl, don't ya' think this is the best coffee the Colbert Mountain green houses have ever grown?"

"I do, Daddy, but it should be, the price at the market is up to 15 credits a pound."

"15? Huh!"

"I wish more regular folks could afford it."

"They have their chicory, Cate."

After a minute of silence, Catherine asked, "So, they attacked us first?"

"Yes, they came across the Singing River Bridge in force and established a bridgehead."

"But we were all set to attack them, right?"

"Well, yes."

"Whatcha' gonna do?"

"Aw, Danny has an elaborate counter-attack all planned out. With most of our Black Force teams and militia already assembled near Nitrate City, he is going to attack Harry at dawn."

"You sound doubtful, Daddy."

"I am doubtful."

"Why?"

"Just this feelin' … I guess." After a long pause he continued, "Harry worries me. He is so damn smart and yet wild at the same time. I remember watching him play sports and compete in scholar bowls when he was a boy… back in The Peace. You just couldn't read him."

"I loved him, Daddy. I saw something different than you … and I guess … everyone else."

"I know, My Girl, and you still do. Don't you?"

"Well, part of me does, but if he was here … right now … he would probably kill us all. We've done so many horrible things to each other. Horrible."

"I guess so, but it's just the way things are."

"Does it have to be that way, Daddy? Does it really?"

Charles did not answer her question, but after a moment he suggested, "Why don't you try and get some sleep, Cate … at least lie down and rest."

With that, she stood and departed the study. Just past the entrance, she turned and asked, "What about you, Daddy? You goin' to bed at all?"

"Oh, I'll be along after a while. I just want to check on a few things."

"Okay, Daddy."

Catherine returned to her bed and curled into a fetal position under her covers. She worried, prayed, and cried a little. Somewhere around three she finally found sleep.

The scramble of servants and her mother's call jarred her awake. She glanced at her bedside clock, and through blurry eyes, saw 7:05 AM. Her bedroom glowed with the morning sun.

At 6:00 AM, they rolled *Knight Killer* out on the Cox Creek Parkway. In the pre-dawn, her silver gray outline became more discernible to the eye. Discovered years ago partially disassembled and hid away under tarps in the back corner of some long-dead East Lauderdale crop duster's barn, the aircraft was a P-51 Mustang. Given the lack of accessibility to the OW's supply of replacement parts and expertise, the P-51 would never fly as originally intended.

Almost written off a half-dozen times, the love and persistence of Crazy Ned Flanagan led to the restored flight readiness of *Jimmy's Gal*. Less her engine, propeller, fuel tanks, and original moniker, she was now the rocket powered *Knight Killer*, and Crazy Ned was going to pilot her.

Ned's nickname was well earned. A gift applied during his youth when he first started working at Wade Smith's armory. His exasperating eccentricities, manners, and demeanor were tolerated because of his unbridled enthusiasm, loyalty to the Smith family, and sheer brilliance as to things mechanical and chemical. His father taught him to build and fly ultralights and even had him stick a crop duster back in the 50's. Ned was a teenager then. He is one of the few ST residents ever to leave the bounds of the territory. In the air that is, and only for short distances. Military operations, lack of appropriate fuels, and just plain time led to the demise of aircraft in the ST over the past decade. Like his father before him, Crazy Ned found a home at Mr. Wade's skunk works. He concentrated on vehicles, weapons, and explosives as directed but always spent an inordinate amount of his spare time tinkering on the Mustang.

Last year, Ned was brought in to attend a planning meeting for *Attack Plan R*. Wade's health was beginning to fail and he had turned the meeting over to Harry — a test for the young heir. Harry decided to include several "outside-the-box" thinkers and Ned could only believe that divine intervention was at play when he saw the role that his pet project could play.

Eyes rolled in the meeting when Crazy Ned began to excitedly ramble about his plane, but Harry slowed him down with direct and intelligent questions. Ned made his case and sold Harry; *Knight Killer* was to be a reality. Ned left the meeting with all his other design and manufacturing duties reassigned. He was to concentrate on the P-51 and deliver death from the air.

The Lauderdale's P-51 Mustang was no longer an example of what may be the most successful piston-engine fighter plane of all time. She was now what Ned called a RATOG-B. That was short for Rocket Assisted Take Off Glide-Bomber.

After the C-130 "Fat Albert" crash-landed at the Muscle Shoals Regional Air Port seventy years ago, Henry Smith and Charles Ragland ordered the remains salvaged. Surprisingly the eight JATO bottles affixed to its fuselage were found to be unused and in perfect condition. They were carefully stored in the Florence Armory and actually forgotten for decades. Crazy Ned happened to be on the inventory team that came across them in 67. His gears never quit turning after that.

He invested two of the JATOs to test his ignition systems and to make sure their solid fuel propellant had not deteriorated during their careful but long storage. The other six were mounted under the wings of the Mustang — three to a side. Ned could afford to further reinforce the airframe given the missing weight of the engine, propeller, and fuel tanks. He hoped the plane would not tear itself apart once the thrust of the JATOs was applied. Ned's geek buddies cautioned that his mission verged on suicidal, but he disagreed. He had logically worked through his entire plan. He had confidence in both his skills and those of the handful of friends he entrusted to assist him with the project.

Knight Killer's ignition system was quite simple. The armory engineers contributed one of their coveted batteries to the project to run the P-51's modified electrical systems. Ned had installed three firing switches with safeties. They were labeled 1, 2, and 3. 1 would fire the two most inboard JATO bottles — just a few inches from the fuselage, 2 would fire the next two — each about two feet from the first two, and 3 would fire the two most outboard bottles — mounted about mid-wing. Ned hoped to just use 1 for takeoff, 2 for acceleration and altitude, and 3 for a final climb enabling him to make a return glide and landing on the Singing River Bridge. To save weight, he had converted the P-51s landing gear from retractable to fixed. Well, not as much fixed as "disposable." Just after takeoff, Ned could pull two levers in the left of his cockpit. Each lever was attached to cables. The cables in turn were attached to a couple of spring-loaded bolts, one for each landing gear strut. After the levers were pulled, the gear would fall free. Ned felt his odds were better for surviving a belly landing whether on the Singing River Bridge, the river itself, or even some bumpy Colbert road or pasture.

Danny Ragland had five of his six militia battalions muster at 4:30 AM; the 3rd West Colbert Militia Battalion was stationed well to the west of Sheffield and Tuscumbia protecting the lightly populated and vulnerable river bank. He ordered the 1st and 2nd West Colbert Militia Battalions to advance at 5:00 while all three of the East Colbert Militia Regiment's battalions held in reserve at the Nitrate City training grounds. Sunrise was at 6:28. It was now 6:25. Not wanting to squander his Black Force Knights and their precious few vehicles as machine gun fodder, Danny thought several of them better deployed to tow and position his new artillery pieces. Pickard Thompson's R&D people recently produced a modern take on the

19th century's 12-pounder Napoleon howitzer. These were muzzle-loading smoothbores capable of relatively rapid-fire, employing black powder charges behind solid cannon balls, exploding shells, or canister shells. Pickard and Danny had cajoled Charles into sacrificing almost every bronze statue and monument in Colbert for the project. Danny had six of the wheeled guns, a dozen iron balls, two-dozen exploding shells, and two canister rounds for each. Pickard promised another hundred rounds in three days, about a third each, of solid shot, exploding, and canister. Danny planned to have his Black Force teams fire all they had on hand at the bridgehead to support his infantry attacks. He was also positioning a dozen, three man, Knight fire teams armed with an assortment of automatic weapons to bring suppressing fire on the bridgehead's perimeter defenses. Danny hoped to have his howitzers, MGs, and infantry all in their assault positions by 6:45. He would start an all-out infantry assault shortly thereafter. His technical people managed to get their ancient radio equipment working and Lawrence was in contact with almost all of their units.

Nitrate City was the site of the Black Force Training Center (BFTC). Danny and Lawrence were high in the facilities observation and review stand looking over his reserves. Danny was prepared to deploy his reserves to exploit a breakthrough at the bridgehead or as a second wave to crack Smith's perimeter. A less than desirable contingency would be for Smith to launch a breakout, no matter the direction, in advance of Ragland's assault. He hoped that would not be the case and they would catch the Lauderdales by surprise. Danny Ragland knew all too well that "hope is great, but it's not a plan." He and Lawrence had their militia and Black Force commanders prepared to shift unengaged and reserve units to address any breakouts by the Lauderdales.

In the stillness of the dawn, Danny heard a distant roar to the northwest. He trained his field glasses in that direction.

Ned's friends helped him into the cockpit of the P-51D. They hovered about strapping him in and patting him on the shoulder while exchanging handshakes, thumbs ups, and high fives. The bubble canopy of the Mustang was already damaged when the plane was first uncovered. Since Ned's airspeeds would be moderate, they decided to save the weight and go with an open cockpit; just the windscreen remained. Cute little Jenny Simmons over in optics had manufactured a pair of flying goggles for Ned. He smiled as he donned the goggles and remembered the kiss on his cheek she added when presenting them.

At 6:30 a.m., a tow vehicle eased forward and took up the slack in the 200-foot cable attached to the undercarriage of *Knight Killer*. It continued its acceleration to 80 miles an hour and Ned's plane left the road. At an altitude of about 50 feet, Ned gritted his teeth, pulled both the landing gear levers, released the tow cable, and hit number 1. The G forces pulled him back in his seat as his aircraft climbed. Prior testing revealed the JATO bottles burned for 20 seconds. The P-51's altimeter and air speed indicators were functioning; they read 2500 feet and 280 knots when the bottles flamed out.

Ned shook his head to calm himself and focus the on mission. Just a slight left bank and he headed towards Nitrate City. The sound of the air rushing around his cockpit filled his senses. A crosswind required another left bank to correct his course. The aircraft was now passing the bridgehead. As Ned banked, he looked down, scanning the enemy terrain. He spotted a Black Force vehicle below. Near it, a couple of hundred foot soldiers moved in double time. The enemy was indeed advancing as Harry Smith predicted at his 4:00 a.m. briefing. Ned hoped that he would have worthy targets remaining at the Black Force Training Center.

Ned mentally checked off the landmarks passing below him: the old aluminum plant and the Muscle Shoals airport. He carefully watched his instruments. The aircraft was losing altitude quickly and its airspeed was approaching his estimated stall speed. Ned hit number 2, and both of the JATOs fired. The aircraft climbed to 3000 feet and attained and airspeed of 300 knots this time. It was quiet again — just the whistling air. Ned shivered under his coveralls and leather jacket. The thermometer at the armory that morning read 39 degrees and it was colder at this altitude — perceptibly colder given the wind.

As intended, *Knight Killer* was south of Nitrate City. Ned could turn out of the glaring sunrise and begin his descent to target. He cringed at the thought of how low he would have to fly to render his weapons effective. The aircraft needed to pass over the Black Force Training Center's parade ground from an altitude of 300 feet. Facing downward, "FRONT TOWARD ENEMY" appeared sixteen times along the centerline of his fuselage. His buddies had rigged a release lever behind his seat. At the right moment, Ned could reach back over his left shoulder and pull the lever forward. This action would release the remaining inventory of Lauderdale's Claymore anti-personnel mines. Weighted to fire downward and parachuted to enhance dispersal, the weapons had mechanically timed detonators set to fire between fifty and seventy-five feet above the ground.

Danny asked Lawrence if he had heard the roar. The adjutant simply shook his head as he strained to hear the garbled messages passing from his headset. Danny continued to scan north and west. Lawrence stood to better join him in the search. A moment later, Danny heard Lawrence speak loudly into his microphone, "Please repeat. You saw a what?"

As Danny caught movement in his peripheral vision, he turned to see a silent aircraft streaking at low altitude from the south. Danny had no time to react; the dull silver plane crossed his drill grounds and bivouacs, releasing a number of small mushroom shaped objects. His reserve militia units were either standing for inspection on the parade ground or on detail, policing their camping areas. As the devices exploded, thousands of steel balls tore into Danny's hapless troops. Pandemonium ensued.

Danny's attention was drawn back to the departing airplane as fire and roar belched from its wings and sent it climbing off and away to the northwest. He uttered, "Those damned geeks!"

Danny screamed at his commanders to restore order. He feared follow on aerial attacks and barked once again, directing them to get their troops to cover. Danny ordered his own Black Force security detail to set up their M60 machine gun. "Get it up on something so that you can fire at a plane."

Lawrence turned on the facility's loudspeaker system and ordered all company commanders to submit casualty reports *ASAP*.

After a few minutes, Lawrence remembered their assault commanders and recovered his headset and microphone. Multiple commanders reported they were in position and at risk of detection. Lawrence firmly ordered them to hold their positions and cease all chatter until further notice. After getting Danny's attention and passing on the reports from his field commanders, Danny simply raised a finger to pause him. The Constable turned and leaned over the review tower's rail to peer down at the handful of officers standing below.

Knight First Class Cecil Morgan looked up at Danny and reported, "Constable Ragland, only a little over half the militia's company commanders are present and their casualty reports are spotty at best.

Danny sighed and said, "Well, give me what you've got so far."

Knight Morgan held up his note pad and read, "Casualties reported so far are, 5 militia officers killed including Colonel Morris, 31 enlisted militiamen killed, 15 officers wounded, 202 militiamen wounded, 4 Knights killed, 18 Knights wounded, and four Black Force vehicles damaged — one beyond repair; it's on fire, sir."

Danny glanced up to see black smoke rising from the far side of the bivouac. He looked down at his reporter and said, "Thank you, Cecil. Keep working on it."

"Yes, sir."

Danny walked over to Lawrence apprehensively waiting at his radio and asked, "Did you hear those casualties, Larry?"

"Yes, sir. What do you think the final count will be, Danny?"

"Uh, I don't know … about twice that … don't ya' think?"

"Yes, sir."

Danny looked about the sky again. "Hell, they could hit us again anytime."

"Yes, sir."

After checking his watch and discovering it was 7:00 a.m., Danny commanded, "Larry, order the even numbered Black Force teams to hold and prepare defensive positions. Assign an infantry company to each one of them. Have the odd numbered teams and the rest of the militiamen withdraw to Muscle Shoals. Order them to stay on full alert and be ready to move. The Lauderdales may break out at any time. Oh, and Larry, explain to all the commanders what happened here — caution them to disperse their troops to lower their vulnerability to aerial attacks."

"Yes, sir."

Danny walked over to a field phone. Clutching the handset, he spoke, "Constable Ragland here. Get me the President."

Crazy Ned Flanagan's third JATO burn turned scary. With the weight reduction incurred from four spent rocket bottles and sixteen released M18A1 Claymores, he nearly lost control of the much lighter Mustang as he fired the last two JATOs. Ned was able to stave off disaster with some quick stick and rudder work, but at a cost; he topped out at only 2,100 feet this time. He made a beeline for Wilson Lake.

Ned struggled to gauge his descent and distance wondering if it might be better to use whatever altitude he had remaining to search for an isolated stretch of Colbert road or meadow to make a more controlled crash landing. However, he abandoned that plan after contemplating his fate at the hands of a Black Force tactical squad or Colbert militia company. He recalled how full the parade ground at the BFTC had been. *Damn, they'll be pissed!"*

Ned had to continually decrease his angle of attack to avoid a stall. Rapidly approaching the big lake on the Tennessee River, the plane's altimeter needle was now dancing just over 700 feet.

Ned began to talk to his precious *Knight Killer*, "Girl, we gonna make it. Yes, ma'am, we gonna make it. I'll miss you, darlin'. But, shit, we really chewed their asses didn't we? Lordy, that water is going to be cold … in the high 30s or low 40s I bet."

His buddies insisted that he wear an aged waterski vest. He protested at the time but was glad he had it now. To further prepare for the water ditching, Ned reached up and pulled a strap dangling over his right shoulder. It ran back to the compartment behind his seat. He tugged on it and felt the weight on the other end. That resistance brought a bit of warmth to his heart.

As a head wind gave the aircraft some lift, Ned's optimism continued to grow. He decided to get as close to the Lauderdale side of the lake as he could before turning left at an altitude of about 300 feet to ditch the aircraft with the current. He planned to nurse his altitude within a few feet of the water and then flare at the last moment causing the plane's tail to strike first to avoid nosing over.

Crazy Ned heard a couple of bullets whiz by as he crossed the Colbert shoreline and yelled, "Hah, missed me, Assholes!"

A small miracle, all the Slingshot teams' radios were working. By 7:30 a.m., the teams had all checked in. After Harry and Ben Smith listened to the teams' reports as summarized by their communications officer, Lieutenant Neva Lazo de la Vega, they could assume that Ned Flanagan's air attack had been successful to some extent. While the Colberts had been amassing for a coordinated attack on the Lauderdales' bridgehead, they now seemed to be standing down, even partially withdrawing.

Ben said, "Harry, if we are going to do what I brought up earlier, now is the time."

Harry considered for a few seconds and replied, "Uncle Ben, they might just send you back in a bag."

Ben laughed, "Nah, that's just not Little Charles's style, Mr. President."

Majors Donna Flurry and William Fuqua entered the bridgehead command tent, and Harry waved them over. "So, is Neva's news correct? Do you two think that Danny Ragland is backing off?"

Donna spoke up, "Yes, Harry. He pulled at least one Knight Team and two companies of infantry out of my area. Thank, God! We'd uh played hell holdin' 'em!"

Harry turned to his old warrior, "Major Fuqua?"

"'Bout the same, Harry. Your crazy ass flyboy musta done his job. By the way, the cavalry's 1st Squad had a guy up in a tree and he saw the plane cross back over the lake. He lost sight after that, though."

Harry turned to Neva, "Any word on Ned?"

"No, sir. I'll try again."

Harry asked his uncle and the majors to join him in the back of the tent. In privacy, he began with glances at Donna and William; "Ben wants to go talk to the Raglands under a flag of truce. He wants to see if we can bluff 'em in to giving up the dam without more bloodshed."

Donna quickly opined, "With all due respect, Ben, I fear it will be a waste of time … possibly a dangerous one. I think we should start our feint right away."

Ben shook his head, "Donna, it will take at least an hour to get ready for the feint and I doubt if my mission will take over two. What have we got to lose, really?"

Donna simply answered, "You!"

Major Fuqua interjected, "I don't think they would hurt Ben under a flag of truce. They would consider that *Tacky*. Hell, the Raglands love this kind of drama. If Ben is willing to go, I suggest we let him."

Harry shifted his position in the canvas chair to focus on his uncle, "Uncle Ben, who do you want to take and how do you want to go about it?"

Ben grinned and replied, "Well, I don't want to invest very much in this … no vehicle or key personnel. I thought about just ridin' over to their lines on Ol' Sam with another horseman actin' as my flag-bearer. How 'bout Cleve Offutt from the 3rd Cavalry Squad?"

"Dammit, Ben, you've probably already asked him about it. Haven't ya'?"

Ben just grinned again.

Perched on her bedroom's window seat, Catherine Ragland was watching the Palace's driveway like a bird of prey. She had been alerted by the sounds of staff member activity emanating from the first floor. Something was up. Her barely touched breakfast tray sat on the window table. She intermittently sipped the black coffee, its mug doubling as a hand warmer.

Just before nine, she watched Cousin Danny's SUV turn in followed by a Black Force Knight pickup. She stood as Danny and Lawrence stepped from their vehicle. Catherine moved to the other side of her window to better observe the occupants getting out of the

Black Force SUV. She recognized the fearsome looking pair of
Knights as Holt and Gruber, but the blindfolded man they
respectfully escorted was dressed in Lauderdale khaki. Holt removed
the blindfold and the enemy looked up at her window. His eyes met
Catherine's. A familiar half-smile followed by a cheerful nod fired a
distant memory. She softly said with a tone of wonderment, "Ben
Smith."

Earlier, Catherine did her hair and makeup and donned jeans and
a sweater to be ready for a day she suspected would hold surprises.
She was now glad of it. She had dismissed Alice after her "lady-in-
waiting" delivered the breakfast tray, and then instructed her to see to
any other duties that were pending. Without Alice to slow her,
Catherine darted out her bedroom door and slipped by the second
floor security guard before he could react. She was down the circular
staircase in a lickety-split. The parties she had seen arrive were in the
Grand Foyer now. Taken aback by the 25-year-old Ragland beauty's
presence, they looked embarrassed and annoyed except for one.

Ben Smith said, "Why Hello, Miss Catherine!"

With a coy drop, she turned her head away from her perturbed
cousin and responded, "Ben Smith, how have you been? You look
well, sir!"

Though they were in a hurry to get to the basement's council
chamber, the Colbert men had no choice but to endure the moment's
pleasantries.

Ben, reveling in their discomfort, kept on, "As do you, and given
this situation, I'm just fine. Fine indeed!"

Pushing her luck, she approached Ben and extended her hand.
Danny nodded for the pair of Knights to allow it. Catherine and Ben
shook hands.

In a serious tone, she said, "Mr. Smith, I'm sorry about the
passing of your brother. I wish we could have attended his funeral,
but given the circumstances …"

Eyes watering, he replied, "Thank you, ma'am. How is your
mother?"

"Oh, she has her good days and bad days. And, the rest of your
family, sir?"

"Pretty good ... once again, considerin'."

To close on an optimistic note she said, "Well, goodbye, Mr. Smith and I hope we can meet again on a better day."

"As do I, Miss Ragland."

The men had started to turn and depart, as did Catherine, but Ben Smith simply had to add, "Oh, I almost forgot. Harry told me to say hi!"

Danny pressed his eyes closed for a second, Ben chuckled, and Catherine's heart skipped a beat. No one paused or broke stride.

Ned Flanagan reveled under the warmth of a colorful quilt. He was safe and sound at a River Watch Station near the mouth of Shoal Creek. One of the men had given him an old but clean pair of pajamas. He was resting on a cot with a hot cup of sassafras tea in his hand and a plate of molasses cookies in his lap.

Crazy Ned had managed to put *Knight Killer* down without flipping her. That enabled him to pull his makeshift folding Styrofoam raft out from behind his pilot's seat before jumping into the Tennessee River. His plane filled with river water and sank a minute or so after it hit the water. He had rested his chest on the raft and kicked with his legs for propulsion. As he feared, the water was brutally cold. His extremities became numb. The situation was exacerbated by sporadic rifle fire from the Colbert side of Wilson Lake. At one point, he felt things slipping away. Then he heard nearby rifle fire from the opposite direction. Some militiamen from the Lauderdale River Watch were close by in one of their biodiesel cruisers. They were firing their rifles at the Colbert shoreline as they approached him for rescue.

Harry walked among his infantry shaking hands, patting backs, and exchanging barbs. As much as he felt loved and respected by them, he still sensed a questioning in their demeanor — a doubt. Harry wondered, *Many of these men and women could be dead tomorrow, would this sacrifice warrant the reward? Would there be a reward? They could fail. The Spared Territory lying north of the river may well become one big shantytown for the Raglands with a proud history forgotten and its heroes dead.*

A boy Harry learned to trap with up near the old Tennessee State line, now a broad shouldered man in his twenties, stood and extended his hand to Harry.

"Tim Gray, how is the trappin' business goin' these days?"

"Hello, Harry. Aw, Hell, I got hitched last year and went to work at the gin. The barter is more steady."

"Oh, really? Well, I bet the fur bearing creatures of Middle-Lauderdale are happy about that."

They laughed, and Harry pointed to Tim's weapon and asked, "May, I?

"Of course, Harry!" As he proudly opened his rifle's breech and passed it to his commander-in-chief, Tim continued, "It's the latest version of Lauderdale Load's striker fired flintlock muzzleloader. All ya' need is some cotton patching, a flask of fffg black powder, some of these ffffg pellets, any kind of scrap lead, a chunk of flint, and a little grease."

"A fifty?"

"Yes, sir. I used one of their first generations in .36-caliber for the last couple uh years an' killed everythang from squirrel to wild pig and deer with it. But this militiaman's .50 caliber makes for a better round ball killer against these Colbert sumbitches. The last of me and Daddy's .22 ammo ran out back 'round the years you used to hunt and trap with us. We couldn't afford that Lauderdale Load fodder, so everbuddy up our way put back what rimfire and centerfire ammo we had and went to these black powder guns. I'm preachin' to the teacher though, ain't I? You and your uncles, helped come up with these didn't ya'?"

Harry just grinned and shouldered the rifle drawing a sight picture off in the eastern sky. "I love those peep sights. They were going to go with open ones, but I pressed for the apertures."

"Aw hell? I didn't know that. Glad you did, Harry. Thar' more 'ficient."

Harry opened the breech and inspected the rifle's firing mechanism. "Tell me, Tim, what's your failure rate with this enclosed flintlock ignition design?"

"I've only had one so far, an' that was my fault. I pushed that piece of flint too far. Twenty shots is about it."

"One due to operator error, huh?" gently teased Harry. "Out of how many shots?"

"Oh, I reckon I've fired fifty or sixty total. We hated to see production of the percussion guns stop, Harry, but I know how scarce the makins' for percussion caps and primers have become. Just about ever-thang has to go for primers to reload centerfire rifle and pistol brass, right? Dangerous work, too. I lost a cousin down at the chemical works last year."

After a grimace and head shake acknowledging the accident, Harry asked, "Accuracy?" Harry knew the man was a crack shot.

"From a bench, she'll put three .490 balls in one ragged hole at 25 yards, an inch and a half at fifty, and three or four inches at one hundred pendin' on the wind."

Effortlessly slipping into his soldier's vernacular, "Them round balls uh'll blow, huh?"

"Yep, an' glance-off on a twig or branch! But you can cast a shitload of balls out of a pound uh lead."

"I directed the armory to get it right on accessories. How 'bout that, Tim?"

"No problem, Harry. They done good. Every rifle was issued with a flinting tool an' a bullet mold — both are cracker jacks. You have to be a real doofus to mess up chippin' a flint with that little tool."

"How about the casting pots and ladles?"

"One per platoon. Sum guys were bitchin' about it and thinking we need one per squad, but I told 'em they were full of it an' would just lose 'em. Besides half the soldiers of each squad are still carrying the Lauderdale Sharps percussion breechloaders and y'all have tons of paper cartridges ready for those folks. They won't need to worry about scrounging for lead and casting .54 caliber Sharps bullets. Their problem is caps. Only a hunnert each? That sucks, Harry."

A listening soldier's jaw dropped at Tim's bluntness. But, he quickly realized the friendship went far back — thus the candor.

"That's an understatement, Tim. It really, really sucks. We have found all kinds of sources for the scrap metal to make percussion caps — landfills, junk yards, and even creek bottoms, but as you said a minute ago, Tim, it's the chemical substances."

The list was daunting: Glycerin, nitrate, nitric acid, sulfuric acid, ammonia, phosphorus, and potassium chlorate — all getting hard or impossible to come by in the ST. Other than charcoal, even the saltpeter and sulfur required for black powder took some creativity and considerable effort to manufacture.

Tim knew it. He was light on formal education, but heavy on intelligence and common sense. He just nodded to Harry in a combination of agreement and frustration.

Moving along, Harry pointed to the rear sight, "When I tested one of these the elevation gradients were dead on. Is that your experience, Tim?"

"Pretty much. Ya' gotta stick with that 60 grain charge though to make the trajectories work, but that's taken care of with these paper cartridges y'all are issuing. They are top notch. We measured the charges in a bunch of 'em at our range session last week. They were true. We'll have to be more careful if the supply of paper flintlock cartridges run out and we go to loadin' loose components. Still, y'all's little flask is a goodun and it throws 60 grains evertime if the rifleman does his part.

At that, Harry chuckled and nodded as he handed the rifle back to Private Gray.

Harry and Tim were surprised to find a semi-circle of soldiers gathered around them, listening. Harry glanced at 1911 and knew his expression meant it was time to head back to the HQ tent. After nodding recognition and a smile around the assembly, he shook Tim's hand once more and said, "It was good to see you, Tim. Good luck."

"Thanks, Mr. President. You, too!"

Before turning to depart, Harry directed in a louder voice to the little group, "Hold 'em an' squeeze 'em!"

Guffaws followed as Harry and 1911 walked away.

Charles's secretary had just finished announcing the arrival of the Constable over the intercom on the council chamber table. Charles, Edward, and Johnny Montjoy stood around the head of the table; it was a goodly 25 feet from the room's entrance.

Edward moved to his father's side and cautioned in a low voice, "Daddy, don't give an inch with these damn Smiths. Self love is not so much a sin as self neglect."

Before President Ragland could respond to his son, the chamber's double doors opened. Danny and Lawrence entered first followed by the two Knights escorting Ben Smith.

Not in any mood for pleasantries, Charles asked, "What news from Lauderdale, Ben Smith?"

Matching his demeanor, Ben said, "Just this, President Ragland. President Smith has an army ready to wreak havoc in old Colbert County, and if need be, bring down its rule unless a single demand is met."

Charles asked, "And what demand is that?"

Ben sternly replied, "Immediately abandon the occupation and operation of Wilson Dam. If you do that, President Smith will negotiate and sign a new treaty which includes a commitment to fifty-fifty power sharing with Colbert."

"That's a bold demand from a kid-president at the head of a force half his enemy's size."

"Kid president? Gentlemen, you are wrong headed if you still see the Harry Smith of his greener days. As has been demonstrated in the past 16 hours, he is fierce, and the events thus transpired will pale in comparison to the earthquake and thunder that awaits."

Edward almost shook with anger and emitted a nervous cough, but Charles and Danny stood in poker-faced silence.

Charles inquired, "Is that it, Ben?"

"That's pretty much Harry's demand, threat, and message unless your son, Eddie, is present. Harry has something for him."

Edward stepped along the side of the long table to close his distance on Ben. A few feet away, he stopped and in a smart tone said, "I'm Edward Ragland, Mr. Smith."

Feigning surprise, Ben exclaimed, "Oh, Edward, I didn't recognize you, son. It has been years though. Hasn't it?"

Eddie scowled and through terse lips, he uttered, "What does Harry have for me?"

Now Ben's face lost all humor. With a cold stare he answered, "Scorn, defiance, slight regard, and contempt."

With clenched fists, Edward added, "I can't believe he rejected the Sheffield Industries tennis balls. I know his pitiful citizenry could never produce the like."

Sarcastically, Ben countered, "Naw, rifled artillery and bomber planes are more their expertise."

Charles cut them off, "Ben, Black Force will see you back to your lines. If we want to negotiate further, Mr. Montjoy will be at your bridgehead at noon. If not, we don't."

Ben responded, "Simple enough, Mr. President."

DAY FOUR
THE AFTERNOON

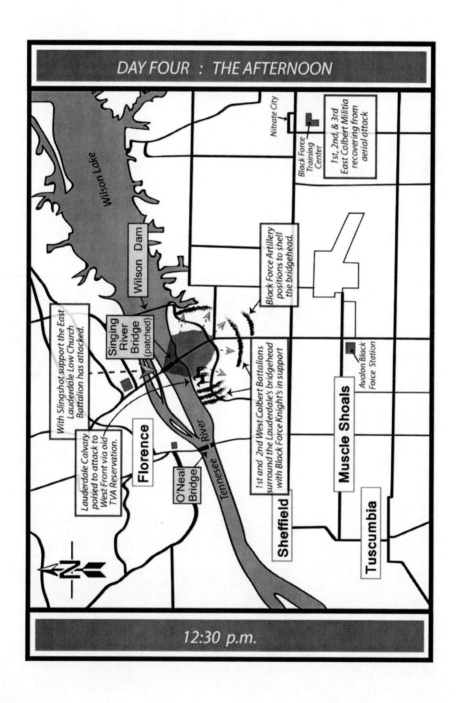

DAY FOUR : THE AFTERNOON

Wilson Lake

Nitrate City

Black Force Training Center

1st, 2nd, & 3rd East Colbert Militia recovering from aerial attack

Wilson Dam

Black Force Artillery positions to shell the bridgehead.

Singing River Bridge (patched)

With Slingshot support the East Lauderdale Low Church Battalion has attacked.

Lauderdale Calvary poised to attack to West Front via old TVA Reservation.

Florence

O'Neal Bridge

Tennesee River

1st and 2nd West Colbert Battalions surround the Lauderdale's bridgehead with Black Force Knight's in support

Avalon Black Force Station

Muscle Shoals

Sheffield

Tuscumbia

12:30 p.m.

Tim Gray's squad, part of the East Low Church Militia Battalion, began to fire on a distant Black Force Knight position at 12:30 PM. His squad leader, Pastor James Dayton, had an uncanny eye for judging distances. He estimated the range to the Knights at 190 yards. With his receiver sight in its second to uppermost position, Tim lobbed his first ball into some unlucky Colbert relieving himself back behind his cover. Tim grimaced as the guy folded from the possible kidney shot. Tim knew the targets would be harder to find after their first volley. Their orders were to pour fire into the Colbert lines and even close with the enemy if the opportunity arose. Their commanders had been straightforward. His battalion's job was to convince the enemy that this was an all-out attack, the first wave of an offensive to expand the bridgehead in all directions. The Lauderdale bridgehead perimeter was soon crackling with rifle fire.

Tim and the others of his squad armed with muzzleloaders found big trees to stand behind. This enabled easier reloading, and they used the trees to support their rifles when aiming. By contrast, the six members of his squad with the Lauderdale Sharps percussion rifles could fire and reload handily from the prone position. He bit off the end of a paper cartridge, poured its 60 grains of fffg black powder down the barrel, flipped the cartridge, and squeezed the greased and cotton-patched ball onto the muzzle. After starting his patched ball with the smack of his combo tool, Tim withdrew his ramrod from underneath the barrel, drove the ball down the 26" barrel, and returned the ramrod. Next, he lifted his bolt handle, retracted the bolt, and inserted one of his little aspirin shaped black-powder pellets in the fire hole chamber. As Tim pushed the bolt forward and turned the bolt handle down, it ground the pellet of ffffg black powder to dust. With his left hand against his big oak tree and his right on the rifle's grip, Tim sought a target of opportunity. They had been ordered to not take over five seconds waiting for a living target. Rather than wait longer, Harry told them to put the shot in the enemy's general area, barricade, or a vehicle. It was suppressing fire, odd work for single shot weapons, but the militiamen had been briefed on the overall strategy for the day, and it made sense.

Raised by his daddy to consider wasting lead a sin, Tim took more than five seconds, but it was worth it. The Colberts in his designated target area had started returning fire with a machine gun and repeaters. A bullet whizzed by his head causing Tim to wince. Just as he was about to fire at a muzzle flash, Tim saw a Black Force vehicle backing out of their line. He quickly put his square post front sight on the vehicle's grill, centered the post in his rear peep, and pressed the trigger.

The trigger's sear released the striker housed in the bolt. The spring-loaded striker travelled forward tripping the twin spring-operated venting gates on each side of the rifle's receiver. The vents were automatically closed earlier when the bolt was retracted — a feature intended to help keep moisture out of the firing mechanism. The file-like striker raced along the flint box causing sparks to ignite the crushed black powder pellet and in turn send flame through the fire hole where the 60 grains of Lauderdale Loads fffg awaited ignition. The rifle's lock time was half that of Daniel Boone's Kentucky Rifle, and far less vulnerable to misfires and the elements.

"Damn, I hope that poked a hole in his radiator!" Tim exclaimed.

A buddy in the middle of a flintlock reload laughed and hollered above the gunshots, "Oh, Hell yeah, she'll be blowin' steam by supper time, Tim!"

The friend was a Rhodes from Zip City. They all called him Jaybird. He was a rather skinny fellow with long legs and a high voice. Jay managed to finish loading in time to throw a snap shot at the cab of the now turned and departing Black Force truck. Tim, already on his next reload, winked at Jay as he tossed away an empty paper-cartridge sleeve.

The two Lauderdale Militiamen were finally driven prone by a burst of Colbert machine gun fire ripping around them. Tim commented while laughing, "That's fine, dumbasses! Just keep bustin' those caps!"

A moment later, Slingshot 7 pulled up behind Tim's squad and the gunner in its ring mount started firing his .50 caliber machine gun at the Black Force position. The enemy soon broke. As they scrambled south, Tim's squad took advantage of the exposed targets by scoring a couple of more hits.

Tim's squad leader, Pastor Jim ordered them to charge. Tim complied and sprinted with his rifle in his weak hand and his personal handgun, a double column single action 9mm, in his strong hand. After clearing the Colberts' light breastworks, Tim spotted two Colbert militiamen lying in a shallow foxhole. Half-a-dozen dead Colberts were scattered about, but these two were alive. One was holding his intestines in his hands and the other was trying to reload his lever action repeater. Tim ignored the torn man, but placed an aimed pistol-shot in the head of the other. They cleared the enemy's former position and pressed on to a high spot behind it. Pastor Jim ordered them to hold there.

They observed some Colbert Knights and militiamen pitching another defensive position a couple of hundred yards away. Tim's squad started the offensive cycle again.

Pastor Jim and his daughter, Mary, hustled back down to the vacated Colbert position to scavenge for any abandoned Colbert ammunition, weapons, or supplies. Pastor Jim mercifully thrust the razor sharp head of his seven-foot-long spear into the writhing Colbert man. Two last jerks and he was gone. Their squad leader carried no rifle — just the fearsome spear and a blue-less double action .38 Special revolver. In effect, Mary was his rifle. She was the only member of the squad with a repeating rifle. She carried an M1 Carbine for which she had hand loaded 60 rounds of FMJ ammo — enough to fill her four 15-round magazines. The five-foot-tall 20-year old with her long brown hair was seldom more than a few feet from her father, and the entire squad knew that she would only fire the carbine to protect the squad and her father as a last resort. The dead Colbert's lever action rifle, a first aid kit, and a cache of black powder hand grenades made the search worthwhile.

After a few minutes they settled into their suppressing fire. Tim and Jay were surprised a bit by the sounds of explosions to the west.

Tim announced, "There goes Scooter again."

"Scooter?" questioned Jaybird.

"Captain Shelton!"

"Oh, yeah!"

The arsenal staff members were better than their word. They delivered 31 Parrott Rifle shells just before noon.

Scooter Shelton, still perched atop the old bank, silently worried that his iron guns might explode. Such an event would surely injure and/or kill the failed gun's crew. His gunners were not just his command. They were his friends.

He and Bill Walker heard the distant explosions from their first salvo of the day, and within seconds saw plumes of smoke rising from the ridges of the old TVA Reservation. The reservation, to the west of the Singing River Bridge, was partially occupied by Harry's bridgehead forces but only about a mile from the bridge. Harry ordered the perimeter set in the west starting at the river on a very high bluff. The site was named the Civilian Conservation Corps Park (Franklin Roosevelt's CCC) in the OW. Harry's real attack was going to advance from this park in a westward direction into the City of Sheffield. Scooter's fire mission was to put six salvos from his four Parrotts onto the rows of hills and hollows running along the river between the bridgehead perimeter and Sheffield. They hoped the barrage would soften whatever defenses Danny Ragland had deployed in the heavily wooded area. After sending those 24 shells on their way, Scooter was to divert his guns to bring the remaining seven shells down on the southern approach to O'Neal Bridge. That was the first objective for the advancing Lauderdale Low Church Militia after clearing the reservation.

Lieutenant Bill Walker was directing his gunners via one phone system while on a new line, Lieutenant Smitty Cox filtered reports from his two forward observer teams across the river. Earlier, Smitty had four members of his 57mm gun crew drive his two guns back to the arsenal and the other eight were transferred to Captain Juarez at the bridgehead to serve as artillery spotters. Harry's engineers had strung phone lines across the bridge and the two 4-man teams were relaying the results of the first barrage back to Smitty. The two would decipher the results and order corrections to the gun commanders.

Scooter saw from his watch that three minutes had elapsed since the first salvo. Just as he started to speak, he saw Bill speaking into his phone. Scooter held back.

Bill barked into the phone, "Gun commanders, fire at will as soon as you have made those corrections."

The four Parrott Rifles fired over a few-second span about a minute later. Captain Shelton thanked the Lord. The breeches of his big guns held once again.

At the Avalon Black Force Station, Danny Ragland mentally processed the latest field reports. His black-clad staff surrounded him in anxious tension. He spoke, "Okay, we have a concerted push from the bridgehead in all directions. They're bound to concentrate their offensive at some point. They may be coming directly for Muscle Shoals to the south and west or our chemical plant and bio-fuel facility to the southeast. There's no way in Hell they'll push east; they won't risk the dam. Artillery salvos are impacting sporadically just outside of their western perimeter. Lawrence, how strong is the southern assault?"

Lawrence quickly requested updated reports from the field commanders. After a minute or two, he relayed, "Constable, their artillery is still falling to the west, but our western defensive positions report very little movement from the Lauderdales. However, our defensive positions along the southern perimeter have begun to fall back after encountering heavy Lauderdale infantry attacks supported by Slingshot Humvees armed with heavy and light machine guns."

Danny calmly laid out his decisions, "Ladies and gentlemen, let's reassess. At most, the Lauderdales have a regiment of militia at the bridgehead. We have the three battalions of the East Colbert Militia Regiment licking their wounds from this morning's aerial attack holding at Nitrate City. The 1st and 2nd battalions of the West Colbert Militia Regiment are here in Muscle Shoals with the 3rd deployed thinly along the river between Sheffield and Mississippi. The West's 1st Battalion is manning defensive positions around the bridgehead. The 2nd is just outside our building.

The Lauderdales seem to be attacking right at us. However, that could be a feint. On the other hand, the artillery fire pounding the TVA property along the river could be a feint. Lawrence, restate the nature of our defenses in that area."

"As you all know, the terrain consists of a series of deep hollows and high ridge tops running towards the river. Any Lauderdale assault would have to go up and down these precarious features. Given the easy defensibility of that area, we have deployed only a company of the 1st's militiamen and three Black Force Knight Teams. They are set up on a series of three ridges — a platoon of infantrymen and a Knight Team on each one."

Danny ran his index finger over the big map on the station's break room table as he considered his options. "Fine! Here is what we will do. Lawrence, which of the East's battalion was most decimated by this morning's air attack?"

"The 2nd, Constable."

"Okay, have the 2nd Battalion deploy three companies to Wilson Dam and one to Wheeler. Next, order the East's 1st and 3rd battalions to march for the intersection of Wilson Dam Road and 2nd Street. They are to hold there in support."

"And the 2nd Battalion of the West Militia and their attached Knights?"

"Order them to join with their 1st Battalion and attack the southern perimeter of the bridgehead en masse, immediately. Use the Knights' vehicles once again to bring up the Napoleons. Have them stop and set up the guns as soon as they are in range. They are to start firing explosive shells as the 2nd's infantry pass and continue to fire until both of those battalions are engaged at the Lauderdales' perimeter.

"Are they to have any holding positions as they advance, sir?"

"Yes, when they hold the south end of the bridge dammit!"

"Yes, sir! Oh, one more thing?"

"Yes."

"Don't forget the 50 or so Tuscumbia Junior Knights we have hidden down in the power room at Wilson Dam."

"Oh shit! Those young fire breathers were going to lead our invasion across the dam."

"Yes, sir."

"Well, I know it's not their forte, but have them reinforce the defenses on both ends of the dam. Hell, they're certainly armed well enough. Tell Smokin' Joe I'll call on his boys if I need them, but in the meantime, he's to hold that dam at all cost!"

"Yes, sir."

"That brings up another opportunity. Are the Sheffield Junior Knights still assembled at the old school?"

"Yes, sir."

"Good, order Coach Hammer to get his kids over to the reservation ASAP. They can reinforce our troops on those western ridges."

Lawrence said, "Good idea, Danny," and busied himself and his staff on the phone and radio initiating the Constable's orders.

When the exhausted adjutant finished his round of commands, he tilted his head forward, closed his eyes, and breathed therapeutically.

Danny Ragland purposely spared him a moment, but soon had to add, "Lawrence, tell the East's commanders to light a fire under 'em. We will need their two battalions soon. We will probably have to commit at least one of them to battle as soon as they arrive."

"Yes, Constable, right away."

Michael Williams, sitting astride Dungee Boy, leaned forward and murmured in his ear. The horse calmed and ceased nervously chopping at the earth with his front hooves. Sitting up, Michael looked around to check on his squad. His scan seemed to confirm they were ready. He turned to Private Alexander Court and asked, "Alex, whatcha' think of that new mount?"

"Aww, he'll do. More docile than I would prefer, but I've rode him before … a good horse."

"Me, too. Once Dungee came up lame during a drill, I had him for a Sunday. Ol' Garcia over at the remuda called him El Truenos."

Alex contemplated a second or two and responded, "Well, maybe Distant Thunder."

The rest of the squad followed the exchange and all laughed at Alex's dry retort.

The 1st Lauderdale Cavalry Squad waited near a crumbling stone picnic pavilion in the CCC Park. The winds had started to pick up. With the temperature in the mid-40s, it was chilly on this high ground above the river. The troopers fiddled with gauntlets, cuffs, collars, buttons, and zippers to fend off the cold. Captain Juarez was fifty or so yards away working with a field phone operator and their platoon sergeant, Mark Gillespie. They had a marvelous view across the river to downtown Florence. They could see the muzzle flashes and smoke plumes at the bank building. Private Betty Sands, mounted on her beautiful brown mare, Double Knot, had been counting the artillery rounds.

Michael asked her, "Betty, how many is that?"

"Twenty, Corporal."

"Damn, I hope they are hittin' somethin' besides trees and boulders," said Michael.

Alex added, "I ain't heard no screamin'."

Chuckles this time.

Horace Bennett observed, "Shit, Alex, you are in rare form today!"

The squad's attention was turned to Captain Juarez. He was signaling for the squad to come in close.

After the entire platoon gathered, Jesus stepped on top of what was once the end wall of the old park pavilion. Even in their saddles, the horse soldiers could clearly see their commander, head and shoulders above them.

Jesus began, "Troopers, the next barrage will be the last one. As I briefed you earlier, we will be leading today's attack. We have to take out the Colbert's defensive positions located on the ridges and behind me." He thumbed back over his shoulder. "Yep ... between this west side of the bridgehead and Sheffield. We have to open the door for the infantry militia that will follow. Otherwise, they will be cut down. Y'all remember. We ease over to the road that snakes through this old reservation. Then we'll ride hell bent of leather along it, and Squads one, two, and three will break off and clear their respective ridges. The weapons squad and my element will hold at the third ridge and wait for you all to recover to that position as our infantry progresses. Any questions?"

There were none.

After a daunting few seconds of silence, the cavalry leader urged, "Very well then! Let's go get one for Trooper Bates!"

The troopers all lifted their hats in the air and yelled, "Trooper Bates!"

As if on cue, the guns from Florence fired once more, followed seconds later by their shells exploding in the woods to their front.

Michael did not hesitate, "First Squad, form up!"

Within minutes the Lauderdale Cavalry were galloping along the road. They were soon taking Colbert fire. Michael heard a scream and looked back to see Private Tim Tate tumble to the road surface. There was no way to stop. They pressed on and Michael soon turned his six remaining troopers north along the first ridge. He spotted a Knight vehicle in the trees ahead. A machine gun crew was trying to turn their weapon towards the 1st Squad. Michael was bringing his revolver on target, but three bursts of full auto fire from Alex's M4 5.56X45mm assault carbine sent the machine gunners tumbling about. He and Alex were on the vehicle in seconds. He slowed to a trot, and ordered Betty Sands and Naddy Smith to make sure the vehicle was clear and to catch up as best they could. He, Alex, and the Bennetts resumed the gallop. Michael shot two fleeing Colberts in the back with his revolver while Alex took out several more with his M-4.

The brush was thickening and they had to slow and begin picking their way through. Enemy bullets were whizzing by. They came upon a low place in the ridgeline. Michael ordered the other three to take their horses down on their bellies and folded legs. Michael did the same. With practiced efficiency, Eulis Bennett did not need a verbal command to gather all four sets of reins and become the holder. Betty and Naddy joined them. A nod from Michael was all they needed to secure their mounts in the same way. Michael quietly instructed Naddy to divide the horses with Eulis. He told Betty to take her M16A1 5.56X45mm assault rifle up behind them and cover their rear and flanks. Michael pulled his Short Magazine Lee Enfield from its scabbard, cycled a round into its chamber, and signaled for Alex and Horace to advance with him on foot. Michael estimated they had another three or four hundred yards to reach the end of the ridge. He reasoned that the resistance could be numerous and fearsome backed up against the river. They eased forward slowly.

A machine gun crew could not see Michael or his men, but the gunner was doing a pretty good job of placing bursts wherever he or she thought his or her foes might be. A couple of times bullets ripped right over the crouching cavalrymen. Spread about twenty feet apart the three men finally saw the muzzle flashes of the machine gun through the trees and brush. Harry signaled for the other two to start firing on the gunner after his first shot. He drew a sight picture on the muzzle flash and pressed the trigger of his SMLE. Alex did the same with his M16, now set on semi-auto, and Horace joined them with his .30-30 lever action carbine. After a few shots each, the machine gun fire stopped. Michael kept crawling forward while firing in the direction of the MG crew. He had directed Horace and Alex to move to each side and flank the position. Michael finally reached the area and found their foxhole, a pile of spent 7.62 cases, and links, but no Colberts.

After Alex and Horace joined him, Horace said, "Oh, me. Lookie here."

The other two joined him to see that he was pointing at a blood trail leading off along the ridge.

Michael commented, "We hit somebody, huh?"

They started advancing again and quickly came across a dip in the ridge.

Michael waited a few seconds for a bit of a lull in the firing on the ridges to his west and blew his whistle. A couple of minutes later, Betty, Naddy, and Eulis arrived with the horses. This dip was low enough to allow the horses to keep standing.

Michael asked Betty, "Did you see any of 'em from the flanks or rear?"

"No, Michael, not a one."

"In that case, Horace, you stay with your brother this time, and hold the stock while Betty and Naddy clear the rest of this ridge with Alex and me." Michael usually tried to spread the risk for his squad, but he knew Alex always preferred to be in the thick of it.

The squad didn't hesitate. They just did as their leader ordered.

As they scrambled to the lip of the shallow, Betty yelled, "Look out, Michael, here they come!"

Michael went prone and looked ahead to see the black uniforms of the charging Colbert militia. He quickly acquired a prone firing position and started shooting. Alex was already firing, and Betty was soon engaged with her rifle, as was Naddy with buckshot from his 12 gauge pump shotgun. The enemy soldiers were shooting as they ran with an eclectic mix of weapons much like the 1st Squad's but to poor effect. By comparison, the cavalrymen were firing from cover and they could shoot very well. The closest the enemy got was about twenty yards. After going seven for ten, Michael was forced to draw and fire his revolver when his SMLE ran dry. He put one more down with multiple shots from the handgun. Suddenly, there were no targets left. The troopers cautiously continued on foot after reloading their long guns. They passed a couple of dozen dead or dying Colberts scattered among the trees.

Just past this killing ground, the end of the ridge was in full view with the Tennessee River appearing in the distance. Three shell craters evidenced the efforts of Captain Shelton. A couple of dead bodies lay to their left. Just past them, an unarmed Colbert medic was tending to several wounded Colberts.

The medic spotted Michael and raised his bloody hands. Michael ordered Betty and Naddy to guard them. He had Alex run back to help the Bennetts bring up the horses. Michael carried a black powder spigot flare attached to his belt. He slung his rifle, unclipped the flare, and drove its sharp wooden shaft deep in the soft earth of the ridge. He pulled a ring attached to the flare's fuse and stepped back. An inordinately large orange ball shot up at a steep angle and then arced towards the river. Michael almost instantly heard the sounds of bugles and whistles from the east. The East Lauderdale Low Church Militia Battalion would soon be clambering over his ridge.

Michael was surprised to find that he had unconsciously drawn his revolver, half-cocked it, swung open the loading gate, and was methodically popping fired cases into his left palm as his right hand operated the ejector rod. He dumped the five empties in his coat pocket and pushed five fresh rounds from the loops on his belt with his right hand. While cradling the three-screw revolver in his left hand, he slid the first cartridge into the chamber exposed by the open loading gate. His left thumb and fingers rotated the cylinder past the next empty chamber, and he inserted cartridges in the next four chambers. He snapped the loading gate shut, cocked the hammer, and finally eased it forward. Given his hundreds of repetitions of the task, he holstered the "five-shooter" with total confidence. An empty chamber was under the hammer.

After nervously checking the time, Adjutant Constable Lawrence Foster ordered a Knight, standing at the Avalon Station door, to have Constable Ragland come back in at once. Danny was outside encouraging the trailing elements of his 2nd West Militia as they advanced into battle.

Danny stepped back in and asked, "What's up, Lawrence?"

"We can't contact anyone on the western flank! My girls started trying them at 1:30 and it's a quarter 'til two now! From outside, could you tell if an inordinate amount of fire was coming from that area?"

"Not really. The noise of battle is coming from the entire perimeter."

Suddenly, one of Lawrence's assistants, Gail Atkinson, raised her hand and waved as she listened on her field phone.

Lawrence walked to her side and asked, "Fresh report, Gail?"

She reported, "Still nothing from the west, but Knight Team 3 in the center reports that large numbers of Lauderdale infantry are moving to the west. Also, the Lauderdales that broke out a little while ago to the south and east are retreating to their original perimeter positions."

"What?"

"Yes, sir! I repeated it back to them and they confirmed."

Danny had been listening and interjected, "I was afraid of this. They are going for Sheffield." He took a deep breath and sat down on a wooden straight back chair, removed his hat, and scratched his head. "Lawrence, have the 2nd halt their attack."

"They're engaged, Danny!"

"I know, but we have to try and protect Sheffield. Have you heard from Hammer?"

"No, sir, but I doubt he's had time to get his Junior Knights to the western lines."

"Crap, when will the troops from Nitrate City be here?"

"Their lead elements are in transport vehicles and will be at the assembly point any moment ... the intersection of 2nd Street and Wilson Dam Road. However, their marchers will not be there for another hour or so."

"I tell ya' what. Negate that order to disengage at the bridgehead perimeter. Let's see if those troops can break through their defenses. Harry won't have as many reserves left to hold it now. I'll take a Knight team up to the intersection myself. As soon as the troops from Nitrate City start to arrive in vehicles, we'll have them proceed to Sheffield via 2nd Street. We'll just have the foot soldiers keep marching in that direction as well. I'll order those drivers to drop their militiamen in Sheffield and immediately turn around to go back and fetch another batch of the marchers."

"Yes, sir. Ya' hear that, Gail?"

"Yes, Lawrence. Do you want me to follow Constable Ragland with a radio crew and see if I can operate a line of communication back to you?"

"Yes, excellent, Gail! Take Ben Sneed and his son."

Danny was already out the door and hollering at his Knights, "Get your butts in gear! We're headed up the road!"

After his 3rd Squad broke off for their assigned ridge, Captain Jesus Juarez had his command element and the platoon's weapon squad position themselves on a slightly higher bit of ground to the left of the road. In a stand of mixed hardwoods, facing west, they set up their two belt fed machine guns. Their recent dash took them through the Colbert's defensive lines as planned, but there were enemy forces all about them at this point. Jesus had his half-dozen riflemen disperse in a circle. If random enemy units approached from a direction other than Sheffield, he could move at least one of his MGs to address them. A pair of holders walked their mounts over to a low-lying area deeper in the woods.

Jesus listened intently to the sporadic small arms fire along the ridges and hollows back to the southeast. He prayed his three squads would prevail and suffer few casualties. After hearing engine sounds, he turned his attention west towards Sheffield. Two box-trucks led by an open bed pick-up appeared shortly.

Sgt. Gillespie studied the vehicles through his rangefinder binoculars, and after a few seconds said, "Captain, I can't see what is in the big trucks, but the pick-up is full of kids. It looks like school cadets. They're sportin' rifles, sir."

"Range, Sergeant?"

"Comin' up on 300 yards."

"Count us down in 50 yard increments, Sergeant. Gunners, prepare to open fire on my command. If they stop, I'll wait to see who or what gets out. If they don't stop, we'll start shooting at around a hundred yards."

"Yes, sir," the two gunners said in unison followed by the simultaneous retraction and release of their weapons' charging handles. A third Bennett brother, Clive, manned the weapon squad's M249 5.56mm MG and Jake Connelly was on their M240 7.62mm automatic weapon.

"250 yards," announced Gillespie calmly.

The vehicles were moving very slowly. Jesus suspected the convoy's commander was spooked. He had probably expected to encounter a Knight Force Team or the like by this point.

"200."

The cavalrymen could now read *Thompson* on the side-panels of the box trucks. The pick-up was sans signage and painted in the Ragland's basic-black.

The captain ordered, "Jake, you concentrate on the rear vehicle first, and Clive, you take out the driver of that lead pick-up and then hit the men in the bed."

"Men?" questioned Clive.

Juarez cut back, "Whatever, Private Bennett. They're here to kill us, so how 'bout we kill them first."

"Yes, sir," complied Bennett in a somber tone.

"150."

Slowing down even more, the trucks curved with the road and angled up a shallow rise in the terrain.

"That's 125! Shit! Captain?"

Jesus commanded, "Fire!"

The staccato of the automatic weapons was deafening. None of the weapons squad's members had ever fired a round in anger. This baptism of fire was exhilarating yet horrifying.

The drivers of the lead and trail vehicles were hit first, but the pickup continued to smoothly roll along, spilling screaming teenagers to either side of the road. The box truck in the rear kept lurching forward like a wounded animal. The driver in the middle of the convoy tried to turn off the road, away from the fire, but was hit by the truck behind him.

Clive was done with the occupants of the pick-up and now let a long burst fly into the cab of the middle truck. He noticed Colbert cadets jumping out of the back and making for the far side of the road and the woods beyond. As Clive shifted his sights to the rear of the truck, he heard his commander order the riflemen to start picking off the scattering youths. As he fired, Clive saw the long dark hair of a female cadet fly in a circle as she spun to the ground. Uncontrollably, he released the machine gun's firing handle and turned his head to vomit. Gillespie shoved him aside, assumed control of the M249, and expended the last of its 200-round belt taking out a handful of cadets trying to return fire from beneath the middle truck.

Jake's larger .30 caliber bullets shattered his target's truck cab. He then raked the side panel, and started shooting the passengers as they fled. None got more than a few feet from their vehicle.

Captain Juarez ordered, "Cease fire! Cease fire!"

The quiet was numbing. At that moment, no fire was even coming from any of the distant engagements. Their nostrils were filled with powder fumes, their burning eyes were fixed on the carnage before them, and their joints were locked. Above the ringing in their ears, they began to hear the cries and moans of the dying.

Alice Boyd, Catherine Ragland's Personal Assistant, stepped out of Catherine's office and looked both ways. She was both relieved and surprised that no servants or security guards were anywhere to be seen. The office was located halfway down a long corridor of offices, supply rooms, and communication rooms that led from the residential sections of Ragland Palace. She hurried along the hallway to the grand foyer. Once again, she found no one there, and without further hesitation, rushed downstairs to the Council Chamber. Her flats tippity-tapped down the marble stairs — she kept heels under her desk, but seldom wore them around the Palace. The chamber doors were closed, but she did not knock. Upon entering, she found Edward Ragland sitting by himself at the big table. His briefcase was open and he had papers spread about — a pretense of purpose.

He stood and exclaimed, "Thank, God! You finally got away from her! I was about to give up."

Alice said nothing. She went straight into his arms and they kissed and hugged for a long minute.

Interrupting the kiss, she softly said, "I'm sorry, Eddie, she had a bunch of letters and notes to get out to auxiliaries, militia widows, and the like. You know."

"Yes, yes, I know my sister all too well. Bless her heart."

In a nervous tone, Alice asked, "Eddie, do you still think no one suspects us?"

"Shh now, darlin'. We are safe as kittens. Everybody is distracted with this damn war. The Lauderdales are in Sheffield, and everybody is in a panic. Hell, my wife won't even leave the house. Harry'll probably be knockin' at the door of Tuscumbia tonight, but he's spread too thin now. We'll crush him in the mornin'."

Alice sighed in relief, batted her dark eyes, and said, "Well, I'm supposed to fix your sister and myself a late lunch or early supper, and take it to her office. I told her my hands were aching from all the typing. Always the sweetie, she urged me to take a short break before

I made the sandwiches, but I better be back up there with the food by three."

They both glanced at the clock on the wall and saw it was 2:20 PM.

Edward commented, "Yeah, and Danny sent me a message asking me to help him out on something pretty urgent."

Alice smiled and nodded as she glanced at his sprawled papers.

They resumed the stares into each other's eyes, and Alice seductively said, "Well then, Mr. Ragland. We best get at it."

He grinned and stepped back ever so slightly, "Yes indeedie! Aren't we a pair ... with the world going to Hell all around us?"

Alice quickly took off her blazer, neatly folded it, and laid it on the table. Next, she slid her waist-band-holstered, aluminum framed, 4.25" barreled, single action .45 ACP semi-automatic from behind her hip, and placed it gently on top of the coat. Now totally enthralled, Edward watched as Alice pulled up her pencil skirt and thumbed down her panties. After wriggling a bit to accelerate their fall, she stepped out of them and returned to his waiting arms. As they locked into another long kiss, her hands went to work on his belt buckle.

Harry winced from the explosion of a nearby artillery shell. The Colberts' cannon fire of the past half-hour was both surprising and troublesome. They were firing from the south at a distance of around 800 yards. Harry's soldiers on the perimeter could only see a couple of the guns. The actual size of the battery was still unknown. Scooter's forward observers had returned to the bridgehead. After analyzing a couple of barrages, they concurred — six to eight howitzers. The explosive black powder shells were damned effective. Harry's list of casualties from the shelling was growing not to mention the loss of supplies and equipment.

Harry and 1911 were at the west side of the bridgehead. They had just watched the last of the East Low Church Militia Battalion advance to the west and now the West Low Church Militia was forming up to follow. The East had just retreated through the perimeter after their successful feint. They received water and food. After resting for a few minutes, they were ready for their next task — taking the City of Sheffield. The High Church Militia had been strengthening their bridgehead perimeter positions since the day before, so the incoming artillery fire had little effect on them. They had stopped the latest Colbert infantry charge dead in its tracks. The attacking Colbert Militia settled into firing positions scattered between two and three hundred yards from the perimeter. For the moment, they seemed content with sniping at the Lauderdale breastworks, trenches, and foxholes.

Slingshot Teams 2, 4, and 5 had departed as well. They accompanied the Low Church Militia to provide mobile fire support and exploit any breakthroughs. Harry kept Slingshot 7 in reserve at the bridgehead.

Bardolph and Nim had been antsy and whining all day about missing the fight. Harry eventually relented and released them to bum a ride with Slingshot 2. He sent them with a message for Captain Juarez and an understanding, "After you relay my orders to Juarez, you two can choose your battle. Just two things, kill as many Black Force and Colbert Militiamen as you can, but comply with my *Directive for Interactions with Colbert Non-combatants.*"

Harry let the pair of miscreants take Slingshot 8's two AK-47 assault rifles and the last of the steel cased 7.62X39 Chinese ammunition. That was enough to load the nine 30-round magazines they shared. He did not allow them to take any of the team's hand grenades or night vision equipment. They trooped off happy and grinning even more so after climbing up into the back of Major Flurry's LMTV to join the women of her tactical team. In contrast, the females looked askance at the pair of miscreants.

As the last of the Low Church Militia advanced, Harry couldn't help but admire the new uniforms of the militia and Slingshot Teams. The Lexington Mill had worked diligently over the past year to outfit them. The militia pants and hooded field jackets were made of heavy cotton duck, and the jacket had a wool lining. They were dark khaki in color. They wore shirts or sweaters of their own choosing. The Slingshots had the same trousers, but their jackets were shorter and dyed mottled green and brown. The militia had the Lauderdale Flag as one shoulder patch and their battalion flag as the other. The Slingshot Team jackets had chest patches consisting of a fabric circle with the letter Y (representing the shape of a slingshot) and each team's particular team number appearing in the fork of the Y — both figures in black. The militia had a cotton duck combat cap the same color as their pants and jackets while the Slingshot teams wore an eclectic mix of headgear — OW baseball caps being most prevalent. 1911 had over a dozen such hats squirreled away.

Harry observed to 1911, "The troops marching and fighting in this November daytime weather may get a little hot but they will appreciate them at night, and even more so, if the rain starts and the temperature drops."

With that the two men looked to the western skies and frowned at the heavy, distant clouds. 1911 held out his right palm to gauge the increasing wind.

"Looks like our luck is running out on the weather, Harry."

"Yep, whatcha' think, Mort? Startin' around dark?"

"Probably. Hey, Harry, it's right at three."

Harry and 1911 next dropped in at the field hospital. The newly arrived Dr. Fulton and his staff were already busy with several wounded personnel, so Harry waited to make eye contact with the physician, nodded, and moved on. Harry noted the medical staff had loaded a Florence Wagon with a couple of the more seriously wounded. He no longer had the fuel or motor vehicles to spare, and was glad they had worked out a means to transport the wounded and dead back to the Florence Hospital.

Harry's logistics officer and first cousin, Major Donnie Smith, hailed them as they left the hospital tent. "Harry, remember I warned you about the condition of the tires remaining in storage? Well, I was right. In spite of all we have done to seal and protect them, even the never used, brand spankin' new ones have degraded. After over a half century, you would expect that, huh?"

"Really, Donnie? That sucks. How bad?"

"In general, if you are real careful installing them they will give some service, but two Humvee tires and three or four truck tires have popped. An' I only have a few left for each."

Harry shook his head in frustration.

"Yeah, that's right, Harry. Not punctured! They just failed!"

"Well, do the best ya' can with 'em, Donnie. I figured we'd be mostly afoot after a few days anyway. What about the solid, recycled fiber tires you came up with last year?"

"We got 'em here, but those fuckin' drivers will have to be careful. They'll come apart at anything over forty miles per hour."

Almost disappointed in Harry's absence of panic, Donnie looked around frustrated and dejected.

Harry thought it best to redirect his cousin, "Donnie, how 'bout the supply lines and your crew? How are they doin'?"

"Aw, my folks are workin' their asses off, and those kids you assigned to me, the orphans, they are a great bunch. Don't have to tell 'em anything twice. That one named Robby, their kinda boss, he's uh good 'un, Harry."

"Good to hear, Donnie," said Harry as he shared a glance and proud grin with 1911.

Donnie started in on a new roll, "Shit, I'm glad y'all have taken the river bank over there towards Sheffield! Those crap hounds have been sniping at my folks crossing the bridge all day. I've lost two people, a horse, and two mules. And had a tire shot out! It's flat stopped now though. Wonder why they ain't been shootin' at us from the part of the river bank runnin' to the dam, or for that matter, the dam itself?"

Harry answered, "I imagine they don't want us to have any reason to shoot at or get any closer to their precious dam ... or our 'precious dam' for that matter." He did not want to reveal his spy's transmission from last year reporting that Edward Ragland had the dam's powerhouse wired with explosives.

"Oh, yeah. I reckon so."

Harry changed the subject, "Where are we on food, ammunition, and supplies?"

"Oh, we'll have it all crossed by tonight. As to your order to get it all out in the field … you know, in the trucks and supply wagons … we're workin' on it. Hey, are you still sure that's such a great idea? Seems kinda' risky."

"Maybe so, Donnie, but I think it's riskier to leave large amounts of it here … all in one location," and Harry pointed off to the south.

Donnie thought a second and caught up, "Oh, yeah. That Colbert artillery is a pain in the ass. What the Hell are you gonna' do about that, cuz?"

"We got a plan, Donnie. Trust me."

"Okay, Harry. I always do. Damn, son, Uncle Wade would be proud of you!"

"Thanks, Donnie."

"Sure thang, Harry. Hey, I best get back at it. It looks like some sittin' around is goin' on down at the depot tent."

"Oh, one more thing, Donnie. Will you send Robby up to HQ? I just need him for a couple of minutes."

"You got it. Good luck!"

The cousins shook hands and parted.

After returning to his HQ tent, Harry went straight to Lieutenant Neva Lazo de la Vega, "Neva, anything from Cheetah?"

"No, sir. Not a thing."

"Hmm, that's a bit worrisome," Harry said as he studied Neva's situational map.

After reading a message from one of her staff, Neva said, "The perimeter runners report they are holding just fine."

"Anything from the lead militia elements or Juarez?"

"Captain Juarez sent back a wounded rider to let us know the ridges were cleared, and the West Low Church Militia and the Slingshot Teams had reached his position."

She pointed out Juarez's position on the map.

Harry looked at the spot and then scanned to the west on the map, "Good, how long ago was the rider?"

"Fifteen minutes, sir."

"Well then, considerin' how long it probably took him to get back, they should be at Woodward Avenue and Jackson Highway by now."

"Yes, sir, and by the way, the rider said, and I quote, 'the cavalry got pretty chewed, ma'am.' I sent him on to the field hospital."

"Oh, me. Well, keep me posted."

"Okay, Harry. I will."

After studying the map for a few minutes, Harry and 1911 sat down on a couple of the folding chairs next to the communication area. Harry sighed with fatigue, looked up, and saw Robby at the tent's entrance. "Robby, come on in, son. Have a seat."

The boy was uneasy with all the officers, radios, and phones. He slowly sat down on the edge of the folding chair across from Harry and 1911.

Harry said, "Robby, Major Smith says you're doin' a good job with the boys over in supply.

Robby smiled a bit and blushed, "Oh, that was generous of him. He's a fine man. Kinda' nervous though."

Those in earshot laughed.

1911 stood and said, "Harry, I'll get those items out of the 8."

Harry responded as 1911 exited the tent, "Thanks, Mort."

Robby gawked around at the goings on and observed, "Harry, y'all were smart to move this tent underneath the bridge. One lucky shot from those Colbert cannons and we'd be hurtin'."

"Yes, indeed, Robby. Oh, here's 1911."

"Here ya' go, Harry," 1911 said as he handed Harry a leather rifle scabbard and a cloth bundle.

Harry stood and began, "Yes, that's them, Mort." He passed the bundle straight over to Robby and retained the scabbard.

"What's this, y'all?"

Harry urged, "Well, untie that rope and see for yourself."

Robby tugged at the slipknot and loosened the bundle. His eyes lit up as he unfolded a Slingshot uniform. "Damn, Harry is this for me?"

"That's right, Slingshotter! Whatcha' think?"

"Oh, Man! These are great! And there's the 8's chest patch and everthang!"

"Yep, they might be a little big, but it's the last set that supply had. My sister sewed that Patch on for you."

"Miss Philippa, did? Really?"

"Yeah, her quilting circle did a bunch of the sewing for us. She was glad to do one more."

Robby gushed, "Will you thank her for me. She's a fine seamstress!"

"I will. Now, I got a new job for ya'."

"Am I gonna' be a real Slingshot 8 Team member now?"

"You are, but when we head out today for Sheffield, I need you to stay here."

"Oh. Yes, sir, he responded with a bit of disappointment in his voice.

"Now, don't worry. We'll be back soon enough and you can ride all the way to Hell with us tomorrow, but I want you to take a special command for me right now."

"A command?"

"That's right. Donnie reported a little while ago that the supplies we have in inventory will be over here and mostly dispersed by this evening."

"Yes, sir. I figured so."

"No small part to the hard work of you and your friends."

"They're a good bunch."

"I agree, and they're your command."

"What?"

Harry laid out Robby's assignment, "Yeah, now listen close, son. We will hold the southern end of the O'Neal Bridge shortly, but it will take a while to make that bridge fit for traffic. Its damage was far more extensive. Our engineers will have to span a hundred foot gap, and the supporting structure is questionable.

"That said, we have to hold this one. I'm gonna need at least two or possibly three of these High Church companies pretty soon to help with the advance. That leaves one Slingshot Team and one or two High Church companies to protect this bridgehead.

"How many are there of your orphan buddies?"

Robby asked, "Boys and girls?"

"Oh, you got girls too?"

"Yes, sir. Eight came over the bridge this morning from Mrs. Chandler's Home for Girls. She told them to stay, but they snuck out before breakfast."

Neva had moved over to the circle and laughed after hearing Robby's revelation. She advised, "If you send them back, Harry, they'll probably just run away again."

Harry shook his head in surrender and moved on, "Okay then, Robby, girls too. How many over twelve-years-old total?"

Robby rolled his eyes up and starred at the tent ceiling as he calculated a figure. After a moment, he answered, "Just one little boy and girl are under twelve. I think they are both eleven, so not countin' them, we got seven girls and nineteen boys."

"26, okay, Robby, there's your platoon. Have they all had elementary marksmanship training?"

"Of course. One of those girls was in the championships last year. Yep, and even the least trained boy or girl in the whole bunch knows which end of a rifle is which and BRASS too."

1911 questioned, "Brass?"

Neva laughingly poked 1911's arm, "C'mon, Mort! You know, BRASS! Breathe, relax, aim, sight, and squeeze."

1911 figured it out and chuckled, slightly embarrassed. The old warrior had been shooting since he could walk yet never had any formal marksmanship training.

Harry moved on, "That's good, Robby. We already have a few rifles racked over by the field hospital. They are weapons no longer needed by our first dead and wounded. There will be more, Robby … a lot more. Armed with these weapons, I would like for your group to stand by here at HQ and the supply area just in case the Colberts make a breakthrough in the perimeter."

"A last line of defense, Harry?"

Neva, 1911, and Harry cringed.

Harry sighed deeply, put his hand on Robby's shoulder, and answered, "Yeah, Robby. 'A last line of defense.'"

143

"We'll do it, Harry. You can count on us."

"All right then. Go over to hygiene and get cleaned up, put on your new uniform, gather your people, and get them organized. Be sure to tell them it is volunteer duty. If any don't want to serve in this new outfit, they can ride back to Florence with Major Smith and the two eleven-year-olds."

"Harry, do I need to go through anyone, to draw those weapons from the field hospital?"

"No, I'll be making an announcement about this in a staff meeting shortly. Actually, I'm putting you in charge of those extra weapons, Robby. As they're racked, you have one of your folks stationed at the hospital to take them back to your area under the bridge. You issue them as you see fit. Make sure each of your soldiers are familiar with his or her firearm, can load it, free a stoppage or malfunction, clean it, and has at least a modest supply of ammunition. Frankly, they'll just about all be the new flintlock muzzleloaders or the older Sharps breechloaders. I'll have supply issue you 200 percussion caps for the Sharps right now. They'll all be gone by the mornin', and hardly any of the caps will make it back here from the front lines."

"Yes, sir. Thanks."

Robby stood to depart. 1911 interjected, "Just a second, Robby. Hey, Harry." After catching Harry's eyes, 1911 glanced down to the scabbard in Harry's left hand.

Harry said, "Oh, shit. I forgot." He reached in the end of the scabbard and slid out a lever action rifle, and continued, "Robby, I wanted you to have a repeater to better lead your folks in battle if or when the time comes. I liberated this rifle from a Colbert militiaman on the O'Neal Bridge back in the Three Day War." I was about your age." Harry handed the rifle to Robby, and cautioned, "The chamber's empty, but the tube is full. Now, here's the downside. It's chambered for a .35 caliber cartridge. Other than the 6 rounds in the tube magazine and the eight more boxed and tucked away in that pouch on the scabbard, there probably isn't another round of that ammunition to be found in the entire Spared Territory. I put a couple of shots through it years ago and then cleaned it and put it in Daddy's vault. Those two shots were dead on at 50 yards. The open sights are good to go."

A tear ran down the boy's cheek. He could say nothing. 1911 just laughed and put his arm around Robby's shoulder to give him a fatherly hug. The orphan seemed to have no shortage of surrogates.

Jesus Juarez watched the Humvee, LMTV, and MTV of Slingshot 2 roll to a stop on the road near his resting troop. As Low Church infantry hustled by her lead vehicle, Donna Flurry stood on the floorboard and surveyed the dozens of scattered and broken Sheffield cadets sprawled about the opposite side of the road. She turned her eyes to meet Jesus's, and simply shook her head — not in incrimination but empathy. Movement from one of her trailing vehicles altered his gaze. He watched Thomas Nim and Chance Bardolph clamber down from the back of the LMTV. A couple of Major Flurry's gals passed them their AKs. Both sides had obviously been trading barbs and waved goodbye sarcastically. The ne'er-do-well pair strolled and smirked. They held the misconception of victory in this most-recent philosophical exchange. The relieved laughter from the Slingshot truck bed indicated otherwise.

As they approached, Bardolph and Nim took in the scene and assessed both the slaughtered and the slaughterers. Bardolph exclaimed, "God Damn, Cap'n, y'all gave more than ya' took, but ya' took plenty, huh?"

"That's true enough Sergeant Bardolph. What are you sightseers up to? Just out enjoyin' the beautiful fall colors of the Tennessee Valley?"

"Uh, naw, Cap'n. Harry cut us loose to go make trouble over in Sheffield, but he told us to deliver you a message on the way."

"I see. Where is it?"

"Oh, it's verbal, sir."

"Well, go ahead, Corporal."

Bardolph's eyes darted about and he leaned in to whisper, "In front of your men, sir?"

Juarez chuckled and responded, "It's fine, Sergeant. We have no secrets. They can handle troublin' news just as well as I can."

"Okay, fine then. Harry, or uh, President Smith wants y'all to head back east and take out the Colbert guns that are shelling the bridgehead. There are around a half-dozen of 'em. They are settin' about 800 yards from our southern perimeter. I went up to the defenses and took a look for myself before we hopped in that truck-full of dykes. I figure their cannons are spread out, side-to-side, over 'bout two hundred yards. Their skirmishers are forward of 'em about a quarter-mile. They still haven't sent any other forces in to back up their assault, but I could see a lot of activity up on 2nd Street. It looked like large numbers of militia marching for Sheffield or Tuscumbia. Harry says you can reconnoiter the gun positions from their left flank, and decide for yourself if you think it's doable. He said not to attempt it if you 'deem it suicidal'."

Jesus glanced back at his men and saw their attentive stares. After clearing his throat, he addressed Bardolph and Nim, "Thank you, men, Sergeant Gillespie and I will check out the map and stir things up shortly."

"You're welcome, Cap'n. I reckon we'll be on our way. Hey, Cap'n did ya' find anything on those kids?"

"They were all armed with Colbert Sharps rifles, so the militia relieved them of their percussion caps and paper cartridges, and my men piled the rifles in one of those shot-up trucks. At least it will keep them dry."

All three men glanced at the steadily clouding sky.

Jesus advised, "I gotta' say, men, you two could probably best contribute by working with one of the militia squads or a Slingshot tactical team. It would be safer for you as well … rather than flat headin' around on your own."

"Good advice, Cap'n. We'll try to do just that. Huh, Corporal Nim?"

Nim finally spoke as he uttered, "Uh … Yes, sir. That's right."

146

Jesus turned to walk towards his platoon, but just inside earshot, he heard the departing Nim, in a mocking tone, say something about the *Directive for Interactions with Colbert Non-combatants*. Jesus paused, considered an ass chewing, but shook his head in disgust knowing further intervention was futile.

Michael Williams and his squad had taken the late Sheffield cadets' water barrel over to water the platoon's horse. Juarez walked over to discuss some changes with the 1st Squad's leader.

"Michael, I'm real sorry about Private Tate."

Michael just looked at him, swallowed hard, and nodded. He continued to lead Jake Connelly's horse, Margie Sue, over to their makeshift trough.

Captain Juarez continued, "The 2nd Squad finally joined us a few minutes ago."

Composed now, Michael said, "Yes, sir. I thought I saw three of those Buffalo Soldiers ride in. Where're the rest of 'em?"

"That's it, Corporal."

"Aw, Hell! No way! They're dead?"

"Well, Corporal Napier and the two Henry brothers were killed, but Tommy Jones and Leticia Goodloe were just wounded. That's what took 'em a while to catch up. They had to find a militia medic. The Knights had a dug-in position on their ridge. Oh, and after sending back Private Jennings from 3rd Squad, that just leaves four of them ... all privates."

"Yes, sir. I saw their leader, Corporal McDonald, on the road after we cleared our ridge. One of his troopers, Bryant, was taking him and Offutt back. Bryant was bleeding from his left arm ... I bet he'll lose it. I doubt if Mac will live. Cap'n, that's some hard luck."

"Yeah, well, that's the situation, and that's why I need to run somethin' by ya'."

Michael stopped fiddling with the horses and turned to give his commander his full attention, "Yes, sir."

"Harry wants us to take out those Colbert guns that are pounding the bridgehead. There are the four of us from my command element, the six of you from 1st Squad, the three from 2nd Squad, and the four from the 3rd. I'm thinkin' we should roll 'em into two squads for the assault. Sneak the weapons squad up on their flank to lay down fire, and then we attack with our two squads from behind their guns. Slip out of that rolling wooded area on this flank and get 'em before they can turn their little guns and put canister on us."

"Sounds good, Cap'n."

"Okay, how about you taking Cameron Brown, Tommy Thirkill, and William Abernathy from the 2nd and I'll take Janie Cooper, Hoop Baker, Bud Counts, and Debbie Felton from the 3rd?"

"That'll be fine, Cap'n. I guess we need to get movin' pretty quick, huh?"

"Absolutely, Michael. Whatcha' think, 15 minutes?"

"Affirmative, sir. My folks will finish up with this waterin', and I'll walk over with ya' to talk to the platoon."

As they returned to the platoon, Michael commented, "This is gonna' be hairy, Captain Juarez."

"Yes it will, Corporal Williams … quite hairy!"

Danny Ragland had quickly surmised that he was not going to be able to beat the Lauderdale forces to Sheffield's eastern border. Reacting quickly he diverted his forces to the center of Sheffield. The 1st Battalion of the East Colbert Militia ineffectively deployed in the downtown area and several residential neighborhoods. By 3:30 PM, he saw that they were not going to be able to hold. He decided that committing the East Colbert's 3rd Battalion to Sheffield was futile, so it was diverted southwest to Tuscumbia. Thank goodness he brought Gail Atkinson's little band of radio specialists along. Danny had Gail relay orders for Lawrence, still in Muscle Shoals, to report to Ragland Palace in Tuscumbia and prepare it as headquarters for the defense of Tuscumbia.

Gail connected Danny with Pickard Thompson around 4:00 PM. The Constable urged him to gather key personnel, communications equipment, boxed ammunition, and portable weapons and depart for

Tuscumbia. He offered a company from the 3rd to assist Pickard, but the Sheffield industrialist politely declined the offer. Pickard assessed the deteriorating situation earlier and already had such an evacuation underway.

After reviewing field reports from his company commanders in Sheffield, Danny saw what was happening. He should have the tactical advantage with his troops fighting from prepared defensive positions. The invaders would be paying dearly to dislodge the Colberts. However, the Lauderdales, whether by design or through luck, had set the stage from the start. Harry advanced quickly and picked the ground. Danny was forced to attack him and got banged up. Harry diverted and moved to new ground. Danny circled to cut him off, attacked, and got hammered again. Danny had even been forced to withdraw the 2nd Battalion of the Western Colbert Militia from the Singing River Bridge to defend Muscle Shoals — leaving just their 1st Battalion brethren and sisters to harass the bridgehead. All told, Danny had suffered seven or eight hundred casualties. He had no way of knowing what Harry Smith's losses were, but Danny guessed they were a fraction of that. This had to stop. Danny was abandoning Sheffield to once and for all box Harry in. Danny's new plan would force the Lauderdales to attack on the ground of the Colbert's choosing. Also, Danny hoped the strategic withdrawal would enable him to initiate a proper and decisive counterattack.

Lawrence Foster and his staff did not arrive at the Palace until after four. Muscle Shoals and Tuscumbia were clogged with fleeing refugees from Sheffield. After two days of sporadic shelling from Lauderdale artillery, the populace was edgy. After word got out of Lauderdale militiamen crossing their city limits, they broke. They took to the streets in droves carrying what they could. Lawrence was embarrassed to witness this — something he never dreamed would happen on his watch.

After entering the grand foyer, Lawrence was immediately waylaid by Knight Second Class Holt. Lawrence glanced at him and curtly asked, "What now, Holt?"

"Sir, I need to speak to you in private about a critical matter."

Lawrence hesitated a moment, reassessed Holt's expression, and turned to his staff, "Go ahead and start setting up in the office and communication rooms next to Constable Ragland's office. I'll be along shortly. Oh, you there, Hughes, stay out front and keep an eye out for the Constable. I want to be informed the moment he arrives."

Knight Sergeant Hughes replied, "Yes, sir!"

After Hughes headed for the porch, and the rest of the staff made for the administrative wing, Holt asked, "How about just steppin' into President Ragland's study?"

Lawrence nodded to his Head of Palace Security, and the two men walked over to the study. After making sure they were out of earshot, Danny asked, "Where is the President, Holt?"

In a low severe tone, Holt answered, "I had to call a Code Alpha, sir!"

"What the Hell? Wait a minute! So the President and his family are in their safe room?"

"Yes, sir, and they are all fine."

"Okay, Knight, you have my full attention. What's goin' on?"

"Yes, sir. Here it is as short as I can make it. You know how I reported to you a few days ago that I suspected an affair between Edward Ragland and Alice Boyd?"

"Yes, I do recall that. Don't tell me!"

"Well, yes, they are."

"Go on."

"I noticed that Mr. Ragland, Edward that is, hung around after this morning's meeting. Around two, he ended up down in the Council Chamber. He said he wanted to go over some operational issues and catch up on paperwork. It seemed strange given the incursion and all. An' he was just actin' kinda' hinky, sir."

"Hinkier than usual? You said short, Holt."

"Yeah. Sorry, sir. I promise I'm gettin' there. I decided to check on him late, round a quarter to three. I used the servants' staircase that comes out at the far end of the chamber and peeked in to check on him. I'll be damned, sir, if him and Miss Boyd weren't goin' at it on the council table!"

"Fucking?"

"Hell, yeah! Right there on Little Charles's prized walnut council table! She was layin' there on her back with her blouse undone an' her skirt up around her waist while Eddie stood on the floor holdin' her legs up in the air, just nailin' her!"

Lawrence responded, "Okay, I got the picture. Now, why the Code Alpha Alert?"

"Well, I didn't linger at the servants' door. I went back up to the main floor and noticed that this room, the study, was empty. I hid in here to observe the council chamber staircase. A little while later, Alice ... Miss Boyd came up the stairs. She was trying to straighten out her clothes and hair as she looked around suspiciously. No wonder, that, huh, sir? Anyway, she went directly to the kitchen. Eddie, I mean, Mr. Ragland, trotted up the stairs a couple of minutes after her and shot straight out the front door. He left heading east with his Knight detail in his big 4X4 SUV."

"Once again, the Code Alpha?"

"Oh, yeah. Alice musta' prepared some sandwiches for her and Miss Catherine. She came through the Grand Foyer right at three with a tray and sodas and went straight to their office. I had Knights Candler and Thorne handle my rounds for me, so that I could keep an eye on her. At exactly 3:26, she returned the tray and empty bottles to the kitchen. I thought she was going back to Miss Ragland's office but she didn't."

"So where did Alice go?"

"After glancing back over her shoulder, she went into the janitorial closet in the business hall; I figured she'd come out with a broom or dust rag or sumpin'."

"And did she?"

"No, sir. She didn't come out. After a couple of minutes, I decided to check on her. Figured I'd use an excuse like I needed a mop to clean up one of my men's spills or somethin' like that. Luckily for me, Candler had returned to the foyer. I got him to chamber a round in his AK and stand ready. I drew my sidearm, but held it down at my side. I told him to stand close and at-the-ready as I opened the janitorial closet door. She was in there settin' up a transmitter."

"A transmitter? God damn!"

"Yes, sir. We really caught her off guard. Thank God! You know how quick she is. I had the pistol on her immediately and Candler was right beside me in a snap with his AK."

"Did you kill her?"

"Oh Hell naw! Didn't have to, but I've sparred with her too many times at the Knight Center to dis' her. She is as quick as a cat. She had both hands holding that transmitter, or she would have probably drawn down on us. I had her ease the transmitter on to a supply shelf, and then pull her weapon, that lightweight .45, with her weak-hand fingertips and hold it out for me to snatch away from her. I had her do the same with her spare magazine. Then, I had her take off her blazer and drop it to the floor. I guess even a she-warrior like her is intimidated by an assault rifle pointed at her chest from ten feet away. I checked her blazer and found her Palace keys in one pocket and a little tactical flashlight and liner lock folding knife in the other."

"So, where is Alice Boyd now?"

"I felt it best to keep this as tight as possible, until you or the Constable got involved. I left all of her stuff in the closet. I used my master key to lock the closet after we got her out in the hall. I broke it off in the lock to keep anyone from messing with the radio or her weapons. Hell, there is no tellin' what all she has in there. From what I could tell, it looked like she had removed a false wall-panel. That musta' been where the transmitter was hid. The only place I could think of to take her was the council chamber. We walked her down there with me in the front and Candler behind. He is with her now. I warned him to not take his sights off of her and not to listen to any bullshit stories she might try to come up with. Candler and I are still the only two that are aware of this entire situation. Upon my return to the Grand Foyer, I found Thorne and ordered him to initiate the Code Alpha Alert. I told him that all would be explained later."

"Is she restrained?"

"No, sir. You'll probably think we're a couple of pussies, but we thought it was too risky to get that close. Me and Candler were worried about other weapons, so we had her strip down to nuthin' to make sure she was totally unarmed, and then let her get dressed again."

"Actually, you did the right thing. That was a smart way to handle it. Okay, I'm going to go over and make sure my people are on-task, feed them some bullshit excuse, and then you and I can go question her."

"Yes, sir. I'll just wait here by the study. Sir, do you think Constable Ragland will be back soon."

"He's supposed to. God, I hope so. What a fuckin' mess! Not you though, Holt. You and Candler did well. Very well."

Taken aback and too moved to respond, KSC Holt just nodded and grinned.

In a trot, Private Cameron Brown brought Sugar Rhea up beside Michael and Dungee Boy, and asked, "Hey, Corporal, did I understand Captain Juarez correctly? These guns are manned by Black Force Knights?"

"Yep, Cam. That's the way the Raglands do it."

"Shit!"

"Exactly!"

"I guess it was nice knowin' ya' then."

Michael laughed and winked at him. He knew any kind of *bucking-them-up* pep talk would be taken for what it was — *a load of crap.*

Michael teased, "Well, Cam, did you get to use that saber today?"

Cam glanced down at the long-bladed weapon dangling in its black scabbard at his side. He chuckled a little and then went somber,

"Naw, that was pretty much a machine gun fight on our ridge. Those Knights had all kinds of firepower. We used those pot-metal grenades on 'em. Surprisingly, they all worked. We fired all of our 5.56 ammo in our two M4s. We went through our casualties and some of the dead Colberts collecting ammo. No 5.56 to amount to anything. But, we collected over a hundred rounds of 7.62X39. We each took one of our squad's SKS carbines and divvied up the cartridges."

"Those are tough little guns."

"Yep."

"Cam, I hate that we lost Napier and your other buddies. They were good horse soldiers. Bad luck runnin' into those clusters of Knights."

"Thanks, Michael. I'll miss 'em. God, I don't know how to tell their kin!"

"Hell, I'll go with ya', man. Soon as we get back."

The sun was touching the western horizon behind them as they slipped around a cluster of industrial buildings long since taken over by woods and weeds. They could hear the Colberts' cannon firing to their front and wished they had been ten minutes sooner to possibly save a Lauderdale or two at the bridgehead. They were getting close — maybe two hundred yards from the edge of the woods. The understrength platoon halted while Juarez and Gillespie rode ahead to reconnoiter. The small arms fire from the bridgehead had declined from steady to sporadic.

Returning a few minutes later, Juarez gathered his men. "Ol' Bardolph was pretty much right on. The nearest gun is about a hundred yards from these woods. There are five more, and they lie side by side, facing the bridgehead. There is about 25 yards between each of 'em, so they are spread out over about two hundred yards total … probably more like 150. There are several vehicles parked behind the guns, and it looks like they are getting ready to load two or three of them in the trucks. I bet they are movin' those to Sheffield or Tuscumbia.

"Sergeant Gillespie is going to take the weapons squad forward and set up a firing position in the woods about a hundred yards behind the row of guns. We found a good spot for you gunners. Corporal Williams, our squads are going to attack from the tree line a little to the right of our MGs. Now listen up, Weapons Squad, Clive you engage the closest three guns with your 5.56, and Jake, you take the three farthest with the 7.62. How much ammo do you two have left?"

Jake spoke up first, "I have a little over four hundred rounds, Cap'n."

Clive answered, "Just the single 200-round belt, sir … in 5.56."

Jesus noticed Clive's pale complexion and asked, "You okay, son?"

"Yes, sir! I won't let y'all down."

Sergeant Gillespie's horse, Noble Deed, was standing alongside Clive's Hector. He reached over, and patted Private Bennett reassuringly on the shoulder.

Still addressing his machine gunners, Jesus added, "Well, don't conserve it. Y'all start pouring short bursts into your closest assigned cannon and then work your way to the farthest. You can start working your way back, but be sure to stop firing before our two squads cross into your lanes of fire. Got it?"

Clive and Jake answered simultaneously, "Yes, sir."

Shifting from the gunners to his other horsemen, Jesus continued, "Troopers, you may be thinking that the machine gunners will kill all the Black Force Knights on those guns for you. Well, it ain't gonna' happen. Those Knights have built up little defensive positions around their artillery positions — sand bags, dirt mounds, and the like.

"We could do this two ways: dismount and attack them on foot, making for smaller slower moving targets, or attack on horseback making for larger faster moving targets."

Private William Abernathy announced, "Dammit, Cap'n, we're cavalry, by God!"

Supportive remarks followed from the platoon.

Jesus looked around beaming with pride, "Hell, yeah, we are! So, here we go. Michael, your riders are the fastest of us. Y'all take the far guns and my squad will take the near ones. I'll leave it up to you how to divvy-up your people, and I'll take care of mine. Any questions?"

There was silence.

"Alright then, let's ease up to our positions."

"Damn, Jimmy! You can't hit shit movin', but any poor Lauderdale bastard that pauses inside of a thousand yards of you is dead meat!" exclaimed Ted Creasy.

Peering through his spotting scope, Corporal Creasy of the Colbert Militia had just observed the results of a shot taken by his fellow corporal, Jimmy Putnam. Their .308" diameter 200-grain boattail bullet had passed through the head of a Lauderdale rifleman at the end of its 275-yard arc. Jimmy grinned with pride as he cycled the bolt of his heavy barreled, aluminum stocked sniper rifle. A fresh belted magnum cartridge rested in the chamber — ready for the next Lauderdale.

Jimmy glanced back to the west at the setting sun, and urged, "Find me another one, Ted. We only have about a half-hour of shooting-light left. I bet we've killed more Lauderdales at that bridgehead in the past hour than those Civil War cannons have all day."

"Absolutely, Pard," agreed Ted.

As Jimmy peered through his scope, he remarked, "Hey, Ted. You sure as Hell got the handle on that wind."

"No problem, Jimmy. I'll cook it and you serve it!"

They were an unattached sniping team handpicked and armed with the best by none other than the man himself, Constable Danny Ragland. The rifle and its reloading dies, brass, primers, powder, and bullets, were discovered in the extensive firearms collection of the late loan shark, Lamar Bonner, of Littleville. Lamar blew his own brains out after his doctor diagnosed him with an advanced case of prostate cancer. His daughter, Lambert, turned her father's weapons horde over to the Raglands for the defense of Colbert County. She wanted to make amends for the years of "greed, victimization, and profiteering" put upon the community by her "Daddy's trade."

The discovery of the rifle in May was fortuitous for the pair. It coincided with the Colbert Militia's annual shooting competition. The big match was held at the Nitrate City Black Force Training Center's big firing range. The facility had several short range firing bays plus four rifle ranges with earthen berms at 100, 200, 500, and 1,000 yards. In the sniper event, with Jimmy on the trigger and Ted spotting, they took the *Ragland Trophy* with a beat up old .308 bolt action deer rifle. Danny Ragland approached them later about manning Bonner's long-range rifle to serve as a special sniping team. They would have to be willing to fight with the units and at the locations of the Constable's choosing. The two unmarried bricklayers from Spring Valley jumped at the opportunity and never looked back. As a secondary weapon, the Constable also presented them with an M4 5.56mm carbine from the same collection.

Danny had sent them in with the Napoleon-armed Knight teams earlier that afternoon. He wanted them to separate from the artillery line and move forward into the trenches, foxholes, and breastworks of the East Colbert Militia battalions. Facing the southern perimeter of the bridgehead, they were ordered to engage any targets of opportunity. Moving and firing for the past hour at distances ranging between 200 and 400 yards, they were 10 out of 11. Jimmy blamed the lone miss on the wind — it was picking up with this front. Ted teased him arguing that the miss was fired at a walking Lauderdale officer.

Jimmy reacquired his sight picture and slowly scanned the trenches, foxholes, berms, and trees of the Lauderdale Perimeter. A bit of movement caused him to pause, but the flash of khaki was gone as quickly as it appeared. Jimmy chuckled and murmured, "We done put the fear in 'em."

Jimmy and Ted turned to look behind them as they heard machine gun fire and yelling from the artillery positions a quarter-mile to their rear. They blinked in amazement as horse mounted troops emerged from the tree line to the west, galloped across the six-lane highway and charged the guns.

Ted loudly said, "It's the Lauderdale Cavalry attacking us from behind! Shit, I thought they would be off fighting in Sheffield or Tuscumbia by now!"

As they spun back around to grab their gear, Jimmy directed, "Forget the spottin' scope, Ted. Un-bag the M4. They could be on us in no time."

The enemy horsemen were riding parallel to the line of cannons and breaking off in twos and threes to attack each gun from the rear. Jimmy went prone at the back of their trench and assumed a firing position. Now the bi-pod height was wrong. Ted observed this, and lunged forward to shorten the legs a couple of notches. Jimmy's hand darted to the ocular end of his variable power riflescope and dialed the power ring down from 20 to 8 to increase his field of view for the moving targets. Obviously, they had not ranged this direction, so he "guesstimated" and dialed in 400 yards on the side focus knob then shifted the same hand to the other side of the scope to the windage adjustment knob. Given that his right cheek still felt the same westerly wind, he simply doubled his last windage correction in the opposite direction.

This was not Jimmy's kind of fight. His heart raced as he tried to pick out a single target. Many of the cavalrymen to his right had dismounted and were engaging at close range with the Knights. He didn't want to hit one of their own guys, so he tracked to the left and caught up with the last of the still-mounted horsemen. However, they were simply riding too fast.

In frustration, Jimmy shifted his optic back to the cannon on the far right. Finally, a standing target appeared. A cavalryman was standing by the first gun fooling with its muzzle. He quickly placed the 400-yard Mil Dot at center of mass and pressed the trigger. Bang, the trooper crumbled after Jimmy's blink. He cycled the bolt. There was nothing else at that gun position, so he swung to the next one in line. A horse soldier and Knight were fighting hand-to-hand on the ground. Evidently, the Lauderdale won and stood. Jimmy rushed the shot and knew it was a miss at the trigger's break. By the time he cycled the action, Jimmy's target was not to be found.

Ted called out, "Heads up, Jimmy! Some of our guys are charging 'em!"

Jimmy glanced to his front-right and saw Colbert militiamen heading towards the rear. Frustrated at not being able to fire into the melee, they were racing back to help.

"Shit!" he exclaimed. "As if finding a target in that mess wasn't already hard enough!"

His militia buddies still had quite a sprint to go, so Jimmy reacquired a sight picture. "All right," he chirped. A cavalryman, sitting tall in his saddle, paused behind one of the middle guns. *Chill, my man*, Jimmy mentally coached himself as he stopped breathing and fired.

"Hit." calmly but loudly said his spotter as the Lauderdale tumbled from his horse.

Jimmy didn't have to look. He realized that Ted had moved the spotting scope to bear on their artillery line and engaged it.

Ted corrected, "By the way, Pard, it's more like 350 yards."

Jimmy tweaked the side focus for the correction in parallax, and sought another target. He was checking down the artillery line. He considered shooting some of the horses milling about, but quickly ruled it out. It would put some cavalrymen afoot, but he only had about twenty rounds of his precious magnum ammo remaining.

Jimmy tried a running enemy and missed. "Fuck that! No more movin' targets! Shoulda' shot a horse!"

Ted declared, "Damn straight!"

Michael Williams had assigned the fourth gun position to Naddy and the Bennetts and the fifth to Cameron, Tommy, and William. That left the sixth and last gun for Alex, Betty, and himself. The machine gunners actually did more than make the Knight artillerymen duck. They hit several Colberts from one end of the line to the other. Jake actually managed to shoot up three of the Knight's vehicles that were hitched to guns. It helped. The chargers got on the gun positions without losing a single trooper. It was after they closed that things went bad.

The Knights had hunkered down behind the earthen defenses, so most of the troopers found their only means of attack was to dismount behind the guns and go in face-to-face against the Knights. They took the guns but lost half their number. These Knights were real scrappers and they dealt it out with rifles, pistols, and blades. Michael emptied his revolver and was forced to gut one Knight with his Bowie knife. He was in good company — Cam got to put his saber to good effect, and virtually all the troopers, still standing, were a bloody mess.

As they went to work disabling the guns, the troopers realized a sniper from the front was picking them off. Other than keeping low and moving fast they had no response. They didn't even know exactly where the shooter was. If that wasn't enough, a hundred or so Colbert militiamen were charging from the same direction. At least nothing was coming from the rear.

Just after Captain Juarez had remounted and started coordinating the destruction of the little howitzers, the sniper shot him out of his saddle. From the edge of the woods, Sergeant Gillespie saw this and the onrushing militia. He ordered the weapons squad to gather their weapons and ammunition and move to the nearest artillery position. Clive and Jake set up their MGs on top of the Knights' sandbags and started firing at the enemy militia.

Sergeant Gillespie was scanning and ranging the enemy lines for the sniper with his binoculars. Aided by the waning light, he caught a muzzle flash in the right center of the line and heard a bullet whistle by one of his straggling ammo bearers as they sprinted the last few yards to the sandbags. Gillespie took note of a big oak tree to the right of the muzzle flash.

As the machine gunners broke up the Colbert Militia's charge, the lucky ammo bearer sprawled face down and panting behind them. Gillespie crawled over to make sure he wasn't hit. He wasn't. He retrieved the man's burden, a metal can of 7.62 ammunition, and flipped the lid open. He withdrew the belt and turned to his gunners.

Clive was staring at him, "I'm out Sergeant!"

Gillespie shifted to the other, "Jake how 'bout you?"

Jake had the top cover of his M240 open and answered, "Me, too, Sarge!"

The sergeant crawled over to Jake and said, "Son, let me borrow your gun for a minute. I saw the muzzle flash of that sniper and it would take me too long to try and explain where he's at."

"I gotcha, Sarge," and Jake instantly rolled away from his weapon.

The sergeant loaded and charged the M240, took a moment to adjust the sight for the longer distance-to-target, and settled his cheek tightly on the buttstock's comb. After locating the distinctive oak tree and tracking a bit to the left of its trunk, he observed another muzzle flash. A second later, Gillespie heard the agonizing scream of one of their horses.

The NCO from McGee Town growled, "Goddammit, that's enough!" He began to lay down fire on the sniper's position. He had every intention of expending the entire belt.

At the other end of the artillery line, Michael Williams heard the machine gun fire resume. He had stuffed a field dressing in the sucking chest wound of Private Cameron Brown. Michael knew the man was dying, but he applied pressure and talked to him between the machine gun bursts.

Cam asked, "Michael, are Tommy and William okay?"

Michael glanced at the two lifeless Buffalo Soldiers sprawled among several dead Black Force Knights. He looked back into Cam's dark eyes and lied, "They're fine, Cam. Just fine."

"Did we take the gun?"

"Yeah, man. Y'all done good."

"Where's my saber, Michael?"

Michael looked around and spotted the saber. He lifted one of his hands from the bloody wound, reached over and retrieved the gleaming edged weapon. Then, Michael laid it gently across Cam's torso, and guided the dying trooper's hand to its handle.

Cameron Brown from the Pisgah community, just south of Cloverdale, asked, "Michael, will you take it to my Momma for me?" Then he smiled and took his last breath.

Ted Creasy advised, "Jimmy, we better change position! You know the drill."

"You're right," agreed Jimmy Putnam.

Jimmy released his grasp of their sniper rifle to rise and prepare for the move, but he unwisely stood a little too high. It was a lapse in procedure caused by two distractions: concern over the deteriorating situation of their artillery position and a charley horse in his left calf. Jimmy's stand took Ted off guard and caused the spotter to glance up. In seemingly slow motion, Ted heard bullets whistling overhead, and to his horror, one struck his friend in the neck. The sound of a distant machine gun burst followed a second later.

DAY FOUR
THE EVENING

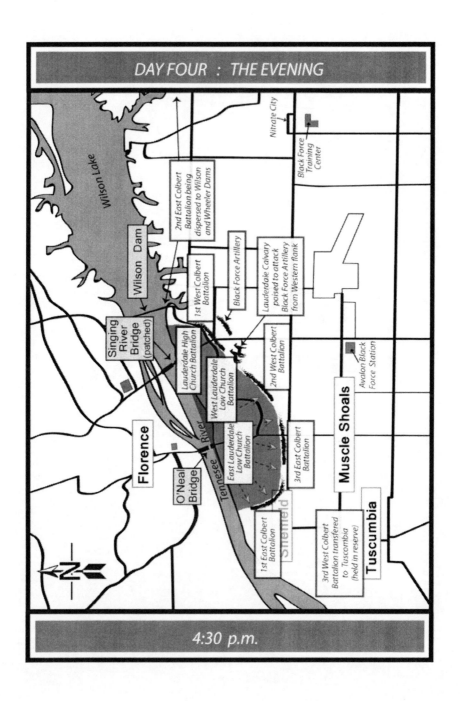

DAY FOUR : THE EVENING

Nitrate City

Black Force
Training
Center

Wilson Lake

2nd East Colbert
Battalion being
dispersed to Wilson
and Wheeler Dams

Wilson Dam

1st West Colbert
Battalion

Black Force Artillery

Lauderdale Calvary
poised to attack
Black Force Artillery
from Western flank

Singing
River
Bridge
(patched)

Lauderdale High
Church Battalion

West Lauderdale
Low Church
Battalion

2nd West Colbert
Battalion

Avalon Black
Force Station

Muscle Shoals

Florence

O'Neal
Bridge

East Lauderdale
Low Church
Battalion

3rd East Colbert
Battalion

Sheffield

Tennesee River

1st East Colbert
Battalion

3rd West Colbert
Battalion transfered
to Tuscombia
(held in reserve)

Tuscumbia

4:30 p.m.

Alice Boyd stopped making eye contact with Knight Candler. There was no hope or opportunity there — just a blank stare from behind the sights of his shouldered AKM 7.62X39mm assault rifle. He sat in one of the sumptuous chamber chairs, and she sat in hers. They were about 20 feet apart. Alice shifted her eyes to the clock on the wall. The past 15 minutes seemed like an hour. She had moved slightly a couple of times. After each move, Candler emitted a slight grunt and tensed his trigger finger — she sat still now. Her hands rested on her thigh, and with her ankles tastefully crossed, she appeared the "perfect little lady." Alice reasoned that a scratch of her nose would result in her death. Did it matter? Short of a miracle, she figured, she was dead anyway.

Mental exercises were one of the important skills taught at the Smith Academy for Adolescents. Alice Boyd was a master. Both at the academy and during her last 15 years as a Lauderdale agent, she had employed the tool to ease bad situations and save her from potentially disastrous ones. Silently, she quoted her academy instructor, *The exercises can be employed to, create scenarios for operational planning; relive stress and cure boredom through escapist fantasy and meandering; or endure capture, intense questioning, and torture via specific mental gymnastics.*

In the last few minutes, Alice had played out five scenarios to solve her present predicament. She chose not to number them but to name them after each scenario's recipient of her first strike: *Candler, Holt, Lawrence, Danny, and heaven forbid, Catherine.* The KISS Principle prevented her from adding any more. She reasoned that Danny and Lawrence would never bring Charles or Eddie in on this until they had the facts and a plan. Charles always insisted on hearing not just the problem, but a solution as well. Plus, bringing in any more of "these dumbass Knights" would simply increase the likelihood of a dangerous and embarrassing security leak.

Even though the past quarter-hour across from the oafish Candler was "torture," it did not rate in the literal sense — unlike having sex with Eddie. Now that called for some "mental gymnastics." She equated their encounters to masturbation. At least Eddie stayed in shape and was well endowed. She never could afford the risk of a real Colbert lover, but the years were long ones. She burned up her sexual energy for years via exhausting workouts, range time, and occasionally "doin' herself" while reading from the randier of Catherine's seemingly endless supply of OW romance novels. In her weaker moments, Alice wondered if this assignment was actually a life sentence to some surreal prison. As for her absence of affection and tenderness, Alice half-filled that void with Catherine. They were together most of their waking hours. On the surface, two loving sisters could never have been any closer. She respected the gentle lady to the utmost. *Cate was just so un-Ragland.* All sisters have their secrets, and if Alice's was a bomb, it was one of the Old World's nuclear bombs. The only guilt she suffered from this mission was caused by the familial love she had for her charge.

To endure what may be the next five minutes or two hours, Alice decided to mentally trace her journey to this point. It was one she hadn't visited in a long time and an exercise she could shut off in an instant — like a water faucet. She imagined herself as author writing the tale as a third person omniscient narrator. The girl she was and the woman she became were the main characters. *That was escapist fantasy and meandering indeed.*

As if sitting at the aging computer in Catherine's office, Alice mentally typed, *In year 55, Jenny Hart was a skinny little thing from a wooden shack on Middle Cypress Creek. It was a sparsely populated area in the middle of Lauderdale not far from Tennessee. She was 13-years-old and the youngest of three children. The oldest, her brother, died as the result of complications from a tree-cutting accident. Jenny's sister married at 15 and moved to Florence with some character almost twice her age; the suitor threw in a shotgun to coax Mr. Hart's permission. Mrs. Hart had died giving birth to Jenny, so it was down to just Mr. Hart and Jenny. Her daddy was a drunk. He made moonshine but consumed almost as much of the liquor as he sold. When he was half-sober he fished and trapped a little. Mr. Hart was a sinning low life. He began to have his way with Jenny after her sister moved to town. Jenny quit going to school after the second time he took her. She stayed home; cooked for him; dressed, cleaned, or skinned his catch, whether from a hook or trap; and generally suffered his abuse. She quit crying after a few weeks.*

One day, Wade Smith, showed up at Jenny's hovel accompanied by his brother Ben and the President's two children, Harry and Philippa. Mr. Wade told her father that reports had reached him of mistreatment. The women of the local Low Church claimed that Jenny Hart was being physically abused and kept from school. Jenny's daddy argued and disputed the reports as lies and fabrications. Ben and Wade examined the residence, and after seeing the girl, they overruled Mr. Hart's protestations. Gently taking the girl by her hands, Ben and Wade led her to Slingshot 8. The sullen father seemed to calm down but suddenly grabbed a nearby ax and came at President Smith. Ben, with a wary eye to their rear, reacted. He passed the terrified girl to Harry and Philippa, and yelled for Mr. Hart to stop while drawing his .357 Magnum. Wade, unarmed, had crouched into a defensive position, but Ben decided there should be no doubt as to the outcome. He emptied the slick double-action revolver's cylinder into their assailant. Mr. Hart tumbled to the ground a few feet from Wade. He struggled up on his knees and palms like a rabid dog. Ben ejected the empty cartridge cases and retrieved a speed loader from his belt. As Ben closed the reloaded cylinder of the revolver, Jenny Hart's daddy coughed out some blood and collapsed.

In the back of the Humvee, Philippa hugged the distraught, crying girl while Harry kept one hand tightly on her arm and the other sheltering her eyes. He did not want her to see her dying parent. Mortimer Johns '1911' drove the kids off while Ben and Wade stayed with the late Mr. Hart. After dropping off Jenny, Philippa, and Harry at the Smith Academy for Adolescents, 1911 headed back for the Smith brothers. Jenny had an object lesson in the power of the Smith Ascendancy; Wade Smith could be judge, jury, and executioner when so moved. Later, Jenny Hart not only grew to appreciate this fact; she respected him for it as well. In fact, she grew to worship the Smith family.

Jenny's life got better after that. Her previous schoolteachers had reported that the girl showed potential in all her studies and athletics, but she was hobbled by her horrible home life. The academy was a dream come true for Jenny. 'Smith's' was established by Wade in year 50 to house, feed, and educate orphaned youngsters or those from dysfunctional homes. The wards had to be at least 12-years-old. The plan was for them to graduate at 17 or 18. Wade's resources were limited, as were the slots at the institution. Jenny was one of 15 girls at the academy and the same number of boys balanced the population. Their respective quarters were in opposite wings on each side of the multi-purpose school building. Wade never failed to fully utilize a resource — the youngsters were being assessed, trained, and filtered for the Teams, the hospital, or his arsenal. They would not be forced to accept a position of service, but Wade had every intention of 'selling them real hard' every chance he got.

Given that it was The Peace, Wade had to handle this strategic resource with stealth. He perceived the growing tension and discord between the two sides of the river and began to discreetly prepare for war. The Florence and Lauderdale schools competed athletically with Colbert teams during The Peace, but the academy's teams only played schools north of the river. He did not want his high performing orphans exposed to any wary Ragland eyes.

In year 58, Jenny turned sixteen. She was 'Smith's' top academic student, a solid softball and soccer player, and a beauty. She even cheerfully endured the course named Finishing School. However, she consistently shied away from leadership positions. A cloud hung over the girl. She avoided dances, teas, and social gatherings other than those required. She was polite to the male students, even proved a natural flirt, but she never dated.

The Slingshot Teams took notice of Jenny in 58. She posted the highest score ever achieved by a woman at the Lauderdale Shooting Championship, but Mr. Kilburn at the Lauderdale Times was asked to kill the story. Jenny graduated in 59 with highest honors but made *sure she scored just low enough on her finals to not be chosen valedictorian. Selected for medical training at the college and hospital in Florence, a promising future lay before her. She was a lean but shapely five-foot-four straight-haired brunette. Jenny was smart, strong, quick, healthy, coordinated, ambidextrous, polished, and lacked a single living relative. She drowned in a water skiing accident the day of her class graduation picnic held near the Smith Lodge on Shoal Creek. 15-year-old Harry Smith was driving the boat. Her classmates and teachers attended the funeral, but memories of the quiet girl, close to no one, faded quickly.*

In year 60, Alice Boyd eased into a factory job in Sheffield, she played just 'good enough' to make the company softball team, attended High Church, kept the boys at bay, and quietly applied for acceptance to the Black Force Academy. It was delayed until further notice for vetting. After the losses incurred during the Three Day War of 61, Black Force contacted Alice and swept her enlistment through. She made Knight Sergeant in 62 and Knight Third Class in 63. She avoided 'brown nosing' as she did not want to accelerate her advancement in the ranks, but she leapt on an open position at the Black Force Training Center. She spent two years there with her days divided equally between instructing on the firing range and teaching hand-to-hand combat in the gym.

Late in 65, Danny Ragland requested her presence at the BFTC admin building. The new constable informed her that his cousin, Catherine Ragland, was becoming active in the greater Colbert community with events such as charity work, speaking engagements, church-congregational covered dish suppers, and visits to schools. President Charles Ragland insisted that his daughter have a personal assistant that could double as a bodyguard. Danny Ragland asked if Alice was interest—

Alice shot a glance at the clock after she heard footsteps from the marble staircase. The therapeutic daydream was blown from her mind as she began to store tactical data, *Eight minutes to five.* The sounds were somewhat muted by the closed chamber doors, but she was quite sure that two men were approaching. Without altering his point of aim, Candler stood.

She heard Holt's voice, "Candler?"

Candler replied, "Yes, sir."

"We're unlocking the door and coming in."

"Yes, sir."

Alice tried to slow her racing heart as she anticipated the identity of the other Colbert. The left of the double doors eased open, and Holt entered followed by Lawrence Foster. Alice's eyes darted past them and noted the empty stairwell.

Holt immediately drew his polymer framed .45 semi-auto, strolled to Candler's side, and assumed a Weaver stance with his sights settled on Alice's center of mass.

Lawrence stared in contempt at Alice then shifted to Candler. "Has she tried anything?"

"No, sir. She's hardly twitched."

"Good job, Candler. Step out and lock the door behind you. I want you to go up that circular staircase just far enough to cover the entire stairwell. No one other than Constable Ragland is to come down here. Got it?"

"Yes, sir, nobody but the Constable ... Uh?"

"What?"

"What if the President wants to come down?"

"He won't. He's in the safe room with his family."

"Safe room? Right! Lock the door behind me ... right, sir?"

"Yes."

Candler cautiously relinquished his position, slung his AK, and stepped out. From the bottom landing, he warily took one more peek at Alice as he closed and locked the door.

Alice heard the large man clomping up the staircase. She mentally crossed off three scenarios, *Delete Candler, Danny*, and *Catherine*.

Scenario Holt called for Alice to aggressively initiate the interview while *Scenario Lawrence* has her wait for them to start.

She thought to herself, *Oh, what the Hell*, and then she asserted out loud, "Really, Lawrence? I just went in that damned janitor's closet looking for something to clean my computer screen. I saw a loose panel in the wall and thought it strange. When I gave it a tug, it fell off and there was some old radio equipment hidden in the wall. I took it out to get a closer look, an' then these two fuck heads come bustin' in threatening to blow my ass away. Hell, I bet it's one of their shit and they are trying to set me up."

"Bullshit!" exclaimed Holt. "You ain't gonna believe that are ya', sir."

Holt had already closed Candler's 20-foot margin to 15 because Lawrence was already that close to Alice and he did not want to be behind him if firing became necessary. The accusation from Alice brought him yet another step closer.

Lawrence hesitantly said, "No, of course not. Relax, Holt."

Noting the decreased striking distance, Alice teased Lawrence, "Ooh, but you're not sure are you? C'mon Lawrence, look how nervous Ol' Holt is gettin' over there."

Holt stepped again, and declared, "Sir, she's a lyin' bitch! God, I wish I had shot her in the head when I found her with that transmitter."

Alice mentally measured the distance, *Ten feet.*

Again she pled her case, "Do you honestly think if I was some kinda' super spy chick assassin, I wouldn't have already taken out both these pogues, killed Little Charles, and been on my merry way?"

Holt was highly agitated now, and as he took another short step with a tightening pointer finger on his handgun's preset trigger, he commanded, "Shut the hell up, you fuckin' whore!"

In an elevated voice, Lawrence coached, "Ease up, Holt! Can't you see she's baiting you? It's okay, man. I believe you."

Alice had already recalled each man's Close Quarters Battle Rating. She had developed the performance measure and its ratings during her time as lead instructor at the BFTC: *excellent, proficient,* or *capable.* You didn't get to leave the center without obtaining at minimum, a *capable* rating. Also, she had sparred with all three of them over the years. Holt was *proficient,* but the bureaucrat, Lawrence, only rated *capable.* Actually, the six-foot-two 300 pound Candler, just outside in the stairwell, rated excellent. He was quick for a big man, very strong, and balanced. He bloodied her nose once. She remembered what he said afterward, *Sorry, Knight Boyd.*

Since Candler exited earlier, Holt's CQBR and his superior officer's holstered sidearm, earned Holt first strike honors. However, he was still 8 feet away standing directly to her front with Lawrence standing to his rear-right. The backs of rolling chairs, pushed up to the square-shaped council table, were to Holt's left, and the chamber doors were to Alice's left — about 12 feet away.

Scenario Holt was on hold. She didn't want to verbally push the big Knight any further. He might just shoot her out of anger and hate. A lunge without the aid of a distraction would definitely get her shot, no matter how quick she was.

Lawrence suggested in a calming tone, "I tell ya' what, Holt. Let's just call Candler back in here and keep her sitting there until Danny arrives."

Alice's heart sank as she noticed Holt's face losing its flaming color.

At that instant, raised voices were heard from the stairwell. Alice did not break her stare at Holt, but she noticed Lawrence turn his head to the door in her peripheral vision. *Scenario Holt is on!*

Almost comically, all three carefully listened and could now identify the arguing parties.

They heard Candler forcefully reason, "I'm sorry Mr. President, but it's not safe for you to come down here right now!"

Charles Ragland declared, "Not safe down there? What the Hell is goin' on around here? Is this my house or what? Am I not the goddamned President? Where is Danny? Catherine is worried about Alice. Why isn't Alice in the safe room like she's supposed to be?"

"The Constable should be here any minute, sir, and I haven't seen Miss Boyd this afternoon. If you don't want to go back to the safe room, why don't you have a seat in your study, and I will get Adjutant Constable Foster for you."

"Foster? Is he down there in my council chamber? Hell, I'm comin' down! Step aside, Knight!"

The parties in the chamber heard Charles' footsteps.

Lawrence headed for the chamber doors. Holt glanced to his right just as Lawrence passed him.

Alice had been primed ever since the argument in the stairwell began — she fired. Her left hand grasped Holt's pistol's slide taking it out of battery, and a fraction of a second later, the heel of her right hand caught Holt under his nose as she thrust it up and into his face. She pivoted into the Knight and after wrenching the pistol back and out of his right hand with her left hand, she slammed the back of its slide into the stunned Lawrence's mouth. She continued the pivot to 360 as she transferred the pistol to her strong hand. The pivot stopped with Holt crumpled at her feet on all fours. The image of her father's grisly death flashed in and out of her mind. With her fingers and thumb in a death grip around the European pistol's slide, she rabbit punched the base of his skull twice. She spun back towards Lawrence, expecting to find him sitting up and bleeding from the lip with his pistol pointed at her. That was not the case. He was on his right side groaning in semi-consciousness with his head towards the chamber doors. She lunged for him, impacting his back with just enough force to roll him on his belly. She repeated the same deathblows that Holt received. Alice Boyd, with her skirt up around her hips and her legs straddling the Colbert Adjutant Constable, repositioned the pistol in her bloody hands. She looked up poised and panting with an isosceles hold on the chamber doors. Her Lauderdale code name, Cheetah, was apropos.

As she took deep calming breaths, the adrenalin subsided restoring her hearing. Charles and Candler were oblivious to this action in the chamber. They still argued up in the stairwell.

The ever more impressive Candler was serving yet another lie to his President. "Mr. President, I'm serious! I ain't got a key to the chamber and the doors are locked! Do you have a key, sir?"

"No, dammit! I don't have a key either! Wait a minute there is one in the desk in my study. You go up there and... Aw, never mind. I'll get it myself."

As Alice heard him pattering up the steps. A thought came to her, *If he comes back, I could kill Little Charles and end this whole damn thing.* Then she reversed, and her mind raced, *No, wait. After*

Eddie got put in charge of operations at the Wilson Dam he had the dam wired with explosives, and there is a standing order to blow the Wilson Dam if it is about to fall into Lauderdale hands. Harry can't take it with force. Charles might bargain with Harry if his back is against the wall, but left to Eddie, it will never happen. Besides, Danny could be walkin' in the Grand Foyer door at this moment. Crap! I gotta' get to the Lauderdale lines ASAP; I must reach Harry! Move, girl!

She looked up at the clock. It was five o'clock. She quietly whispered, "You gotta' be fuckin' kiddin' me. Eight minutes? All this in eight minutes." It also occurred to her that in spite of all her daunted fighting skills, these were her first kills, "Hmm!"

Lawrence hadn't even drawn his handgun. She pulled it and cursorily examined the shiny pistol, but scornfully dropped it on his back reasoning, "Some piece-uh-shit 9 I don't even recognize — can't even use the ammo for Holt's weapon."

Alice rushed to Holt's side. She rolled him over and removed the Palace keys from his belt clip and pulled his spare pistol magazine from its holder. She had noticed on occasion that his keys were both labeled and color-coded. "Thank goodness, you fastidious prick," she whispered, and continued, "I wish I had my little .45. I hate these fuckin' plastic guns."

As an afterthought, she slid the combat folder from his pocket, flipped open the blade, cut the hem of her skirt, and then ripped the right side open all the way up to her hip. A whisper again, "Now I can run!" The knife had a pocket clip, but Alice had no pockets. She slid the knife in her waistband at the small of her back with its pocket clip snapping over her narrow belt. Alice considered stripping one of the men's pants, boots, and shirt to fend off the declining weather. *Negative! You got no time for that, girl.* She wedged the fat polymer magazine under her waistband behind her left hip. *If it falls out, fuck it!*

Alice hustled back to the doors. After press checking Holt's pistol, she quietly unlocked the dead bolt on the right door with her weak hand. The chamber doors were of the outwardly opening type. She had to be ready. She couldn't ease it open and peek first or anything like that; Candler could be standing there aiming at the door. She had to open and shoot in one smooth motion.

Her life story from earlier bounced into her head and she thought, *Okay, Jenny, here we go, Sweetie!*

Luckily, Alice caught Candler halfway up the circular staircase with his head turned up facing the Grand Foyer. *Looking for Little Charles no doubt*, she thought. He was holding his AKM at port arms and used a chest rig to hold his spare magazines. Thus, much of his center mass was hard-covered. She took a head shot just as he glanced down and saw her. *Poor bastard*, she thought as his rifle fell to the stares and rattled down a few steps towards her. *Glad there was enough light to see the sights*, she thought as she raced to retrieve his rifle. Alice grabbed his AKM and glanced up the stairwell as far as she could see. Since she couldn't see all the way to the foyer, she passed on traveling the extra distance for another magazine or two. As she turned to go back down the stairs, she slid the handgun under her waistband behind her right hip. An alarm sounded. *I figured.*

Alice took the stairs three-at-a-time, broke right at the bottom landing, and entered a little hallway. After a few feet, she stopped and swept open a maroon curtain exposing a steel door. She had located the escape tunnel key back in the council chamber, *Hah, the maroon one. Holt, I love, ya'!* Alice opened the big door flipped on the escape tunnel lights, returned the curtains to their original position, closed and relocked the door, and sprinted along the 130 yards to the outer door. She knew from numerous security drills the same key opened the outer door. After turning off the tunnel lights and securing the outer door, she turned away from the exit and carefully scanned her 180. By design, the tunnel exited from the face of a little bluff in a wooded area. *Cheetah* was done with Ragland Palace.

Alice was about a mile southwest of downtown Tuscumbia, and she estimated that Harry's troops were about the same distance north of same — she could hear the battle raging in the distance. It was twilight, cold, windy, and spitting rain. Her outfit was a torn skirt and a blood-splattered, white blouse. She accessorized the ensemble with an assault rifle at low-ready-muzzle-down plus a sidearm, spare magazine, and knife shoved in her waistband. She turned into the wind and let the rain sting her face for a moment. Alice smiled. She was alive.

Nim said, "Ahm glad we found this fine house to hole up in for a while. It's really comin' down out there." He took a long draw on his cigar, turned away from the last light of the living room window, and slowly let the smoke pass out his nostrils.

Bardolph pulled his unlit stogie along the bottom of his nose and asked, "How many of these did you find?"

"Four."

"I'd heard that the Raglands' buddies up at their green houses were growing some quality tobacco now. They weren't shittin'. What are you going to do with the other two?"

"Keep 'em for trade, I reckon."

"Yep, Cold Zee would ride ya' all night for just one of 'em."

That suggestion brought a big smile from Nim, "Fer two, I bet Ginger woulda.'"

"Fuck that, Nim. No way. Besides, ain't you got no respect for the dead?"

Nim shot a look at Bardolph. A smirk from Bardolph brought Nim realization of the bad joke, and he chuckled in acknowledgement.

Bardolph drained the glass in his hand, licked his lips, and commented, "Damn, I wish there woulda' been some more of this corn liquor."

"We ain't checked the basement."

"I hate goin' down in strange basements — you never know what yer gonna' find."

"We might find sumpin' good, you big wuss!"

"Or not!"

"Come on, Chance, let's check it out. There is no tellin' what these rich river rats have squirreled away down there."

Bardolph reluctantly rose from the sumptuous chair and picked up his AK. "Okay then, my friend, you lead."

Oblivious to the sounds of battle outside, they left the room. Nim stepped over the body of an elderly man in the hall and headed for the basement stairs' door.

Nim remarked, "That ol' fart thought he had you — sneakin' up from behind ya' with that hog leg."

Bardolph nervously chuckled and said, "Yep, I'm sure glad he didn't check his flank. You put that bullet right through his ear."

"He had some balls, huh? I mean that ol' cowboy gun just had two rounds left in the cylinder!"

"True enough. I guess his kids just left his ass."

"Ain't no tellin' with a stubborn ol' bird like that. They might have come for him and he told 'em to 'take off!'"

"Yeah, well, come on let's see what's down here." Nim had the door open to the basement stairwell.

Sheffield's power had finally been cut, so the two pillagers lit a hurricane lamp they found in the house's kitchen. Bardolph handed the lamp to Nim. Nim took it in his left hand, leaned his AK against the wall, and drew his 9mm pistol with his right. There were four steps down to the landing and then four more to the left ending at the basement floor. He proceeded to the landing, peered around, and then looked back up at Bardolph.

"Okay, I'm comin' growled Bardolph."

As Bardolph stepped down to the landing, Nim reached the basement floor. A shot from the far corner rang out. Nim pressed his back to the wall and let several rounds fly in the direction of the muzzle flash. A woman's scream came from the corner then there was silence.

Bardolph asked, "Holy shit, Thomas! Are you okay?"

Nim, in between pants, answered, "I think so … the slug whistled by my head. Fuck! That was close!" After a moment staring into the offending corner and hearing more muffled conversation, he barked, "Alright goddammit! Throw out your guns and come on out in the light with your hands up."

Despite his fear, Bardolph had come down to the landing and was pointing his AK's muzzle at the corner as well. He commanded loudly, "Did you hear him? Come on out!"

Shortly thereafter, a woman said, "We only have one gun!"

Nim and Bardolph exchanged glances and Bardolph commanded, "Well, throw that one out!"

A long gun struck the concrete floor.

"Okay, I'm steppin' out," said the woman.

A well-groomed lady, in her 70s or 80s, stepped into the light. She tightly clutched a bit of cloth wrapped around her right hand. Blood was already soaking through the makeshift bandage.

Nim asked, "What about the others?"

"There's only me," answered the old woman

Angrily Nim said, "Bullshit, Lady! I heard at least two females talkin'!"

"It's okay, Granny, they know I'm here," said another voice from the dark.

A woman, perhaps in her twenties, emerged from the shadows.

"Well, lookie here! What have we got us now, Chance?"

Bardolph just stared for a moment and then eased by Nim. He took the lamp to the far corner and checked the rest of the room as well. After a thorough search, he walked up in front of the women. Nim joined him.

The matron curtly said, "You Lauderdale trash. I wish I had aimed at your gut instead of your little head. Shame there was just one bullet left for that twenty-two."

Bardolph finally said, "Thomas, be a gent and lead these ladies upstairs."

Nim did so and after clearing the landing he waved the women to follow.

Bardolph took a bit of a bow and extended his lamp hand towards the stairs. He sarcastically followed with, "Ladies?"

The sole remaining troopers of the Cavalry's 1st Squad, Michael, Alex, and Betty, covered the rear of their platoon as it worked its way back to the relative safety of the bridgehead. Fortunately, they avoided losing any troopers to their own sentries. It was something they were concerned about, given the darkness and pouring rain. Sergeant Gillespie sent Jake Connelly out ahead to alert their perimeter guards of the cavalry's approach.

Their first stop was the field hospital where the wounded and dead were delivered. Sergeant Gillespie led two horses in. One carried the body of Captain Jesus Juarez and the other the body of Private Cameron Brown. Dungee Boy was one of the few uninjured mounts, so Michael had kept his horse and hands free for defensive action. This enabled Betty to lead a horse with the bodies of Horace and Eulis Bennett strapped across its back. Alex did the same leading a limping horse carrying Naddy Smith. Most of the surviving troopers had some kind of injury, but the three seriously wounded ones were riding in the supply wagon. Due to the loss of horses, two members of 3rd Squad doubled up on one horse and led another carrying the bodies of privates Bud Counts and Debbie Felton.

Captain Juarez had ordered the remuda back to the bridgehead before their assault on the enemy guns. After the field hospital, the troopers filtered over to the remuda. Ben Smith was there with Garcia and quickly assessed the state of the Lauderdale Cavalry. He realized they could no longer function as a mounted force. He had them unbridle and unsaddle their mounts and load all the tack in a supply truck. Ben sent the truck, the supply wagon, and the remuda to Lauderdale under the capable supervision of Corporal Garcia accompanied by his remuda handlers and the platoon's two cooks.

Michael hugged Dungee Boy's neck and gently said, "You be a good boy for Ol' Garcia, ya' hear? I'll be along in a day or so." After a final pat goodbye, he walked over to Garcia and handed him

Cameron's saber. "Garcia, this is Cam's. I promised to take it to his momma. If somethin' happens to me, will you see that she gets it?"

"Will do, Michael."

Ben ordered Sergeant Gillespie and Corporal Williams to take their nine remaining troopers over to the mess tent for some hot chow, see to any flesh wounds at the field hospital, and then go to his personal tent and try to get some sleep. "It will be a little crowded but it's dry and warm — it has a little wood burnin' stove. Just shove everything in there off to the side and stretch out on your bed rolls as best ya' can. I'll come check on y'all later."

Gillespie said, "Thank you, Mr. Smith. We appreciate that."

"No problem, Sergeant. Hey, obviously you disabled their guns. It has been a blessing since the shelling stopped. I'll let you make a full report to Harry later, but I'm curious — how did you destroy the guns without explosives?"

Gillespie smiled and answered, "Hell, Mr. Smith. Three of those Knights' vehicles would still run, even after we shot 'em up, so we just jumped in 'em and shoved all those cannon into one big pile. Then we crashed the trucks right up on top of the busted up guns, punched holes in their fuel tanks, and set the whole mess on fire."

"So that's the glow in the distance reported from the southern perimeter?"

"Yes, sir."

The 11 troopers sat at a long table in the mess tent. They were the only occupants at this time. Plates of chicken stew and cornbread steamed on the table before them along with mugs of hot chicory and shots of Petersville Hooch. The exhausted horse soldiers had little appetite. Michael and Betty consoled the distraught Clive Bennett. Clive held it together to this point, but once seated with the others, the loss of his brothers hit him. After sobbing uncontrollably for a few minutes, he was quiet. Betty hugged him and Michael gently patted him on the back.

The man of few words, Alex Court, cleared his throat and spoke, "Let us pray."

Startled, the troopers exchanged glances, noticed Alex's bowed head, and then joined him.

Alex continued, "Our Heavenly Father, we thank You for seeing those gathered at this table safely through this day. We pray that You receive our fallen sisters and brethren. We thank You for the feast set before us. Now bless this food to the nourishment of our bodies and in service to Thee. It is in your name we pray. Amen."

Most repeated, "Amen."

Straggling refugees and entrenching militia were all over Tuscumbia. Alice Boyd could make little headway. Even in the rainstorm, there was much foot and vehicular traffic in the town. She would hide behind some shrubs or a low wall, shiver in the rain and cold, and then once a clear path presented itself, Alice would make her way to her next cover. She considered entering one of the Hook Street residences she passed to search for some warmer clothes and sturdier shoes, but she was afraid a stubborn resident would be in the house. She would probably have to kill them, and she did not want that. After she entered the center of town, Alice realized Tuscumbia's electrical power had been cut. The flicker of candles and lamps from some windows indicated many citizens chose not to flee.

It wasn't freezing, but Alice felt the temperature had to be in the low 40s. Given the wind and driving rain, she knew hypothermia could set in. Alice came across an old tarp. She wrapped it around herself and crawled in the back seat of a blocked four-door sedan that had weeds growing up all around it. She clutched the AKM to her chest and maintained a fetal position until the shivering stopped. Her muscles, joints, cuts, and bruises ached as she stood, but Alice had to keep going if she was to deliver her dire warning in time.

After Alice crossed North Commons Street, she peeked through a residential window and read the time off a grandfather clock. It was almost eight. She could only guess the distance to the Lauderdale lines — not knowing exactly where they were. Taken by surprise, she looked up just as three Colbert militiamen jogged by her heading in the direction of Sheffield.

One of the soldiers turned his head back towards her. She must have been quite the sight. He laughed and loudly said, "Way to go, lady, give 'em Hell!"

The black uniformed figures faded into the darkness like ghosts. She hurried along in the same direction.

1911 negotiated Slingshot 8 around a couple of Lauderdale militiamen's bodies on Hatch Boulevard in Sheffield. It was the first of many such scenes. Both khaki and black clad corpses littered the lawns and streets of the town. As they approached Montgomery Avenue, Harry scanned ahead with his night vision gear. He spotted the Humvee and support vehicles of a Slingshot Team. It was Major Flurry's Team 2. They were preparing a new HQ at the old Sheffield City Hall.

After getting the all clear to advance, 1911 drove them up to the cluster of vehicles and tents. Yet another field hospital was set up on the ground floor of the government building. Medics were doing what they could tending wounded soldiers from both sides of the river.

Donna Flurry walked up and gave Harry a hug. She reported, "As you can see, Harry, I decided to set up the next HQ here. We actually got Neva on the radio and informed her of this location. She said that her staff just about had the communications and command group packed and would be here by 8:00 PM. Oh, she also reported that the enemy's shelling of the bridgehead had stopped thanks to the assault by our cavalry. Unfortunately, the cavalry lost most of its personnel including Jesus."

Harry sighed and looked down then lifted his eyes back to Donna's and asked, "How many troopers are left?"

"Just a handful, Harry. Your Uncle Ben deactivated them and ordered Sergeant Gillespie to hold in reserve at the bridgehead."

Harry contemplated in silence.

Donna added, "Harry, as thin as we are at the bridge, it will be good to have the troopers back there. How many did you end up leaving on the perimeter?"

Harry responded, "Just two companies of the High Church Militia Battalion, some kids from supply, and now the troopers. Oh, and Slingshot 7 of course."

"Chester has his team's single set of night vision gear, right?"

"Yes, he was going to try and bounce around the perimeter to keep an eye on the Colbert forces still entrenched to their east and south."

"How many Colberts are there, ya' think?"

"Two battalions at least, but we have shot them to pieces today."

"Where are the other two companies of High Church Militia?"

"They are not far behind us ... should be arriving anytime. I'm not in contact with them. Donna, how 'bout sending some runners back to lead them in."

Donna addressed Sergeant Annie Slocomb, who had just joined them. "Annie, you hear that?"

"Yes, ma'am. I'll send Privates Gillespie and Joiner back to find them."

"Fine, Annie, and by the way, Bonnie Gillespie may hear scuttlebutt about the cavalry. Be sure to tell her that at last report her daddy is okay and standing in support back at the bridgehead."

"Yes, ma'am, will do."

As Annie hurried off she passed by the 8. She jibed at 1911 standing by the driver's side door, "Hi, handsome!"

He laughed and replied, "Hi, cutie!"

She stopped and asked, "Where are your ugly friends?"

"Oh, kicking around up here somewhere, I reckon. You had 'em last; what did you do with 'em?"

"We dropped them off back at the reservation. I have not seen them since."

"Hmm, they'll probably be along sooner or later."

"Sure, Mort. Those two SOBs always land on their feet, huh?"

"Absolutely."

"Well, I gotta run. See ya' around."

"Yeah, see ya', Annie."

Back with the commanders, Harry asked Donna, "Whatcha' think, Donna?"

"I don't know, Harry. There seems to be a Colbert rifleman behind every damned tree. The Low Church losses are piling up. Hell, I have two killed and three wounded from my TAC-team. These Colberts never seem to surrender and they are dying in droves. Shit, Harry, they have a lot of people. Our militiamen say that the Colbert ranks are refilling with armed civilians from their southern mountain chain … old men, boys, and women."

Harry glanced over at Donna's team area, assessed her folks then asked, "Do you think we will hit our objectives tonight?"

"I do, Harry. We should soon have the Low Church Militia in temporary defensive positions from the river to the western bend in the railroad tracks then all along the tracks and 2nd Street to Woodward Avenue in Muscle Shoals."

"Any specifics yet on losses, Donna?"

"No, sir. Not really. Heavy."

Harry stood in concerned silence with the rain beating down on him.

Donna said, "Come on over to my tent, Harry. My girls found some coffee in their town hall building. I about forget what real coffee tastes like. I'll get ya' a cup … Ol' 1911, too."

Harry smiled, wiped the rainwater from his face, turned back to Mort, and commanded, "Mort, shut 'er down. The Major has invited us for coffee."

Danny Ragland arrived at Ragland Palace at 7:45 p.m. Edward Ragland got there a few minutes earlier. Edward was standing with

Charles and Catherine in the Grand Foyer. Danny could tell by their facial expressions that things were very wrong.

Dispensing with any greetings, Danny asked, "What's happened?"

Charles and Edward Ragland had the demeanor of a couple of whipped hounds.

Charles responded, "Danny, I hate to be the one to tell ya' this but Lawrence Foster is dead. So are Knights Holt and Candler."

Still trying to process the troubled state of the Colbert front lines from which he had just returned, Danny took the news in disbelief. Lawrence and Danny had been close friends since childhood.

Edward spoke up, "Daddy, let's go in your study for a minute, sit down, and catch the constable up."

Surprised by the stoic calmness of his son, Charles said, "Good idea, Eddie. C'mon Danny."

Instinctively, Catherine walked to Danny's side and took his arm in hers. She led him to the study following her brother and father.

Already in the study was Johnny Montjoy. He had arrived around seven. Montjoy quickly announced, "Charles, I'll step out and—"

"No, Johnny. You stay. I insist you stay. We need you. Now everyone sit."

Charles got Danny reengaged by asking some basic questions about the deployment of their forces and the current battle lines.

Danny wiped his rain soaked face and hair with a towel delivered by a servant. Catherine handed him a small glass of Barton Brandy. He kicked it back, embraced the burn, and handed the empty glass back to his pretty cousin.

She asked, "Another?"

"No thanks, Cate."

Edward said, "Danny, we'll miss Lawrence. He was a good man and fine adjutant."

Danny shifted his eyes to Edward then Charles, "How did he die?"

Charles replied, "Here at the Palace. In the Council Chamber."

Disbelief again, "What? Here? But, who—"

Charles raised a calming palm and began, "Danny, it seems we had an assassin or commando in here. Best I can tell, Holt and Lawrence might have very well caught him and were questioning him in the council chamber. To protect the family, they declared a Code Alpha Alert and had Cate, Miss Izzy, and me go to the safe room. You know me, Danny. After a while, I got tore up and went to investigate. I ordered the guards to let me out of the safe room and came down right in the middle of things going to hell. The assassin must have gotten the better of all three of our people and escaped the Palace. It looks like he murdered Lawrence and Holt with his bare hands in the chamber; and then shot Candler in the head. He was standing guard on the chamber steps ... I had just spoke with him. God damn, what a mess."

Danny was more himself again, "Wait a minute, Uncle Charles. How did this mystery assassin exit? Was anyone in the Grand Foyer? Weren't guards outside the entrance to the foyer?"

Eddie interjected, "Danny, I don't see how anyone could have come up the stairs and slipped out without security seeing them. They had to use the escape tunnel in the basement."

Charles blurted, "But the tunnel was locked at both ends with no sign of being used, even the curtains were undisturbed."

Eddie countered, "Yeah, but Daddy, they could have put that all back the way it was to cover their tracks."

Catherine asked, "Would that not have required that the killer or killers have a key to the tunnel?"

Unusual for the normally composed constable, Danny went off in a ramble, "Shit, I wish that ol' digital video surveillance system hadn't given up the ghost! Just too bad! Anyway. Okay, let's break this down — who all has keys to the tunnel?"

Charles listed, "You, Edward, Me, Catherine, Holt, and Alice."

Danny asked, "Were Holt's keys still on him?"

Edward and Charles shared an embarrassed glance and Charles confessed, "We didn't think to check."

Danny looked at Catherine, and asked, "Where is Alice, anyway?"

Her eyes watered as she answered, "Oh, we haven't even told you, Danny. She's missing."

"What? Missing?"

Charles blurted, "Oh, yeah. These murderin' bastards must have either killed or kidnapped her. I have had these Knights turn the whole joint upside down looking for her or what's left of her. Uh, I'm sorry, Cate, that was thoughtless."

Edward added with an air of sadness, "I looked for her, too. Took my men around the grounds, with flashlights, no luck, no sign of tracks or blood. By the way, the ground around the escape tunnel's exit is rock. Of course this rain and darkness, made it all even worse."

Danny had not noticed Eddie's soaked clothes and muddy shoes until this point.

Danny stood and hugged Catherine. He said, "Don't worry, sweetie. We'll find her."

He said to Eddie, "Okay, Eddie, let me go have a look at the chamber for myself."

Edward and Danny left the study to Catherine, Montjoy, and Charles. As they walked across the foyer, Danny, now back in the groove, asked, "Eddie, did you get that job done?"

Pulled from the distraction of the Palace massacre and his missing lover, Eddie shook it all off and answered weakly but proudly, "Oh, yeah Danny. It's done. The East Colbert Militia Regiment's 2nd Battalion has been alerted at the Wilson Dam; they are relieving the Junior Knights guarding the dam with one of their companies. Their detached company at Wheeler Dam has been ordered to join them. However, that Wheeler bunch won't arrive until dawn. As for your Knights, I contacted the Black Force commanders and ordered them to have all non-essential combat rated Knight personnel report to the Tuscumbia Knight Station if they are in the center or west, and to Wilson Dam if they are coming from the east. I stressed 'non-essential' and told them that request applied to tactical vehicles and weapons as well. There are over a hundred Knights waiting in those two places already. Oh, and we can add the Junior Knights platoon to that number. A few more might filter in. Damn,

Danny, they are ready to go for whatever mission you have in mind. One commander told me that his guys got in a fight over who would go. That was Ol' Carl Storm from Barton. He finally gave up and sent them all, saying, 'To Hell with my section of the river. Sounds like all the Lauderdales are in Sheffield anyway.'"

DAY FOUR
THE NIGHT

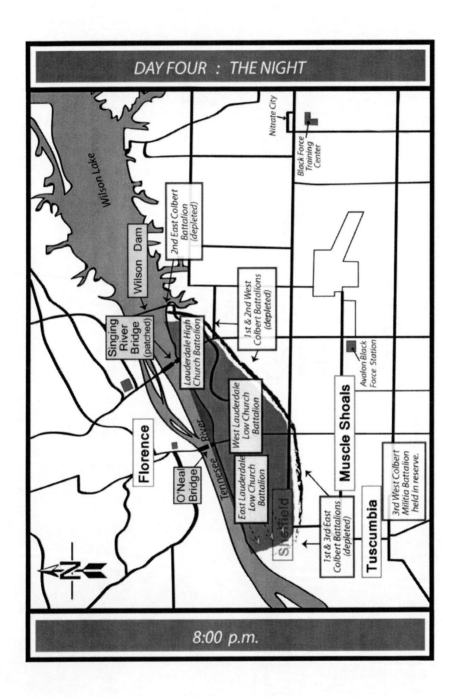

DAY FOUR : THE NIGHT

Wilson Lake

Nitrate City

Black Force
Training
Center

2nd East Colbert
Battalion
(depleted)

Wilson Dam

1st & 2nd West
Colbert Battalions
(depleted)

Singing
River
Bridge
(patched)

Lauderdale High
Church Battalion

West Lauderdale
Low Church
Battalion

Avalon Black
Force Station

Florence

Muscle Shoals

East Lauderdale
Low Church
Battalion

O'Neal
Bridge

Tennessee
River

Sheffield

1st & 3rd East
Colbert Battalions
(depleted)

Tuscumbia

3rd West Colbert
Militia Battalion
held in reserve.

N

8:00 p.m.

Tim Gray's Low Church Militia squad was miraculously intact. Other than a scratch or two, all twelve members were unharmed. Yes, they were tired, hungry, wet, and cold, but nonetheless unscathed. They knew how high militia losses in Sheffield's street fighting had been. The costly day wasn't over. They and their fellow squads, platoons, companies, and battalions were still pressing to reach their objectives. Their mission was to clear a couple of residential blocks. Tim and Jaybird Rhodes had nary a timepiece between them, but their squad leader, Pastor Jim, did.

He had them gather in a Sheffield carport to escape the rain for a few minutes while he briefed them, "Listen up, people. We are in the northwest end of Sheffield. It is a few minutes past eight o'clock. I'm very proud of the way y'all performed today. Truly outstanding! I'm blessed to have such a good group of soldiers. We did a real number on that little pack of Knights back there. Now, Tim, are you sure you can operate that weapon?"

"Yes, Pastor. I got it down pat. I shot one of these FAL rifles at militia camp a few summers ago in a familiarization course."

"How much ammo have ya' got?"

"Me and Jaybird only found two magazines on the gunner's person. They hold twenty 7.62 rounds each. We did find another thirty or so loose rounds in their vehicle. They look serviceable as well, so about seventy rounds all together, Pastor."

"Very well. You okay toting Tim's regular rifle, Jaybird?"

Private Rhodes answered, "Yes, sir. Just fine."

"Those Knights had some canned meat in their vehicle. In a minute, Mary's gonna' divvy it up to go with our hardtack. We'll eat, drink, and rest for a few minutes and then keep movin'. Y'all go ahead and take a load off. I'll keep watch."

Mary spoke up, "Daddy, whadaya' think that automatic weapons fire is that keeps moving ahead of us?"

"I don't know for sure, Mary, but they must be Lauderdales. We keep comin' up on dead Colberts. Heck, I'd call 'em angels if I didn't know better. They've sure lessened the burden for us. I've counted nineteen dead Colberts since that shooting started, and there is no tellin' how many bodies we haven't even seen. It does worry me some. The last little cluster of dead men appeared more like civilians. No guns at all, but they might have been armed before. Our shooters probably took their weapons rather than leave them for others to use against us."

As she walked around spooning the meat in the squads mess kits, she said, "Just wonderin', Daddy."

"I understand, girl. Maybe we'll catch up with 'em in the next block of houses."

"These are some fine houses ain't they, Daddy?"

"Yes, fine indeed. Rich folks."

About ten minutes later, Pastor Jim had the squad gear up. They spread into three assault elements and started advancing west again. Soon, a flickering light in the front picture window of a big two-story house caught their attention. Pastor Jim had his element stop. He ordered Tim and Jaybird to ease up on the porch and peer in the window. He and Mary followed a few yards behind. However, all four stopped well short of the porch after they heard a lady screaming and a man shouting from within the house. They listened intently, and heard the lady's voice, "Please, you men, go ahead and kill me if you want, but stop that with my granddaughter. Please, I beg you, stop."

The man's response was heard as well, "Shut the fuck up you old bitch!"

Then another man's voice, "Chance, I can't concentrate with Ol' Granny caterwaulin' over there!"

The first man again, "Okay, I will find somethin' to shut her yap. That girl is a goodun' ain't she, Nim."

Pastor Jim had heard enough. He signaled his two outlying elements to watch the flanks. He leaned in and whispered to Tim and Jaybird.

A moment later, Tim and Jay burst through the front door followed by the Pastor. Tim held the FAL on Bardolph who was standing in the living room near an elderly woman trying to gag her with a strip of sheer cloth — she was tied-up in a straight-backed chair. Jay and the Pastor quickly moved to a bedroom across the hall and found Nim with his pants down going at a naked woman. She was sprawled across a four-poster bed with her hands tied to the far side posts.

Pastor Jim loudly commanded, "Get your hands up! Boys, watch 'em now!"

Bardolph scowled at the militiamen and yelled, "Get the hell out of here. This is none of your concern, Preacher."

Nim stood, turned, and raised his hands. His BDUs were all clumped down around his ankles weighted by the belt-holstered handgun on his right and magazine pouches on his left.

Bardolph angrily spoke again, "I know you, Preacher. Do you know who we are? Get them damn guns off us" — he pointed — "right now!"

Pastor Jim responded, "Hold your weapons right where they are, men. Yeah, I know who you two are, Corporal. You there, Corporal Nim, move over in here beside your buddy. Take it real slow now."

Nim protested, "I can't walk with my pants like this. I'll trip, dammit."

"Well, then, I suggest you just shuffle real careful-like," countered Pastor Jim.

Nim started baby stepping out of the bedroom — thump-clump, thump-clump, went his weapon and magazines on the old house's hardwood floor.

Nim stopped in the hallway and complained, "Goddammit, I'm gonna fuckin' trip. Look, I gotta reach down and pull up my britches. I'll do it real slow. His eyes darted to Bardolph's.

Mary had stepped in the door.

Pastor Jim, noticed her and barked at Nim, "Corporal, you best watch your tongue in front of my daughter. Private Rhodes, if the Corporal stops again, blast him."

Jay replied, "Yes, Pastor."

"Honey, I hate that you have to see this scene of debauchery, but I need for you to be strong," Pastor Jim softly said to Mary.

Mary stood, jaw agape and a white knuckled grip on her M1 Carbine. She quietly replied, "Okay, Daddy."

Nim assessed the demeanor of Jaybird and the .50 caliber muzzle pointed at him. Corporal Thomas Nim resumed his shuffle.

After Nim joined Bardolph in the living room, Pastor Jim directed, "Mary, go on in that bedroom and see what you can do for that poor woman."

"Yes, sir," complied Mary. She moved to the room checking her nine and three as she entered. She checked behind the door as well. Satisfied, she slung her little semi-automatic rifle over her shoulder and moved to the sobbing woman's side.

Embarrassed by Mary's presence and frustrated by the militia's refusal to lower their gun muzzles, Bardolph firmly repeated, "I told you folks that this was none of your concern. Y'all need to move on."

Pastor Jim calmly replied, "Well, we're making it our concern. Private Gray, would you say this activity is a violation of President Smith's directive regarding treatment of Colbert non-combatants?"

A bit taken aback, Tim Gray glanced at his squad leader coughed and said, "Yes. I guess I would, Pastor."

Bardolph, seeing the writing on the wall, glared at Pastor Jim and growled, "Go to hell, Preacher."

Pastor Jim considered a second, and responded, "I might someday. It ain't my call, but I suspect one thing; you two are going there shortly."

He lowered his spear, drew his revolver, and pointed it at Nim, "Private Rhodes, I got this one covered. You go back outside and gather the squad. Post four lookouts and have the rest come in here to help us bind this pair of snakes."

Danny Ragland had his suspicions, but he felt time was running out. Charles, Edward, Montjoy, and he had spent the better part of an hour hashing out possible acts that may have played out in the council chamber. The Constable dealt with interruptions from his dazed staff members. The death of Lawrence Foster was almost as daunting for them as it was for Danny.

Danny said, "Uncle Charles, it's almost nine. I simply have to move on to have any chance at pulling off my operation tonight."

Charles glanced at the clock on his study wall, and then rested his face in his palms for a few seconds. He glanced at Danny and asked, "Do you really think it will work, Danny?"

"I do, sir. I have had scouts out pulling recon missions in Sheffield all evening. The intelligence indicates that the Lauderdales have indeed dug in along the tracks and 2nd Street in Sheffield. With the rain and the heavy losses in personnel they have suffered, I believe they are done for the night. However, they will resume their attacks in the morning if we can't hurt them somehow — a critical blow. My attack will do that."

Edward cautioned, "Danny, you have done a great job positioning our forces in Tuscumbia and Muscle Shoals. Our small harassment teams will start working the far ends of Lauderdale's shoreline in about an hour. Haven't you finally forced them into the position of attacking you on your own terms? It seems like we can slaughter them tomorrow as they advance against our prepared positions, and we still have a two to one advantage in number of troops."

"Eddie, what you say is true in theory, but Harry has done the opposite of what we expected so far, every time. I just know, deep down in my gut, that this may be our last chance to cripple his invasion. Besides, our inventory of centerfire ammunition is critically low. There is virtually none left in the militia units, and what the Knights have remaining is literally 'on their person.' I also received word that the Lauderdale Cavalry destroyed all our Napoleons just as the Knight artillerymen were about to transport them to Tuscumbia. We never got to fire a single one of their deadly canister rounds. My casualties — killed, wounded, or captured — are well over a thousand. The good people of Colbert are refilling the ranks to some extent, but they are mostly too young, too old, or too poorly trained. We have lost over half our vehicles to enemy fire or the lack of spare tires and other critical parts. No, Eddie, we must drive them off the southern end of the Singing River Bridge, and then they will be forced to sue for peace."

Eddie asked, "But, Danny, can't they just start using O'Neal Bridge?"

"No, Eddie, I have two of my best Knight scouts well hidden in a cave on the face of the river bluff. They have a spark-gap transmitter and my personal hand-held night vision device. They are keeping my staff abreast of the Lauderdales' progress on the bridge. At the moment, it still isn't even safe for foot traffic and vehicular traffic is out of the question for days."

Charles sighed and said, "Okay, Danny, I trust your judgment. Go ahead with your plan. Take Johnny with you in case you force them to surrender. As to this crap at the Palace, it'll have to wait."

Danny asked, "Back to that, you know what bothers me the most about not knowing the truth of the Palace killings?"

Charles knew, "The fact that the assassin might still be in the Palace among us."

Danny replied, "Exactly."

Eddie suggested, "I have an idea. Pull all the Knights that were on duty here during the time of the killings and add them to your assault force, Danny. Let my Knight security detail guard the Palace. There're only four of 'em, but they'll do for this evening. An' Daddy, you may not like this, but let's just send the servants home for the night — eliminate that possibility altogether."

Charles and Danny stared in near disbelief at Eddie and wondered who this clear thinking man was.

"Damn, son, if that ain't a dandy idea," exclaimed Charles; "and with you here to cover your sister, Momma, and me, we'll be fine."

Eddie paused, looked at his father, and said, "Well, Daddy, that is something I want to ask about."

"What's that, Eddie?"

"I want to go with Danny on this attack. I can be of more use there than here."

"I don't know, Son. The risk would be too great. Your mother and—"

"No, Daddy. I've got to go on this mission. I mean it. It's really important to me. I have some things to prove to myself and everyone else."

Danny asked, "Eddie, if you go with me, who will give the family the kind of indisputable, close in, protection required given this internal threat?"

"I will," said Catherine. She had quietly entered the study without the four men even noticing. Catherine was dressed in her Knight-blacks. She held her four-inch, nickeled .38 Special in her right hand. It pointed towards the floor at her side. In her left hand was her father's gleaming six-inch, blued steel .357 Magnum. She walked between her cousin and brother, straight to the front of her father's big desk and laid the Colbert President's favorite sidearm in front of him. She added, "And, Daddy."

Robby had suffered the adolescent, homophobic banter of Mickey Sarnes and Bret Haley all evening. After finishing their supply details and supper, Robby's orphan platoon huddled under the bridge to escape the rain. A couple of Harry's engineers had hung a lighting system below the bridge for the headquarters detachment. The HQ folks had departed for Sheffield almost an hour earlier, but they left one diesel generator to run the lights at the field hospital and a couple under the bridge for whatever needs might arise. Robby took advantage of the lighting to give individual firearms instruction to his crew.

Half the time Mickey and Bret behaved like best friends, and the other half was spent acting like a pair of angry twins. Just as Robby thought the two were over it, they started again.

Mickey punched Bret's arm and blurted, "Fuck you, Haley! You queer!"

Bret slapped at the retreating fist and dove into his oft heard, disgusting poem, "Eat me raw, balls and all. Leave my hair, I like it there."

Without hesitation, Mickey fired back, "I got a better idea. Let's play battleship. I'll lay down and you blow me up."

"Oh, that's very original, Sarnes!"

"As original as your shit, Haley!"

Robby was done with it and shouted, "Will you two shut up! Please! I think everybody has heard enough of this! Besides, there are girls here and you two need to watch what you're saying."

The two boys went sullen for a moment then Bret mumbled, "Sorry, Robby. We'll watch it. We didn't mean to piss anybody off."

One of the girls, Camille Ledlow, loudly said, "Thank you!"

They all turned and stood as Ben Smith approached.

He walked into the center of the youngsters, and announced, "Folks, you people have done well. Your hard work is appreciated."

Robby said, "We're glad we could help, Mr. Ben. What do you need us to do now?"

Ben replied, "The perimeter has really quieted down. Maybe because of the rain or maybe they have pulled troops to Tuscumbia and Muscle Shoals. We're not sure. However, we are staying alert. Y'all take advantage of the lull and try to get some sleep. Just stretch out down here in the driest spots you can find. I'll send for you if we need more shooters on the perimeter. Donnie Smith left a couple of hundred blankets up at the field hospital. They can spare enough for each of you to have one for the night. Robby, send a handful of your folks back with me, and help them pick out some dry ones."

"Yes, sir. Thank you." Robby scanned his command and continued, "Bret, Mickey, Brud, and Camille, y'all go with Mr. Smith and get the blankets."

Later, around ten o'clock, the rain stopped and the cloud cover began to break up. Intermittently, moonlight bathed the bridgehead. Robby had turned off their lights, but the generator still hummed for the hospital tent. The sound droned the exhausted young man to sleep.

A little while after Edward, Danny, and their accompanying Knights left the Palace, Catherine and her parents decided to finally eat something. Isabel was having a rare moment of clarity. That was at least one thing that Catherine and Charles could smile about. Catherine made them some ham sandwiches and coffee. They ate in the study.

Catherine stacked the dishes on a tray and returned them to the kitchen. Thinking the Palace only contained the three Raglands and four Knights standing guard outside, she was shocked, upon exiting the kitchen, to find their little night-servant, Rebecca Sullivan, standing just outside the kitchen door. Becky had curly, white hair, but judging by the freckles covering her pale complexion, one could easily assume it was once red, "Oh, me! I'm sorry I scared you Miss Catherine."

Catherine's strong hand was already on the grip of her holstered revolver. She quickly assessed *Non Threat* and released the grip as subtly as possible. "Becky, what are you doing here? We sent all the servants home."

"What? Oh, that explains why I can't find nobody. I'm sorry, ma'am! I came early for my graveyard shift because of all this ruckus in town. I was afraid things would get worser, an' they'd keep me from making the start of my shift. Well, I never been late, Miss Catherine. You know that. So, I just came in around eight o'clock an' told Mr. Glenn that I was here. He told me to go take a nap in the side quarters an' set the alarm clock to wake me in time for my shift."

"Oh, Darlin'. Mr. Glenn must have forgot about you."

"Seems so, ma'am."

"Well, I can't send you home with those trigger happy militiamen standing watch all over town."

"No, ma'am."

"Well then, I'll tell the guards that we're making an exception and letting you work tonight, or would you rather just go back to bed in the side quarters for this one time?"

"No, ma'am. I'm slept out. I'd rather work."

Supportively, Catherine said, "Very well, Becky, if that's what you want. Let's go tell Knight Collins at the front door," and she escorted Becky down the hall.

Becky halted abruptly, "Oh, Miss Catherine, I mus' ask ya'."

Catherine stopped as well, "Yes, Becky?"

"Well, Mr. Glenn told me to go clean up that ungodly mess on the marble staircase as soon as I finished my nap."

"Oh, dear!"

"Yes, ma'am."

"And I bet you'd as soon not tackle that tonight, huh?"

"No, ma'am. I'm gonna get right on it."

"And what's the problem, darlin'?"

"Well, as soon as I left the side quarters a minute ago, I went straight to the janitorial supply closet. You know, Miss Catherine, the one near your office in the business wing?"

"Yes?"

"Well, I couldn't get in it."

"Did your key not work?"

"No, ma'am it weren't a problem with my key.

"Really?"

"Yes, ma'am. It seems as though somebody done hammered their key in the lock and then broke it off. I tried and tried to dig it out with my little penknife, but after a while, figured I was doin' more harm than good."

Hearing the sound of conversation, Charles stepped from his study, massive revolver in hand, and asked, "Cate, what's goin' on out here? What's Becky doin' here?"

"Well, Daddy, let's just say she slipped through the crack."

Becky giggled, and that induced the same from Catherine.

"Hah, hah. Very funny, ladies. Now, tell me what's goin' on."

"Oh, Daddy. I don't have the energy. Why don't you just help Becky and me with the door to the janitor's supply closet."

"The one in the business wing?"

"Yes, Daddy. That's the one."

"Well, what about your Momma?"

"Is she still with us, Daddy?"

"Yes, she is quite lucid."

Catherine called into the study, "Momma, come on with us. We need to help out Little Becky with a problem."

Isabel hopped up from her chair and replied, "Oh! Help Little Becky? For heaven's sake, yes, I haven't seen her in years!"

Becky giggled again, while Catherine and Charles exchanged grins and raised eyebrows. Then all four walked across the Grand Foyer to the business wing — Isabelle and Becky arm-in-arm following Catherine and Charles.

Harry and 1911 actually managed to nod off for a little while on the floor of an office in the Sheffield City Hall building.

Harry was jolted awake by Donna Flurry's voice, "Harry, Mort, I hate to bother you two, but Clara Smith has sent one of her team members back for you."

Harry groggily asked, "Clara? She needs us to go to her team's location?"

Donna answered, "Yes, Harry. The runner indicates it is urgent. I don't know what it's about."

"Okay, c'mon Mort. Let's roll."

Harry had Clara's runner stand in the 8's ring mount and direct 1911. They ended up in a residential area near the river. It wasn't far from the western battle line. The rain had stopped, and with the sky clearing, the light from the moon presented them with a far different setting than the one they fell asleep to.

The runner announced, "There she is. There's Captain Smith — straight ahead."

Harry squinted and spotted the unmistakable gait of his first cousin.

She greeted him after he stepped out of his Humvee, "Hey, cuz. You doin' okay?"

He hugged her and replied, "I'm fine Clara. How 'bout you? What's up?"

"Well, Harry, I hate to be the one to show you this." She turned and waved him to follow.

1911 and Harry walked behind her and grimaced as they worked the kinks out of their leg muscles; keeping pace with the fast walking Slingshot 5 commander.

After a couple of hundred feet, Clara stopped by a big oak tree, and she said, "Here we are." Her Slingshot Humvee and several of her team stood about the area.

Harry stopped and looked at her questioningly. She pointed up to her right. Harry looked up to where she pointed. He saw two human shapes hanging from one of the tree's limbs.

Clara commanded, "Ruff, get a light on 'em!"

"Yes, ma'am!"

The hood spotlight from Slingshot 5 blasted the tree with illumination.

Harry peered up at the bodies, and his eyes concentrated on signs affixed to the chest of each one. The one on the left read, *Looter*, and the one on the right read, *Rapist*.

Harry's eyes jerked to 1911 as his old soldier exclaimed, "Oh, my God!"

Harry moved to 1911 to shore him up and grasped his arms firmly. Harry agreed it was a gruesome sight, but after the sights they had seen this day, he looked into Mort's eyes.

Mort gazed back and realized Harry didn't get it. He cried, "Harry, it's Bardolph and Nim! It's them hanging up there!"

In denial and confusion, Harry returned his attention to the gently swaying corpses. This time, he studied their faces. Harry stopped his upward gaze after a moment, turned, and walked over to Slingshot 5. He leaned forward, pressing his palms on the hood, with elbows locked.

Clara stepped to his side and gently rubbed and patted Harry's back. She softly ordered Corporal Ruff Creasy, "Kill the light, Ruff, and y'all find some way to cut 'em down."

The darkness returned. In that moment there was no sound of battle. The distant hooting of a Great Horned Owl broke the silence. Unusual for this time of night, Harry wondered if the fighting had separated the night-raptor from its mate. He hoped they found each other.

 &

Alice finally came across a lightly guarded spot in the Colbert line. She slipped into the killing zone that lay beyond the old railway lines. She was glad she didn't have to kill anyone else to escape from Tuscumbia, but she would have. She belly crawled in the darkness to a point about fifty yards from a line of Lauderdale foxholes. She saw a head periodically rise and fall. She figured it must be a militiaman that drew the watch.

She contemplated at what volume she would need to call out to alert the sentry and yet avoid the Colbert counterpart behind her. That decision was made more difficult by the fact that she had not spoken in hours and the exposure to the cold and damp might have done a number on her vocal cords as well.

Alice softly called out, "You there! Lauderdale Militia!"

There was a shuffling in the foxholes and several heads popped up and down. After a few seconds, a man's voice responded, "Who goes there?"

"I'm a Colbert soldier that wants to surrender."

"That's a first. We haven't had a Colbert surrender all day. What makes you different?"

"It's complicated. May I approach? I need to speak to an officer."

"Negative, Bitch."

"C'mon, Asshole. It is very important that I surrender."

There was more shuffling and mumbling from the foxholes. The same voice asked, "Are you armed?"

"Yes."

"Leave your weapons and crawl on in, Lady."

Suddenly a shout came from behind her, "You God damn coward! Get your traitorous ass back over here, woman! We'll open fire if you don't."

The Lauderdale voice countered, "We'll open fire if you do!"

Alice hollered, "Look here, Lauderdale! I'm comin' in, but I'm not leaving my weapons, but they're cleared. So, heads up!"

A shot rang out from the Colbert lines. The bullet screamed away from one of the rusty tracks. A volley of fire from the Lauderdales tore into the Colbert line. Alice kept elbowing and kneeing her way to the foxholes. The top half of a human silhouette appeared ahead of her. In the moonlight, she could see the soldier beckoning to her. She shoved her AKM and its detached magazine towards the figure, and dove into the foxhole. The single exchange of gunfire must have been all the ammo either side wanted to invest; there were no more shots.

A new voice said, "What the fuck, Lady? Are you crazy? Check this out, Bill! She's dressed like a secretary of somethin'!"

Alice quickly disclosed, "I have a cleared pistol in my waistband along with its two magazines, and a knife."

"What? Dammit, Lady — if you don't beat all! You got'em, Bill?"

Alice was standing in the foxhole and could only make out shadowy figures — one to her front and one to her back. The one in front held a long gun with the muzzle pressed against her chest. From behind, she felt big, strong hands at her waist. The knife, slide-locked handgun, and both its magazines were gone in seconds. Next the hands ran up her ribs and reached around, covered her stomach, gently squeezed her breasts, and then retreated to pat down her back. She braced herself for what she assumed was next. The hands ran over her buttocks, hips, the surface of her legs, and finally, they shot up between her thighs all the way to her crotch.

After a cursory, almost gentlemanly, feel-about, the hands pulled away, and her frisker announced, "She's clean, Toby"

Alice said, "Nice to meet you too, Bill."

Toby snickered, "She's a pistol ball. Huh, Bill?"

Bill wasn't quite so jovial, and murmured, "Sorry, ma'am."

A head appeared at the edge their foxhole. The owner asked, "You men search her?"

Bill answered, "Yes, Sergeant. Nothing but a shitload of weapons was on her."

Toby added, "Sarge, she had a fuckin' AK!"

Their NCO responded, "An AK? Damn! Much ammo?"

Bill answered, "No, just one AK magazine and a couple of pistol magazines."

"Pistol? What kinda pistol?"

"Hard to tell exactly in the dark, but I think it's a nice one — it don't weigh much, plastic frame."

"Geez, that's some top-end ordnance! Is she wearing a dress?"

Bill seriously answered, "No, Sergeant, a skirt and blouse."

Sarcastically, the NCO responded, "Well, excuse me, Bill, I stand corrected — 'a skirt and blouse'."

Toby snickered again.

After a long silence, the sergeant commanded, "Lady, I'm gonna have these boys hoist you up here. I heard you holler that you want to talk to an officer. Well, I don't much care what you want, but I do need to get you off of my line. I'm going to take you back and hand you over to an officer. Bill, you're actin' corporal since Barney was wounded. Can you handle things until I get back?"

"Yes, Sergeant."

Toby asked, "Sarge, can me and Bill keep her guns?"

"No. Here, I got a burlap bag I was going to use for scavenging grub. Put everything she had on her in it, and I'll take it back with me and turn it over to the commander of that Slingshot team."

After filling the bag and handing it up to his squad leader, Bill asked, "Sergeant, she is soaked to the bone and shivering. If I put my coat on her, will you make sure I get it back?"

The sergeant said, "Bill, if you ain't the southern gentleman? Yeah, sure, put your coat on her."

The Sergeant pulled and the two privates lifted and Alice slid over the lip of the foxhole and was soon crawling along in a northeasterly direction.

After they passed the first line of structures, the sergeant told Alice that it was okay for them to walk upright. She clutched Bill's giant coat around her. It smelled like burned wood, perspiration, gun smoke, and dirt, but it was magnificently warm.

About a quarter mile behind the line, Alice and her escort approached a cluster of vehicles. Alice remembered seeing the Slingshot teams from her early days in Lauderdale. She anxiously sought a team number plate on the vehicles. She made out the number 5 as they got closer. According to her recollection of Colbert intelligence reports, the Slingshot commander was Captain Clara Smith, Harry Smith's first cousin. A Slingshot sentry spotted them and after the militia sergeant responded to the Slingshot sentry's challenge, they were waved into the bivouac.

The sergeant reported the reason for their presence to his Slingshot counterpart. Captain Smith was retrieved from a small, single story house located across the street from the vehicles. The stocky, thirtyish officer looked fatigued and a little sad at first, but upon viewing the unlikely pairing, her demeanor changed to one of an alert field commander.

Clara addressed the militia NCO, "Sergeant, my teammate says this woman is a Colbert and wants to surrender to a Lauderdale officer?"

"Yes, ma'am. That is correct. She presented herself to our line, gave up her unloaded weapons peacefully, and has been most compliant every step of the way. One of my men loaned her that coat. She is dressed like a civilian underneath it — like an office worker, Cap'n. I have all the weapons she had on her in this sack."

Clara directed them to follow her inside the house. The team was using it for shelter for the evening. They had a fire going in the fireplace and several lanterns burning. Clara looked at Alice then the sergeant. "Sergeant, set that bag of guns on the floor and help the lady off with that coat."

Almost hesitantly, Alice gave up the coat.

Clara took in the Colbert's attire right down to the almost full slit running up the side of her skirt.

The sergeant folded the coat over his left arm as his Lauderdale Sharps rested in the crook of his right. He looked at Alice and said, "I'll get this back to the private, ma'am."

Alice said, "Thank your Private Bill for me, Sergeant. That was most gracious of him."

"I will, ma'am," replied the sergeant as he lingered at the sincerity in her beautiful eyes.

Clara did too. She told Alice to sit. Alice sat down at one end of a love seat.

The sergeant asked Clara, "Captain, will that be all?"

She hesitated a moment and reached down into her field bag and lifted out a large flask. She turned to the Sergeant and said, "Sergeant, there's a couple of glasses on that table behind you. Hand them here and I'll pour us a snort."

"Yes, ma'am!"

Clara poured two shots, gently passed one to the sergeant, and then presented the other to Alice, saying, "Miss Boyd?"

Shocked, Alice tried her best not to show any emotion, but as she accepted the glass, her hand quivered.

Clara poured herself a drink in the cap of the flask. After setting the flask on an end table, she raised her makeshift cup and said, "To peace."

The sergeant and Alice had matched the gesture and now brought their glasses to their lips. The sergeant tossed back the whiskey in one gulp, closed his eyes, and moaned in the seconds of fiery pleasure. Alice just took a sip. Clara met them in the middle and drank half of hers.

Clara asked the sergeant, "Robison, right? From Whitehead?"

"Yes, ma'am. Good memory."

"Well, Sergeant Robison. I'll take it from here. You can return to your squad."

"Thanks for the drink, Cap'n." He saluted and was on his way.

Alice watched him exit then focused on the Slingshot commander, she noticed the captain no longer had her drink in her hand, but a .45 compact 1911 instead.

Clara politely said, "Pardon the .45, Miss Boyd, but I have to cover security myself since I have chosen to conduct this interview in private."

Alice calmly replied, "I understand, Captain Smith."

"I imagine you do," said Clara as she took a seat on the couch across from Alice's loveseat.

The hours of terror and exposure had caught up with Alice; she had no scenarios ready. She simply begged, "Please, Captain Smith, I have to get to Harry Smith as soon as possible. I have critical information for him. It could determine the outcome of this entire conflict."

"And just why would Catherine Ragland's personal assistant and body guard want to share such information with President Smith?"

"Ma'am you obviously recognize me from intelligence briefings or the like."

Clara nodded affirmatively with a smirk and raised eyebrows.

"Damn, I don't know any other way to explain this but straight out."

"That works for me, Miss Boyd."

"Well then, here it is. I'm an agent for the Smiths. I have been operating undercover on this side of the river for ten years."

"Ten years? Did you grow up in Lauderdale?"

"Yes, Captain. My real name is Jenny Hart."

"Jenny Hart! Wait one damn minute, Sweetie! I remember that name. It can't be. I attended Jenny Hart's funeral with Harry, Uncle Wade, and my Daddy after she died in a horrible boating accident.

Harry was distraught with guilt over that. He blamed himself. I thought he'd never get over it."

"It was all faked, Captain. Just Harry, Mr. Ben, and President Wade were in on it with me. I was secreted away down at Waterloo, trained, and then inserted into Sheffield in 60."

Clara was staring intently at the striking woman sitting before her. Yes, striking, in spite of the dirt, mud, wet hair, scratches, and abrasions. Clara almost triggered a headache trying to pull from the recesses of her brain any mental image of the young Jenny Hart. Clara had only encountered the girl a few times during the 50s. "How in the Hell did you land the position you held with no family history in the ST — especially a Colbert family history, or schools, chur—"

"I did have a history, all that, but it was a lie — a brilliant deception!"

"What? Given the Raglands' caution about such matters, that's hard to believe."

"Wade Smith had a dear old Colbert friend, Rebecca Boyd. She was a widow that lived a sheltered life deep in southwest Colbert; it was literally the middle of nowhere. She was once a teacher in Tuscumbia, but after the questionable death of her husband, she became a recluse. She hated the Raglands — blamed 'em for the death of her husband that occurred in 39. She started spying for the Smiths in the 40s ... just little stuff like reporting activity along the Southern Wall. She eagerly took on the task of selling Alice Boyd to the Colberts mainly fueled by the fact that her health was failing, and she loved the idea of getting one last significant jab at the Raglands. The Smith's intelligence folks created an entire background for me centered on the falsehood that I was her illegitimate daughter — conceived, born, and home schooled without public knowledge. Thus no forged documents were needed. She used the excuse of her failing health to reveal my existence to the authorities, so that I might make a place for myself in regular society. Charles Ragland's people out that way were so suspicious of her, they eagerly bought the story. It validated their long-existing animosity. They fell all over themselves making sure I got a proper start in the real world. A group of High

Church ladies even brought me in to Sheffield to apply for work at Thompson's mill. The rest was up to me after that."

"So, did Rebecca Boyd die?"

"Yes."

"How convenient."

A little anger flushed Alice's pale cheeks, but she swallowed it down and calmly continued, "But not until 63. I actually grew quite close to her. She was the only person in that whole fake world that I could be honest with. Rebecca Boyd became my mother. The mother I never had. I loved her. After I became a Knight, I moved her into town and we shared a crappy little apartment till the day she died."

Feeling quite guilty for her last remark, but still deeply suspicious, Clara held her cold, tough line, "That's quite a tale, Miss Boyd."

Noticing a clock on the desk in the house, Alice saw that it was approaching eleven o'clock. In spite of her considerable skill set and mental toughness, she felt panic arising. "Please, Captain Smith. I remember you, don't you remember me?" She pulled off her dark-rimmed glasses. Look, I don't even need these to see. I just wear them as part of my disguise. They aren't corrective lenses. The Smiths issued me three pairs just in case I lost or broke them over the years. I got to the point of wearing them all the time, not just to keep up the look, but for eye protection as well."

Clara was conflicted. She had indeed been shown pictures of Alice Boyd in an intelligence briefing and a threat briefing as well — this appeared to be her. Alice Boyd was an apex predator, and without proof of this bizarre cover story, letting her get anywhere in the proximity of Harry was unfathomable. She said, "I just don't remember Jenny Hart's face, Miss Boyd, and your story is questionable at best."

With watering eyes, Alice asked, "Clara, do you remember the Lauderdale Softball Championship of 56? It was your senior year at Florence, and you were their ace. It was the bottom of the seventh and y'all had a 5 to 4 lead over Smith's Academy. You had not given up a run since the third, so your coach left you in. You struck out the first two batters, Barb Hovater and Glenda King. Next, Sammie

Crow reached second off a throwing error by your shortstop, Nannie Farris. You walked the next hitter, Joan Gunderson, a lefty, to get to their skinny little freshman. But you underestimated her and ended up with a three-two count. You couldn't afford to walk her because Ann McCoy, Smith's best hitter was on deck. Shocking to you I'm sure, the little girl moved to the other side of the plate. You tried to burn her with your fast ball."

Tears were now in Clara's eyes, and she interjected, "Right across the plate."

Alice finished, "With a full count, my girls were on the run. I hit a liner between your first and second basemen, beat out the throw to first, and both our girls scored."

Context burned through the clouds of time, Clara marveled, "You're that switch hittin' little filly?"

"Yes, ma'am"

Clara stood and lowered her pistol. She said, "Our old tube radio has crapped out, but I can get a quick message to Harry on the spark-gap transmitter. What should I tell him, Jenny?"

Jenny considered and then answered with both relief and joy in her voice, "Tell him you have Cheetah!"

Cam Blakely and Joe Candray had passed by around nine just after the rain stopped. Tassy Williams heard the horses of the two old River Watch soldiers and stepped out in the cold darkness to say hi and let them know she and the boys were fine. It was good to have an adult conversation, even a short one. Little Mike was 8-years-old and his brother, Wade, was only five. With Michael off to war, the mother had long days and longer nights with her sons.

The Lauderdale River Watch veterans had little fresh news from the front, but they did pass along disturbing reports of small Colbert raids along the Lauderdale shoreline from one end of the ST to the other. They proudly claimed that all had been thwarted with the traditional harshness such missions carry. It was policy on both sides of the river to kill all interlopers. No quarter was expected or given relative to such raids.

These pairs of seasoned watchmen, like Cam and Joe, operated on horseback and were usually issued a .30-30 lever action rifle and a 12 gauge pump shotgun. The River Watch maintained its own arsenal and kept them in tip-top condition. A Tennessee River sector would have four such two-person teams assigned to it. The pairs would share the two firearms throughout the day, and rotate among four or five mounts — every team working a six-hour shift. Older men and boys tended to carry the burden of these patrols, but a scattering of women of all ages filled some of the slots. Tassy had been watching Cam and Joe work the eight-to-two shift ever since she and Michael moved to the remote location back in 62.

Michael and Tassy grew up in Waterloo, proper, but they dreamed of having their own place "out in the woolies." When the Smiths offered to pay for the construction of cabins in the more remote Lauderdale areas, the young couple jumped on the opportunity. With their thinly spread neighbors, they trapped and hunted the woods and streams of McKelvey Hollow, Panther Creek, Cedar Fork, and Shaw Hollow. They fished the river with the dark and mysterious Mississippi shoreline looming to the west; and maintained a solid little garden and a couple of fruit trees. Michael's barter-pay for his cavalry service was considerable. The Smiths rewarded the part-time service in the elite unit generously. It was a rich life, but a lonely one at times.

Tassy heard automatic weapons fire around ten. She thought she recognized the distinctly different sounds of the River Watch guns as well. The shooting only lasted a minute or so. She knew the drill. She grabbed a lamp, their single shot 12 gauge, and her Short Magazine Lee Enfield. She then roused the boys and headed for their hideaway. It was behind the cabin, just beyond the garden and orchard. Generally, she only used their diesel generator sparingly, but she started it as they departed.

"What you doin' that fer, Momma?" asked Little Mike.

"Just as a precaution, Son."

The sleepy-headed boy suddenly realized the severity of the situation and he grasped Wade's left hand tightly and pulled him along. Wade used his other hand to wad-up and clutch his quilt.

Little Mike asked, "Can I carry the shotgun for ya', Momma?"

"That would be sweet, Son," she replied, and carefully handed him the long, slender shotgun freeing her hands for the lamp and rifle.

A steep hill lay behind their cabin and a small cave was located a short way up its face. The resourceful couple had worked on the cave and turned it into an emergency site. Nestled among trees and undergrowth, it was indistinguishable when viewed from the cabin. A sealed tub in the back of the cave contained food, water, medical supplies, and blankets. Tassy hoped that she wouldn't have to break the seal.

She quietly told her boys, "We'll just be here for a short while. Ol' Cam and Joe will be along shortly to whistle from the dark and let us know everything is fine."

She wrapped Wade's quilt around their skinny little shoulders and had them huddle, side-by-side, on the sturdy log bench Michael had hewn for them.

"Y'all be quiet as a mouse now, ya' hear."

"Yes, ma'am," said Little Mike.

Tassy settled in behind the low stone wall that Michael had carefully built across the entrance to the cave. She clutched the shotgun and had the rifle leaning on the wall at her side. She peered into the darkness.

After an hour or so, she was fighting the terror that worked its way into her mind like the water that dripped in the far back of the cave. A cloud obscured the moon. It moved on and the back of her residence became a shadowy scene albeit one with distinguishable features. Her terror was replaced by adrenaline-fed resolve after Tassy saw dark humanoid shapes moving around the cabin.

One entered the cabin and a moment later came back out. The Colberts huddled.

"There's three of 'em, Momma!" whispered Little Mike.

She did not even realize he was beside her.

213

"Son, I told you to watch your brother."

"I had him get under Daddy's bench, and covered him with Granny's quilt. I wanna help, Momma."

She glanced back to see the little mound under the bench, looked at the face of her brave boy, and whispered, "Okay, Mike. Here, you take the shotgun. Don't cock the hammer until I tell ya' to. It's loaded with a buckshot-shell. You remember what your Daddy taught you about how far buckshot will kill?"

"Yes, ma'am."

"Okay, no more talkin'."

The three Colberts talked for what seemed like the longest. She wondered if they were perplexed by the sound and location of the generator. They finally began to move. Evidently, they decided to search the grounds more thoroughly. All three approached the hill. One came down the left side of the garden between it and Dungee Boy's vacant stable and corral, another traversed a row in the middle of the garden, and the third moved through Tassy's apple and peach trees on the right.

She whispered to Little Mike, "Get ready, Son. Look up at the moon for a couple of seconds to get your eyes ready. Aim for the one in the orchard, Honey— just like that chicken-thievin' coyote you shot last month."

He nodded and glanced up at the bright moon — his eyes blinking.

After Tassy brought her gaze back to the garden from the moon, she hit the electrical switch nestled in the wall before her. Light flooded their back yard. The enemies covered their eyes in shocked blindness.

The moonlight had already given Little Mike a sighting plane along the top of the worn shotgun barrel; the Colbert in the orchard stood at the end. Little Mike fired first. The distance to target was only about 20 yards. The enemy stumbled and then lunged behind their apple tree. The young Lauderdale thumbed the breech's lever, broke the action — ejecting the empty hull, and reached for a fresh shell from the little cotton bag his mother had positioned to his side.

Tassy took a second longer to aim and acquire a sight picture on the Colbert in the middle, but her chest shot was true and the target collapsed. She cycled the bolt expertly and sought out the invader on the left. A burst of automatic fire ripped into the surrounding flora with one round whizzing over her head to ricochet around the cave.

"They're good," thought Tassy as she acquired a sight picture. Fortunately, the garden had been cleared for winter and there was no cover for the assailant. The shooter was prone and directly facing the cave — about 50 yards away. Tassy aimed at the center of the black oval and fired. In a blink, she cycled another round and repeated the shot.

At Donna Flurry's command post, Harry Smith met Jenny Hart as she stepped from the back seat of Slingshot 5's Humvee. He greeted her with a hug, and said, "Jenny, Lauderdale is greatly in your debt. I'm greatly in your debt. It is so good to have you back."

Jenny tried to say something appropriate or witty or even smartass, instead she hugged Harry again and started sobbing.

Clara emerged from the front passenger seat and stood staring at them. Donna Flurry soon joined her, and hooked arms. The Slingshot commanders exchanged teary-eyed glances and smiles.

Harry looked over her shoulder during the long hug, and laughingly asked Clara, "Whose Slingshot 5 uniform is she wearing?"

Clara chuckled and answered, "Oh, that's a spare set of Debbie's, uh, Corporal Debbie Tanner's. She had some extra thermals, as well, and boots and socks. Hell, I'm glad Debbie had spares — nothin' of mine would have fit her."

Donna laughed.

Jenny stepped back with her hands grasping Harry's arms just above his elbows. Her demeanor became all business, she said, "Harry, we have to talk — right now!"

215

The four of them walked towards the Sheffield City Hall. Donna, walking beside Harry, leaned in and softly said, "Harry, Clara's people got Chance and Tom back here a little while ago. I put them on an ambulance wagon heading to O'Neal Bridge. We've decided to start holding bodies there until we can get that bridge ready for traffic. It may take a couple of days, but the engineers think they can have it capable of handling at least our lighter wagons."

"Thanks, Donna."

They stepped into a clerk's office at the Sheffield City Hall. Before Harry could ask a question, Jenny said, "Danny Ragland is going to hit your bridgehead any minute now."

"With what? He is spread from one end of Colbert to the other."

"This afternoon, I read a freshly decoded memo sent from Danny Ragland, in the field, to Edward Ragland at the Palace. Danny was strongly requesting Eddie's assistance in gathering every Black Force Knight available for use in a concentrated assault. Not only the ones in the lines of Tuscumbia and Muscle Shoals, but those from their eastern and western assignments as well."

"Did the message state they were going to be employed to attack the bridgehead?"

"No, sir, but he was having the Knights from the east assemble at Wilson Dam, and those close by and to the west at the Tuscumbia barracks. If Danny was going to use them against your— I'm sorry … our, troops in Sheffield, it would seem logical to have this Knight-army all gather in Tuscumbia. Oh, and the memo directed Eddie to have a militia company previously sent to guard Wheeler Dam rerouted to Wilson Dam. That would place the entire 2nd Battalion of the East Colbert Militia Regiment at Wilson Dam.

"I see your point, Jenny. When would this memo have been sent?"

"Early this afternoon. Eddie departed to fulfill his cousin's request in the middle of the afternoon. Oh, an' get this, Harry. Danny stated in the memo that he would personally command the assembly."

Donna looked at Harry and asked, "What do you think, Mr. President?"

As Harry considered, Jenny added, "By the way, are y'all aware that the Tuscumbia Junior Knights have been cloistered away down by the generators in the dam's powerhouse for the last five days?"

Donna answered, "No! Hell, I wondered why we hadn't run into those kids yet. I figured they were being held back for the defense of Tuscumbia."

Jenny commented, "I don't know where or if they deployed the Sheffield Junior Knights."

Captain Smith curtly stated, "Oh, our cavalry killed every damn last one of that Sheffield bunch in an ambush on the reservation."

Jenny paled, obviously stunned.

Clara noticed and asked, "What?"

Jenny despondently responded, "I accompanied Catherine Ragland to their selection ceremony in August. They were such babies."

Clara, trying to reason the tragedy of the slaughter, stated, "Well, shit! They should've never have been committed to that hot of a sector. What a stupid-ass move!"

Harry said nothing but was reminded of Robby and the orphans in that moment.

Jenny, back in intelligence spouting mode, commented, "Well, I personally witnessed a Tuscumbia Junior Knights training exercise last spring. Charles Ragland had me run a CQB class for them. That whole junior program was his pride and joy, and the Tuscumbia bunch was the flagship. They are organized into a platoon with three squads, a command element, and a weapons squad. Little Charles's buddy, Pickard Thompson, had his arms division build Sten Gun clones for them in spite of the critical shortage of 9mm ammo. I fired one. It looked like crap and was woefully inaccurate, but it didn't malfunction. Their weapons squad has a couple of old U. S. Army automatic rifles; they are .30-06 weapons from the WWII era. They came from some loan shark's gun collection. Anyway, they are half-a-hundred young toughs that fancy themselves as some sort of shock troops. I taught them a series of basic hand-to-hand disarming and killing moves. Unfortunately, they were quick-learns."

Harry blurted, "God damn, Jenny! Any more cheery news?"

She blushed after realizing just how robotic she must have sounded. "No, sir."

Donna had been studying Jenny with a wary eye, she said, "Ten years, darlin'? Ten years in this muddle?"

Jenny glanced back at the Slingshot 2 commander, but could not bring herself to respond other than a half-nod.

Harry said, "Sorry, Jenny. Excellent report, analysis, and conclusions."

He looked at Donna, "To answer your original question, 'What do you think, Mr. President?' I'll tell ya' what I think. Danny Ragland is going to hit the bridgehead with every Knight he and Eddie have been able to scrounge, a fanatical bunch of submachine gun totin' adolescents, and the better part of a fresh battalion of infantry. They could be attacking as we stand here, but I doubt it."

Donna guessed why, "Because our bridgehead perimeter contains the main road to the dam."

"That's right, Donna. From the first night of our invasion, they have had to use a loop of back roads and possibly even cut some new ones to reach the dam. It will have slowed them down tonight — I hope. But, we've got to move quickly."

They all glanced at their timepieces, except for Jenny — Holt had made her remove her cherished watch, a gift from Catherine, and hand it to him along with everything else. She glanced over at Clara's watch.

Harry announced, "It's a quarter to midnight. Major Fuqua and the 4 are backing up the line at Muscle Shoals. I can't afford to pull him for this. Donna, you're gonna have to do the same for all of Sheffield with only Slingshot 2. Clara, get your people ready to roll. We're headin' to the bridgehead ASAP."

Clara asked, "Slingshot 8 and 5 are all we send? Against all those Knights?"

Harry thought for a second and asked, "Does anybody know where the two companies of High Church Militia are located — the ones I pulled from the bridgehead earlier?"

Donna answered, "You're in luck, Harry. I ordered their company commanders to hold them in reserve near the Sheffield end of O'Neal Bridge. I was going to hand them off to Major Fuqua at dawn to help with the assault on Muscle Shoals. Screw that, huh?"

"Exactly, Major. Can you spark-gap the bridgehead and alert them to this new threat? Then send a courier to O'Neal and order those High Church company commanders to double-time back to the Singing River bridgehead. Oh, an' tell 'em that Harry said to forget all their shit. Just grab their weapons and ammo, and go. Get word to Donnie to watch over the stuff they leave behind. "

"Consider it done, Harry," said Donna and she immediately turned to exit the office.

Clara caught her sleeve, "Whoa up a second, folks. I have issues."

Harry asked, "How big?"

Clara answered, "My LMTV was hit badly this evening. It is short on tires and I have no spares plus its radiator is toast."

Donna said, "Get your people to hoof it over here, Clara. Y'all can take my old deuce and a half, and I'll send my mechanics over with what few spares we have left to try and get your LMTV running. We'll swap back when you get back."

Clara smiled and asked, "Get back?"

Donna lightly punched her bicep and growled, "Hell, yeah!"

Jenny blurted out, "Harry, I wanna go!"

Harry saw by the look in Jenny's eyes that there was no way he could deny the request.

"Okay, Jenny the 8 is down to just me and 1911 now. We'd love the company. You want the passenger seat or the M240 in the ring mount?"

"Hell, an M240? I've never had the pleasure. I'll figure it out during the ride over."

"That's my girl!"

Clara caught Jenny's sleeve this time. "Jenny, don't forget your weapons in the 5. I've got a couple of more more magazines for your AK too."

Clara glanced at Harry and gave him a sad nod and wink. It only took him a second to realize whose magazines they had been.

DAY FIVE

"Constable Ragland, may I speak with you for a minute?"

Danny, standing near his command tent at Wilson Dam, turned to see Ted Creasy approaching him from the shadows. Ted was carrying a rifle case that Danny recognized. "Of course, Ted. I heard about Jimmy. I hate that, he was a good man and an exceptional marksman — such a loss."

"Thanks, Constable. He was that."

Guessing that the spotter was turning in the long range rifle, Danny wanted to show him proper respect. "Are you going to pick up the flag, Ted, and become our shooter? We can find you a decent spotter."

"Uh, no sir. I can dope the wind and figure distance with the best of 'em, but I'll never be the sniper Jimmy was. I just wanted to turn our rifle in."

Danny noted the man's resolve. He commanded his driver, "Knight, take this rifle and put it in my vehicle."

After Ted passed the case to Danny's man, he asked, "Sir, I'd like to keep the M4 and help with this assault y'all are puttin' together. Would that be possible?"

Danny, without hesitation, answered "Why yes, Corporal. Edward Ragland and I are running a little short in our command team. You want to gun-up with us?"

"Absolutely, sir!"

Danny saw renewed vigor in the warrior's expression, and extended his hand to the corporal. Ted shook it.

Edward had walked up to them, and Danny turned and asked, "Eddie, Corporal Creasy wants to join our command team. Do you think we can put him to work?"

Edward had seen the sniper team at work in the past. He was familiar with Creasy's record, and was aware of their top sniper's death. Edward smiled and extended his hand as well, "Hell, yeah, Danny. Corporal, we need a tail-end-charlie. Can you cover our six?"

"Sounds like a job I can handle, Mr. Ragland. I'd be honored."

Edward responded, "Good enough, Corporal. Welcome aboard. Report to Knight Kirkland over there and he will bring you up to speed on this op."

"Yes, sir. Thank you."

After Ted walked away, Edward turned to his first cousin, "Danny it's midnight. We are ready for final briefing. Our count is two companies of militia infantry, 122 Knights, the platoon of juniors, and one ex-militia spotter with a score to settle."

Danny chuckled and said, "That's great, Eddie. Hey, man, before we get too wrapped up in this operation, I—"

"Yeah, yeah, you want to thank me for being a stand-up guy for once and doing such a great job assembling this badass assault force."

Danny grinned and man-hugged his cousin, "Well, I was going to say that you are a pretentious, stuck-up, elitist, loser, douchebag brat, but 'stand-up guy' will do."

They laughed and stepped off for the briefing.

"Hey, Asshole. You be careful."

"You too, Eddie. "

After receiving Harry's alert, Captain Chester Hayes, the Slinghot 7 commander, informed Ben Smith, and they awoke and dispersed all of their perimeter personnel to thwart the impending Colbert assault.

Chester had lost his two trucks to Colbert artillery fire the day before. He had his driver pull their still-intact Humvee with its .50 caliber machine gun into a defensive position about 100 yards behind the eastern side of bridgehead. Preparing for the worst, he had ordered their engineers to backhoe up three sets of earthen berms — one behind each side of the perimeter. His vehicle was hull down with only the heavy MG in enfilade.

The entire perimeter would have benefitted from the presence of a bulldozer, but even after being reinforced, Harry's Bridge could not handle the weight. Two hardworking excavation crews were performing near miracles with their backhoes.

Ben Smith and Chester had divided commands. Ben would cover the southern and western sides of the perimeter. He relinquished command of the eastern side to Chester and his Slingshot NCOs.

Chester was wearing the bridgehead's only set of night-vision goggles with the eyepieces flipped up towards the sky. He inserted one of his two remaining M14 magazines into his rifle, racked the bolt handle, flicked on the safety, and stepped off to move forward into the busy collection of berms and foxholes running along the eastern perimeter. He advanced with his sixteen remaining team members — half the original number.

His gunner, perched in the ring mount of their Humvee, said, "Y'all let some through for me, ya' here."

No one else from Slingshot 7 found it amusing.

After awakening and readying his kid-soldiers, Robby led them off to reinforce a squad of militia located on the side of a steeply sloping hollow off to the east of the bridge. The High Church Militia had dug a 50-yard trench. Obviously its purpose was to defend against an infantry assault from the riverbank. They dispersed into the trench, shoulder to shoulder with the militia, and peered into the darkness. Most of them were terrified; so was Robby.

Robby had managed to arm the entire bunch with Lauderdale Sharps breech-loaders. He was glad none would have to deal with the more complicated flintlocks. He had asked and received permission from Ben Smith to have his teens load and fire two shots each into the river. At least each was now acquainted with the feel of the trigger, lock time, and recoil.

Scooter Shelton arrived at the bridgehead at sunset. After word of the pending attack reached him at midnight, he had his artillerymen immediately start setting up a dozen pipe mortars. The mortars were not designed to lob explosives, but rather to fire star shells to light the battlefield. He anxiously looked at his watch after he saw the Slingshot 7 Team advance into the line. It was twelve-thirty.

Danny and Edward Ragland commanded the Knights advancing from the dam. Their people were to hit the left and center of the eastern Lauderdale perimeter. Seventy-year-old school principal, Smokin' Joe Barnes, led his Tuscumbia Junior Knights along the old Rock Pile Fishing Area to strike the perimeter just above the river's edge. One company of militia was left guarding the dam and the two others were advancing more slowly behind the Knight spearhead.

Captain Hayes ordered skirmishers out to detect the approach of the Colberts. The first skirmishers fired at the Colberts and started sprinting back to the perimeter from points as far as a quarter mile out.

Through his night vision eyepieces, Chester saw the skirmishers racing back. He yelled for Scooter to begin firing star shells. The first two of the comets shot up and over the defenders igniting at an altitude of around 200 feet — about 100 yards in front of the line. They slowly drifted down on their little parachutes.

Shockingly, the illumination revealed black uniformed attackers already within one to two hundred yards of the perimeter. Chester had given orders earlier to fire at will as targets presented themselves. The eastern line opened up from one end to the other. The black powder booms of the single shot rifles contrasted with the sharp cracks from the centerfire repeating weapons. Dozens of Knights fell as they neared the lines, but more filled their sprinting ranks from behind. They were on the perimeter quickly. The Colberts' Thompson hand grenades began to explode in and around the Lauderdale earthworks.

Harry saw the first star shells rise and burst in the east. He arose to squeeze in the ring mount beside Jenny. 1911 slowed their Humvee as they caught up and passed the jogging companies of Harry's High Church Militia.

Jenny gestured to the south and asked, "Do you hear that?"

Harry turned and listened. At first, he heard small weapons fire from Muscle Shoals, and then it was joined by more back to the southwest. He concluded, "They are firing into our lines along the entire front — all the way from Muscle Shoals to Tuscumbia. I guess they are hoping to keep us from transferring any more troops to the bridgehead."

They both glared into the east again. After clearing the foot soldiers, 1911 did not need to be encouraged. He depressed the accelerator. Harry glanced back to see that Slingshot 5's vehicles were passing the infantry as well.

Jenny nudged him and nodded to their front. He turned his head to see another LMTV up ahead pulled to the side of the road. As they closed on it, Harry recognized it as Donnie Smith's lone supply truck; Donnie used wagons for the majority of his work. The back was jam packed with High Church militiamen. 1911 slowed to a stop beside the LMTV.

Donnie sat in the passenger seat next to his driver. He leaned out the window and yelled to Harry. "Hey, cuz. I thought I'd give some of these folks a lift up to the fight. I figured you could use the help. Oh, and how sweet, you arranged for fireworks."

Harry responded, "Donnie, smartasses die from bullets just like everybody else. Are you sure about this, pogue?"

"Hell, yeah. Lead on, Mr. President," Donnie said as he threateningly shook the riot gun standing between his legs.

Harry laughed and slapped the roof of his vehicle. 1911 depressed the accelerator.

A second pair of star shells went up. The M2 gunner on Slingshot 7's Humvee was surprised to see enemy soldiers already breaking through the lines. He racked his machine gun's bolt and started firing bursts at the darting targets. Some he hit. Some he missed. The militia's black powder rifles were creating a cloud. It was eerie in the flickering light as was the red mist that sprayed from the recipients of his 709-grain projectiles.

Observing the enemy sporadically breaking through the perimeter, Scooter Shelton hollered for his mortar men to keep firing the flares at thirty-second intervals and to keep their firearms close. He stepped forward, shouldered his Daddy's old M16A1, worn silvery over the decades, and began firing at the shadowy figures exposed by his manmade twilight. He rolled two Knights quickly. Thus imbued, he started firing more rapidly, but the rest of his magazine found no more flesh. As he reloaded, he reminded himself to fire more deliberately.

Intensely focused forward, Scooter was surprised to hear muzzle blasts to the left and right. He glanced around to find he was now in the middle of a skirmish line made up of the surviving troopers from the Lauderdale Cavalry.

Robby's orphans did not begin firing with the first star shells. The first enemy soldiers from the river did not appear until the second pair of star shells went up. In the thicker brush of the river's edge, these assailants were only a couple of hundred feet away when first detected. The orphans and their handful of militiamen volley fired. As they reloaded, the enemy began to pour a hail of automatic weapon fire upon them. Two kids screamed as 9mm bullets connected with their bodies. Robby could not turn to check on them. He just kept firing, levering, and firing his rifle at the onrushing enemy. His hammer dropped on an empty chamber and he fumbled in the right pocket of his jacket for his remaining .35 caliber cartridges. The concussion from an exploding hand grenade knocked Robby to the floor of the trench. He could hear nothing save the ringing in his ears, but he smelled the damp earth into which his face pressed. Someone stepped on his back and another on his leg. His hearing began to return. His hand flailed for his weapon unsuccessfully.

He rolled over and saw a figure kneeling on the crown of his trench. Another star shell burst and transformed the silhouette into a darkly clad teen. The Colbert was firing automatic bursts from a long shoulder arm. Surreally, Robby recognized the weapon from the old war movies he watched at Captain Jacks. Scared that the boy would see him, Robby froze. He watched as the boy ejected a magazine, pouched it, and then withdrew another and inserted it in his weapon's magazine well. The automatic rifleman stood, stepped back, and then leapt over the trench. Robby just lay there listening to the cries and moans of his friends.

Ben Smith's southern perimeter forces were receiving a heavy volume of small arms fire from what was left of the shot-up Colbert Western Militia in front of him, but he ordered every third man to form three fire teams to address the breakthroughs from the east. His soldiers were engaged immediately. The action deteriorated into hand-to-hand combat in some instances. Ben moved to Slingshot 7's Humvee and yelled up to the gunner, "Son, why aren't you firing?"

"I'm out of .50 cal', sir."

The gunner pulled his M16A4 up from the interior, spun his Ma Deuce to the rear, and leaned forward assuming a firing position. Ben rushed to the back of the vehicle's earthen bay, and then slipped along its side to crawl up on the front berm. He went prone with his bullpup 5.56mm assault carbine and joined the gunner in his search for targets of opportunity.

From behind and to the left, Ben heard the gunman comment, "You're pretty spry for your age, Mr. Smith!"

The old warrior growled in response, "Shut up, smartass, and don't accidently shoot me in the back of the head."

After being waved through by sentries in the west, Slingshot 8 covered the last few hundred yards to the bridgehead at breakneck speed. They careened over the last little hill, going slightly airborne. 1911, Harry, and Jenny took the landing pretty well. Jenny saw it coming, locked her gun mount, and grasped the sides of the ring mount with her gloved hands. She managed to move with the jolt pretty well — absorbing the impact. Inside, Harry and 1911 incurred a good jostling but no injuries.

Harry quickly assessed the dire situation on the perimeter. He yelled, "Jenny, shoot anything in black. Mort, swing around to the right of Slingshot 7's Humvee and get us in the thick of it."

Jenny was frustrated trying to select a target for her 7.62 MG that would not compromise a khaki-uniformed Lauderdale. Finally, a three-Knight element to the right was in her sights. She fired a long burst, missing at first, and then walking the rounds into the cluster. The FMJs tore the Knights apart.

1911 sped by Slingshot 7's bay giving Ben Smith and the gunner a heads-up wave. Harry had his LLSR-10 at the ready. Jenny cut more Knights down in front of them. Harry glanced back and saw Slingshot 5 entering the bridgehead. 1911 slowed the Humvee down as they got within 50 or so yards of the breastworks.

Harry yelled, "This is close enough, Mort. Jenny, get your AKM and come with me."

Before they left Sheffield, Clara had handed Jenny an AK mag-carrier complete with a universal pistol holster. She had strapped it on during the passage through the reservation. Now her assault rifle magazines, loaded pistol, and its spare magazine were fully secured and at the ready. She came down and out of the Humvee in seconds grabbing her AKM along the way.

Harry commanded, "Mort, man the MG and shoot till the ammo's gone."

"Gotcha, Harry."

Harry leapt out to join Jenny. "C'mon, girl!"

They sprinted towards the eastern defensive positions. A round or two whizzed by them on the way. Mort provided covering fire as they reached the main trench. Harry hand-signaled Jenny to clear the right end of the trench as he cleared the left. They jumped down in the hundred-yard trench to find Knights in both directions distracted with everything from finishing off wounded Lauderdales to tending the wounds of their buddies. Oblivious to the deadly couple's presence, the Knights were shocked to find themselves being shot.

Neither weapon was selective-fire, but in their highly trained hands, semi-auto was the option of choice.

Jenny killed at least a dozen Colberts, double or triple-tapping them on her way to the south end of the trench. She recognized some. She even liked a couple of them. Her section snaked along with two blind curves; she ambidextrously passed her AK from one shoulder to the other as she cleared the trench. Harry killed half that number in his beeline to the north end of the trench. He recognized the bodies of his first cousin and at least a dozen other members of Slingshot 7 along his gruesome path. At the end, he stepped up to look back into the perimeter. Clara had deployed her tactical team and things appeared to be under control.

Danny and Edward climbed to the top of their hard-won earthworks. A moment earlier they would have seen victory in their grasp. Now they peered over the breastwork to find Slingshot vehicles tearing about the bridgehead. Also, an LMTV pulled right up to the perimeter a hundred yards to the south of his position and disgorged a couple of dozen Lauderdale militiamen. His command team Knights prepared to fire at them, but Danny had them hold off so as to not announce the command team's presence.

Danny looked back to the East and by the light of yet another Lauderdale star shell, he could see, dishearteningly, that his two infantry companies were still a couple of hundred yards away. Edward tapped his shoulder and pointed to the northeast. Danny saw the platoon of Junior Knights approaching after their successful breeching of the defenses nearest the river.

"Eddie, we have to retreat and hit them again as soon as that last company of Western Militia arrive. Shit, I'm gonna pull all but a single squad from guarding the dam as well."

"Are you sure, Danny? I mean ... we are so close!"

"Yeah, Eddie. The Lauderdales still have control of the perimeter and most of our Knights are dead. The militia will be slaughtered. I didn't count on those big-ass flares turning night into day, and the militia were not following closely enough."

"Okay, Danny. How do we handle it?"

"Stay here and have Knight Harper whistle retreat until you see that the militia has turned back. I'm going over there to those Junior Knights and talk to Smokin' Joe about having his kids cover our withdrawal. I think it will be best if the command team and any remaining Knights head back along the river with those kids."

"I gotcha, Danny."

Unable to find his rifle, Robby pulled the stainless .38 from his coat pocket and crawled south along the floor of the ditch. He passed several lifeless bodies in search of Camille Ledlow. He recognized her voice weakly calling for help from the darkness before him.

An exploding star shell momentarily lit the recesses of the trench and Robby recognized the faces of Mickey Sarnes and Brett Haley before him. Obviously dead, the two friends' noggins now touched and their bodies sprawled along the feet of the trench walls, sandwiching Robby. He gently separated the heads and squeezed between them. Seeing the dead friends made him think of his friend Brud. He remembered that Brud was at the other end of the trench when they jumped in earlier. Robby hated to think of what may have happened to him, so he didn't.

Before the light faded, Robby came upon Camille. She was sitting upright with her back to the eastern wall of the trench. Her legs were crossed, Indian-style, and one of her schoolmate's shoulders and head rested in her lap.

"Robby, she's dead. Sibby is dead. What are we gonna do, Robby? Everybody is dead."

"I know, sweetie. I know," whispered Robby as he gently squeezed her arm. "Listen girl. Are you injured?"

"No, I don't think so. I played dead after those boys tromped through shooting everybody."

"Well, that's good, darlin'. Real good. I want you to lie back down and play dead again. I'm gonna cover you with your friend, and you just don't move. Okay?"

"Okay, Robby. Where are you going?"

"Don't you worry — I'm going for help. Alright?"

She drew into a fetal position facing the eastern side of the trench and Robby slid Sibby's body next to Camille. He placed Sibby's bloody arm over Camille's upper arm and pushed Sibby's hand down between Camille and the wall.

After a final pat of her shoulder, Robby whispered to Camille, "Not a word. Not a sound."

He continued to crawl towards the end of the trench. He was glad he passed a few dead Colberts along the way. At least his charge had given back some of what they got. He was sure he hit two or even three of the Knights with his rifle as they had emerged from the riverbank's foliage.

It was damp and somewhat muddy along the floor of the trench, but there weren't any puddles of water. Robby suddenly wondered why his side was soaking wet. As the next pyrotechnic went off, he touched his right side, felt the liquid and brought it back to view. It was red. He realized he was bleeding, heavily. Hurting in so many places, he hadn't distinguished the dull ache in his side until this point.

Robby heard voices coming from beyond the end of the trench. He cautiously eased to the crest of the trench's entrance and peeked to the south. A couple of dozen teenaged Colberts had all grabbed a knee and were attentively listening to two men standing in front of them. Robby listened intently trying to hear the speakers. The gunfire and explosions in the perimeter indicated heavy fighting.

The gunfire briefly lulled, and Robby heard the speaker say, "Now, boys, I know y'all want to keep mixin' it up, and we will again in a couple of hours, but right now we need to escort the

Constable and his command team back out the way we came. Constable Ragland, would you like to add anything, sir?"

The other man spoke up, "That's right, Mr. Joe. I'm very proud of these young warriors for what they've accomplished here tonight, but we are going to withdraw and strike them again at dawn. They have gained a tactical advantage at the moment, and incurring any further losses would be foolish right now."

One of the youngsters towards the front began to address the two men, but Robby could not make out what he was saying. Suddenly, a feeling of light-headedness came over him. He started to slide back down in the trench and play dead like Camille. Adrenalin raced through his body as the injury to his side fired a sharp pain. He had to stifle a scream. It passed after a few seconds. With his back pressed against the sloping entrance, the boy from Florence felt a combination of fatality, anger, and resolve. Robby repositioned the little revolver in his hand, rolled over to all fours, and thrust up and out of the trench to complete his new self-assigned mission — killing Danny Ragland.

It was only a distance of 50 feet or so. None of the enemy could react fast enough to stop him. Robby dodged over and around the kneeling young Knights.

Nim flashed into his mind, *That's a nice piece, Kid. Just remember — never show up at a rifle fight with just a handgun, but if push comes to shove, stick it in their gut or face and let 'er rip!*

Robby wasn't really sure which back-lit figure was the Constable, so from a distance that narrowed from ten to three feet over a couple of seconds, he put two of his cylinder's five rounds in the shorter silhouette and three in the taller.

Constable Ragland's bodyguards riddled Robby with 5.56 projectiles. Robby hadn't noticed the pair of bookends, nor perceived he was being shot until his severed spine stole his legs. His finger continued to double-action on spent primers — *click, click, click.* Robby's momentum carried him into a collision with the taller man. Tangled together, they tumbled along on the ground for a few yards then separated. Robby's roll stopped with his face to the sky. He watched a star shell flicker out.

Jenny Hart had sprinted back along the trench to join Harry. They heard a Colbert whistle, and Jenny grabbed his arm. "Harry, that's retreat! They are sounding retreat!"

But Harry's blood was up. "Hey, I saw a couple of Knights, just for a second, up at the top of this breastwork. Let's ease up to the corner of this berm and see if we can catch some of 'em jack-rabbittin'."

"Yes, sir."

As they moved along the back of the breastwork, Clara Smith and Ruff Creasy joined them. Jenny led the way. Just as they reached the end of the berm, she spotted the Junior Knight platoon to the north. They seemed to be uncharacteristically milling about.

She halted her group, "Harry the Tuscumbia Junior Knights are over there about 50 yards to the northeast."

Without hesitation, Harry commanded, "C'mon Clara, let's spread out a little and all take this corner at the same time. That star shell just went up. Me, Clara, and Jenny will fire on the Knights. Ruff, you keep moving all the way around to the face of this breastwork and make sure we don't get blindsided."

The ladies nodded, and Ruff said, "Yes, sir."

Harry, Clara, and Jenny took out several of the Junior Knights before they could flee into the darkness. Ruff broke around the berm and caught a Colbert militiaman taking 'giant-steps' down the face of the berm. No doubt, he was headed for the woods to the east. They were only a few yards apart and the Colbert glanced towards Ruff just as the Lauderdale fired his M16. The Colbert began to lose his footing as he took hits but managed to swing his weapon up and fire at Ruff, pistol-style, with one hand. The Colbert's burst of automatic weapons fire put several bullets through Ruff's torso and one clipped his neck. He collapsed and began to slide and roll down the face of the steep breastwork right along with the militiaman.

The two ended up at the bottom of the dirt mound on their sides a few feet across from one another. Neither had their weapon in hand, but they could both see that the other was alive.

Ted Creasy recognized Ruff first, "Hey, Cloverdale. It's been a long time, cuz."

Ruff replied, "Well, I'll be damned. Hey, yerself, Spring Valley."

"If this ain't a goddamned cluster, I don't know what is."

"You got that right." After a few pain filled seconds, Ruff corrected, "Actually, I ain't lived in Cloverdale since 63. Daddy moved us to east Florence … 'cause of a job. How're your folks, Ted?"

"Aw, hell, Daddy died of the cancer in 66, but Momma still lives in the same ol' place."

"Damn, I use to love those visits with y'all back durin' The Peace."

"Absolutely, weren't we some little hellions — just tearin' about them hills and hollers?"

"Yep. Those were some good times. Good times, indeed."

The star shell burned out. It was a step away from pitch-black at the base of their dirt slope.

A female voice could be heard from up above, "Ruff, you down there? Hey, Ruff, are you hit?"

From the dark, Ted teased, "Yer girlfriend's callin' ya, Cloverdale."

"Fuck you, Spring Valley. That's my boss, Captain Clara Smith."

"The Slingshot Clara Smith?"

"One and the same, Bubba."

"Well at least I'm goin' out with class — killed by a Slingshot Team Member. Which number?"

"Five. What outfit are you in, Ted?"

"Aw, I was the spotter on uh two-man sniper team. Ya' might say we were floaters."

"Were?"

"Well, my sniper, Jimmy Putnam, was hit yesterday. He died last night."

"Aw, man. You don't mean Jimmy Putnam from Spring Valley do ya'? He used to hang around with us. That little squirt was yer sniper?"

"Hey, he was the best."

"I do recall he was a squirrel killin' son of a bitch with an air rifle."

"Yep." Changing the subject, Ted asked, "Hey, Ruff, are yer folks still livin'? Gawd, I used to love the cakes and pies your Momma would bring when y'all visited."

After getting no response for a time, Ted called once more, "Ruff?"

A few seconds later, the next star shell ignited, and Ted saw a Slingshot-uniformed woman kneeling over his cousin performing CPR. He closed his eyes and faded away to images of a distant, sultry August day; Ruff Creasy was swinging out over Little Bear Creek on a rope then letting go to cannonball into the cold water. Ted and Jimmy Putnam laughed in sheer delight from the creek bank.

Danny Ragland died just after four in the morning. He was in his command tent close to Wilson Dam with his cousin Edward at his side. Edward grasped his hand tightly at the end and felt the life pass. He moved the hand to his cousin's bandaged chest, released it, arose, and departed the tent. Every remaining Knight must have been standing outside the tent including the Junior Knights.

Edward asked, "Who is my ranking Knight now?"

"I am, Mr. Ragland."

"Well, Knight First Class Martin, give me the report."

"Sir, there are 22 Knights still standing including myself. My subordinates are Knights Second Class Ferguson and Claggett; Knights Third Class Dobbs, Brody, Hewitt, and Jackson; and the sixteen remaining are Knight Sergeants. We have 26 of the Junior Knights present. Smokin' Joe died while his boys and girls were carrying him back."

"Claggett? Knight Claggett!"

"Yes, sir. Juanita Claggett, here."

"Juanita, one of the men we lost the first evening was a Claggett. He was manning one of our bunkers … I think."

"Yes, Mr. Ragland, that was my little brother."

"Your little brother?"

"Yes, sir."

"How many of the rest of you have lost a brother or sister to the Lauderdales? C'mon, raise your hands, Junior Knights as well. Good, how about cousins, moms, dads, aunts, and uncles? That's right. Hell, I bet some of you have even lost a grandparent."

Most of the Knights had their hands raised now.

"Alright then, who is ready for some payback?"

Now, all the hands were up. Edward raised his as well.

"Good, put 'em down. Martin, has the last militia company from Wheeler arrived?"

"Yes, sir. They are resting after marching all night."

"Well, they are going to have to rest quickly. We're gonna attack again at six o'clock. Have my two bridgehead battalion commanders and their company commanders meet me in the Constable's tent at five including you, Ferguson, and Claggett."

"Yes, sir."

"Oh, Martin, what were the militia's losses from the bridgehead assault?"

"They had not engaged, sir. We caught them in time. Just a handful."

"Good. Are the Constable's staff members here yet?"

"Yes, sir. It's the tent with the blue trim — right there, sir." He pointed out the staff tent. "They should be receiving the action reports from all battle fronts shortly, sir."

"Good. Y'all are dismissed."

Edward turned to the command tent to find Danny's aide waiting with a tray.

"Henderson, is that coffee?"

"Yes, Mr. Ragland. Colbert's best ever. And some bacon and eggs, sir?"

" Well, Henderson. I have no appetite, but I'd love the coffee."

They walked in the command tent and Henderson said, "Sir, we'll move the late Constable's body out shortly."

Edward paused a few seconds, and said, "No, Henderson. Leave my cousin Danny right there."

During your staff briefing, sir?"

"Absolutely, perhaps it will inspire those militia commanders."

After pouring the coffee, Henderson asked, "Anything else, Mr. Ragland."

"Yes, is Johnny Montjoy handy?"

"Yes, sir. He couldn't sleep. I took him some coffee a half-hour ago."

"Good, will you have him come see me immediately."

"Immediately. Yes, sir."

Harry and 1911 lifted Robby's body, placed it on a litter, and began to carry him towards the bridge.

1911 said, "Those fuckers shot him to pieces, huh Harry?"

"Yep. Is there a body wagon up on the bridge or is it at the field hospital?"

"Both. There're two, Harry."

"Oh," Harry said solemnly and maintained their original course.

As he walked in the cold darkness, Harry kept seeing the fresh young faces of Robby's orphans. What a miscalculation. He thought at most the kids might be called up to the perimeter to fire a few shots at another of the half-hearted assaults from the exhausted and depleted Colbert militia to the south. *My, God!* he thought. *One little girl.* "The only survivor was one 14-year-old Girl."

"What's that?" asked Mort as he limped along on his arthritic knees.

Harry didn't realize he must have verbalized the last few words. "Nothing, Mort. I was just thinking out loud."

"I thought you said 'Girl' and wondered if you were talking about that gal that we found playing dead in the trench."

"Well, yeah."

"You know, Harry, her name is Camille Ledlow. She is the daughter of John and Birdie Ledlow. You remember them, don't ya', Harry."

Harry's toe caught a rock and he stumbled a little. Fighting to maintain his balance with the weight of the corpse. He grimaced and fought off the pull of gravity, stopped for a moment, adjusted his grasps, and stepped off again.

"Dammit, Harry, you can stop and rest a minute, son." That was something he hadn't called Harry Smith in years.

Harry liked hearing it. It brought memories of lighter days in happier times. "No, that's okay, Mort. I'm fine."

"Anyway, then, that John Ledlow ran the bar down on Mobile Street. You remember him, now, don't ya' Harry."

Harry focused out of respect and affection for his old friend and soldier. "Uh, yeah, I remember the Ledlows. They were both killed in the Three Day War."

There was silence for a few moments, and then Mort said, "Crap, that war made a lot of orphans."

Harry couldn't respond. He just kept walking.

A former girlfriend of Harry's, a nurse named Elizabeth Hughes, ran over to Harry and 1911. She said, "Harry, I was taking a smoke for just a minute and saw you two. I just had to let you know that the doctor says that Chester Hayes should make a full recovery. Captain Hayes has awakened from his concussion and his shoulder wound was a clean shot … straight through."

Harry stopped with his burden for just a moment, gazed at her blood smeared but beautiful face, and leaned over to exchange busses. "Thanks, Liz. You doin' okay, Honey?"

"I'm holdin' up okay, Harry. That Colbert tobacco certainly helped. Somebody took a pack of cigarettes off of a dead Knight and passed 'em around." Her wedding ring glinted as she flicked a wayward strand of hair from her eyes — then tucked it back up under her surgical cap. "Is that poor little, Robby?"

"Yep."

"Oh, my God. What a sweet kid! I'm sorry, Harry. Very sorry." After a pause and sweet smile to both men, she touched the back of Harry's hand and said, "Well, I gotta get back. Bye-bye, Y'all."

"Bye, darlin'," said Harry as he stepped off again.

After she was out of earshot, 1911 said, "Shit, Harry, that's one good woman... an' cute, too. What were you thinkin' … breakin' up with her?"

Harry plodded on towards the bridge and answered, "I wasn't, I guess. As usual."

At the body wagon, Harry's stomach turned as he saw all the bodies neatly stacked in the wagon.

"Got one more, there, President Smith?" asked the driver of the wagon. "I'll take him, sir."

"No, I'll do it, Huey."

Huey could tell by his leader's tone, that it was best he stand clear.

Harry lifted the boy up and over the sideboard, but did not lay him flat. He stepped up on the tire and carefully arranged Robby in a sitting position. He propped Robby's head up with it facing east. Harry rubbed away some of the dirt and blood from the boy's face. He tousled the boy's hair like they had all done so many times before. They would tease him and say that it brought the team good luck. He would act annoyed. Harry smiled at the images and stepped down.

"I'll take good care of him, President Smith. I promise."

"Thanks, Huey, but be sure he stays sitting up like that. He always said he wanted to look out over the river while crossing one of the bridges. We came over after dark the first night. Will he catch the sunrise?"

"Yes, sir. I won't be headin' back until first light."

1911 blurted out, "Well, lookie here!"

Harry and Huey looked at 1911 and turned to the direction he was gesturing. Emerging from the murky light of the oil lamps strung along the Singing River Bridge was a sizeable column of foot soldiers.

Harry stood in awe; all his reserves were committed. He walked off towards the unidentified Lauderdales. Harry closed the distance, but he still couldn't see the end of the column. He thought, *There must be a couple of hundred or more!*

He was only a few yards from the marchers when he recognized the faces of Arthur Canterbury and Eli Stram. Other familiar visages appeared as well after he closed to hand-shaking distance. The entire group consisted of old men carrying longbows. It dawned on him just what this group was.

The Ecumenical Archers were a group of older Lauderdale churchmen, both Low and High. They began decades ago with friendly yet competitive archery matches serving as a lure. The men would have an opening and closing prayer but purposely made the archery their focus; thus, avoiding petty squabbles or heated disagreements over differences in their disparate forms of worship.

As such things go with the games of the male gender, firm rules were tweaked and hammered into a set. These rules were followed like biblical verse. Not to rob the state of any strategic resources, they prided themselves on using handmade longbows of yew or Osage orange. The shafts of their arrows were carefully turned from yellow cedar or maple. Those unblessed with the skills of handicraft, clustered around anointed teammates that could build a proper longbow and arrows, or those with deeper pockets, or simply more dedication, traded with a handful of professional bow makers.

Ironically, the most esteemed bows were those of a Colbert tradesman. During The Peace, many the Lauderdale archer crossed the river, converted precious barter for Colbert credits, and bee-lined it to Pipe Marston's place on Hawk Pride Mountain. The old master-of-his-trade died one morning while working in his shop the week before the Three Day War. Some say he was in is his nineties. A rookie Ecumenical Archer might question the high asking-barter for a Marston longbow; that is, until he loosed an arrow from one.

Stram and Canterbury proudly stood before their young president with Marston Bows in their left hands and heavy quivers of arrows belted at their strong-hand sides. Eli reached out and shook Harry's hand. "Hi, Harry. God bless ya', son."

"Hello, Brother Eli, and God bless you, sir."

Arthur Canterbury was waiting with an extended hand as well. "Hello, Harry. The Archers are at your disposal."

Harry smiled and wiped the moisture from his eyes. After gathering his emotions and processing their courageous offer, Harry said, "Gentlemen, I'm honored. Dang it, I'm humbled. But I just can't let y'all cross; the risk is too great."

Arthur countered, "Harry, c'mon now. Just let us over and we'll—"

"No, Reverend Canterbury, no. Your bows against their guns will be too much of a mismatch. I know you men are good. Hell, I've … pardon, me…I've seen y'all shoot. I've joined in your matches a couple of times, much to my personal humiliation. Y'all are extraordinary archers, but you could be slaughtered come the mornin'."

Eli firmly interjected, "Now, Harry. You haven't heard us out. We have come up with somethin' that may be of great service to you and our troops. Let us come over and Arthur and I will explain it … tell you of our plan. Whatdaya say, Harry?"

Harry scanned the eager faces of the old men. Scores of them he had known and loved since his earliest memories. They were pillars of the community and friends of his father. Relenting, he leaned in to Stram and Canterbury, and quietly said, "Okay, gentlemen. I'll hear y'all out, but first I need to address all of you right here. My medics and your chaplains are working overtime back there at the bridgehead. We have suffered a costly pre-dawn attack. Many of the men I see here have members of their younger generations stacked in body wagons and laid on the road behind me. I need to tell them what transpired here tonight and prepare them for the sight of the dead and dying."

Arthur said, "Thank you, Harry. That's wise. We'll call everyone up in to earshot."

After Arthur directed the columns of archers to come forward, Harry asked Eli, "Brother Eli, just how many folks do you have?"

Eli laughed and proudly announced, "Brother Smith, we are 331 strong."

Harry smiled but was too moved to say anything. He was confused when one of the archers said, "Best Feast, Harry!"

Seeing Harry's expression, Eli asked, "You've lost track of your days haven't ya', Harry?"

"Yes, sir. I guess I have."

"Yes, Harry, its Friday morning — the third Friday of November. Forty-four years ago, your father and Little Charles signed the Treaty of 26 - the beginning of The Peace."

Harry thought, *Spared Territory Day and the Feast of Peace.* The irony was poignant.

Harry's attention turned to Reverend Canterbury.

The old High Church minister stood on the top of a handcart, and announced, "Archers, listen up. President Smith wants to bring us up to speed on the situation here. Harry?"

Shivering in the pre-dawn cold, Tassy heard the sound of approaching vehicles above the hum of her generator. The vehicles stopped in front of her house. They shut their engines down.

After a few seconds, she recognized the voice of Bedford Smith calling out, "Tassy! Tassy Williams, are you out there somewhere?"

"Yes, Captain! We're here."

"Thank, God! Stay where you are. We'll come to you."

"Hold up, Captain! We had to shoot some Black Force folks back in here. I'm not sure they are all dead. I've been hearing the one by our apple tree moaning for the past hour." After no response for a few seconds, Tassy added, "Here, Cap'n Bed, you might want to shield your eyes. I'm gonna hit the floods again."

"Okay, Tassy, we're ready."

After the floodlights washed the garden, Tassy and Little Mike, now awake, watched members of Slingshot Tactical Team 6 work the garden.

Captain Smith called out, "Okay, Tassy, you can come down now. We got 'em covered."

Tassy looked back and saw that Wade was fast asleep under the bench. She took Mike's hand in her left and grasped her SMLE in her right. Little Mike carried the shotgun in his left hand. They stepped over the little stone wall and walked down to join Captain Smith and his team.

District Leader David Smith's son greeted her. "Damn, Tassy Girl! You got all three of 'em!"

"They all dead?"

"Yes, ma'am. Well, sorta, this one is still hanging on," and Bed pointed to the base of the apple tree. "Tassy, where did y'all get these flood lights?"

"Oh, those? Michael and I found 'em on one of our hoard hunts."

"If that don't beat all! Huh, Guys?"

Nods and chuckles came from the surrounding tactical team.

Tassy led Mike around to the front of the tree and saw the victim of Little Mike's shotgun blast. He was sitting upright with his back to the tree and legs spread out in front of him. It appeared that four of the .33-caliber 00 buckshot had caught him: neck, chest, abdomen, and bicep. The Knight's AK lay off a few feet to his right where a Slingshot had kicked it.

The Knight opened his eyes and winced at the light. His eyes widened with obvious surprise as he viewed Tassy and Little Mike standing in front of him. After coughing a bit of blood to clear his throat, he asked, "Did you shoot me, Lady?"

"No, my boy did."

The dying man's eyes shifted to the child.

"Hell, I been killed by a little kid. How old are you, son?"

"I'm eight, sir."

"That was a good shot. My boy would be about your age."

Tassy sternly inquired, "About? Don't ya' know for sure?"

"Well, I ain't seen him in years. His momma up and run off with a merchant from Town Creek years ago. She took the boy. I've lost track."

Softening, she empathized, "That was sorry of her — I reckon."

"Well, I don't know. I can't say as I blame her much. The life of a Knight's wife can be a rough one, especially, if they're married to an unfaithful SOB. Oh, sorry, son."

"That's okay. He's heard worse. What's your name, Knight?"

"Caleb, ma'am. Caleb Houston Brown to be exact. I heard them callin' 'Tassy' a minute ago. Where's yer ol' man, Tassy?"

"He's in the Cavalry off fightin' the Lord-knows-where somewhere on your side of the river."

"I hope he makes it home, Tassy."

Deeply moved, Tassy asked, "Would you like for us to pray with you, Caleb?"

"That would be nice, Tassy. I'd appreciate that."

Tassy and her son laid their weapons on the ground and stepped towards Caleb.

Bedford moved to stop the mother and son, but he could see that Tassy was determined. Bedford eased back out of their way while darting cautioning glances to his nearby teammates. They cinched up their gun-holds on the Colbert.

After they knelt at his sides, Tassy held Caleb's left hand and Little Mike grasped his right.

She closed her eyes and bowed her head. "Lord Jesus, thank you for watching over my boys and me and sparing us for another day in your service. Be with Brother Caleb here and forgive him of any sins he may have committed in weaker moments. I pray that some glorious day he can reunite with his son in Heaven. Now, Lord Jesus, please let him pass quickly to ease his pain and suffering. Amen."

A couple of long minutes later, Caleb stopped breathing.

Tassy released his hand, but while still staring at his lifeless, bloody face, she calmly said, "Cap'n Bed, I think you'll find 'Ol Joe and Cam down by the river — not far to the southeast."

Major Donna Flurry dismissed her staff after their 5:00 A.M. briefing. Sergeant Annie Slocomb lingered after the other women departed. She walked over behind her commander and started massaging her shoulders and neck.

"Darlin' did you sleep any?"

"Oh, Annie, I don't know. I might've dozed a little at one time or the other."

"It sure has been quiet at the bridgehead for the past couple of hours."

"Scary, huh?"

"Actually, the whole front."

"No probes or anything?"

"Yes, ma'am. Nuthin' but that gunfire during their assault on the perimeter."

"Annie, do you think they might have pulled some of their people from our sector to strike somewhere else? They seem obsessed with the bridgehead. I know the obvious reason would be to cut off our connecting route to Lauderdale ... but really ... Harry has turned it into a fortress. It's a hard nut to crack."

"It sounds like they came close though, Donna. I dread seeing those morning reports. Frankly, if they hit us with a couple of their battalions, right now, here in Sheffield, they could drive us back to O'Neal Bridge."

"True enou—Damn, girl, that's the spot. Mm, yep, right there."

"God, I miss you, Donna."

"What the Hell. We're together 24-7, Annie."

"You know what I mean, Babe."

"Yeah, I know what you mean. I'm being obtuse on purpose. I'm sorry."

Annie abruptly stopped the massage, and moved in front of Donna's little folding field desk. "Will that be all, Major?"

"Look, Annie. I said, 'I'm sorry'. Don't be mad."

"I'm not mad. I gotta get after these bitches or they'll go to sleep on us."

"Shit, it's quiet. Let 'em sleep if they want to."

"Very well, ma'am. If there's nothing else, I'll go tuck 'em in." She stood at attention and saluted.

Donna stood, and barked, "Yes, Sergeant Slocomb, that will be all. Dismissed."

Annie stubbornly waited. Donna finally answered her salute. Annie snapped her hand down to her hip, performed a flawless about face, and exited the Slingshot 2 command tent.

Privates Deb Romine and Judy Kelly were sitting cross-legged on a tarp cleaning their M16A4 rifles. They watched Annie slap the door flap closed and stomp away. The soldiers looked at each other and giggled.

"Lovers' quarrel?"

"War is hell."

Their giggles turned to laughter.

"Harry, there's a Colbert up on Reservation Road, at the edge of the eastern perimeter."

"Well, shoot his ass, Clara! What the fuck?" Stram and Canterbury had just departed Harry's tent, after a lengthy debate that ended with him granting them the right to stay and fight. He was exhausted, worried, and depressed. Cranky felt good.

Knowing her cousin all too well, she knew it was best to throw it right back, and responded, "He's under a white flag, Asshole."

"Oh."

"Yeah, 'Oh' is right. I haven't seen him myself, but the militia runner's description of him makes me think it's Johnny Montjoy."

Harry popped up. "Johnny Montjoy? Maybe they finally want to talk some reason."

She shrugged, "Do you want me to go find Daddy?"

"Yes. I'll head on up there and wait on the two of you. We'll go out and talk to him together."

A few minutes later, Harry, Ben, and Clara walked out to meet with Johnny Montjoy.

Johnny began, "Once again, President Smith, I wish the circumstances were different."

"As do I, Mr. Montjoy. What word do you bring from the Raglands?"

"Withdraw."

"You or us."

"Come now, Mr. President, your defenses were breeched in the wee hours, and if not for a lack of timing on our part, you would have found yourself in the river. Hell, Harry, negotiate, agree to pay some symbolic reparations, and withdraw. Both armies have suffered horrible losses. You have made your point. You and your Lauderdales can still hold your heads high."

"Who sent you?"

Strategically lying, Johnny answered, "The Constable."

"The Constable? I tell ya' what, Johnny. Go back and tell Danny Ragland that he can come kill me and sell my bones. How's that for some goddamn reparations?"

"Harry!"

"No, you've delivered your message. You've done your job. Don't come back, Johnny. There's no need."

Catherine was awakened by a knock at the study's door. She looked up to find her parents sound asleep, her mother curled up on the couch in an afghan and her father asleep in his corner recliner. She went to the door and softly asked, "Collins, is that you?"

"Yes, ma'am."

She opened the door and stepped out pressing her finger to her lips then she closed the door and moved a few feet away from the study.

"Sorry, to wake you, Miss Catherine, but a courier just brought this sealed message from the dam." He handed her a simple beige envelope.

Catherine recognized the hand on the front as that of her brother's. "Thank you, Collins, that will be all."

"Yes, ma'am."

She slit the seam of the envelope with her perfectly manicured thumbnail, removed the note inside, and read of her cousin's death. She looked up and about the Grand Foyer. She was reminded of a colorful little beetle she once dropped in her kill jar while completing a "bug collection" for high school biology. It seemed so alone and pitiful in the relatively large space. Before the acetone had taken effect, she impulsively turned the jar upside down and shook the insect free. It fell for a few inches, engaged its stubby little wings, and buzzed to freedom. She wished someone could turn the Grand Foyer upside down and shake her free.

Catherine numbly returned to the study-door and eased it open. After slipping in and returning to the loveseat, she wondered how to share this news with her father. She glanced at his peaceful countenance, and decided there was no rush. After reading the note once more, Catherine put her face in her hands and began to quietly cry.

Now twilight, Harry asked 1911, " Did I hear vehicles to the south?"

"Yes, sir. Clara went to the southern perimeter to check it out. After she got back, she said it was either trucks or buses on 2nd Street. They were probably unloading some more Colberts from Tuscumbia or the like."

"What's goin' on out there, Mort?" asked Harry, gesturing at their operational tents in the center of the bridgehead.

"It's quiet on the battle lines. Most of our folks have walked over to the mess tent and are in line for short rations and chicory."

Harry rose and exited his tent. He quietly approached a cluster of his commanders. Hoping to gauge their attitude, he stopped to listen a moment.

He heard Scooter say, "Over 200 lost last night. Damn! At this point, I imagine they have us three-to-one here at the bridgehead — even counting those stick-shootin' old men."

Ben Smith, referring to the enemy, added, "And at least half of 'em are fresh."

Clara responded, "Oh, Daddy. If we only had a tenth of those able bodied men and women asleep north of the river."

Harry darted past them and in two leaping steps he stood atop the torn remains of Slingshot 8. Almost yelling, so that the few-hundred breakfasters could hear him, he asked, "Who wants more help from north of the river? Clara?" He pointed to her and smiled affectionately. "No, girl. If we gotta die, there's enough of us, and if we live, the greater the honor. I didn't undertake this war to gain wealth or power. Those mean little to me. But if it is a sin to covet honor, I am guilty. No, cuz, have faith. Don't wish for one more from Lauderdale. As a matter of fact, I'll provide transportation across the bridge for anyone who has lost his or her stomach for this fight. Let 'em go with my blessings. We'd rather not die with them if they are scared to die with us."

Harry had been pivoting as he spoke. Abruptly, he stopped, facing the red dawn and rising sun to the east. "Earlier, I almost forgot this is Spared Territory Day. Y'all that survive this fight, and return to your homes will stand proud on each anniversary of this celebration. As you grow old, your loved ones will annually sit at the Feast of Peace with your neighbors, and when this victory crops up in the dinner conversation, you can pull up your sleeve and proudly show your scars. Your grandchildren's eyes will grow wide as they ask, 'You got those on ST Day?' You'll forget a lot in your life but not today. In your mind, you will see the faces of those that fought and died by your side. Also, you'll remember the names: Harry, Clara, and Ben Smith; Hayes, Fuqua, Flurry, and Juarez. You good men and women will tell your children this story, and we'll be remembered to the end of time. We will be a family. I guarantee that those who fight with me today, even the sorry lowlifes among you" — Harry paused and cast a sarcastic grin about the listeners — "will always be my brother or sister. And any Lauderdale all cozy in bed at this moment will cringe when anyone says, 'I fought on ST Day'!"

As a cheer arose from the assembly, Gunfire rang out from the east.

"That's the skirmishers!" hollered Clara, "We better get ready!"

Harry exclaimed, "We're ready, if our minds are, Clara!"

"To hell with the Lauderdale whose mind isn't ready now!"

"You don't want any more help from Lauderdale, cuz?"

"Dammit, Harry, you and I alone could fight this battle!"

Laughter and hoorahs erupted.

Harry shouted, "You know your places! God Bless you!"

Edward Ragland double-timed along the rocky fishing area below the dam. He jogged with two depleted companies of Colbert Militia spearheaded by the Junior Knights. Two similar companies and about half the surviving Knights commanded by Knight Martin advanced through the woods along the north side of Reservation Road. The other half of the Knights under Knight Claggett held with what was left of the Colbert Militia battalions south of the perimeter. She had received another company of militiamen around four o'clock. They were pulled from the defensive line north of Tuscumbia and bused over to Muscle Shoals. Her force numbered around 300. She was to attack from the south after Ragland and Martin reached the eastern side of the bridgehead perimeter.

The Lauderdale advance skirmishers took out a couple of Edward's lead Knights and then fled for their perimeter defenses. Edward did not let his charges slow down in the least. He just raced up to the head of the force and waved for them to follow. Edward shunned rifles; he was armed with Danny's polymer framed 9mm in his right hand. Before the assault started, Edward had strung a command whistle around his neck. The prior owner no longer had a use for it. He blew shrill attack commands vigorously as he accelerated their advance to a run. The sun was now well over the horizon to their backs. Edward laughed to think of the Lauderdales trying to draw sight pictures into the blinding glare.

Arthur Canterbury took his company of High Church Archers to a sloping area just to the east of the bridge's approach. Eli Stram had his third-again-as-large group of Low Church Archers at the southeast corner of the perimeter. They would be directly behind Harry's command parapet in that same corner. Harry wanted the Low Church archers to have the option to lob arrows to either the east or south as needed. Eli had divided his archers to address threats from both directions.

Arthur waved to Eli in the distance. Eli pointed back to the west. Arthur turned in that direction and discovered that the earlier winds were the harbinger of a front. Heavily laden rain clouds were moving in from Mississippi. He grimaced considering the rainwater's potential to abate his black powder warheads.

Each archer had his regular sheaf of steel pointed arrows in his quiver. The members with machining skills had produced several thousand steel arrowheads for the archers. A hunter's broadhead was deemed too fragile for combat. They settled on a variation of the medieval bodkin point with three sharpened, but sturdy, edges rising from the point to the base. The designer whose drawing was selected was given the honor of naming the new arrowhead. Thus it was dubbed the Broadkin point.

Off to the side in a ground quiver stood three very special arrows with points up. These had exploding fragmentation warheads. The Lauderdale Pottery Association had spent weeks throwing more than a thousand little oval shaped shells with open ends. Shredded metal and broken glass was worked into the clay before it hardened. In lieu of their regular competitions, the archers had met and formed assembly lines. They took the hardened shells, glued an impact igniter in the front hole, filled the shell with blasting-grade black powder, slid the arrow-shaft in the other, and secured the shaft to the warhead with a plant-based epoxy-impregnated felt ring. In tests the exploding warheads would reliably shatter a fruit jar up to ten feet away.

The igniters were strokes of both luck and genius. A few years ago, one of the members had found a large box of flashcubes in the back of a dry and temperate old storage building. In the Spared Territory, anything of this nature, no matter how useless it seemed was hoarded. Usually, a use would surface. A couple of octogenarian archers were former Florence College chemistry professors. After hearing of the flashcubes' discovery and inspecting the cache, they designed the exploding arrows. They put the word out among the Ecumenical Archers requesting donations of any aged cans or jugs of nitrocellulose-based smokeless gunpowder, even if it was deemed unreliable for cartridge use. The powder came in from the rank and file. The cubes were disassembled, and each one's four little flashbulbs were removed. The bulbs' plastic coatings were chemically removed. The old chemists dissolved the gunpowder in acetone and made a paste. Quickly, before it could dry, they painted the bulbs with the paste. After drying, the bulbs were inserted and cemented, in the forward holes of the shells.

In fear of veto, Stram and Canterbury had pulled off this entire stratagem without Harry or any of his family catching wind of it. They had seen the war clouds brewing and wanted to contribute in some way if the need arose — a need they felt likely. Few had any viable stores of ammunition for their old firearms, so they chose to increase the lethality of their recreational arm of choice.

With Jenny Hart and Mortimer "1911" Johns at his sides, Harry gazed out to the east watching his skirmishers reenter his lines. He glanced back to see the Low Church archers behind him, and then off to the north to catch the High Church archers already nocking their first arrows. A bullet from the as-yet-unseen enemy whizzed into the parapet. They stooped down a bit. Distant fire from the south and west started.

Jenny surmised, "Harry, they seem to be repeating the last attack."

"Well, they came close to breaking us with it, and now they're reinforced."

"They can't have many Knights left though. What did we count, over a hundred of their bodies this morning?"

"Yeah, Jenny, but we lost almost twice that many militiamen and nineteen Slingshot team members in the same few minutes."

"Well, we sure can put those Black Force weapons to good use."

"Good use? Yeah, I guess so." He had noticed her change in weaponry. "You like that M4, Jenny?

"Yes, that AKM was fine, but we seem to have a lot more 5.56 ammo than 7.62x39. And it's a bit more ... uh ... surgical. Captain Smith said the Colbert that killed her Corporal Creasy had it. It is in really good condition — like new!"

"Good decision, Jenny. All told, Donnie took inventory — bless his heart. He estimates we only have 2,000 rounds of 5.56, 700 rounds of 7.62X51, and about 700 rounds of everything else remaining here at the bridgehead. I figure we'll run out of centerfire before this fight is over."

"Well, I gotta hand it to your militiamen, Harry. They went down and grabbed every black powder weapon in the perimeter, loaded 'em, and now have two, three, and even four leaning to their sides in their rifle pits."

"Yeah, I noticed that too. Nobody even had to suggest it to them. Hell of a bunch!"

"Harry, who did you say has that trench to the far left — the one the kids were in?"

He paused and lapsed into sorrow for a moment, then cleared his throat and said, "There's a squad of infantry from the Underwood High Church, but the real anchor there is the handful of surviving troopers from my cavalry platoon."

"That would be the Sergeant Gillespie and Corporal Williams you introduced me to earlier?"

"Yep, their weapons squad survived and they have at least a couple of hundred rounds each for both their M240 and M249. God help the poor bastards that try to attack from the river bank."

"Whoa, there they are, Harry!" Jenny leaned on the top of the parapet and fired a single round.

Harry saw a distant black uniformed soldier slump to the ground. He noticed the Colbert fell near a 200 yard ranging stick. Harry stared for a minute at Jenny as she sought out her next victim. He could almost feel the intensity radiating from her slight frame. *Damn, I love her, but she is one scary woman!*

Harry noticed Colbert militia advancing from the south as well. He turned and waved to Eli Stram, then shouted, "By the time you've nocked an arrow they will be in range from both directions. Let 'em fly, Preacher!"

Arthur Canterbury kept his gaze on Ben Smith. Ben was waist high in a little foxhole to Arthur's front. He was located halfway between Arthur and the 50-yard trench that covered the woods above the riverbank. Arthur saw a cavalryman wave to Ben from the trench and then Ben turned to Arthur and gave him a thumbs up.

Already nocked, Arthur took a firm grip on his bow with his left hand and yelled, "Ready … maximum elevation … aim … fire!" and he released his arrow just as his men did. Over a hundred of their egg-shaped, terracotta-colored bombs arced over the front line to descend into the woods along the river. A firecracker-string of explosions ripped through the trees and underbrush to their front. Screams and curses erupted from the area of impact.

Danny Ragland's security team had shifted their coverage to Edward Ragland upon the death of their beloved and respected Constable. They were shocked when Edward sprinted off ahead of his assault force to lead by example with pistol in hand. They caught up to him just before the ascent to the Lauderdale bridgehead. Just as Edward started racing up the hill, one Knight Sergeant tried to grab his shoulder and hold him back. He wanted to let the Junior Knights pass by his new field commander so that they could absorb the first Lauderdale volley and then repeat the same spray-and-pray sub-gun-onslaught from earlier. The Knight's hand found no purchase, and Edward raced on.

Flashes and bangs erupted in the tree limbs above their heads and the ground at their feet. Edward felt a blanket of searing pain thrust upon the back of his legs. He fell face forward and a Knight tumbled over him screaming with his hands on his face. Edward reeled; it was as if someone had just ripped the skin off his legs. His dedication to duty forced him to all fours and then he arose to a shaky stance. After a few stiff-legged steps he fell again. He managed to take a knee and yelled encouragement to the few unscathed Junior Knights. They pressed on ahead and he heard their machine guns begin to chatter. Edward looked back to find the first of his militia companies entering the woods. He waved them forward.

A couple of them stopped and bent to lift Edward, he ordered, "No, no, go on, get out of these damned woods, hurry!"

The next rain of mutilation hit. Dozens of Colbert militia screamed and fell as the flame and shrapnel tore through the woods. The air was thick with smoke from the black powder. It burned the attackers' eyes, and the spoiled egg smell of sulfur filled their nostrils. Small fires started among the trees and bushes. The bed of fallen leaves, still saturated from yesterday's rains, prevented an inferno.

Knight Claggett heard the furor to the northeast and surmised that Ragland and Martin were engaged. She blew the attack sequence into her whistle and her brave hundreds rushed forward. The distance to the Lauderdale lines varied from 200 to 300 yards. Withering machine gun fire started cutting into her ranks immediately. The first Lauderdale rifle volley felled as many again. Colbert suppressing fire silenced the Lauderdale riflemen and machine gunners for a moment.

In spite of the losses, her troops filled the open ground before her. Juanita's heart soared with optimism and pride at the sight of her Knights and militiamen running to engage the enemy. Juanita's attention shifted to two clouds of tiny objects rising from behind the Lauderdale's breastworks; one arced to the east, and the other towards her. In horror, she realized it was hundreds of arrows. In what appeared to be slow motion, the arrows spread and turned down. Juanita's knees almost buckled from emotional shock as the arrows exploded on impact. A few seconds later, two more volleys of the exploding arrows had decimated her militia. Wave after wave of farther ranging steel-tipped arrows followed. They rained down for several minutes pelting not just the struggling few in the no man's land, but her trenches, foxholes, and breastworks as well. Trying to assist a wounded Knight sergeant, Juanita was struck in the middle of her back. Lacking the velocity to carry through, the sharp-edged Broadkin point lodged in her kidney. Writhing in agony, she ordered retreat. There was no one to relay the command. The remnants of her determined force pressed on into the Lauderdale revetments where they inflicted much but received more.

The day before, Donna Flurry had been torn whether to disperse her Slingshot team throughout Sheffield to add some back-up firepower to their militia, or to keep the team intact to respond to any serious enemy breakthroughs. She kept them together and they never really engaged. At dawn she chose to deploy her team in their two-member elements. She and Annie Slocomb would remain at her command post by the Sheffield City Hall and cover the communications staff.

Slingshot privates Deb Romine and Judy Kelley were ordered to find a two or three story building on Montgomery Avenue, position themselves on the roof, and fire on the enemy if they attacked from Tuscumbia. They were a bit too late. The firing from the enemy lines began as they moved south on Montgomery. They quickly chose a two-story office building, broke through the front door, and made their way to the top floor. They found a pull down staircase under a roof hatch.

Once on the roof, they kept low and moved to the southern side of the building. There was only a low parapet, about two feet tall, for cover. They positioned themselves at the two southern corners of the building. They peeked over and saw that the Colberts were attacking their militia's lines.

Deb tried to rise up and acquire a hold and target. A rifle bullet shattered the top of the brick parapet a couple of feet to her left. She slid back down behind the wall and yelled to Judy, "Girl, did you see that?"

"Yep and I heard the report too. It was a .50 cal'!"

"One of their Barretts no doubt!"

"I'd rather not die here, Deb."

"Fuckin' A, Jigglypuff, let's get the hell off this pedestal."

"After you."

They crawled back to the open roof hatch and scurried back down the stairs to the ground floor. A few feet from the front door, they saw black uniforms dart by heading north.

"Shit, Deb, they've broken through the lines already! I'm gonna aim left and take those runners. You aim right and cover me."

"Done."

Deb sliced the pie at the doorjamb and employed two short bursts to gun down the two militiamen. Judy caught four more coming north up the street and had to use an entire magazine to put them all down as they either went prone on the road surface or tried to dodge for cover.

Deb looked back over her shoulder to see the results of Judy's fire. "That was fuckin' awesome, bitch!"

"You like that, girl?"

"Yep, but you better watch that ammo. Hell, what does that leave you, four mags?"

"Nope, three. Remember the Knight recon vehicle on Hatch yesterday evening?"

"Oh, yeah, I forgot."

"How much you got, Deb?"

As she tactically swapped out her partial for a full magazine in her M16A4, Deb answered, five and a half."

Judy glanced around performing a broken 180 of their world, and then gazed at Deb. "Whatcha think?"

After performing the same assessment, Deb replied, "This doorway is pretty solid ... brick and mortar. How 'bout you stay here and I'll ditty bop across the street to that green doorway and pull the same stance. We'll both concentrate on the south, but keep our third eye on our six in case they flank around."

"I like it, Cherry Delight, but how 'bout I cross the street?"

"Cherry Delight? That's a new one. Where'd you come up with that?"

Judy nodded her head to what was obviously a receptionist's desk a few feet from the building's entrance. Deb glanced at the desk. Questioning for a moment she finally zeroed-in on a black and red, half-empty bottle of Colbert Soda. She read, *Cherry Delight*."

Deb chuckled, smirked at Judy and commanded, "Fine! Get on outta here!"

Judy crouched for the sprint, took another look each way, and as Deb covered south, Judy undertook the 100-foot-dash across Sheffield's main thoroughfare. About halfway across, they heard the sonic crack of another Barrett round. This was followed by the combined sounds of its distant muzzle blast to the south and the whine of its ricochet off the street just north of their position.

Judy dove into the opposite doorway, pressed her back against the door for maximum cover. She pulled off her faded baseball cap, and whisked her weak hand through her dirty-blonde hair. After tucking it back in her cap she snugged it all back down, and yelled "That goddamn motherfucker! I felt the breeze off that one!"

Deb tried to laugh at the reaction, but she was just too overcome with relief. She gave her friend a sweet smile and hunkered down on her rifle to await the next target of opportunity.

The three salvos of exploding arrows winnowed down Edward Ragland's assault forces, but the determined Colberts took their losses on the chin and reached the perimeter. Scattered raindrops greeted them initially, but by the time the fighting drew to arm's length, there was a torrential downpour.

Once again, the crucial northeast corner of the perimeter was nearing collapse. The Lauderdale Cavalry were being tested once again. Clive Bennett tossed his empty M249 into the muddy soup at the floor of his trench and pulled his M9 pistol. He expended his entire first magazine killing the last few Junior Knights in front of him. Jake Connelly was dying in the mud to his right sprawled between his smoking M240 and their empty ammunition cans. Michael Williams had switched from his SMLE to his big revolver as the fighting got close and heavy. He prayed the single heavy bullet he invested in each attacker would be enough to take the fight out of them. Mark Gillespie's right arm was hanging limp and bloody as he weak-handed shots at the Colbert stragglers with his big double action .45 ACP revolver. Betty Sands was out of ammunition for both her long and short weapons. She scrambled among the dead and wounded for something with which to fight. Alex had just finished strangling the life from a Knight and was trying to regain his feet. The rest of the Lauderdale Cavalry plus the entire squad of Underwood infantrymen lay still, bleeding, and lifeless along the trench's floor mingled with a like number of black-uniformed bodies.

Betty grasped a submachine gun from the hands of a fallen Knight. The little weapon fired from an open breech, and rounds gleamed at her from the magazine's feed lips as she glanced through the open ejection port. She thrust herself up to the edge of the trench to fire then froze in astonishment and disbelief. To her left, Clive had reloaded his handgun but held the same motionless stance. To her right, Michael and Alex stood standing, staring, and panting. Between them, Sergeant Gillespie leaned into the trench for support. There was no fight left in front of them. Only dozens of Colbert fallen occupied the tortured ground.

At the opposite end of the perimeter, Harry and Jenny were shooting from kneeling positions, Jenny picked off interlopers along the eastern perimeter while Harry did the same along the south. 1911 stood between them with his matched pair of .45 pistols. He had not drawn the U. S. Government Issue Model 1911s once since this war began, but they were out of his shoulder holsters now. He moved back and forth along the parapet firing at any soul that entered Jenny's or Harry's blindside. Like Jenny, the old warrior was ambidextrous and no finer pistol-fighter existed in the ST.

The rain adversely affected the aged archers. Their arthritic fingers struggled and fumbled to nock the dripping Broadkin tipped arrows and draw the slippery bowstrings. As Harry had demanded they were slowly withdrawing to the bridge, stopping to loose a volley of arrows over the defenders, stepping back a few yards, and repeating. While not nearly as effective as their exploding arrows, the steel often found Colbert flesh. Some of the archers had scored direct-fire low-trajectory shots on a few of the Colberts that fought their way through the breastworks and trenches. One victim of the Lexington contingent looked like a pincushion.

Donnie and his supply workers joined Scooter with his artillerymen to form an outwardly facing circle around the field hospital. They each had small stacks of discarded single shot breechloaders and muzzleloaders at their sides. They prayed that the powder in the chambers would remain dry until called upon.

Clara Smith and Team 5 in the center of the eastern perimeter were trying to preserve their centerfire ammunition by only engaging the close-in attackers. By protecting her assigned militiamen, the citizen-soldiers could concentrate on more distant targets with their Lauderdale Sharps rifles. The strategy was mostly working.

Sheffield, the most thriving city in the Spared Territory, was being ravaged for the second day in a row. The East Lauderdale Low Church Militia fell back from their positions, initially, to settle into a new battle line nearer Donna's HQ. The surge by the 1st and 3rd East Colbert Militias ran out of momentum about the time Slingshot 2 started running out of centerfire ammunition. Major Fuqua and Team 4 backed up the West Lauderdale Low Church Militia companies on 2nd Street and were never really pressed. The Colberts only had scattered forces opposing them in that sector.

Edward Ragland made his way back to Wilson Dam limping along through the rain with the remnants of his Black Force Knights and Colbert Militia. Some medics put him on a stretcher and carried him the last quarter mile. They toted him to his tent and he rolled onto his cot. Henderson brought him a glass of water in one hand and a shot of whiskey in the other. He took the whiskey in one gulp, but nursed the water. One of the medics said they would bring a doctor to look at his legs, but he insisted they leave the doctors alone to tend to the more seriously wounded.

Gail Atkinson came over from communications and gave him a condensed report on the Sheffield operations.

Edward painfully uttered, "Henderson, please try and find Mr. Montjoy. I need to speak with him."

Harry, Jenny, and 1911 shifted from one area to the other as they visited with the survivors of the battle. As they left the field hospital, he couldn't believe Johnny Montjoy was standing there with his mocking white flag again. Ben, standing to his side, must have let him pass through. Jenny subtly ducked back into the tent then stopped, just out of Monjoy's sight, to listen.

Harry lost it, rushed towards Johnny, and thrust his arms to Johnny's chest grasping the envoy's coat with his fists. "I told you to not come back, Montjoy! What does Danny want now? Our first born?"

"No, no, Harry, you misunderstand! The field is yours."

Stunned, Harry couldn't believe what he had heard. He eased his grasp and let go of Johnny's coat numbly patting the man's chest. "The field is mine?"

"Yes. And the Constable is dead."

"Dead? Then who sent you? Charles?"

"No. Edward Ragland is in command of our forces in the field."

With disgust, Harry said, "Edward."

"Yes. He is badly injured, but still commands."

Harry, hearing of the injury and what it implied, softened his expression.

"Harry, Edward Ragland realizes that there is still too much bad blood and mistrust to have either president go to the other's ground for a discussion of terms and the negotiation of a treaty. He suggests you allow us to set up a large field tent just south of your breastworks. Charles, Catherine, and he, the Lord willing, can be there tomorrow at 10:00 A.M. to meet with your contingent."

Harry gazed about the slaughter around him, pushed down the anger, and calmly said, "That will be fine. We will see them then." A second or two passed. "Oh, Johnny."

"Yes, Mr. President."

"Will you be there?"

"Of course."

"Good."

DAY SIX

It was a beautiful, clear and cold Saturday morning. The storm had been ahead of a cold front. Now the Spared Territory seemed freshly washed at least symbolically. The Lauderdale contingent consisted of Henry Wade Smith V, Benjamin Smith and his daughter; Major Clara Smith; David Smith, Clifford Hayes, Peter Hayes, Colonel Phillip Goins and his daughter; Major Donna Flurry; Major William Fuqua, and the Reverends; Eli Stram and Arthur Canterbury. The distantly located Slingshot commanders were not in attendance. They stayed with their commands. Harry did not want all the eggs in one basket.

The Lauderdales walked through a freshly cut gap in the bridgehead perimeter's earthen mounds and made their way to the Colbert's big white tent.

Donna, walking arm-in-arm with her father, leaned to his ear and whispered, "Daddy, I'm surprised it's not black, but I guess they had to run out of that dye at some point."

Colonel Goins squeezed her arm with his to punish her for her bad form, but a sheepish grin revealed his amusement.

Jenny Hart watched from a firing port in the breastwork. She fixed on the departing party until they neared their destination. Then, Jenny turned, cleared her M4, slung it over her shoulder, and stepped down from the bloody walls towards the center of the bridgehead. There, 1911 was waiting with the engine running in the last functional Slingshot vehicle extant at the Singing River Bridge, Slingshot 7's Humvee. He had orders to drive Jenny Hart to Smith Lodge. There the staff had been notified that they were to spoil her rotten. Harry had ordered her to relax and enjoy some tranquility, a time of letting go. Jenny Hart took it as a joyless assignment another at which to work and master. The idea of "letting go" of anything was a stranger to her.

As the Lauderdales entered the tent they passed through a wind breaking canvas foyer possessed of large flaps at both ends. Upon exiting the tunnel, they found two sets of folding chairs facing one another. An aisle ran down the middle, akin to a prayer meeting save for the fact that the chairs did not face the front. There was no table or podium. Charles and Isabel Ragland were standing to the left front of the tent, just beyond the chairs. Behind them was, Edward Ragland; he was sitting in a wheel chair with his legs heavily bandaged. Catherine Ragland stood at his left side, and Pickard Thompson and Midge Burkett to his right. Standing in the back, the Reverends Donnie Butler and Thomas Utter completed the Colbert assembly. Neither side was armed nor had any guards in attendance.

Johnny Montjoy stood in the center of the aisle. He gestured for the Lauderdales to come forward and stand opposite the Colberts. A devotee of situational awareness, Harry glanced to his right and left. He noticed a man standing behind the chairs on the left. A second look brought recognition. It was Clement Applewhite, a successful farmer and influential Colbert citizen from the Leighton community. Harry knew Mr. Applewhite from The Peace as he had been a friend and business associate of President Wade Smith; one of the few that called himself a friend to both Charles Ragland and Wade Smith. He was a hardworking and learned gentleman known of great character.

The attendees' dress was casual and warm to match the 38-degree temperature with the warriors present still wearing uniforms.

After the Lauderdales gathered in the front facing the Colberts, Montjoy began, "President Smith, the Ragland family has asked Mr. Applewhite to serve as a mediator of these proceedings. Does that meet with your approval?"

Harry's eyes met the old friend of his father's and they exchanged nods of recognition. With little hesitation, Harry said, "I will be honored to have Mr. Applewhite serve in that capacity."

Montjoy said to Harry, "Thank you, Mr. President." Then he turned and said, "Mr. Applewhite, would you come forward and lead us in the task at hand?"

The old man strode forward and loudly stated, "It will be my pleasure, Mr. Montjoy." Upon reaching Johnny Montjoy, he shook hands with him. As on cue, Johnny moved to the rear of the Colbert contingent.

The mediator began, "With all due respect to the four clergymen in attendance, I will ask the Lord's blessing from my position of self-imposed neutrality. Let us pray. Our heavenly Father, God in Heaven, we humbly ask that You bring peace and love to this gathering and guide our negotiations to a reasonable and just conclusion. Please be with the souls of the recently and tragically departed soldiers and civilians whose earthly vestiges lay cast about these very fields and streets. Amen."

Those present raised their eyes to exchange child-like, anxious glances at their opposites. Harry purposely avoided Catherine's and she his.

"My heart soars to see you rulers, Colbert and Lauderdale, come together at last. Why can't blessed peace come to our land — the last home of humanity? She has been chased for too long. Instead of raising our children in joy, happiness, and enlightenment; toiling for abundance in our fields; and driving our industry towards progress and earthly comfort; for most of these seven decades, we have instead maintained an air of savagery, as soldiers, meditating on nothing but blood, full of swearing and stern looks, to the point when all seems ... unnatural. Why can't blessed peace finally visit us with her gentler qualities?" Applewhite pointedly looked to Harry.

While Harry carefully avoided eye contact with Catherine, he tried to measure the intentions of both Charles and Edward Ragland with mutual visual exchanges lasting pregnant seconds. Edward Ragland was still angry but now sat disillusioned and beaten while his father seemed to be drifting with age, fatigue, and fear. Finally, Harry spoke, "If the Ragland family wants the marvelous peace you describe, Mr. Applewhite, they must buy it with full accord to our just demands."

Lauderdale eyebrows went up as the Colbert's fell.

Applewhite, expecting such, looked to Charles Ragland as a straight-laced older brother might gaze at his misbehaving younger sibling.

Somewhere in his mind an assistant slapped the side of his skull, just enough to force a reasonable state of reality to the Colbert ruler of forty-five years. "Harry, I've only glanced at your advance articles. Would you appoint some of your council to sit with us and fully discuss the details and ramifications of the treaty as submitted? I am quite optimistic that upon complete explanation, we will pass our acceptance and provide the positive answer you seek."

Applewhite moved with vigor, "Very well, then. Let's all have a seat and discuss these articles."

Harry was humbled. He had not expected such at this juncture. He finally glanced at Catherine and saw her watering eyes. Recovering, he said, "That's fine Mr. Ragland, but I must insist that I leave my entrusted friends and family to assist you and your council while I take your leave."

Surprised and confused, the factions shot glances across the tent.

Harry noticed and regretted his misperceived dismissal as insult, "Oh, I'm sorry to cause y'all such angst. I ask, not only, that you excuse me, but Catherine Ragland as well. If I had such power and guile, I would have included her as the capital demand in the articles. As such, I humbly ask, that she suffer my company, alone, for a few minutes. What do you say, President Ragland?" Harry shifted to the daughter, "Catherine?"

Father and beloved daughter shared shrugs and sighs with each other, and then Catherine said, "Okay, Harry, I'll talk with you. Daddy, are you okay with that?"

"Very well. Where are y'all gonna be?"

Harry interjected, "Just outside, sir, we'll take a short walk."

Charles just nodded in agreement while Edward squeezed his eyes shut whether in pain or disgust.

Catherine squeezed her brother's shoulder as she passed by him to join Harry. Edward seemed to take solace in the tender, physical contact and determinedly asked, "Reverend Utter, how 'bout pushing a crippled Knight over to the chairs."

Harry and Catherine departed the tent; both were visibly apprehensive.

1911 had managed to salvage Harry's only clean uniform from the remains of Slingshot 8. Harry had the single Slingshot jacket, and its appearance reflected his activities of the past few days. A cursory glance would find oil stains, dried mud, and blood. He chose to leave the coat at his command tent and suffer both the cold and the somewhat bland khaki attire. However, the young president would have had to really work at being unattractive. Even the Slingshot 5 girls did double takes when their president came around. He had shaved and raced through a tepid field shower, while Mort knocked the dirt from his boots.

Catherine was quite the contrast. She had changed from her Black Force uniform to civilian attire. *It is over. Further fighting is futile and stupid.* Almost unheard of for a public appearance, she skipped makeup; a natural beauty, she didn't really need it, plus the wind and emotion of the day gave her some color. Ever the lady, she wore her long blonde hair up, under a tan fedora that matched the color of her tall riding boots. They sported lacing-detail up the backs. One of Mr. Thompson's dye-line workers must have had a good day with the walnut as her winter-weight skirt looked like chocolate. It ended below her knees where the tops of her boots stopped. A beige turtleneck sweater accentuated her long, thin neck and a string of aged OW pearls peeked out at the margins of her black leather coat's lapels.

Both sides had worked diligently the afternoon before and earlier that morning to remove the dead from the field, but evidence of the preceding days' slaughter abounded. Harry tried to gently take her arm and guide Catherine in the least bloody direction.

She pulled her arm away and took a path of her choosing. "Don't worry about it. I have been seeing your slaughter for two days."

He wanted to defend himself, but he had no real defense.

She looked at him fumbling for response and curtly asked, "What do you want Harry?"

"What do you think I want, Catherine?"

"That crack in there was either a bad joke, bad taste, or if serious, outrageous."

"Why outrageous?"

"Are you serious, Harry Smith, you meant that?

"Well, it's what I want."

"You've got to be kidding me. We haven't seen each other since we were kids, and you want to marry me?"

"But I—"

"'But' nothing, 'Mr. President!'" She turned away, and continued, now addressing the vacant southern horizon, "Oh, I see. You're so obsessed with your own power and revenge, you would force my marriage to you; cementing your control of the entire ST and for the first time in post-pandemic history, the joint ascendancies would become one — a single bloodline ruling the entire Spared Territory. Yes, Edward is my twin brother, but it was administratively witnessed and recorded that I am the first born by ten minutes — ten fucking minutes, Harry. The Spared Territory's Rules of Ascendency do not specify a first born son, simply, the firstborn. Only a handful of people were privy to this knowledge, and only four of those are still living: my parents, my brother, and Reverend Ut—"

"And, me, Cate!"

"'Cate'? Only my clos…"

Harry grabbed her shoulders and rotated her back to face him, "Shhh! Hush, Cate! May I speak…for just a moment?"

A tear glided down her left cheek betraying the damage to her feelings and pride. She stood tensely with her arms tightly crossed.

Harry gently intercepted the drop with his right thumb, and massaged it between his index finger and thumb, watching until it evaporated from the friction and cold wind. "Your father told mine about it during that lazy, wonderful summer vacation at Smith Lodge. The shared secret bound them to keep us apart. My father told me about the secret and their conspiracy years later, with a sense of guilt, I might add." After a pause, he turned his eyes back to hers, and continued, "I was close to you once, Catherine. I called you Cate. You didn't seem to mind then. As a matter of fact, it made you smile and scrunch-up your nose."

She laughed and began to cry at the same time.

"There it is"—he whispered—"there's that cute nose. I fell asleep many a night and woke many a morning seeing it. That memory has never faded, Miss Catherine."

"'Cate', is fine, Harry."

He leaned in and kissed her. She did not back away, but pressed in and wrapped her arms around his neck. They swam in the kiss and embrace, escaping the horrors of their mean little world and sank dizzyingly into a pool of renewed passion and love.

She finally broke the kiss, and looked into his eyes.

Harry urged, "Take me, Cate. Take a soldier. Take a soldier. Take a president. Say yes, my love."

She pondered and then her expression fell back into sadness, "Is it possible that I can love the enemy of Colbert — marry him and bear his children?"

"No, Cate. It's not, but in loving me you would love a friend of Colbert, because I love it so much, I won't part with a single crossroads, township, or city of it. I am a citizen of the Spared Territory and will see it united once and for all. I firmly believe that the Territory will not survive our future trials unless we unite as a single people."

She smiled and pulled him in for another long, tender kiss.

They had heard some elevated voices from the tent, but now, for the first time a bit of subdued laughter.

Harry broke the kiss this time and, displaying the smile that Cate remembered so well, said, "You have witchcraft in your lips, Cate Ragland. There is more eloquence in the sugar touch of them than in all the waggin' tongues of our respective councils."

Her eyes sparkled and Harry asked, "Will you marry me, Cate?"

She turned serious and with a slightly embarrassed expression said, "Now, Harry, I must tell you. I haven't spent the last dozen years pining away for you. There have been a few other men in my life."

Harry's heart broke a little once again, just like it did each time Cheetah tapped in a coded message reporting the strategically important identity of the latest suitor to the future Colbert President.

Harry countered, "Well, darlin' I've kept company with a girl or two along the way myself."

"Yeah, Harry Smith, I've heard. Girl or two, my—"

"Aw, now, Miss Catherine, let's not dwell on the past. It's time to move forward."

"Fine, I'll marry you, Mr. President. If nothing else, it is our best hope for peace. I do believe we can make it something special. Don't you, Harry?"

"Absolutely, Cate. Very special."

A few minutes later, Ben Smith appeared at the tent's entrance and waved Harry and Catherine back in. As the couple walked back into the canvas council chamber, they both perceived an air of optimism and sheer relief the likes of which neither ever thought possible — well, maybe in their dreams.

Charles stood with his arm around his beloved Isabel. He addressed the Lauderdale President, "Harry, we have consented to all terms of reason. Most notably, I will abdicate the presidency to Catherine, and we will carefully begin the removal of explosive charges from Wilson Dam. I'm a tired old man, Harry. This killing has to stop."

Charles and Harry signed the treaty.

Before the ink was dry, Harry asked, "Mr. Charles, President Catherine Ragland has consented to marry me. May we have your blessing?"

"I always knew this would come to pass. Hell, I feared it, but not anymore. Yes, Harry and Catherine, y'all have my blessing."

Isabel, in another moment of clarity, said, "Why, Little Charles, this is so exciting. We're going to have a grand marriage of state!"

Catherine went and hugged her mother, "Momma, I hate to disappoint you, sweetie, but we aren't. Well, not the 'grand' part." Next, Catherine surprised everyone, including Harry, after she turned to Reverend Utter and asked, "My dear Reverend Utter, please marry us."

The High Church preacher quickly smiled and complied, "Of course, I am honored."

He stood sharing grins all about.

Catherine, grasping Harry's hand tightly, had not altered her gaze on her High Church leader. She repeated, a bit louder this time, "My dear Reverend Utter, please marry President Smith and me. Now!"

"Oh, now! You mean, right now?" He laughed as did most of the others present, and he said, "Of course, right away."

Isabel impulsively strode over and hugged Harry's neck saying, "Be good to my little girl, Lauderdale."

Harry replied, "I will Mrs. Ragland. Oh, and by the way, since we cheated ya' out of a big, fancy weddin' of state, we'll throw a Hell of a celebration in a couple of weeks." He looked back at Catherine, and asked, "First, we have some work to do, right, Cate?"

"Yes, a lot of work, Harry Smith, but we'll find some time for us. We'll make the time."

Reverend Utter moved to the center of the aisle and asked the two councils to go turn their respective chairs facing front. "Here let's make a proper church out of this place. Uh oh, I don't have a Bible with me. Brother Donnie, may I borrow yours?"

The other three church leaders shared the joke at Utter's expense as Butler handed him his Bible with a cautionary note, "Now, Thomas, it's the King James version."

Wounded but not down, Reverend Utter said, "Oh, thank you, Brother Donnie, I'll manage."

A few moments later Charles Edward Ragland VI clasped together the hands of Catherine and Harry. He looked at her lovingly and said, "From your blood, Catherine Isabel Ragland" — he turned with a smile for Harry — "and Henry Wade Smith V, bring forth progeny to unite Colbert and Lauderdale for once and for all. May this union cease hatred in the Spared Territory and bring Christian accord to the known world. We pray that war will never return."

Charles released their hands and stepped back. He beamed, "Reverend Utter?"

About the Author

After his short story, *White Flour*, was published in the *Savannah Anthology 2015*, Danny Creasy was imbued to self-publish his work of creative non-fiction, *Jim & Nancy: Two Paths Merged by War*. *Slingshot 8* is his first work of fiction. Slingshot *8: The Old World* is in edit, and Danny is 10,000 words into *Slingshot 8: Colony.*

Danny is a retired community banker and lifetime resident of Florence, Alabama. Over 38 years, he worked in several different locations throughout the "Spared Territory" aka "the Shoals." Danny holds a BS in economics and history from the University of North Alabama (1979) and a MBA from the same institution (1989). He is also a graduate of the United States Air Force Officer Training School (1982).

An avid marksman, Danny finished in the gold medal tier four consecutive years at Camp Perry's CMP National Rimfire Sporter Championship. While only a "middle of the packer" in the International Defensive Pistol Association's discipline, he is proud to have competed in three of its challenging "Nationals." Keeping it simple these days, Danny enjoys his club's local matches. He maintains that the best part is the fellowship with his long time shooting friends.

Danny has a loving and supportive wife of 33 years, two sweet daughters, two great sons-in-law, and an adorable granddaughter.

CPSIA information can be obtained
at www.ICGtesting.com
Printed in the USA
BVOW01s1111141216

470789BV00001B/105/P